THE
CALLING
OF THE GROVE

CALLIE PEY

Cover Design by Sleepy Fox Studio
Chapter Inserts and Page Breaks by Etheric Tales and Edits
Original Edit by Enchanted Author Services on 2022 Update
And first draft of 2025 edition
Final Edit and Proofread by Samantha | Radiant Editorial

Dedication

*To those with the courage to fight for those they love, even
when the road ahead is filled with danger.*

*To Chrissy-
Trust in the calling of your heart ♡*

*Special thanks to my partner, Steve, for your support on this
journey. To the readers who followed each new update as I
found my author's voice. To my critique partners Kat B &
Tati A, & Reema C. To my amazing editor Samantha for
joining my team. And to the betas who stepped up despite
the crazy timeline: Maeva & Amanda C.*

*Allie ♡
Puy*

4

Helpful Terms Guide

Vasilissa – Mother tree of a grove.

Druwid – A bonded mate to a vasilissa.

Contessa – Daughter of a vasilissa with the magical alignment for the element of the specified grove.

Ryne – Protector designated to watch over a specific contessa.

Arati/Aratian – High Elf
Eryni/Erynian – Wood Elf
Rava/Ravaian – Wild Elf

Nymph – Encompasses all types of nature spirit. The type of nymph may be called another name:
Dryad (Tree), Nereid (River), Oceanid (Ocean), Aurai (Wind or Breeze), Oread (Stone), Flora (Flower)

Fae – a winged race that has a powerful tie with magic
Fey – A general term for the races that live under fae rule.

Voreios – Northern Grove
Anatoli – Eastern Grove
Notos – Southern Grove
Dytika – Western Grove

Watchtower - a powerful elemental warrior, usually a dryad, that protects the portal guardian

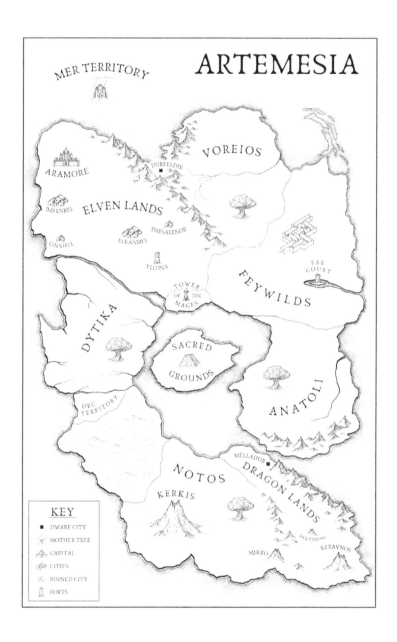

ARTEMESIA

MER TERRITORY

VOREIOS

ARAMORE

DURFELDIR

IMRENBEL

ELVEN LANDS

THESALENOR

ONSHIL

ELRANMEL

YLLUNA

FAE COURT

FEYWILDS

TOWER OF THE MAGES

DYTIKA

SACRED GROUNDS

ANATOLI

ORC TERRITORY

MELLADUR

NOTOS

DRAGON LANDS

KERKIS

MIKTYSMENO

MIKRO

KERAVNOS

KEY

- ■ DWARF CITY
- ✦ MOTHER TREE
- 🏛 CAPITAL
- 🏘 CITIES
- 🏚 RUINED CITY
- 🏛 FORTS

Contents

Chapter 1 – Kelan

I hadn't made it in time to save her.

The time to cross from Voreios to Dytika had felt like nothing at all, and yet. . .she was gone. I couldn't find the watchtowers either. Had she gone back to Earth? But why would she be so terrified then? Too many questions flooded my brain, and I didn't have a clue how to get the answers.

I must have checked inside and outside the tower three times already. The guards from Voreios also looked for any sign of where Melissa might have gone. One of them discovered fragments of shattered glass lying in front of the steps to the tower. The shards and the body of the Dytika guard leaned towards foul play.

She couldn't have left. Not of her own will after she'd been so excited to join me in mating. She'd never even talked about going back. This had to be the work of the gods. . .and by that I meant the Shadow God. If it was the other gods, then they would have to send me with her. I didn't care what I'd have to give up in exchange.

"Kelan!" one of the satyrs shouted, their voice shaking me out of my spiraling thoughts. "There's a magic ring forming!"

11

I sprinted to where the group of men stood, hand on the hilt of my blade, ready for anything. Yellow etchings covered the ground in a circle, and four beings manifested in the center of the wind-wrapped bubble. As they took solid shape a small piece of me relaxed, recognizing the powerful dryads.

Lilise's gaze turned to Ferox as the spell ceased, before she shouted at him. "Where is she?!"

She? Melissa?

I raced to where the freshly arrived group had clustered together to catch any details they might share.

Ferox frowned at his empty arms as if he'd been holding her. "The gods are the only ones who could have snatched her from me. She was tethered in my robes."

The water watchtower stared at her partner, horror and sadness etched across her face at this new turn of events. Ferox met her look with sympathetic eyes.

"You saw Melissa?" I needed clarification. Needed to know she was safe. "Is she safe?"

Surprisingly, Cassie was the one to approach me. "I'm not sure how you knew she was in danger, but Cholios had taken her. We were bringing her back, but it seems our gods may have intervened. I see you came through Voreios—"

The ground trembled, and the sonic booms of loud explosions forced us all to cover our ears. Ferox put up a shield to catch flying debris from the grove.

"What was that?" Minithe asked.

"I haven't heard that sound since Heliria closed the planetary portals. . ." Lilise started to say, but then a messenger approached from the bridge out of the grove.

12

He paused only a moment when he noticed his deceased friend, then turned his full attention to Lilise. "Hairiko said we need you urgently. The ritual failed. Graak didn't show, and even with Zoq's help, the elements wouldn't take hold. We think the magic might be unraveling."

"I will be along in a moment. Tell her to keep everyone away from all portals until we can figure out what is stable and what is not." Lilise turned to the four guards from Voreios. "That goes for you too. When you need to return, do not use a portal."

They all nodded, even if they didn't appear happy with the news.

"There hasn't been a solstice ritual mishap in centuries. What do we do now? There's not a guardian. . ." Cassie mused aloud, and I hoped someone could answer her.

"One thing at a time." Lilise closed her eyes and took a deep breath before letting it out slowly.

A sizzling crack in the sky above tore open, and a small form fell from the darkness within. Melissa tumbled around, trying to right herself before Ferox's winds caught her.

My heart lifted as soon as I caught sight of her. She'd not been sent back to Earth after all. In this moment, I decided I was never going to let her out of my proximity again. If she was to do any more portal hopping, it would be with me at her side.

As I moved around the group to catch her, Lilise sighed, echoing my relief.

"Thank the gods," I uttered.

With Ferox's aid, Melissa was easy to snatch from the air, but I did not like the state she was in under the yellow robes she wore. Her blue dress was torn with dried blood and scratches marring every inch of her skin that I saw. Fresh purple and blue bruises blossomed.

"Kelan." Melissa's voice was so soft that I almost missed it. She looked at all the watchtowers with a small, comforted smile before blacking out. Her head rolled back, as though she had barely enough energy to make sure we were all okay first.

"Melissa!" I cried, trying to manage my panic.

Lilise was at my side in an instant, water magic coursing over her. "She is alive. She's weak but will survive. We cannot wait any longer. Bring her into Dytika's border and get her to the other healers while I figure out the portal situation. I will return to her side as soon as that issue is managed."

I nodded. There were faint signs that she was breathing as I carried her across the bridge.

I shouldn't have left her. If I'd been here, this wouldn't have happened. Her light skin was far paler than normal, a sight that tore at my heart. But she was breathing, and I needed to focus on the positive. I would not return to the elven lands again. Not if this was the price I might pay.

The healers' pools glowed with a blue luminescence that resonated through my being as I stepped further and further in. The nereids turned to face me, but their eyes were on her immediately.

"Lay her here," the first one urged as golden light radiated from her fingertips.

I was remiss to set Melissa down on the smooth stone, but another nymph placed a pillow under her head. This was the worst feeling. I didn't know how to help them, but I couldn't step away from her.

"Kelan." The woman to my left drew my attention. "Sit down next to her and calm your energy. She is safe now, but you are turbulent."

The woman tore open what little remained of Melissa's dress. "Lilise will have to get these wounds. The shadow energy is still pooling from them. How is she internally?"

"Still flooded with adrenaline, but the major damage seems to be to her bones," a second nereid replied.

"Bones can be mended."

They decided collectively to sedate her so that she wouldn't wake up while the bones were reset and regrown. Each sound gutted me like a fresh blade. Once they'd healed her hands, I kept one in between mine, rubbing my thumb over the top of her fingers. She likely couldn't sense my attempts to comfort her, but being able to touch her soothed my soul.

The ground tremors continued throughout the night. I anxiously waited for Lilise to return with the other watchtowers. They would know what was going on with the portals.

My bond confirmed Graak and I were feeling similarly about the new turn of events. I'd told myself before that I would stay out of it and let Graak make up with her on his own terms, but with each passing moment, my resolve grew—I needed to reunite these two as well. Whatever happened. . .she was going to need him to heal afterward, and he would need her.

As the sun climbed in the early morning sky, the legendary dryads appeared, each looking exhausted. Cassie made her way over to sit beside me before stroking Melissa's hair. Then her gaze caught on the mark between Melissa's breasts.

"When did she get that?" Cassie's eyes flew to my chest, but my shirt fully covered my marking.

"The autumn equinox," I admitted, still not sure what I would say about Graak's role.

"Who's the other mate? Where has he been?" The dryad's full attention was on me now. Cassie hadn't made me nervous like this before. I had a feeling she wouldn't be happy to know about the ryne's involvement.

I kept my eyes on Melissa, but in my peripheral vision, I noticed Lilise also glance at the mark before she began working on the bloody wounds on Melissa's shoulder blades.

"I'm not sure," I said carefully. "He hasn't seen either of us since that night."

"That's not possible," she muttered, lost in thought for a moment. "I take it you didn't know him? You probably wouldn't have recognized a guard from Voreios. It could have been that messenger. If he seriously abandoned her, I *will* kill him."

Somehow, she knew that our other mate was from Voreios as she answered the other question for me. It had to be because of the color. Everyone in Dytika had blue marks, but ours were green.

"I would prefer if you didn't. Despite how he left, I believe Melissa cares greatly for him. The bond indicates to

16

me that he misses her. I think they need time to sort it out between themselves."

"Forest folk don't abandon their fated! He's been away from her since autumn? I won't have it," Cassie replied stubbornly. "I am kind of glad he's from my grove though. Almost like this will tie us together officially as sisters."

"Why didn't either of you tell us?" Lilise interrupted as a large puff of smoke drifted up between us.

"He seemed conflicted that morning, and I didn't want anyone forcing him to come back to her while I wasn't here to help her through any upset it might cause. She also doesn't seem to understand the bond mark," I reasoned, and the two dryads nodded as if that made sense to them.

For a few moments, Lilise worked in silence, but the tension between the three of us didn't lessen.

"Should we take her to Voreios since he is there?" I asked, trying to be subtle.

"Melissa will not be traveling for a few weeks." Lilise shook her head as she twisted her wrists, and a fresh strand of water twirled around Melissa's body. "Honestly, I'd still prefer he relocate here to begin with. Voreios is complicated enough with their situation. Hairiko is in a better position to help me protect her."

"I feel like she will heal better if we are all together, though I'm not sure why. Are we able to have him come visit now?"

"That's likely the bond pull you are sensing," Cassie agreed. "But it won't be easy for him to travel either. The portals between the groves have collapsed. I'll send a message to Graak that he needs to find the dumbass and send him here immediately. It'll still be a few weeks on foot for the messages to get there and back."

That wouldn't work. Even I knew Graak wouldn't be able to leave Voreios.

"Perhaps Graak already knows," Lilise mused. "The guards he sent with you through the portal yesterday requested we bring Melissa to Voreios immediately. We can send a message with them now since they are about to return. If he truly hasn't seen her in months, he must be starving. At this point, he may not survive the winter."

I frowned, not sure what to say to that. If Graak died, would Melissa still recover? Or was I destined to lose them both?

Chapter 2 – Graak

The earth around us trembled, and green energy pulsated from the vasilissa. Her pained screams were torture to my very soul. The gut-wrenching sound caused nearby wildlife to flee in all-out panic. Flower nymphs on the edge of the field wailed in distress at the state of their mother tree. I couldn't think clearly with all the noise, but my heart knew exactly how they were feeling.

I summoned forth all my abilities, every magical spell I knew, and attempted to channel myself into the earth to determine the issue. I couldn't find anything. Nor could I see what attacked her, but her terror told me all I needed to know. There was a threat, but how could I possibly protect her from what I couldn't detect?

"Vasilissa. . .please calm down. . . You are safe. I promise I won't let anything hurt you." I attempted to calm her, yet my efforts fell flat.

She screamed louder as the ground shook violently again. Her branches rustled with nonexistent wind as she struggled to break free from what had a hold on her mind.

"Montibus!" I cried. Surely the god wouldn't entirely abandon us now. "She needs help!"

Despite all the chaos around me, I noticed immediately when my tie to Melissa stilled in my chest. Her terror vanished, leaving an absence that rang above all other sensations. I should have spoken with Kelan as he passed through Voreios. I knew it was urgent, but I could only hope he'd made it in time.

There were no impressions of emotion. No pulls in a direction that would lead me straight to her. I tore through all the potential reasons for this change. Had it been the fae, the elves, or Cholios? In the end, it didn't matter. If Melissa were gone, only the gods could save Voreios now.

Knowing I could do nothing to save my true mate, I focused on what I *could* do to protect my sweet dryad. In desperation, I placed my hands on her bark.

I swore I would never use this particular ability, but if she wouldn't come out, I was going to go into her tree essence. Earth magic allowed me to uniquely connect to things associated with the element, including some limited tree walking. My gifts were primarily catered to working with stone and earth for defense and strength, but I could also tap into the spirit of plants when I put in enough effort.

"Vasilissa, I'm coming in there," I announced before endeavoring to shove my way in. I really didn't want to do this to her, but how else could I help if she fought something so deep inside and couldn't tell me what she needed?

My hands emitted a white glow, and our connection flared to life in an instant sign that the vasilissa was welcoming me. She wanted me to come in and protect her. This new insight allowed me to push past my trepidation of attempting to invade her space.

I didn't get far before I knew something was amiss. A shadow barrier sliced through our connection, searing me with jolts of icy fire across my entire torso. The more I pushed, the more resistance I felt until the invisible barrier threw me back from the base of her tree. I slammed into the snowy ground as if I'd been thrown by thirty men, my body leaving a deep groove in the soil.

That shouldn't have been possible. Other rynes could use this technique. I'd never attempted it before, but there was a shield in my way, something blocking me from her essence.

The nymphs wailed again. Though I couldn't see them as I pushed myself up off the ground, I heard shuffling in the snow as they moved closer.

"Stay where you are!" I demanded with a snarl, every muscle in my body aching as I stood on my hooves.

I was back at my dryad's side in an instant. Her musical notes sounded like sobs, and the grass around her tree shriveled, as if scorched by the sun. The natural magic surrounding her seemed unsure how to behave among the chaos.

Pure fear radiated from every crevice of her bark, threatening to consume my very emotional soul. I'd never felt so powerless in my life. Not since Baccys had died, but this was so much worse.

"I'm here. I know this is scary, but you must let me in so I can protect you. I need to know what's happening," I begged the vasilissa, hoping I sounded braver than I felt at this moment.

The oak tree suddenly fell silent. The movement, the crying, the energy—all stopped at once. When I touched

21

her, I no longer felt her essence swirling under the bark. The shield protecting the grove flickered with the residual power from her magic, but it would only be a matter of time before it fell if I couldn't wake her.

My chest seized with dread as my breath came out in staggered pants. Was this really happening? Was I going to lose both of my women with no knowledge of what took place?

"Vasilissa. . . Vasilissa."

Nothing. No response. No blurry images imprinting in my mind. No musical greeting. I would even take the crying so long as she responded. My heart sank to the pit of my stomach with the realization of what this meant. I'd lost her to an enemy I couldn't see. None of my training had mattered. A light breeze rustled her leaves, but nothing stirred within her.

"Graak! We have an urgent problem."

I'd hardly recognized Zoq's voice with all the anguish in his tone. Great. Now there was something else to deal with.

If Zoq had returned from the winter solstice ritual already, then he should have the watchtowers with him. They could fix this and tell me what happened to Melissa. I still couldn't feel her, but I needed to get as much information as possible before I panicked.

But Zoq was alone. The flower nymphs continued crying in small groups, forcing him to wade through as he approached me far slower than I liked. He did his best to appear expressionless, but something broke through the cracks of his facade. Horror.

"What happened? Spare no details!" I snapped harshly before I could stop myself.

22

To his credit, Zoq didn't flinch at my tone before he began his debriefing. "All of us had to flee the sacred lands. The ground shook violently, and the elemental powers would not take hold. Even the gods were not present. Something very foul hung in the air. I brought everyone back so they would be safe before the portals between our groves collapsed. No one can celebrate the solstice tonight. How can they? With what happened on the sacred grounds and this situation with the vasilissa. Please tell me something has changed here. Is she recovering? Or is it the same?"

The ritual failed?

My mind staggered while digesting this information. There had never been a failed ritual, even after Voreios burned to nothing more than ash.

The gods hadn't mentioned this as a possibility, had they? Combined with the death of our mother tree. . .was this all my fault?

I took a deep breath as I figured out how to deliver the news. The truth meant damnation of our grove for sure, but I had to tell him regardless. The rest of the groves might be in danger now. My failure would cost us all, and I couldn't even explain how it happened.

I struggled to string the words together. "She—"

Soft musical notes interrupted my update. My breath hitched in my throat as I turned back towards her. Her tones were nervous and more like a whisper in the breeze, but she was alive. She sounded confused, like she'd been startled awake. Everything else slipped away as I approached her again.

23

"You're still with me. . .oh, my vasilissa," I cooed, in a tone reserved only for her. I stroked her bark gently. "You're safe. I will find help."

Zoq stood beside me, relief clear on his face as he studied her. "She seems to have settled. I will take that as one blessing from the gods. The rumblings of the sacred grounds, however, are not a good omen for the future. The planet will be out of alignment now that the ritual has failed."

I didn't care about anything except my beautiful little dryad singing to me. She told me a long story at an unhurried pace. Even knowing I wouldn't understand the full extent of her tree speak, she sounded like she needed to get it off her chest. Her singing trembled, however, and whatever occurred could not be allowed to happen again. I listened to her as dutifully as I could even knowing Zoq still needed to speak with me.

My magic had not protected her from whatever this event was, and I needed to get to the root of the reason after I met up with Melissa. My fingers caressed the grooves in her bark to offer her comfort, and she accepted it warmly. Pink flashes of light entered my mind again as the vasilissa finished her thoughts.

"These are extraordinary circumstances. Did the watchtowers come back with you? Melissa? I need to see them all immediately," I pressed, processing everything.

With Ferox and Lilise, I could learn how to prevent this. The gods would be appeased for my delay once I'd spoken to and claimed Melissa as my true mate. It would have to work. This couldn't happen again.

"I forgot to mention that part." Zoq coughed and shifted nervously on his hooves. His eyes kept trailing back up to the vasilissa—who wasted no time in reestablishing her link to the illusionary rock border around the grove. Our connection to the magic of Voreios strengthened with every moment. "They were not there."

I furrowed my brow at my advisor. "What do you mean by 'they were not there'?"

"The gods *and* the watchtowers were missing. Hairiko had been talking with Lilise as they came through their portal for the ritual, and then they couldn't find Melissa. The watchtowers left immediately for Dytika, but they did not rejoin us. A few minutes into the ritual, Sabina stopped everything and let us know the portals were collapsing. I made the call with the vasilissas to return at that time."

A string of curses flew through my mind. This was much worse than I thought possible. "The inter-grove portals are truly down then?"

He nodded. "Yes. We cannot access any of the others any longer. Everything will have to be traveled on foot. I have already sent messengers to all the other groves for updates. It's not ideal, but we all can manage for a few weeks on our own."

"I need you to send another messenger to Dytika. We need the watchtowers and Melissa to be found and brought to Voreios right away." I paused and closed my eyes, bracing for the honesty I was about to expel. "I feel I might be responsible for this."

"That is impossible. Whatever goes on with our planet is beyond any of us." Zoq easily dismissed my worry, but I needed to come clean.

I pulled my coat open to show him my mate mark and to his credit he managed to mask most of his shock.

"But you'd said she hadn't come out."

The fact that the mark hadn't faded told me my mate wasn't dead, but the silence stretched on. I needed to see her. To make sure she was all right. And now I was hundreds of miles away without any easy way to get to her.

"This isn't about the vasilissa. Melissa is my mate and I'm running out of time. I'm not ready to tell the elders until we can get Cassie here, but Melissa needs to be brought to Voreios immediately or the consequences will be dire."

The portals between the groves failed because the magic hadn't taken hold during the ritual this evening. The troubles with the balance of the planet were only beginning. If this had something to do with Melissa, then I needed to get to the bottom of things before it was too late.

Chapter 3 – Melissa

I'd been lingering in the darkness for so long that when my body finally started to stir, I refused to open my eyes at first. Memories of what had happened on the solstice came floating back to me as the grogginess lifted.

The guard's dying face as he told me to run. The infernal attackers around the tower. Xernath and Cholios fusing. Flares of bright colors as the watchtowers charged into the dull garden. The gamayun's singing as I pressed my hand to the portal. I couldn't remember anything else, and I wasn't sure how much I wanted to remember.

Where was I now?

I'd chosen to return to Artemesia instead of Earth. This world felt more like home than the one I'd left behind. I sent a silent prayer that the gods truly honored my wishes, and that I wouldn't wake up to find this had all been a wonderful, terrible dream. Would I awaken to find that I could only truly be loved in a place that never existed to begin with?

The soft, unhurried rush of waterfalls filtered through my melancholy thoughts. Clean, fresh air filled my lungs rather than the sterile, stagnant air that lingered in most hospitals.

A firm but gentle pressure held my hand. There was no one on Earth to offer me comfort like this.

I took a deep breath and counted to three before opening my eyes and turning my head to see fingers intertwined with mine. Looking up past our linked hands, my heart immediately lifted at the sight of the person sitting beside me.

Kelan.

My soon-to-be mate dozed quietly, but he didn't loosen his firm grip on my hand. Handsome—even in his disheveled state from whatever had happened to get me here—his long, whitish-blond hair fell perfectly around his face in a way that seemed unfair.

As glad as I was to see him, I didn't understand how he was here now—we still had months before spring. Just one more question to add to my growing list.

"Ah, you are finally awake," a woman's voice said jovially, entering the room with a brisk swish of her skirt. "Call for Lilise."

I gave her a wary smile. I'd never met her before, but the longer I looked around, the more certain I became—I was back in Dytika. "How long have I been here?"

"Three days. With the extent of your injuries, that's not uncommon. I told the watchtowers it could take a week or more for you to wake up." Her eyes drifted to my shoulders, and immediately, I remembered—the poles that had impaled me to the oak tree. I forced myself not to follow her gaze down. "We managed to heal most of your injuries, but it required a bit of sedation."

I grimaced before forcing a smile. "I'm grateful for all your help."

28

"Melissa," Kelan whispered, brushing the hair from my face. Our talking must have woken him. "Thank the gods."

Relief laced every word. For a moment, I wondered how bad I must look as he gazed down at me, love and concern warring in his eyes.

"I'll give you two a few moments. Call me if you need anything." The nereid drifted out of the cave, vanishing as if she'd never been here at all.

"I thought you weren't coming until the spring?" I leaned into the kiss he placed on my forehead.

"I knew when you'd been taken. I couldn't get to you fast enough."

There was a subtle hint of ferocity in his voice— something I wasn't used to. Beneath it, I caught a trace of disappointment.

"It all happened so fast, Kelan. This is not on you," I said, pointing out the easy fact. I didn't need him to shoulder that burden when I was the one who made the mistake. "I shouldn't have left the grove."

He didn't seem to be listening; his only reply was firm. "I'm not leaving you again. Is there anything you need right now?"

I sat in silence for a few moments, unsure how to respond. A flurry of emotions, far more complicated than I normally allowed myself to dwell on, took hold. The weight of my insecurity left me uncertain, grasping for what could possibly come next.

Cassie's smiling face spared me from having to answer Kelan's question. All four of the watchtowers gathered in the small cave. It should have made me feel trapped, yet somehow, it was the most natural thing in the world.

I had decided to stay for exactly this—Family. A future.

Unfortunately, I now had more time to process what had happened with Cholios. It hadn't been some grandiose dream—it was real. Perhaps I should have spent more time with my decision, instead of just signing up for it, forcing all the people I love to fight with me. I'd not even asked the gods what they suggested. I chose with my heart and now they were all in danger.

"I'm so sorry, everyone. I shouldn't have left the border."

"Melissa, don't apologize," Lilise said softly, cutting off that train of thought. "I don't think we properly stressed the dangers to you when Cholios made his declaration at the world meeting. We also found a letter from Avia in the tower among your things. That was quite the dire warning to process alone. Were you going back for the letter?"

She paused for a moment, and I nodded, confirming her assumption.

"Were you thinking about returning to Earth?" Her question didn't sound like an accusation but hurt underlined the words. "I hope you know that you can talk to us about anything. We only want to support you with whatever it is you desire."

I knew that was true. Not sharing the letter with them hadn't been the best decision, but sometimes, old habits died hard.

"I'd already made up my mind—I wanted to stay," I whispered, looking down at my hands. "I wanted to give the letter to the fire as an offering, a thanks to Avia and the gods. You are my family. I will choose this—choose you—

every time, no matter the danger to myself. But it's not fair to all of you."

"What's not fair?" Cassie asked, settling in the seat opposite Kelan next to me. "We claimed you as ours too, and family will always fight for one another."

I didn't bother trying to hide the heavy tears pooling beneath my lashes or the thick trails they left as they rolled down my cheeks. I didn't even want to vocalize it—for fear speaking it made it real. "Any who protect or shelter me are in danger. I can't do that to Dytika or to you. No amount of training will ever make me strong enough to stand beside you in that fight—not after what I witnessed. I will only be an anchor, and I don't want to be the weight that will bring you down."

Minithe tapped my foot with her fist, drawing my attention. "The guards coming in for back up disagree with your assessment," she said. "You took on *five* of the infernal guards on your own. Four are dead. You did that with minimal support. They've already stated that they would be honored to fight alongside you."

I shook my head in protest. "But Cholios—"

"Gods are different, and there is no way you would be expected to defeat him alone," Lilise interjected. "Not even we could handle him one-on-one. But there is another matter we need to discuss: your mate."

I glanced at Kelan, but he was frowning at Lilise. "He's right here."

"Not Kelan. Your other one—from Voreios. I've already sent word for him to be summoned from the grove and relocated." Lilise carefully considered her next words before she spoke, which only heightened my anxiety.

31

Why were they calling Graak my mate?

"With all the turbulence in the world, I must insist that you stay here in Dytika instead of relocating to Voreios. With the portals down, you'd have to travel through forests and some elven lands. Hairiko is prepared for battle with the infernals, and while Voreios is secure, it is still much safer here."

"I don't want to go to Voreios," I answered quickly, cutting Kelan off before he could speak. "We've been talking about moving into this grove. I don't see why that must change. Kelan is my mate, and he's here."

"Melissa, we know about the bond mark," Ferox said gently from over Lilise's shoulder.

"Oh, you mean the tattoo?" I tugged my shirt forward to look down at it, only to notice additional circles along my collarbones. The pain of the memory flashed through me, radiating outward from the fresh scars. I quickly dropped my shirt, forcing my thoughts away. "I'm a bit embarrassed we did it, to be honest. It was a wild night, but a little ink doesn't mean our plans need to change."

"It's not a mark that we chose, my love—it's a bit of forest folk magic, tying our fates together." Kelan leaned in and soothingly caressed the side of my arm. "All *three* of us."

"No, but he. . .that can't be true." I shook my head. How could I get them to drop this?

"It is. Don't worry, Graak will make sure your mate gets his shit together and returns," Cassie promised. "I left very explicit notes, and I will have a very lengthy conversation with that guard when he arrives."

I was going to be sick. Kelan hadn't told them that Graak was my other mate—thankfully. I guessed all I could do was wait to see if he would fess up and claim me. Not that I expected him to. He had a decades-long love who needed him.

I wouldn't out him. If he had wanted to acknowledge this mate nonsense, he would have come back on his own. Clearly, he was doing well enough without me.

"Please don't force him to come," I pleaded, pushing myself up. "It was one stupid night and I—I can't deal with this right now. I don't want to go to Voreios, and he doesn't need to come here."

"Melissa, you need to rest," Lilise protested as I swung my feet over the edge of this smooth, surprisingly comfortable rock.

"I *need* some air."

The rounded room shimmered with cascading water, streaming down every single surface. Placing my hands on the edge of the window-like opening in the cavern, my fingers were instantly submerged in cold water, the shock making me yank them back.

As my mind drifted back to the incident with Cholios, I wondered if I would ever be the same again. I wanted to withdraw, to disappear into a cave where no one could find me. I wanted to sleep—maybe then I could erase everything that had happened.

"Did you find anything out about my blood?" I asked, speaking more to the room than to anyone in particular.

"What do you mean?" Lilise asked cautiously.

"I know you were testing my genealogy and all that, but after the incident with the wild elf—and now the dead tree. . .I'm curious if anything else came up." I shrugged.

"Nothing that seemed unusual," Ferox answered as he considered me.

I chewed on my thumbnail, turning the words over in my mind. "*He* called me a daughter of Earth. Maybe it's just a reference to my human blood, then."

I was ready to dismiss my musings when something more urgent pushed its way to the front of my mind— something that mattered even more than the mysteries of my blood.

"How about Aurinia? Do we know who she is?"

The dryads stilled, their silent communication passing through their root network. I turned, meeting Kelan's gaze. From the way he perched on the edge of his seat, I knew he wanted to come to me, but I'd asked for space. I gave him a soft smile. I really was glad he was here even if that was going to be another interesting development.

After a few moments, Ferox finally spoke. "That is not a name we are familiar with."

A sigh escaped me. Of course, it wouldn't be that easy. "We need to find Aurinia before Cholios does. I can't shake the feeling that she's my only chance."

Chapter 4 – Kelan

Weeks passed after Melissa fell through the portal into my arms. Physically, her recovery was on the right path, however, her mental well-being had been completely shattered by the experiences from that night.

I could scarcely be pulled from her side. Sleep eluded her until exhaustion won out, only for nightmares to awaken her long before dawn. Even when awake, she was far quieter than I'd ever known her to be. Her spark dimmed as her mind traveled to a place I couldn't follow.

We'd moved into our new cave along a beautiful stream, but most days, she didn't venture past the stream except to walk with Cassie. The earth watchtower would give me a subtle shake of her head, indicating that, once more, Melissa had said nothing.

I'd never felt so powerless in my life. Even beside her, I couldn't end the nightmares or ease the lingering pain in her memories—the true fear she now felt from coming face to face with an evil god.

Graak and I exchanged a few messages, but the secrecy it required, along with the lack of portals, often delayed responses for weeks at a time. Graak had sent one to Cassie immediately following the solstice, urging us all to come to

Voreios, however, Melissa and Lilise would not budge. My lover wasn't ready to leave the protection and comfort that Dytika offered.

The scars on her beautiful shoulders glared at me in the flickering torchlight. Lilise had managed to fade them into slight discolorations—perfect circles on both the front and back of her shoulders.

I replayed what I'd experienced through our bond that night, wondering exactly which moment had left these twin marks. Cassie had pulled the metal rods from her, but Melissa remained silent about what had happened before they arrived. Anger and grief warred within me.

Could I guide her back to that easy smile she'd once worn? Without Graak, I wasn't even sure if the two of us together could help her. Lilise and Ferox insisted she just needed time, that her spirit would return to us when she was ready. In the meantime, I would be her anchor while her mind healed.

I gazed down at Melissa's sleeping form, running my thumb along her cheek as a shiver ran down her slim figure.

"Is she finally asleep?" Cassie asked, her voice barely above a whisper.

"Yes," I answered quietly, leaning over to place a kiss on Melissa's forehead.

When she slept, all my perfectly controlled emotions unraveled. Anger, grief, and frustration seized my mind until I channeled them into something else—just to face another day of "I'm fine" and silence.

The dryad placed her hand on my shoulder and squeezed in quiet comradery. "Minithe's coming up to meet you. Get out all the tension. We all understand this isn't easy."

Silently leaving the cave, I forced myself not to look back, instead turning my eyes above me. My lightning raged in the clouds that rolled by in the night sky. For all the emotion not reflected in my face, I couldn't hide what moved beneath the surface.

"Are you causing this weather?" Minithe's question startled me from my thoughts. "There was no indication of rain from the roots."

I grimaced. "There's so much turbulence in my mind, but I keep the clouds away for her."

It wasn't an apology, but I felt I owed her an explanation anyway. Minithe wasn't the biggest fan of water events given her proclivity for fire.

"I can sense it in your flames, even when you think you are disguising it." The dryad leaned against a nearby tree, eyeing the clouds with mistrust. "Have you been honest with her about how you feel?"

"I can't put that burden on her." I dismissed the idea immediately.

"Some vulnerability on your part may allow her to follow suit," she replied with a shrug. "How about you keep the rain over the beach while we spar it out tonight?"

I raised an eyebrow as I considered her request. "I can agree to those terms."

"Swords?" Minithe proposed, excitement bleeding into her voice as she beckoned me to follow.

"That works for me."

She led me to a clearing a few streams over before unsheathing her sword with silent grace. Fire danced along the tip of the blade, illuminating the surrounding earth. With a nod, she urged me to do the same. Lightning crackled under my skin as I withdrew my own weapon.

I wasn't as nervous as I should have been against such a formidable opponent. With a deep breath to steady the surge of energy at the challenge, lightning coursed over my steel, readying me for combat.

Minithe feigned an attack to set us into motion. There was no room for hesitation. With a rapid deflection, I twisted my sword into an upward diagonal swipe. Our blades scraped, scattering sparks of flame and lightning. Neither of us could be burned by the energy of our attacks, thanks to the fire running through our veins.

Minithe tried to bend my magic to her will as we tested our strength against the blades. As I blocked her attempt, sinking into my own fiery resolve, she smirked in approval and spun away. The dryad moved as if this were a dance, each step perfectly choreographed. The fae moved in a similar fashion when they weren't flying, so I was used to this tactic on the battlefield. I wouldn't be distracted. When she launched at me again, our swords clashed—one, two, three times—before I shoved her blade to the side. With a quick sidestep, I struck at her exposed flank.

She would not be taken that easily, and flames licked up around me as she blocked my attack. I surged forward, unafraid of the fire encircling us. While pressing the attack, I kept my energy focused on the right target. Lightning always knew where it was going, even if no one else did. I was used to combat on multiple fronts, but against such a powerful foe, I couldn't afford to miscalculate.

Then she shoved me back with sheer strength, forcing me to stumble a few involuntary steps. The shift in momentum gave her the opening she needed to go on the offensive. Her strikes came swiftly, as if she already expected them to be blocked. The lack of weight against my own sword dulled the effectiveness of my defenses.

The fire warrior pushed me to my limits, forcing me to concede that this was not a fight I could experience anywhere else. She managed to nick me a few times when my blocks weren't quick enough. My breath grew heavier with each exchange, but she remained as fresh as when we began. While I fought with everything I had, the dryad was still in training mode against me.

I knew the true class difference between my trainers and a watchtower. With all four of them determined to protect Melissa, I shouldn't have any doubts about her safety, and yet, she'd already been taken once.

The watchtower met me with as much force as I gave her—until she finally took a step back.

"Feels like this is a draw." Minithe gracefully slid her blade back into its sheath. "I think we should do this again."

She was offering me a way to decompress. The thrill of facing a strong opponent could transport the mind elsewhere. Now, though, I was ready to get back to Melissa.

Except my beautiful mate was not in our cave.

As expected, she hadn't slept for long and now sat on a rock by the entrance of our cave. The winter winds still lingered in the air, and she had no cover. Ferox stood protectively at her back, but I didn't linger on him long—because she smiled at me.

It was a sleepy one, but it was the first genuine smile I'd seen in weeks. I strode right to her, my heart swelling at the amusement in her eyes.

"She trains differently with you than she does with me," Melissa said wistfully, drawing a chuckle from Ferox. "Definitely flashier than when I use blades."

"It would be riveting to watch you perform even a kata with Ares." I tilted her chin up, placing a gentle kiss on her forehead. Ferox stepped aside. The watchtowers were all observant enough to give us privacy without being asked. "You are going to catch a chill."

"It would be worth it. You know, I've never seen you fight before. . ."

Was that a hint of a tease? Maybe Minithe was right—I needed to create the space for her to heal. Not by smothering her with defensiveness, but by being honest with her. She noticed immediately when I frowned.

"Are you okay?"

I hated the worry in her soft voice.

"Honestly, I'm angry that I left you behind," I admitted. "I'm distraught that you went through something so horrific, and I couldn't protect you. I couldn't get to you. Maybe it wouldn't have happened if I had stayed."

"Kelan, they found a very tiny window. It's not your job to be my bodyguard. It's not anyone's job, really," Melissa said gently, her fingers gripping my arms in reassurance.

"You are my whole world. Nothing matters more than you. I felt you here." I gestured to the bond mark beneath my shirt, knowing she felt it too. "All I wanted was to be by your side—to keep you safe. Not out fighting a stupid, endless war for Queen Neia. I don't care what's frightening you. I just never want you to feel alone again."

"I'm sorry. . ." Melissa buried her face against my chest, pulling me closer. She still wasn't ready to talk about it. "I don't feel alone. Not with you. Not with them."

"It warms my heart to hear that. You are my everything." I brushed my thumb along the scar on her left shoulder in a soft caress. "Our future together is going to be so bright. Just know—I'm here for you when you're ready."

Chapter 5 – Melissa

Waking up, I was surprised to find myself alone in the cavern I shared with Kelan. If he wasn't here, usually I'd find Cassie, Lilise, or Ferox nearby.

They were as afraid to leave me alone as I was to be left alone. Or at least, that's what I'd thought.

Sunlight streamed in through the entrance, casting a warm inviting glow over our home.

I rubbed the sleepiness from my face and climbed out of bed. Even though I was alone, I felt safe—so I'd take advantage of this rare moment to myself. Then I noticed a leaf dancing on a string in the center of the room. A note!

With more excitement than I'd felt in weeks, I grabbed the leaf and turned it over, my heart racing as I recognized Kelan's beautiful penmanship.

"Good morning, my love. I have a surprise for you. Meet me at the southern river when you awaken. You'll find a friend outside to guide you."

A surprise? What was he up to? I smiled, pressing Kelan's note to my chest. I hadn't realized how much I'd missed these sweet messages until we were reunited. So much had changed, but this was something I hoped would always stay the same no matter what happened.

I had chosen to remain in Artemesia because my family and future were here. I couldn't let Cholios take that from me. And I couldn't allow myself to become a shell of who I was—because if I did, he would win, even if I survived.

As I gazed at my reflection in the basin of water in our small bathroom, a new fire ignited inside of me. I brushed through the tangles in my dark brown hair, murmuring whatever cheesy mantras came to mind.

"Today is going to be a fantastic day."

"Life is what I make it."

"I am going to be happy."

I didn't know why saying these things out loud worked, but somehow, they did. With each word, the weight on my chest eased, and I started to feel lighter.

It was still winter, but I was ready to wear something other than the practical leather uniforms and baggy shirts I'd been hiding under. I chose a thick, shorter blue dress and paired it with pants that felt more like leggings. After some searching, I found my boots and grabbed my cloak.

Taking a deep breath, I embraced the flutter of excitement still dancing in my chest. If Kelan wanted a date, then he was going to get one—with the woman he proposed to, not the ghost of her.

When I stepped outside onto the recently fallen snow, I expected to see a watchtower. But once again, there was no one.

A soft nicker from my left lifted my spirits.

"Mirage!" I exclaimed, hurrying over to her.

I stroked down her neck with my gloved hand, and she bumped me with her head, searching for any treats I might have.

"Silly girl, I didn't know you'd be here." I turned my pockets inside out, showing her they were empty. She snorted in disappointment, making me laugh. "Kelan will have some for you, though. Can you take me to the southern river?"

I wasn't sure why I expected her to answer, but Mirage simply shifted, revealing her saddle was already in place. Well, all right then. Climbing up with snow covering the ground was a challenge, but one I was up for. Nothing was going to get in my way today.

Mirage took an easy path down the cliffs where our cavern sat. I had been living here for weeks among the snowy hills, yet I'd seen none of it. Lost in the haze of my own nightmares, I had missed out on so much of life's simple beauty. The rising sun glinted off untouched white mounds and icicles chimed softly as the wind passed through them—a song I had been too lost to hear before.

Lilly had told me Dytika was a land of water, but I hadn't expected quite this much. Fresh snow blanketed everything, reaching up to my calves, while a thick layer of ice coated the world above. I couldn't help but wonder how the forest survived, trapped in this frozen embrace. Was this how the world behaved inside Hairiko's protective boundary?

The farther down the hill we ventured, the more activity I heard. Children tossed snowballs at each other as they leapt in and out of high snowbanks. Adults offered me friendly waves and warm smiles, but no one approached me as Mirage carried me forward.

I hoped she knew the way—because I certainly didn't.

I closed my eyes, savoring the gentle sway of her gait as the sun warmed my face from the winter breeze tickling my cheeks and nose. Mirage stepped over sparse foliage before beginning a sharp descent. Her sudden whinny snapped me from my thoughts, and I opened my eyes to see what had caught her attention.

Kelan gave me that breathtaking smile, and through the bond mark on my chest, I felt his exuberance at seeing me. I was torn between wanting to cry because he'd been so patient with me and beaming back at him.

I choose a life with you. Over and over again. You will always be my choice.

His white hair lifted in the breeze, slipping off his shoulders as he caught Mirage's reins and offered her an apple slice. His golden eyes never left me, and I could positively swoon.

"You look radiant, my love." He offered to help me down and I wasn't about to miss that chance. Placing my hands on his shoulders, I swung my leg over and let him set me down easily.

I fought back a blush as I lifted my gaze to him. Tugging on his uniform, before sliding my hands into his pockets, I grinned. "You aren't so bad to look at yourself. Why are we standing on a frozen riverbank?"

His eyes dropped to my lips. How long had it been since I kissed him? Really and truly kissed him? *Too long.* In this moment, I wanted nothing more. He glanced over his shoulder at the frozen river, breaking the tension between us.

"I thought we could start the morning off with ice gliding." Kelan reached back and pulled some thin blades out of his pocket.

"Ice gliding?"

He only smiled before guiding me to a fallen tree. Gesturing for me to sit down, he took my left boot in his hands and began attaching one of the blades.

"We're going to use these so we can glide on top of the ice," he explained as he fastened the other one.

Ice skating. He wanted to go ice skating.

Looking out over the frozen water, I noticed several grove members already out on the river. Twisting my loose hair into a quick braid, I tried not to groan at his gentle caress up the side of my thighs as he rose to sit beside me.

"On Earth, we had special shoes for this. It seems here we use our boots?"

"It seems impractical to have shoes just for this when snow and ice only last for a season." Kelan put his own blades on with refined efficiency.

I couldn't argue with that. He took my hand and together we made our way onto the ice. I wobbled on the thin blades, but he moved with that perfect elven grace of his. I'd never been great at this activity—especially without a wall to crash into. I needed to remember to let go of his hand if I thought I was going to fall so I didn't take him plummeting down with me.

Kelan on the ice was just as unfair as everything he did on land. He skated forward or backward with no awkward transitions. For me, it was like learning to walk all over again. He waited patiently with nothing but adoration in his expression. Others skated by us, but he only had eyes for me—like I was the only person in the world.

Once I finally worked up to a normal speed with a shaky but confident cadence, Kelan slid his arms around me and pulled my body flush against him.

"Lean right," he murmured in my ear.

I let go of my fear of falling and let him guide us. With his coaching, we twirled around the river like a couple of professional skaters. Before I knew it, I was smiling so hard my cheeks hurt.

Then I twisted my ankle the wrong way and instinctively tried to pull away, not wanting to drag us both down. Kelan reacted instantly, twisting on the ice as he caught my hand. I braced myself for the inevitable impact, but it never came.

"What happened?" I gasped.

Opening my eyes, I found Kelan holding me up mere inches from the icy surface. Gently, he lifted me back upright and smirked.

"I've always got you, my love."

He cupped my face, his fingers warm against my chilled skin, and waited until I met his gaze. His eyes searched mine as he checked me over for ice burns.

"I'm never going to let you fall," he swore.

He had promised that—on our first date with Sabannos. Wrapping my arms around his neck, I pulled him down to my lips. He seemed surprised at first, before settling his hands on my hips and pulling me closer. I loved the way he groaned as I melted against him, his tongue brushing against mine.

I'd missed this—the experiences, the letters, the feeling of him against me.

Kelan started gliding along the ice again, but I couldn't take my eyes off him. I was making him skate at an awkward angle, so I pressed a trail of kisses down his neck, allowing him to focus on where he was going.

"Take me home please. To our home," I begged between kisses.

He swallowed hard, his hands slipping down to grope my ass as he kept his eyes ahead. "I have a few more things planned for us today."

"A future date," I insisted, kissing up his jaw line. I wanted his mouth again and it was all I could think about. "I *need* you."

He weighed the decision a moment longer, then lifted me off the ice and into his arms. I didn't even have time to worry about throwing him off balance—he stepped off the ice and detached his blades with one hand before I could blink.

Kelan pressed me up against a tree, lips hovering over mine as he tugged on my boots behind his back. "A compromise then?"

"What did you have in mind?" I purred the words as I realized he'd pulled the blades off my boots. How was he this damn smooth?

His kiss in response was gentler than the last few as he set me on my feet. He laced our fingers together and led us around a bend in the river. More trees clustered here, and it didn't take long to see where he was leading me.

A private tent and small fire awaited, complete with blankets and a pot for a warm drink. A savory stew simmered nearby, its enticing smell reminding me that I'd skipped breakfast. . .and dinner.

When was the last time I ate?

"This is perfect," I said, praising all the effort he'd taken. "How about I make—"

I didn't let him finish before I dragged him down to the blankets and climbed on his lap. My lips met his a moment later. He tugged on my braid before tangling his hands in my hair, pressing me down on his growing erection. Logistically, I looked cute, but damn, there was no easy access.

"Are you sure?" Kelan asked, pausing for us both to catch our breath.

"Please. . ." I begged again.

He flipped me beneath him, and I whimpered into his mouth as his hand slid up my covered thighs. His hand slipped under my dress at a torturously slow pace, caressing under the waistband of my leggings. He cupped my sensitive heat, and I rocked against him as he pushed a finger into my entrance. He pressed a kiss to my temple as he slowly pumped in and out.

"Patience." His command was reinforced with phantom touch to my clit. "I have a lot of plans we didn't get to play out the night you agreed to be mine."

A small electric shock massaged my clit in time with his movements as he added another finger. I jolted against his thrusts, screaming into his shoulder—partly in shock, partly on the verge of coming entirely undone. And he'd barely even touched me.

"Oh, I see you like this," he murmured, his voice husky as he continued to tease me. "You're so wet already."

"Kelan," I mewled.

He alternated his tempo between slow pulls and hard thrusts, pushing my legs farther apart to press in deeper. He brushed his thumb over my clit, trailing kisses along my neck and up to my ear as I gasped for air. My body tightened around his fingers. "Say it again, love."

I panted and shuddered as he hit that perfect spot deep inside me.

"My Kelan."

"That's right." He claimed my next moan, driving me over the edge. My breath was his as he stole the very soul from my body. "I wish you could see how beautiful you look right now."

He slowed his fingers as I came down from my euphoric high.

"I need to be inside of you." It wasn't a question, yet his eyes searched mine, seeking any trace of doubt or uncertainty.

I immediately nodded. "Yes. I need more."

With snow blanketing the ground around us, the fire alone wouldn't be enough to keep me from catching a chill. Even so, I wanted to strip down, to feel him the way I hadn't in months. Kelan must have been thinking the same thing, because he scooped me up, wrapping us both in the top blanket as he carried me towards the tent. Inside, he'd already laid down thick woolen layers, and when he set me down, it felt like sinking into a warm cloud.

Watching me with molten eyes, he quickly unbuttoned his leather shirt.

"You're going to get cold!" I protested, but that didn't stop my hand from trailing down his chiseled chest as I sat up.

"My magic is tied to fire. Don't worry, I'll keep you warm." Kelan guided my hand to his lower abs, and I shivered at the heat radiating from him.

He didn't have to tell me twice. I flicked open the top button of his pants as I kicked off my boots. He shed his clothing and leaned down, capturing my lips as he laid me back to peel off my leggings. We continued exploring each other, our hands roaming and our mouths colliding once more. Cocooning me in his warm embrace, he slid his cock through my sensitive folds before pressing the head to my entrance.

I never understood how he had so much control. I certainly didn't. Sliding my hands down his back to his tight ass, I urged him on. The groan he let out as he filled me completely was everything. I gasped, momentarily forgetting to breathe as my body adjusted to him. I loved how utterly full I felt—with him in and all around me.

Then he began to move—slowly at first. His eyes tracked my every movement as I lost myself to the sensations of pleasure and warmth.

"You feel so good, Melissa," he whispered as he thrust again, picking up his pace.

I encouraged him, my nails digging into his skin as I tried to drive him deeper. My mind was so blissed out that I had no words to give him in return. I squeezed him with my thighs trying to hold on as he worked me towards another climax. He didn't stop as I cried out.

"I think you have at least one more for me." Kelan's breath teased my ear as I panted.

He sat up between my thighs, that beautiful cock still inside me. Running his hands over my legs, he chased away the sting of the chill that had settled in his absence. I ran my tongue over my dry lips as he started pumping into me again. His eyes locked on where we joined as one as he built back up to a steady rhythm. He pushed my knees up closer to my chest, deepening the angle, making us both moan in unison.

The soft caress of his hand, trailing from my knee to my clit, stirred me once more to his call. Kelan's hips made a circular motion as an electrical pulse shocked me, and I came instantly with a startled cry. Kelan growled as my body clenched him tightly.

With a sensual smile, he released me from the vibrations as I climbed another peak of pleasure. Kelan leaned in, catching my lips in a heated kiss. His thrusts grew more erratic, each movement sending us spiraling closer until we shattered together.

Sweaty and sated, I knew I could find my way back to myself—right here, in his arms.

Chapter 6 – Melissa

"Maybe I should go to the border with you?" I asked, following Kelan out of our cavern.

The last twenty-four hours felt like resurfacing after being buried in a hole for far too long, and I was reluctant to admit I didn't want to be parted from him so soon. I sheathed Ares in my holster and looked at Kelan expectantly.

"As much as I would both love and hate that," he said with a teasing smile, "I think you have other important things to attend to today—if you're feeling up to it."

"What other things?"

"Like getting back to your morning training regimen with me," Minithe replied from the other side of the spring. "I should make you run twenty laps just because you forgot about me."

She was joking, but I shook my head at her anyway. "We haven't set up a new track yet, so I guess that will have to wait."

"Hmm, fair point." Minithe conceded, but she paused as Lilise came up the trail.

"Good morning, Lilly," I greeted, and she gave me a warm smile.

"Well, isn't this a nice surprise?" Lilly gave me a once-over as she often did to check for any signs of illness or injury. "Prafrum has requested that you meet with him on the main grounds, if you are able."

I raised an eyebrow at Kelan, who leaned in to kiss me before he departed. "Prafrum? Is this because I missed the winter solstice?" I asked.

The satyr priest had told me I was supposed to meet with all the gods during the solstice—before I fell into Cholios' trap. I should have known this would come back up.

"I believe so. Things are kind of a mess right now with the portals down," Lilise answered, following me down the trail. "Hairiko will be with you at the meeting as I'm not supposed to attend. She understands your wishes not to be relocated from the grove and will back you in my stead."

"Thank you for that," I said. "I'm just now getting to really explore what life here looks like, so I'm definitely not interested in relocating anytime soon."

"We still need to talk about your other mate," she pressed. The watchtowers had been trying to get his name for weeks now.

"I don't want to see him." With all their messengers, if Graak hadn't fessed up about me by now, then he was doing just fine.

I knew this trail we were walking on. It wound back towards the main grounds, where most of the social activity in the grove usually took place. Once the familiar firepit came into view, we took a sharp left into a more secluded clearing where I'd seen Hairiko and Rhiap entertain the most important visitors.

Lilise didn't press me any further on the mate thing, just as I expected. They still hadn't figured out how to approach the topic with me, and I wasn't exactly making it easy. I also didn't understand why it was so dang important.

Prafrum appeared on our path as soon as we crossed the tree line. I offered him a polite nod.

"Melissa, you are looking well." Prafrum's soft charm was typical of satyrs, as I'd come to learn. "Please come join us. Lilise, I would like to speak with you and Ferox after this before I leave with Aconi to Notos."

"Of course." With that, Lilise vanished into a tree.

Instantly, my nerves rose. I hadn't been around many others besides the watchtowers and Kelan for weeks.

"Melissa!" Hairiko rose from her seat on the other side of Prafrum and gave me a warm hug. "It soothes my soul to see you out and about in the grove. The children were so excited to see you ice gliding yesterday!"

"It was a lot of fun," I replied shyly. "I should get back to story time by the end of this week."

"Take your time. You know they love to hear them, but I fear that once you start, they may never let you go again." She laughed and guided me by the elbow to where two other women sat. "Melissa, I don't believe you've met the other mother trees yet."

A woman in burgundy, with vivacious flaming-red hair gave me an amused smirk. She reminded me a bit of Minithe, and from the color of her wardrobe, I assumed she was from Notos.

"Hi, Melissa. I'm Aconi. I've been looking forward to meeting you. Minithe is quite impressed with you and your mate. I hope you will let us host you both."

55

I smiled at her, but before I could reply, the other woman jumped in.

"I'm Sabina, the vasilissa of Anatoli." Her long blonde hair framed a face with yellow eyes that studied me far too closely, and I quickly averted my gaze. "You're a small thing—now that I can see you without Ferox standing in the way."

Taking a deep breath, I sat beside Hairiko, unsure how to feel about the commentary on my height.

"It's a pleasure to meet you both," I said, deciding to be polite.

"Prafrum, why did you say the gods wanted us to meet with her?" Sabina asked as the priest joined our seated circle. "We all met her at the world meeting already. Right now, we need to address what happened at the solstice between ourselves—that is far more important."

"I believe everything is connected," he explained, clearing his throat. "The situation is far worse than we feared. Your spring rituals will be of upmost importance in buying us time before the summer solstice. If they're not completed, elemental magic will collapse entirely by summer."

Sabina gasped, and I stared at Prafrum, eyes wide. I didn't understand why he wanted me at this meeting. He needed Lilly and Ferox—not me. There was nothing I could do to fix this situation.

"Things haven't been the same since Amalithea passed on, but why now?" Sabina asked, glancing in my direction again. "Is it because of her arrival?"

"Now wait a minute, Sabina," Hairiko cut in. "Could you let the man speak before jumping to wild conclusions?"

The impatient woman glared at Hairiko but stayed silent. Prafrum waited another beat, then leaned forward, resting his elbows on his knees.

"I'm not entirely sure how Melissa fits into what occurred at the winter solstice, or what role she plays in our future seasonal events. As far as I know, you don't possess elemental magic." He paused to look at me, and I shook my head. "But the gods have spoken of an unlikely union—one facilitated by Melissa moving through the groves."

I frowned at this new information. Did Prafrum know about my situation with Graak? A union implied much more than a one-night stand amid festival revelries. I wouldn't be entangling myself further with Graak. He was in love with another woman for goodness' sake. I was doing everything possible to avoid seeing him again—even as Kelan and Cassie pushed me to go to Voreios.

"Perhaps she can finally convince Graak to take one of my daughters." Sabina almost seemed relieved at this notion. "Celeste would be perfect for him, and she's ready to take the reins of a grove. I'll find a new contessa to take my place."

I should've been impressed with myself for not reacting. Instead, I stewed silently, consumed by irrational jealousy at her words. If I couldn't have him, I certainly wouldn't advocate for anyone else. Graak was far from available.

A dryad no one knew about, and a protector patiently waiting for her. It would have been a romantic notion if it didn't make me want to rip my heart out every time I thought about it.

I didn't understand how could I feel this way when I shared such a powerful bond with Kelan? Kelan constantly reinforced the idea that we were a triad, and my heart seemed to agree. Selfish or not, I wanted them both—but Graak wasn't mine. He never had been. Still, I sure as hell wasn't going to let this Celeste have him either.

"I don't agree that it should be Celeste," Aconi snipped, drawing everyone's attention. "Graak has been doing something to keep our magic in alignment with the seasons. We need to ask him directly what Voreios is hiding."

"Don't you think I've tried?" Sabina shot back. "He won't tell me anything. He keeps insisting I mind my own grove."

"As you should," Aconi quickly agreed, crossing her arms. "I'll ask him myself. Notos will only follow Voreios in matters of this nature as has been the history of our people. If given the chance, you'd drag us straight back to fae rule—and that's not a risk I'm willing to take."

"And what would be so wrong with that?" Sabina countered. "Perhaps it's time we gave that option more thought—before we lose all our magic anyway!" Sabina shrugged as if it were a minor concern, but even I knew that returning to fae rule wouldn't bode well for the groves' autonomy.

"Did you seriously just ask, 'what would be so wrong with that'?" Hairiko's quiet voice radiated a fury I'd never seen from her before. "I agree with Aconi. Magic or no magic, I will fight against any reunification with the fae."

"That's only because of your love for the elves—"

"Ladies," Prafrum interrupted, inserting himself back into the conversation with calm authority, "I think we're getting off track. Graak was also absent from the solstice ritual, so there is indeed something that needs addressing—

and it has nothing to do with which of your daughters moves to Voreios. If we lose all elemental magic, we'll have no magical defenses left against the fae or the rise of infernals. After this summer, none of this may even matter."

"I still don't see how I fit into all of this," I said cautiously.

As if responding to my confusion, my moldavite necklace flared a brilliant green. I quickly trapped it between my hands.

"Earth magic," Prafrum mused, staring at me far longer than I liked. "Perhaps you do have it after all."

"I don't have magic," I protested. "Maybe the stone does, but I don't want to go back to Earth. Silva said I could stay—I want to stay here." My voice trembled as I pleaded with the priest, hoping desperately he could prevent whatever was unfolding.

Prafrum placed a hand gently on my knee and gave me a reassuring smile. "You aren't leaving us, but you have been summoned. Voreios is calling you. Montibus and Silva will be there to receive you."

I felt the blood drain from my face. Hairiko wrapped a protective hand around mine, stepping up just as Lilly had said she would.

"Surely the gods understand she should stay in Dytika for now," Hairiko argued softly. "With the portals down, and no mother tree to protect her. . .she's safer here. Let's at least wait until spring to see if we can stabilize the portals."

Yet, in my heart, I knew it didn't matter what she said. Everything was pushing me towards Voreios—towards him.

"Melissa will have all four watchtowers and her mate escorting her. Voreios will be as safe as the other three groves once they arrive at the border." Prafrum never took his eyes off me.

"How does this help the elemental magic situation?" I asked, tucking my necklace inside my shirt so it would stop blinding everyone.

"I don't know," he answered honestly, but he might as well not have answered at all for how helpful that was.

I wet my drying lips and swallowed my anxiety about the situation. One problem at a time. "How long do I have before we need to leave?"

The forest around us went unnaturally still as we waited for his answer, as if everything hinged on his response.

Why couldn't the gods talk to me about this privately? Then I could yell at them, beg them to take this burden from me. Why let me return to Dytika if they were going to force me onto Graak anyway?

"Tomorrow," he finally replied. "With spring on the way, you need to be in Voreios before the full transition. With Cassie as your guide, Graak will let you in."

I chuckled, but it wasn't a pleasant sound. Of course he would let me in. So much for staying away from Graak. I hoped that his prestige within the grove and whatever task I was given would keep us apart—but I very much doubted it. He may love his dryad, but our chemistry had been undeniable. I wouldn't be able to avoid him. There wasn't a forest big enough to keep me away if the gods forced us together.

"I'm sorry to interrupt this meeting," Mebsec said, emerging from the forest behind us, "but there are elves at our border."

Hairiko tilted her head, narrowing her eyes in confusion. "During the winter? Let them in, of course. I think we are almost finished here?"

The question was directed at Prafrum, who nodded. "For now. I think more will come to light once Melissa is in position in Voreios."

"All right, then we shall wait for direction from the gods. I will go with you to greet them."

"Unfortunately, they are not here for a visit." Mebsec tossed a frown in my direction. "They are requesting our assistance with arresting Kelan."

Chapter 7 – Kelan

I'd read the demand letter at least five times before crumpling it in my hand and burning it to ashes with a flicker of lightning.

Of course, the elven guard would retaliate for the way I'd abandoned my post. But I hadn't fathomed they would approach Dytika with a request like this. Glaring at Fenian and Captain Beren through the illusionary border Hairiko had placed around the grove, I tried to ignore the conversation Rhiap was having with them.

The demands were simple: turn myself in, admit to treason and abandoning my oath, and be tried as a spy for a foreign kingdom. If I surrendered immediately, they would take a few years off my sentence.

"General treason? What kind of charge is that?" Lilise asked, mostly to Ferox as they both weighed the accusations. "It's like they've never seen an elf move into a grove before! Have you heard about them doing this to others?"

"I didn't go about this the proper way." I hated having to admit it. "They hadn't approved my request to court her. But when she was in trouble, I couldn't wait for their permission to leave—not when they already refused to acknowledge our relationship."

"We will fix this." Ferox's grip on my shoulder was firm, his voice unwavering. "Melissa needs you while she recovers. You may have to give up any claim you have in the elven kingdom, but—"

"Done. Nothing matters except her," I agreed easily. Melissa was the only thing that mattered. After my mother's passing, there wasn't much I truly owned while in the guard, but all my savings I'd built up were meaningless in grove life anyway.

Rhiap shook his head and gestured for Fenian to wait, crossing the bridge with a sigh and an apologetic glance in my direction.

"It's worse than I expected. They're demanding we aid them in pulling you out of Voreios." The satyr pinched the bridge of his nose and sighed again. "They will not listen to reason."

They didn't realize I had only gone to Voreios to reach Dytika through the portals. Well, that might clear up some of this.

"I'm sorry to have brought this to your border, especially with your allies. I should have sent them my formal resignation right away." The last thing I wanted was to create more problems for the leadership here. Cholios was bad enough—they didn't need trouble with their allies too. "Let me talk to them. I'm sure we can smooth this out and come to some kind of agreement."

"They are not here to negotiate, Kelan. They might arrest you as soon as you cross that bridge," Rhiap warned before turning to exchange a few quiet words with Mebsec, who had just arrived from the main grounds.

"They will not touch you with us here," Ferox said firmly. "We won't let them get close enough."

Mebsec appeared to be struggling the most with the situation. "If they know you have a mate, they should have expected you to move. I've known these men since they were barely adults, and I don't like being taken by surprise. Fenian, out of all of them, must understand how bad this looks—yet he's treating Rhiap with indifference. I don't like it."

"I hate to go against Hairiko, but we can't let them in with this attitude. Any talks will need to take place outside the border." Rhiap gestured for me to follow him across the barrier.

Crossing the bridge, it took everything in me to appear calm. Yes, I'd left the guard from the war front, but I had never betrayed their secrets to an enemy force. I was living in Dytika, their ally.

"We knew we could count on you!" Fenian exclaimed, bowing his head at Rhiap.

"Hold on just a moment, he came out here of his own free will because he wanted to talk to you—nothing more than that." Rhiap waved off Fenian's enthusiasm. "I don't appreciate this display of force on my border when we have always welcomed you with grace."

Lilise and Ferox positioned themselves to my left, standing in front of the gathered guard.

"I agree," Lilise said, echoing Rhiap with a sourness in her voice. "It is entirely uncalled for."

"This wasn't meant to threaten the grove, but we cannot take any chances with him." Fenian's disapproving tone practically dripped with disdain as he spoke in my direction. "To have two guards in a row behave so deplorably, the queen has asked that we review how we spend our time in the grove."

I frowned at him. How dare he lump me together with Neldor. I didn't have a chance to reply before Rhiap spoke again.

"We will gladly welcome you for as long or as little as your queen allows—so long as you do not bring this hostility with you." Rhiap gestured towards me. "Kelan mate bonded with Melissa. That would have happened whether he had been here for a week or for years. This is the highest honor among those who live within the groves. He returned because she was in danger, and she is still recovering. Leniency is required in this situation."

Fenian winced at the cultural nuances the druwid had referenced. "Rhiap, this is, unfortunately, a matter our code cannot overlook so easily. Reports claimed you had defected to Voreios, so I'm surprised to see you here, Kelan."

"I passed through Voreios so I could return to Dytika. The grove guards understand the urgency when a mate is involved, and they respected my request. Melissa needed me, and I didn't have days to delay," I answered dutifully, staying on the path Rhiap had laid the groundwork for.

"Since the danger to the human has passed, we need you to return immediately to Aramore," Beren said, glaring at me. "I'm sure we can find a way to navigate this so you can return to your post."

"I'm not leaving *Melissa* again." I emphasized her name, making no effort to mask the irritation their dismissal caused me. I would not tolerate their classist arrogance when it came to her. "She is recovering, and I will not be persuaded to leave her. I can prepare a formal resignation letter if so desired."

"We will arrest you if you do not return as commanded." My former captain gestured towards the guards behind him, though they didn't seem particularly inclined to act. I had trained most of them when they joined the ranks after all.

"I don't understand why. You can clearly see I didn't defect to Voreios. I am here for my mate, in a grove that you have an alliance with." I pressed for them to elaborate—none of this made any sense. "The normal punishment for resigning without process would be to eliminate my stipend, which you can have. Why must I be arrested?"

"Were you intending to return to your post if she had been safe?" Beren countered.

I considered the question, though I knew it was rhetorical. We both already knew my answer. "What had the council decided about my request to court Melissa?"

Fenian answered for the captain, casting a nervous glance at Lilise. "I don't believe that has been reviewed yet."

"Then you know my answer. Melissa accepted my proposal according to our customs, and as such, she is my mate."

"Unfortunately, that's not how it works." Fenian cleared his throat. "Come back with us now, and let's find a solution that works for everyone."

Before I could refuse him again, hurried footsteps echoed from the bridge.

"You can't arrest him!"

Melissa burst into the center of the gathered group, placing herself in front of me as a small shield. Her arms wrapped around me, pressing me tightly against her back, as if she could hold me in place and keep me from vanishing before her eyes.

"I won't let you," she insisted.

She might as well have whispered the last sentence, her gaze sweeping over the gathered elven guards. Beren frowned at her before shifting his focus back to me with a raised eyebrow. Having Melissa in the middle only made the tension spike. It put me on the defensive in a way I hadn't expected. If anyone so much as moved wrong, my charged lightning bolts were already locked onto them all.

Ferox shifted closer to where Melissa and I stood as I struggled to stay calm with the way this conversation had turned. It was a subtle gesture assuring me that the elves wouldn't touch her either.

"She appears to be fine," Beren said before shifting his gaze to Fenian. "I think the charges should stand."

Fenian looked between the two of us, then nodded. "Indeed. Kelan, we need to go. If you come with us, I will do my best to negotiate a plea bargain."

"Wait." Melissa paused to check something with Lilise, then turned back to Fenian. "I'm an ambassador too, right? What do you want in exchange for letting him stay?"

"Melissa," I warned, reaching to tilt her face towards mine.

Unfortunately, Fenian took the bait and immediately seized his chance.

"Agree to go to the fae court for a year to end the war." He took a few steps closer to Melissa, his serious expression an attempt to intimidate her.

"No," I growled, but I wasn't alone. Ferox echoed my word—not in the same tone, but with the same unwavering emphasis. Melissa would not be going to the fae court.

"Then we have no further need to negotiate with you," the ambassador said dismissively.

Sadness tugged at my bond as Melissa considered his words. "Then I will go with him. I'm his mate, and where you take him, you will have to take me."

"Melissa, that's not a good idea," Lilise interjected, but Melissa shook her head at the dryad.

"I'm sorry. I know this is confusing for you." I didn't like the condescending tone Fenian used with her, and I glowered at him. "Kelan didn't have permission to court you. There's a process."

"He didn't need it from anyone other than me," Melissa replied immediately. "I decide who gets that chance."

"She's right," Lilise agreed. "According to elven customs laid out two centuries ago, the woman is the only one who gets a say in who courts her and who she chooses to mate with."

"This is a special circumstance, and that law does not apply here. Melissa is not a nymph, so other rules apply." Fenian argued again.

"Your law does not indicate a species in the clauses." Lilise dismissed the rebuttal entirely.

"Kelan was given specific orders while in Ylluna not to pursue this further without express permission from the council." Fenian took another step closer, and my lightning crackled across the darkening sky in warning.

Melissa glanced up, an amused smirk tugging at her lips as she processed this new information—realizing that I had, instead, proposed that very night.

"I still don't quite understand how a council that has never met me gets to decide what future I do or don't have with the man I love. If I can't go with him, how about you entice the fae with my presence so we can sit down and negotiate a peace?" She glanced towards Lilise as she offered, likely checking to see if this could work.

The dryad didn't look pleased with the suggestion, but I caught the subtle nod she gave Melissa.

"You would assist us with negotiations?"

"Yes. In exchange for Kelan's release and all charges being dropped. It must be on neutral ground and away from the war front."

I watched her with pride as she navigated the terms. She was quick and thoughtful. The two ambassadors considered each other for a long moment.

"He comes with us now to settle his remaining affairs, and we arrange the talks for ten days from now. When you meet us at the world meeting hall in Melladur, he is yours."

"I will be at the station *tomorrow* morning at first light," I cut in. I wouldn't leave her at this moment. Not like this.

"I do need to stress that I will only be there as a witness. There is no chance that I will reside in the fae court for any length of time," Melissa added.

Fenian nodded in acceptance. "Very well. Kelan, we will see you in the morning."

I didn't bother with pleasantries as I scooped Melissa into my arms and carried her back across the bridge into Dytika. Rhiap and Mebsec waited until the elven guard had fully retreated from the border before following us.

"I don't like this plan, my love," I murmured as I set her on her feet.

"Yeah? Well, I don't like imagining that they're going to keep looking for you. Let's be done with all of this." Determination settled across her face as she stared up at me. "After this, we can focus on our future together."

I wasn't going to win this with her. I hated the thought of overriding her decision, but I had to try. Turning to Lilise and Ferox, I asked, "Is there any way you can take her to Voreios instead?"

If I was being taken from her, then she needed to be with Graak. Perhaps he could stop these negotiations from happening.

"No, I'm not leaving without you," Melissa said firmly. "It can wait a few days."

"What can wait a few days?" Lilise raised a brow, giving Melissa a look I didn't quite understand. I must have missed something since that almost sounded like resigned agreement to go to Voreios.

"Prafrum says I have to leave for Voreios in the morning, that the grove is calling or some other nonsense, but I'm not leaving without Kelan." Melissa glanced down at her hands. "Please don't make me."

"If the gods are saying you are needed in Voreios, we can't delay that," she replied gently. "With the portals down, we'll have to travel on foot. If the meeting is in ten days, that doesn't leave much flexibility on time."

Melissa's breath hitched. "If the portals are down, how will we all make it to the meeting? Why can't I stay here?" Panic washed over her, and I hated that it looked like I would be leaving her again—especially when everything around her was changing.

"Graak is anchored to the magic of Voreios. Once we're in the grove, I'll be able to teleport us in and out as needed—but we have to get there first," Ferox explained. "The elves have transports they use. What else did Prafrum say?"

Melissa hesitated. "He said elemental magic is failing. If the spring and then summer rituals don't go well, then all will be lost."

"Prafrum said that to you?" Lilise asked, exchanging a quick glance with Ferox.

"Yeah. The three vasilissas and I are tied to whatever happens next, I guess. Even he doesn't know how, but the gods should be ready to speak to me once I arrive in Voreios. I didn't get to hear more of the plan because somebody was getting arrested." Melissa teased me, the playfulness in her voice making my heart sing.

71

Chapter 8 – Kelan

The sweetest sensation roused me from my light slumber.

Warm lips pressed a soft kiss to my lower abs, followed by another, trailing lower. Melissa brushed my loosened pants aside, her breath teasing my skin as she knelt between my legs. Her bare breasts peeked through the cascade of her loose, dark hair, and my cock immediately stood at attention as realization dawned. Lowering her head, she grazed the base of my shaft with her lips as she freed me from my clothes.

"Melissa. . ." I groaned, threading my fingers through her hair. The sight of my cock disappearing into her mouth sent a charge racing down my spine. What a way to wake up.

What she couldn't take into her mouth, she stroked with her palm, coating me with her warmth. The caress of her tongue along the underside of my shaft had me tightening my grip. Melissa eased her lips back and licked me from base to tip, her eyes gleaming with mischief. I was painfully hard at this point, aching under her slow torment. Then, with a flick of her tongue, she tasted the bead of precum at my tip, and I nearly came undone.

It felt so damn good, and on any other morning, I would have let her have her way. But today, I needed more than just her lips wrapped around me. Today, I had to leave her again. Today, I was sending her off to reunite with her other mate. I wasn't jealous—she needed to be with him. But the selfish part of me ached to remind her that she was mine too.

She squeaked in surprise when I lifted her effortlessly, her lips slipping free from my cock with a wet *pop*. I laid her down beside me, pressing her into the mattress on her stomach. Flipping onto my knees behind her, I grabbed her hips, pulling that perfect ass of hers up, exposing her glistening core.

"Kelan," Melissa purred over her shoulder, arching her back into my touch. My little temptress was breathtakingly gorgeous, and she knew it.

The way she said my name was the strongest aphrodisiac on the entire planet. She moaned softly into the pillows as I rubbed my tip through her slick folds.

Her fingers fisted the sheets the moment I pushed inside her. The gods must have made Melissa just for me— no other explanation made sense for how perfectly she took me. I didn't worship the forest folk gods, but for her, perhaps I should start offering them my thanks.

I thrust all the way to the hilt, one hand anchoring her hip to mine as I pinned her to the bed. Brushing the hair from her face, I drank in her rapture. Melissa had long accepted that I couldn't take my eyes off her—how could I? She was the brightest light I'd ever known, and the rest of the world paled in comparison to her radiance.

73

She cried out in pleasure, her body surrendering to me with each deep thrust until she fully opened to me. Every muscle clenched and quivered, meeting my movements with equal intensity.

When she gave in to her orgasm, I let my own consume me a few thrusts later. I rolled us over, cradling her back against my chest. With gentle hands, I cleaned us both with soft towels that I kept in an opening in the wall by the bed, the soothing touch helping to steady her breaths. Slowly, her heartbeat synced with mine, and I knew I'd never get enough of this.

"Do you have any idea how much I love you?" I murmured, stroking the curve of her face with my finger.

Melissa's cheeks flushed brightly as she buried her smile in our shared pillow. "I know," she whispered.

"I'm not sure you do." I smiled as our bond rippled with the silent warmth of her affection. "You are everything to me, Melissa. For decades, I wondered what it would be like to have a mate. I knew I would cherish her, but I never imagined this—this overwhelming need to see you smile, to hold you close. I never could have comprehended how full my heart would feel just because you are near."

Those beautiful brown eyes met mine over her shoulder, and I pressed a gentle kiss to her nose. She didn't say much, but through our markings, I could feel it—her mind was healing.

Her next words were so soft, it seemed as if only my heart could hear them. "I love you too."

Outside, the world remained cloaked in darkness as we quietly dressed in our traveling leathers, each lost in our own thoughts. Her eyes were heavy with exhaustion, as if she'd not slept much the night before. Yet, with the absence of her usual nightmares, a new concern settled in my chest.

"You didn't get enough sleep last night, my love. Perhaps Cassie can rest with you a bit longer."

Melissa only shook her head as she fastened Ares' belt around her waist. "I want to see you off. There will be time to rest on the road."

Traveling was never an ideal time to rest, but she seemed to have forgotten that detail from her trip to Thesalenor.

"What is troubling you?" I caught her hand before she could turn towards the entrance. Melissa spun around without hesitation, burying her beautiful face against my chest.

"I'm going to miss you," she whispered, her voice muffled against me from how tightly she clung to me.

"You will be the only one on my mind. I hate that I must leave you." My jaw clenched. "I will find another way. You don't need to handle the negotiations—they only want to make an example of me for the way I left."

Melissa shrugged. "It still feels like the right decision. I have the fae king's attention, and the elves have you. It's the leverage we need. In a strange way, this has given me a sense of purpose. . .and that's kind of cathartic." The corners of her mouth pulled down into a frown.

"I understand." I brushed a lingering kiss to her forehead, hoping to lift her spirits.

I would never discourage this newfound drive—not when she'd just begun to emerge from the shell she'd been locked in for weeks.

75

"Promise me you'll listen to everything the watchtowers tell you. No wandering off on your own until you reach the borders of Voreios."

Melissa bit her lip, hesitation flickering in her eyes. "I'll listen. I have no interest in seeing how fast *he* can find me again." She sighed, shoulders drooping. "I just wish I could go anywhere but there. I don't want to see him."

Finally.

Getting her to talk about Graak was about as easy as hunting down an infernal mage. I quickly realized I would have to wait for her to bring him up on her own.

"I know you think you don't want to see him. But Voreios is very beautiful—at least from what I can remember from my childhood. The mountain scape will take your breath away."

She shot me a feisty smirk and pushed against my chest. "This isn't about the grove, and you know it. I'm sure it's stunning. But it won't be big enough."

"Big enough for what?" I asked, pulling her back into my arms.

"To escape whatever this is all leading to."

Silence settled between us. The day after the autumn equinox ritual, Mebsec had suggested that Melissa's other mate might have been running from her perceived destiny. I hadn't given it much thought since then. I knew the real reason why Graak had not stayed—but that didn't mean my friend wasn't also right.

"No matter what it is, we'll face it together. Keep your guard up on your journey, okay? I will see you at the negotiations, and then. . .we'll never have to be separated again."

"Never again," Melissa agreed, her brightest smile breaking through the lingering weight of our farewell.

General Brokk sat behind his desk and eyed Lilise with unease.

He obviously had not expected her to be present for this meeting, but no one had been able to persuade her to leave. She politely declined every attempt and followed me into the general's office. Now, she sat like a queen on the cushioned chair to my left, pouring herself a cup of tea as if we weren't here to discuss my disgraceful discharge from the guard.

I had been surprised when she'd decided to accompany me to Aramore. I didn't like that Melissa would now only have three watchtowers, but if nothing else, Lilise's advocacy on my behalf might make this go smoother than I anticipated.

"I guess we will begin." Brokk shifted in his seat, finally dragging his eyes from the dryad to me.

"Will there not be a trial?" I asked, raising a curious eyebrow. Not that I wanted one, but this seemed informal for the charges they were throwing at me. I'd also assumed that was why they had demanded I leave my mate for so long.

"The council would prefer to avoid a trial in your case, considering all the mitigating factors. Even the queen wishes to keep this quiet, so we will handle it without the fanfare." Brokk cleared his throat and opened the file in front of him.

"And what, exactly, does Neia need to keep quiet in regard to Kelan?" Lilise asked. Her tone remained light, polite even, but the question was pointed.

"I'd prefer not to get into that while we have other options on the table first." General Brokk studied the papers in his hand, refusing to make eye contact with either of us as he continued. "A woman has come forward to claim you, Kelan, as a mate. Though unconventional, this must be given all the respect it is owed."

Melissa's declaration had worked! Even if delayed, this could unravel most of the charges against me. The tension in my shoulders eased, and I leaned forward. "I know this isn't how the council wanted things to unfold. And of course, I apologize for the burden my departure placed on you. That was not my intention."

Brokk shook his head and gestured for me to stop. "I'm not sure you are fully understanding what I'm presenting. This is a reverse proposal. She's asked to skip courting. If you accept, all charges will be dropped, and we will restructure your assignment to Aramore permanently."

I frowned and glanced at Lilise. There was no way I could accept those terms.

"We didn't skip courting and I cannot relocate Melissa to Aramore," I insisted. "With the infernals chasing her, she

78

isn't safe outside of a grove. Cholios all but declared that anyone who shelters her is a target. The groves have honorably taken up this mantle, but we'll need to find another agreement to settle these charges."

Brokk narrowed his eyes at me. "That's where the confusion is coming from. Siraye has come forward and asked to have you as her mate."

"Siraye?" I echoed dumbly, the name feeling out of place, as if none of this made any sense.

"Yes, she's in the next room, waiting to speak to you."

"That won't work," I said with a shake of my head. "My heart belongs to another, and she has accepted my proposal."

For emphasis, I lifted my wrist, displaying the bracelet that matched the one I had given to Melissa.

"I would ask you to reconsider." Brokk exhaled slowly, leaning forward onto his elbows. "If you accept, I will also name you as my sole successor. You know I never had children of my own, but many of you in my ranks are the sons and daughters I never got to have. I've always thought you took after me."

He paused, studying my reaction before adding, "You and Siraye would make a fine match. She is aratian, and her children would hold privileged status, given her blood and your prowess."

The general gestured towards the door on the left. "Please speak with her, at least. It's a good arrangement, Kelan."

I swallowed my fury as I considered how to respond to this blatant insult. Being erynian, they likely thought they were offering me the deal of a lifetime—status, a mate, and security I'd never had. Too bad it meant absolutely nothing to me.

Lilise remained still beside me, but the weight of her disapproval thickened the air with new tension.

"As I have already stated," I said, my voice steady despite the fire in my chest, "I am mated. I have asked Melissa, and she has accepted. Thank you for your offer—I'm sure it took a lot of time and effort to arrange—but it doesn't begin to hold a candle to what I have with my beautiful *mate*."

"Please." The older elf finally met my gaze, his voice carrying a hint of desperation. "Truly consider this offer. The human will not live as long as you. A relationship with another elf would be far more fulfilling. Plus, there is the issue of offspring—"

"What specific issue are you referring to?" Lilise's clipped tone cut through his words like a blade, halting whatever point the general had been about to make.

I could have sliced through the tension with my sword, but even steel wouldn't have stopped it from closing in around us.

"Their children would be half elf."

That was apparently the wrong answer for Lilise. She shifted in her seat and narrowed her eyes before speaking again. "And what, exactly, is wrong with that?"

"Lilise, this is delicate," Brokk replied softly—a tone he never would have taken with me. "You know the divisions in our society. Every union of this nature must be carefully considered. Perhaps the queen would feel differently if Melissa were being courted by someone of aratian lineage, but even that is tricky ground. If Kelan and Melissa agreed not to conceive offspring, then perhaps this could be overlooked."

"No. The council and the queen have no say in the future of my family," I growled at my former general. "How could you even think I would agree to something like that?"

Lilise's lips pressed into a thin, displeased line. "I am disappointed that we are even having this conversation. Children are to be cherished, no matter what combination of blood they carry."

Brokk's expression darkened. "As forest folk, you don't understand. Your children are born with pure distinction."

"I think this phase of the discussions are over. This is none of their concern—or Neia's," Lilise said firmly. "By that very understanding of our culture, you should not consider Kelan anything less than an elf. Your divisions based on lineage are flawed, and you cannot have it both ways."

"I think you're oversimplifying the situation." The general leaned back in his chair, exhaling slowly before turning his attention back to me. "At the very least, you should discuss this with Siraye. She's one of your closest friends—and she's been harboring feelings for you for some time."

My jaw tightened. "Siraye was a friend, but she knew I intended to mate another. I can't be responsible for her feelings when I was always clear on my own." I held his gaze, unwavering. "Melissa is the mate I choose to give my life to."

Lilise rose from her seat and moved over to the window overlooking Aramore. "I believe this conversation is finished. I will speak with Neia—if she will see me. There is much to discuss before your meeting with the fae, and I will not allow Melissa to be put in more danger due to lack of preparation."

I offered the general a polite bow. "If there is nothing else, I'll tie up my loose ends. I do apologize for letting you down. But this could have gone differently—if our society had respected my worth and my intentions for my mate."

"If you continue down this path, you won't be allowed to step foot in elven lands again." Brokk almost sounded sad.

"So be it," I replied, though a small pang of nostalgic pain lingered at the thought.

My life here had always been complicated. I had sacrificed decades for the queen's war, yet in doing so, I had seen more of the elven lands than most common folk ever would. I would miss my friends, but they could come visit me in the groves—especially if the war was truly coming to an end.

But beyond all of that, there was a world of new experiences waiting for me and Melissa to discover together. And that was more than enough for me.

Chapter 9 – Melissa

Each day after we left Dytika bled into the next. Every rolling hill of snow, every cluster of hibernating trees looked the same as the last.

We crossed the elven lands without much commotion, slipping past unnoticed as we made our way towards the border of Voreios. Ferox teleported us around any clusters of guards we encountered, but exhaustion clung to me.

Still, I would have given anything to turn back—to run straight to Dytika if it kept me from *him*. Ferox tried his best to distract me with stories as we walked, but I barely heard him over the sound of my own thoughts. They assumed I was nervous about the shadows, and perhaps I should have been. . .but instead, *he* consumed my mind.

Anxiety flooded me when I thought about his reaction to seeing me again. Perhaps he hadn't even thought about me since the equinox. I wasn't sure what response would hurt worse. In the end, maybe the gods really did know best. In just a few short days, I would know exactly where I stood with him. I had always sworn I wouldn't be the girl who got clingy after one night—but everyone kept telling me this stupid tattoo was supposed to mean something. Except to him, it hadn't.

The time away from Dytika had done wonders for my mind. Not that I minded our cavern, but out here, everything felt new, even beneath the endless blanket of slushy snow.

I started training with Minithe again in the evenings. The first two days left me barely able to walk by morning, but now my body thanked me. I was finding my footing again. The encounter with Cholios had changed me, that part was undeniable, but I refused to flinch at the shadows ever again.

The watchtowers discussed the situation about the seasons, but it all went over my head. What I did understand was that Graak hadn't gone to the winter solstice either, and the magic from the ritual didn't take hold as it should have. Now, we were on a countdown to some elemental calamity.

Which was why I had to reach Voreios before spring. And spring was next week.

Not that I could confirm that—the further north we traveled, the more winter clung to us. My nose and cheeks felt like they would never defrost.

"This is your home, Cassie. What should I look forward to seeing most?" I asked as we trudged over yet another snow-covered mound. Our white cloaks blended seamlessly with the frozen landscape, but I could still make out her dark hair ahead of me.

"Home. . ." she mused, thoughtful for a moment. "Well, once all the snow melts, I think you'll love our mountain ridge. Oh, and the beaches—they're even better than Dytika's! Ours are rocky, with cliff ledges that form special rose rocks."

"I think Lilise would disagree with you about the beaches being better," Ferox said, teasing the young woman. Cassie scrunched her nose and stuck her tongue out at him in response.

"Is it common to have snow this late in the year?" I asked.

"For Voreios and parts of the elven and fae lands, yes. The snow comes earlier every year and lingers longer than in the other groves." Cassie shrugged, as if it hardly mattered.

"I don't enjoy it," Minithe muttered as she moved up on my right. "In Notos, it only snows around the equinox, and then it's gone for another year."

I flashed Minithe a broad smile. "Sounds like my kind of place. Why aren't we going there again?"

"Because we'd have to cross the desert instead, and that's far more unpleasant," Ferox shot back before abruptly falling silent as Cassie raised her hand, signaling for quiet.

Whispers wove through the wind around us, elusive and chilling. I couldn't quite make out the words, but a familiar dread coiled down my spine. I should have known we wouldn't make it all the way without them finding us.

Minithe's sword flared to life just as an infernal lunged from the tree's shadow. Then another. And another. Too many to count. Cassie fired off a rapid series of arrows and yanked me into a full sprint. Behind us, Ferox covered our escape—but it wasn't over.

The whispers surged into a deafening hum as a massive clawed hand erupted from the snow under our feet. Cassie

85

shoved me aside, and I hit the ground rolling as she grappled with the largest beast I'd ever seen.

I unsheathed Ares, steel singing against its sheath, and ducked beneath the strike of another infernal lunging from behind.

"Melissa, keep moving towards Voreios!" Cassie shouted as the earth trembled, splitting apart beneath her.

Everything happened in flashes as the elements roared to life. Minithe and Ferox hurled fire and gusts of ice, carving a path through the chaos. Still, three more infernals rose from the scorched, soaked ground.

Swinging with everything I had, I sliced cleanly through the first one in my path, blocking the claws of the second one. I used my blade to push it off balance, bolting right under the swipe of the third. The beasts were terrifying, but after everything my dryads had told me, I had become almost desensitized to them.

Then a skeletal figure staggered out of the forest, its flayed skin hanging in tattered ribbons over exposed bone. It raised a boney finger at me—laughing.

It was unnerving. My brain stalled, causing me to hesitate as the skeleton lunged.

A hand shot past me, catching the creature by its rotting throat. The most enticing scent flooded my senses as an arm coiled around my waist, pulling me flush against a broad, solid chest.

The thing thrashed and roared before the hand in front of me twisted quickly, snapping the skeleton's neck. The body immediately fell limp before dissolving into dust.

I dared a glance over my shoulder. No mirrors had appeared yet, so I wasn't as scared as I perhaps should have been.

Thick curved horns peeked through strands of his dark, wind-tossed hair. The stranger easily loomed over six feet tall. He wrapped his green cloak around me, hiding me from sight. A spark of light ignited in his dark eyes as they met mine.

"Terra Rupti Sunt," he intoned, his voice laced with a subtle fury. The earth trembled.

Ghastly screams ripped through the air, rising from all around us, but I couldn't take my eyes off him. Somehow, I knew—I was safe here. His fingers dug into my hips as he tore his gaze away, another flash of green magic exploding behind us.

Satyrs dashed by us, jumping into the fray alongside the watchtowers in their battle against the infernals. It was almost enough to snap me out of the trance. Then I realized I hadn't understood what he said. That wasn't Druidic.

"Did you just speak Latin?" I asked, as if that was the most important question right now.

"It's one of the many languages of magic," he replied evenly. "You will be safe now, Melissa."

Melissa.

I loved the way he said my name. His grip hadn't loosened, even as the danger passed, and now a new fire threatened to consume me—leading down a path I might not recover from.

Mine.

I knew exactly who was holding me. His hair was a bit longer, and he hadn't been wearing a cape before, but I would never—*could never*—forget how his body felt against mine.

Graak.

I wasn't sure whether to curse him or let him keep caressing my sides the way he was now. I hated how much I loved his touch. So instead of doing anything, I watched him, drinking in every detail of his face until his gaze returned to mine.

What should I say?

"Melissa! You hesitated *again*," Minithe shouted. I flinched so hard that I stumbled back into Graak. He barely reacted, his hands easily adjusting to my movements. "This was an act first type of situation."

"She did fine," Graak replied smoothly, making no effort to mask the heat in his voice. He looked at me like he was about to devour me, and gods help me—I was pretty sure I would let him. "Not everyone is suited for combat, and those types of infernals are the most off-putting."

As the watchtowers gathered closer, I realized I was still tucked up against him. My skin burned with embarrassment, allowing me to finally tear my gaze away as I took a step back.

"Thank you for your help. Minithe's right, though—I should have known better."

"You can climb into my arms anytime, beautiful." His deep voice brushed against my skin like a caress.

He didn't seem to have any misgivings about our night together. If anything, I'd wager he was flirting with me. Maybe I had overthought behind everything or blown it all out of proportion. But regardless of how I felt, or how he acted now, I couldn't forget the most important thing—he was in love with someone else.

Even knowing that, I still wanted to touch him. And if he kept looking at me this way, I'd end up climbing him like a tree. It would be inevitable if we remained this close. Turns out, I had been right. Voreios wasn't big enough after all.

Why did he have to feel so right?

"Graak," Cassie said with a hiss. "You know she is matched."

The earth watchtower yanked me away from the handsome satyr who made me swoon with barely more than a few heated glances. The mark on my chest burned, a chaotic mix of emotions warring within.

Still, he said nothing. He didn't claim me. I winced at the truth his silence revealed. I couldn't be more than what I was to him. A one-night stand.

When we were far enough away, Cassie stopped and spun me around to face her. "Are you okay? Any injuries we need to check when we get inside?"

"No," I answered, though my gaze flicked back to where Ferox and Graak stood talking.

Green and yellow runes swirled between them, glowing faintly as they clasped hands. As the magic faded, Ferox turned towards us with a smile.

"No more walking," he announced with far too much enthusiasm. "Into Voreios we go!"

Graak and I locked eyes one final time before a green rune circle flared beneath him and his guards. In the next instant, they vanished. I drew in a deep breath, swallowing against the lump in my throat. Ferox murmured a few chants, his voice low and steady, as yellow runes appeared beneath our feet. And then, in a flash of magic, we vanished.

As the bright light faded around us and the forest came into view, a new sensation stirred deep in my gut. A humming. A vibration, rolling through me in waves, from my core to the soles of my feet.

I had lived in Dytika for weeks now and had never experienced anything like this. It left me wondering whether each of the groves felt different or if this was something unique to Voreios.

As soon as the barrier fell, signaling that Ferox's magic had ceased, I stepped away from the group and placed my palm to the nearest tree.

The movement inside me surged towards my hand, racing up my arm until the tree's energy met mine.

"Melissa?" Cassie's voice startled me from the strange connection, and I yanked my hand back. "What's going on?"

"Nothing," I said quickly, rubbing my hands together as if I could erase the sensation. "It's nothing. I think I'm dehydrated."

Lilise always said I didn't drink enough water, but somehow, I knew that wasn't it. Up ahead, Graak addressed a crowd of grove members. Cassie gave me a searching look before gesturing for me to follow.

A trail in the snow to my left caught my attention just as the humming drowned out the world around me. I couldn't see anything but snow and trees, yet I suddenly felt an undeniable pull to know what lay beyond that path. Sunlight splintered through the canopy, breaking the shadows into shifting patterns along the frozen ground. The wind rustled through the branches, tousling my hair like a personal greeting.

"Finally," Graak announced, his voice carrying over the crowd. "I know you've all heard about her, but Melissa has arrived in Voreios." He turned to me with a pleasant smile. "I trust you'll all make sure she feels welcome here."

Friendly cheers and a lively toasting of my name erupted across the main grounds. I recognized the rhythm of it—just like in Dytika, the warmth of nightly fires and easy celebration.

When I turned back, Graak was suddenly in front of me. That troublesome smile of his and the heat in his smoldering gaze sent a furious blush racing down my neck. Before I could react, he lifted his hand and traced the back of his fingers across my cheek. I nearly melted.

"I can't express how relieved I am to finally see you," he murmured, studying my face for a moment before speaking again. "I know that was quite the journey. Let me help you get settled in—maybe massage out some of the soreness."

A small smile tugged at the corner of my lips. "I'd need a lengthy bath before I let you anywhere near me."

This wasn't how I expected our first conversations to go. I had thought about him too much instead of just adjusting to their culture. Realistically, he probably didn't even realize he'd hurt me when he left. It was only one night. And for them, why would it have to mean anything more?

"A bath can be arranged," Graak stated, his voice laced with amusement. "Though I'm quite sure you aren't leaving my sight again anytime soon." His thumb brushed over my bottom lip, and a breathy sigh escaped before I could stop it. "Where is Kelan? I'm surprised to not see him with you after I read through his last letter."

The mention of Kelan was like a bucket of cold water over my head. I stepped back from Graak, even though it was painful. "He left for Aramore the morning we set out for Voreios. Why is he sending you letters?"

Graak's expression hardened. "What do you mean he left? He's supposed to be taking care of you."

I glared at him, fighting the urge to raise my voice. "Excuse you? Kelan has a life outside of me. There were things he needed to address before the negotiations."

Anger that was not mine rippled through our bond as Graak shook his head. "Do you have any idea how dangerous the world is for you? You shouldn't be running around without protection. That's just reckless—"

"What, *now* you care?" I scoffed, crossing my arms. He had no right to say any of this. "It's none of your business what happens between Kelan and me. The watchtowers are here—I'm hardly unprotected."

"Little firefly, I do care." His voice softened, the sharp edges melting away. "It's complicated."

Graak gripped my hips and pulled me into him, almost cradling me. I wanted to let him hold me. I wanted him to tell me it had been a mistake, that he shouldn't have run. But he wasn't going to.

"Don't call me that. It's not complicated," I shot back, shoving against his chest. "Let's not make this into something it's not."

"You don't understand—" Graak started, but I didn't want to hear another word. I already knew he didn't care about me the same way.

"I understand perfectly," I cut him off, my voice cold. "It was meant to be one night. Nothing more. I've played this game before, so I'll behave while I figure out what the gods need me to do. I should have stayed as far away from you as possible. Don't let me distract you from your responsibilities."

"Please. Let's talk about this—"

"Graak." Cassie's voice cut between us as she reappeared at my side. "Why are you touching her again?"

I seized the distraction she provided to do what I needed in that moment. Without another word, I turned on my heel and bolted.

Chapter 10 – Graak

Well, this was off to a great start.

Cassie's eyes snapped to me, blazing with silent fury. I could feel the weight of the other two watchtowers pressing in as I pinched the bridge of my nose.

One thing at a time.

If I wanted to talk to Melissa, it was clear I'd have to go through them first.

"Rehk," I called to the nearest messenger just as Melissa disappeared into the tree line. "Inform all border guards that our guest is not allowed to leave the grove. Report to me immediately if she appears near the borders."

The young satyr nodded and darted off to deliver the message. Melissa likely wouldn't intentionally leave, but if she stumbled across an inner grove portal by accident. . .I needed everyone on high alert.

Being this close to her, being able to touch her, I couldn't think straight. My hunger was all-consuming. Keeping my hands off her was already a battle—maybe it was for the best that she ran. I had expected her to be upset with me, but every single one of her responses was laced with arousal and confusion.

"I'll follow her. Clearly, there's a lot that needs to be discussed here." Minithe raised an eyebrow at me before vanishing into the tree beside us.

"What part of *matched* do you not understand?" Cassie's growl was low and lethal, her patience entirely worn out. "I swear, I'm going to strangle you—and her mate."

Kelan and Melissa must not have explained our dynamic to the watchtowers so I was going to have to break the news.

"I'm her second mate. Melissa is mine," I announced, relishing the words as they settled between us. While there was attraction between us, she also had a fire in her that made me smile. "There is no other match for her here in Voreios. That is why I urged you to bring her here."

I should have expected it, but Cassie moved so swiftly I didn't have a chance to defend myself before her fist slammed into my gut. I caught her second punch in my palm and held her firmly before she could swing again.

"How?!" Cassie's voice cut sharp as ice. "I told you to stay away from her! How could this have even happened?" Her glacial glare was hard enough to freeze lakes, but I knew my sister.

"The autumn equinox," I answered plainly. Those were very pleasant memories, and once I made things right with Melissa, there would be many more. "It's not like it's easy to ignore a call that strong," I added. "And now, the pull is even stronger."

With a wave of my hand, my cloak vanished, revealing the mark of fate bestowed by the gods. The cool air against my skin felt as light as my heart did with the truth finally set free.

"Why wouldn't any of you say anything about this?" Ferox cut in before Cassie could shout at me again. "It's hardly a small detail."

"I asked Kelan not to, the morning I left," I admitted with a frown. "I wasn't sure how to approach the bond with the vasilissa."

"Does she know?" Cassie lowered her voice so only Zoq behind me could hear her.

"I've tried to tell the vasilissa. She doesn't understand that it means I *can't* be with her. I know it's unfair to Melissa, but I must make sure the vasilissa is secure first. If I can do that, I'll have a better chance at coordinating everything for the transition—while keeping an eye on my mate at the same time."

"This is really unfortunate timing to re-anchor your mother tree. The spring equinox is only a week away, and it must go to precise order." Ferox rubbed his chin and furrowed his brow. "That's the other piece we need to uncover while we are here. How are you able to do these rituals without her?"

I opened my mouth and closed it a few times. For once, I didn't know what to say. No other ryne or druwid seemed able to do what I could, but I had never given it much thought. "I assumed that I was delivering her magic in her stead."

"That shouldn't be possible. You aren't a dryad." Ferox countered, puzzling over it a bit more. "We should wait to do anything until at least after the spring ritual. Given the state of everything, I'm inclined to push for the summer solstice as well, but I doubt we can keep the secret for that long."

I glanced back at Zoq before saying, "I already have a meeting with the elders in the morning. If I stand any chance at fixing the pain I am causing Melissa, I cannot keep hiding our bond."

"They will try to remove you immediately," Cassie murmured. "You never made any friends among them."

I shrugged and gave her an easy smirk. "Now that you are here, it doesn't matter. They will have to listen to you. I can manage this role while working for Melissa's forgiveness. I'll host the trials, and we can find a new ryne."

"You know it will not go that smoothly," she said with a growl.

"On top of negotiations." Ferox let out a long breath. This had to be the most emotion I'd seen from him in a long time. "I don't like it, but we will have to do what we must."

Melissa had mentioned negotiations as well. What else had I missed? "What negotiations?"

"In exchange for the elves dropping the treason charges they levied against Kelan for leaving the guard, Melissa is hosting talks between the elves and the fae," Cassie replied, her expression relaying that she was not thrilled about this.

"Yeah, that's not happening." I dismissed the idea immediately. "Given Helio's declaration, I won't have her anywhere near the fae."

"Good luck telling her that." My sister only offered me another glare. "Don't you think we understand the risks? She's convinced this is the only way she can have a peaceful life with Kelan. Once you talk to her, let me know if you can change her mind—but I doubt it."

"Kelan agreed to this plan, then?"

"No, he didn't. He told us to bring her here and that we'd find another way." Ferox paused. "Clearly, none of us are capable of telling her no."

"Fine, I'll talk to her about that as well and see if I can get her to budge." In the end, Melissa would do whatever she wanted, but I'd have to secure her safety. "What happened at the winter solstice? Zoq was advised to bring you all back with him, then Kelan mentioned that she was recovering but didn't tell me what from. The messengers I sent never saw her."

Cassie's demeanor instantly changed—shame and guilt clouded her features.

"You will need to let her tell you about her experiences. When she fell out of the portal, her injuries were substantial. As awful as they were, the ones we couldn't see were far worse. Melissa only started leaving their cave about half a lunar cycle ago."

I had so many questions. Melissa hadn't appeared injured when I saw her a moment ago, but she was also covered from head to toe in leather and a cloak. "What portal? Does she need a healer? You know more than you're saying. What exactly happened?" I pressed.

Ferox's hand landed on my shoulder. "There will be time to discuss that, but not this evening. We are going to visit the vasilissa, but I think Melissa needs your attention. The longer you delay, the more time she has to make up her mind without you."

He wasn't wrong about that. The watchtowers could explain the situation to the vasilissa better than I could and I was the only one who could fix this with Melissa.

"I will handle everything in the grove for the next few days," Zoq offered, and I gave him a grateful smile.

Outside of my meeting with the elders, I needed as much time with my new mate as possible. There was a lot I had to make up for and explain. Even if she had been a surprise to me, I needed to show her that I would cherish her.

Following the internal compass that constantly tugged my heart in her direction, I stepped off the path to the north of the main grounds, crossing through the brush. Minithe passed me slowly, heading in the opposite direction to rejoin her team. With each step, I knew I was getting closer. She hadn't run far—just far enough that she wouldn't have to see me, it would appear.

The trees opened into a small clearing beneath the darkening sky. Melissa had found the hammock. Days of travel must have caught up to her because she was fast asleep, her soft breaths the only sound she made.

Whispers from my left drew my attention away from her sleeping form, and I frowned immediately when I saw the two gods watching her. My patron, Montibus, stood close enough to peer down at Melissa, his long antlers blending into the leafless branches around him. Silva's smile glistened, reflecting the quarter moon in the sky above. I couldn't understand what they were saying, but surely, they wouldn't disturb her now. She was finally here.

I had never seen the gods behave like this in all my life. Sure, they would manifest to pass along messages—mostly to the priests and druwids—but never like this, as if I had caught them in the act of plotting. What was it about my

Melissa that had them so enthralled? Had she seen them before? Even more things to consider.

The gods vanished as I took another step closer, but in their place, a multicolored glow appeared. Pastel lights flickered around Melissa's head and a soft song filled the space between us. Pixies were braiding pieces of her hair as they sang.

"Little Lissa was lost in the woods."

"Little Lissa, so far from home."

"The breeze leads the way through the trees."

"Little Lissa has found her voice."

"What are you all singing about?" I asked softly, careful not to startle them.

Pixies could behave in the most peculiar ways to bring about mayhem. They didn't care about order or balance. However, their songs often held varying degrees of truth— or warnings of things to come. Even the most adept scholars couldn't decipher their meanings until it was far too late.

It didn't matter, though; she was with me now. And this song didn't sound too ominous.

The pixies only responded with tiny giggles before flitting away into the night, leaving a few half-finished braids throughout Melissa's hair.

So, they would not reveal their secrets this evening.

I hated to rouse her when she looked so peaceful, but it was far too cold to sleep outside.

Tucking the braids behind her ear, I squatted down to her level and whispered, "Melissa. Come here, my little firefly. I'm going to take you to bed. We have a lot to talk about in the morning."

"I'm not tired," she mumbled, shifting away and burying her face into the fabric of her cloak.

"Yes, you are." I scooped her up, pressing her lightly against my chest.

Surprisingly, she responded better than I expected, wrapping her arms around my neck.

The press of her weight against me warmed my heart. Succumbing to our fated bond would be far easier than running from it, and I didn't want to push her away again. I wasn't sure how she would take the next few days, but for now, holding her was enough.

Chapter 11 – Melissa

Chirping birds woke me from the most peaceful night of sleep I could remember.

As I pieced together everything that had transpired yesterday, I realized I wasn't sure how I had gotten to this cave. I remembered entering Voreios, my fight with Graak, wandering through the woods, and feeling the hum under my skin before passing out in the hammock.

Panic washed over me. I hadn't awoken in the middle of the night and moved—I should still be outside. Someone must have touched me. Even without a mother tree, I was supposed to be safe in the grove.

"Easy, little firefly." Graak's voice poured over me like smooth water. I found him watching me from the opposite wall of the cave, leaning back like a carved Greek statue, every muscle on display. "You're safe. I didn't want to startle you. Good morning, beautiful."

His compliment sent a flicker of irritation through me, a desire to dispute the statement—but I pushed it aside for the more pressing concern. "Where am I?"

"My cave. I found you asleep in the hammock. It's comfy for a little while, but if you stay all night, it'll give you quite a crick in the neck." His tone was casual, as if we hadn't been fighting just a short while ago.

I was in his bed. I shot upright, a sudden sense of confinement tightening around me as I wrestled with the emotions of yesterday tumbling through my mind. I certainly hadn't expected to be here—but I'd be the first to admit my self-control was lacking when it came to him.

"Did we. . ." I hesitated, my heart skipping as I glanced down and realized I was still in my traveling leathers. Everything appeared completely innocent. The small pang of disappointment was entirely uncalled for, especially when I took in the respectable distance he had kept between us so far.

"Did we what?" He leaned in on his knees with a sinful smirk I felt between my thighs.

Damn these internal desires.

". . .finish the conversation we started yesterday." I completed the sentence weakly, pulling my legs beneath me and straightening my back with a long stretch.

"No. That's the answer to both of your questions." He let out a soft, sad chuckle. "We do need to continue the discussion before things start happening. I have a meeting with the elders, and I'd like you to come with me."

"Why?"

Would the elders be able to break the bond? Trepidation settled into my nerves as I braced for the words I knew had to come. He was in love with someone else, and I had to let him go. I wanted this, right? I just wish the thought of that didn't hurt so much.

Graak brought over a plate of cooked meats and vegetables, setting it on a ledge beside me. "You will play a

103

big role in the future here, and you are entitled to be part of those dialogues."

"Did the gods already talk to you, then?" I asked as I grabbed the plate.

Breakfast in bed. Either he was trying to spoil me, or he really needed to make sure there was no interruptions to this conversation. I hadn't experienced satyr morning etiquette, so there wasn't any way for me to tell.

"I have not spoken with the gods since before your arrival in Voreios." Graak moved his rock seat a bit closer, though he didn't have any food for himself.

"Are you going to eat with me?" I asked, suddenly feeling shy about eating in front of him, even though I hadn't had a full meal in days.

"I've already eaten. I have a feeling I'm the one who needs to do more talking, but I suspected you'd be hungry," Graak said with that smooth charm that had gotten me into trouble to begin with. The sound of his voice melted my core.

Despite saying he'd already eaten, some internal pull told me he was still hungry. Every instinct urged me to move closer to him, but I forced myself to stay put. If he was here to dump me, I didn't need to make a fool of myself before then.

Graak stared down at his hooves for a few moments. Even without his usual confident posturing, I couldn't help but admire the sight of his tanned skin and dark brown fur. Even the curve of his horns, glinting in the reflected light, captivated me. Growing up, if someone had asked me whether I had ever fantasized about being one of those women ravished by satyrs in ancient tales, I wouldn't have understood it. Now, I couldn't stop thinking about it.

The silence lingered. Though it wasn't entirely uncomfortable, I wasn't sure if he was waiting for me to say something.

"Do you have coffee here?" I asked, surprising myself that this was the first thing out of my mouth despite my laundry list of far more important questions.

"Coffee?" Graak seemed momentarily thrown off course. "I've heard of it, but I don't think we grow it in Voreios. I'll investigate for you."

"Thanks. . ." I hummed quietly and took a bite of the food. The char marks on the veggies were delightful. The silence stretched between us again, this time growing more awkward—like a one-night stand where one person didn't know how to take a hint and leave. Except, in this case, I was the one in his cave. "I'll finish this and—"

Taking a deep breath, his eyes met mine with a resolve I hadn't expected. "The first thing that needs to be said is I'm sorry. I shouldn't have left you that morning. I should have returned to you much sooner—before the portals fell."

"It was one night—" I started to protest with my usual argument. We had made no promises. Even I knew that in my heart.

"I have a lot more to say. Please, let me finish." The pleading in his tone made me hesitate.

"For you, it was one night. For me, I dreamt about you every night after I saw you at the world gathering. From that day, you were my heart. It terrified me. I'd had my whole life mapped out for seventy years. There was no world where this was the outcome in my plans. Even still, I should have expected what happened at the autumn equinox. I had never felt more complete than when I had you in my arms."

I set my plate down, unable to even consider taking another bite. What was happening? I knew women were rare on this planet, but he was in love with someone else. Everyone who knew about the dryad also knew how he felt. How was it possible that I slept with two men, and both ended up declaring their love? It was a good thing I'd only slept with two—if this was going to be a pattern.

"Graak," I began, hating how right his name felt on my lips, "you don't have to do or say any of this. I know about your true love. I know that you are tethered to another here."

He frowned. "No matter what I thought before, it was not destined to be. I've known it for months, even if I wasn't ready to face it."

"You can't be serious. You have a life here. You are a leader. Just because the gods say I must come here to learn doesn't mean you need to throw everything away. I am fine. Kelan is fine. You don't need to bother with this." I gestured between us, hoping that he would see reason.

As much as I felt like he was mine, I wouldn't have another man throw away his life.

His face became contemplative, his brow furrowed in thought. Was there any expression he could make that wasn't gorgeous? "Do you know what happened that night?"

"Well. . ." I hesitated. "I took some of your magic mushrooms. Then you danced with me in a way that should have come with a censorship warning. Then Kelan showed up. . ."

Graak's sexy smile told me he was thoroughly amused by my retelling of events. "Did Kelan explain to you about the markings?"

"What markings. . .?" I started, before my gaze landed on the intricate design covering the right half of his chest. It matched the one on Kelan's body—and it was far too big to ignore. "Oh. You mean the tattoos we got that night."

He stood and slowly closed the distance between us. With every step, my heart raced faster. He left an ample window of time for me to stop him, to reject his approach— but I didn't want to.

When his finger traced down the side of my neck to the center of my throat, I leaned into him. Slowly, he caught the fabric of my shirt and pulled it further down. With the faintest touch, he caressed the mark we both knew was there. A quiet groan escaped me, as if he had stroked me between my thighs.

"Yes. This one. Did he explain?" Heat laced every word.

"No. I thought we were too drunk or high, and we got tattoos like stupid teenagers."

I closed my eyes as Graak tenderly ran his fingers over the mark again. Kelan had enjoyed kissing it too, but I had assumed the pleasure came from the things we had been doing—not just the simple act of touching it.

My chest heaved, breath coming faster. I panted with a growing need to drag him into this bed with me.

"Hmm. These marks indicate that you are ours—that you are mine. They also claim us as yours. This is a significant occurrence in forest folk culture. It means our

107

union has been blessed by the gods. Our fates are tied together. I will never want another."

With each word, he leaned in closer, his lips hovering just above my tattooed skin. Graak's hot breath tormented me in a new way, heightening my anticipation. If he touched me now, I would surrender to him in every way. But instead, he only prolonged the moment, pushing me straight into insanity.

"You and I are tied, or all three of us?"

I shifted away, just enough to bring his face up to meet mine. That turned out to be a terrible plan—with his lips now within reach. Oh, my gods, I wanted to kiss him so badly. We could talk later, right?

Graak straightened, releasing the tension of an imminent kiss. "The three of us. I can sense you both now, even when we're far apart."

"But you did leave me. Do you just not want me?"

"Oh, I want you. I was barely able to leave that morning. . . The bond was new. I rationalized that you were safer with him. I didn't think to ask him what role he played in Dytika. But through the bond, it was immediately evident that he adored you immensely. I didn't think you would need me—and why would he leave? It was stupid logic."

He didn't think I would need him? I had thought of him endlessly every day, even when I tried to convince myself otherwise. Was there a deeper word than need? I needed to touch him with every fiber of my being. Unable to hold still any longer, I ran the back of my hand along his cheek. He leaned into my caress. Through my tattoo, I felt his elation from that simple touch.

"I was so worried after that morning you left that I was falling back into old behavior patterns," I admitted slowly. "I thought my attraction to you meant I was having commitment issues with Kelan. I have trouble with trust—because of my past. But Kelan returned to the border for a few months, and outside of you two. . . I haven't wanted another either."

Graak gave me a soft smile. "Another sign of the bond then."

"How does it work? Do the gods go 'Hey, this group looks like they'd be good together'? Or, 'Hey, want to cause trouble today? Let's match these three and see how fast the world implodes'?" I used exaggerated male voices to imitate my point, but it was a serious question. Did any of us have a say in how this played out?

He did laugh at my little act, but a new gentleness settled in his eyes. "After I felt the pull of the bond at the world meeting, I wondered the same thing. I've never questioned it before. You were, without a doubt, the most beautiful thing I'd ever seen—but I'd been so sure I was waiting for someone else."

He exhaled slowly, as if sorting through his own thoughts. "I know we haven't had much time to talk, but the more we do, the more I feel as though the bond is an indicator of the other person who can complement your missing pieces. I am complete as myself, but I will be the best version of myself beside you. I have to choose it, though. And, Melissa, I do."

I couldn't argue with any of his reasoning on this, even if I was still wary of the whole situation.

His words sank straight to my very soul, warming me in a way I hadn't expected. Choice had to play a role in this— beyond attraction, beyond fate. Since neither Kelan nor Graak was asking me to choose between them, why couldn't I be open to the possibility of loving them both?

"Okay. If I want to give this a try. . .what do we do now?"

"We're going to speak with the elders of Voreios. They need to be advised of our bond, and then we'll need to put a new plan in place for our vasilissa," Graak answered succinctly. He paused, his lips curling into a smile. "But first, we get you settled and cleaned."

Chapter 12 – Graak

She had agreed to give our bond a try. I could barely believe it. She was far more gracious than others might have been—far more than I deserved after leaving her following the autumn equinox.

Her agreement did not mean my groveling was over. Satyrs were trained from an early age in the arts of courtship and flirtation. It was both a means of survival and a way to bring ultimate pleasure to our mates when we were blessed. I would spoil her in every way possible—so she never once felt like she had made the wrong decision today.

Even with my heart still warring against my devotion to the vasilissa, I needed to show Melissa that I could put her first. My—no. I couldn't keep thinking of her as mine. The vasilissa would be guided by the community until she found the ones meant for her. My true future lay with the woman in front of me.

Melissa stretched out her arms, then, as she got out of bed, rose to the tips of her toes with a satisfying hum. Without even trying, she was temptation itself—the effortless way her body moved beneath the leather she wore only adding to it.

"I'm glad you thought to move me from the hammock," she said wistfully, flashing me a dazzling smile. "I would have been so sore. And probably cold."

I'll always have my eyes on you from now on.

The thought settled deep in my chest before I rose to my feet to assist her. "Are you familiar with how to use the water in the caves?"

I did the best I could not to stare as she walked past. She'd been very clear—even in her earlier flirtations—that all she really wanted right now was to feel clean after her travels. How was it possible that she was even more beautiful since the last time I saw her? Maybe it was my hunger, but there was something different about her.

"Do these work the same as the showers in Dytika? Kelan and I have a cave there, so if they're the same, then I should be good."

Shower?

That was an unusual word choice. Members of the grove considered it more of a controlled waterfall, but she spoke about it as if it were a rain shower. It wasn't an unreasonable comparison—except there wouldn't be a sky above her.

A flutter of something—nervousness, maybe anxiety—rolled through our bond. She bit her lip, glancing around the wash cavern.

"What's wrong, little firefly?" I asked.

"This space is huge. Ours was much smaller."

"Kelan was staying in a guest cave, if I remember correctly," I said, but she shook her head before I could continue.

"Lilise found us a permanent one by a stream. We were making that our official home."

"I see," I murmured.

Kelan's letters had mentioned that both the watchtower and Melissa had refused to come to Voreios, but I hadn't given it much thought at the time. I hated that it hadn't occurred to me how deeply my leaving had hurt her—that I had thought the pain of that night was mine alone to bear.

I closed the distance between us and wrapped an arm around her waist. Her brown eyes met mine, surprise flickering in their depths, even as her fingers grazed over the top of my hand.

"This cavern is specifically meant for druwids, and we are often not small men."

A blush crossed her face as she worked through her own interpretations of what I'd just implied. Oh, my sweet mate was not a nymph—and it was adorable. Sure, I would never be a druwid now, but I had been conditioned for that role all my life.

She glanced towards the bathroom with longing.

"I miss having a bath," she said softly. "There was one in the tower, but I. . ."

Her voice trailed off.

I knew, without her saying it, that this had something to do with the events that no one would speak of. I really needed to know more. But I couldn't push her. Not now. Not when we were finally settling into something good. This, however—this, I could fix.

I stepped closer, lowering my voice. "You want a tub?"

113

"It's okay. Maybe something to figure out in the future. I really don't mean to sound ungrateful." Melissa slipped out of my grasp, moving towards the nooks to hang her clothes. She began working the belts and buttons securing her leathers loose, and I forced myself to focus on the task at hand.

"I don't need to go anywhere."

Calling on my nature with ease, I willed the rocks in the cavern to mold to my command. I shaped the stone with practiced precision—smoothing the inside so it wouldn't scrape her skin but leaving the edges firm enough for her to easily climb in and out.

I had been playing with stones since before I could run, but when her eyes lit up, glowing with pure joy at my power—that alone was worth everything.

"How are you doing this?" She paused in her undressing to run her fingers along the smooth edges of the newly formed tub.

"My mother's magic," I answered. "There's a lot we still need to learn about each other. I'd love to continue talking, but I understand if you need some time to yourself."

Offering her space was the right choice—even if all I really wanted was to watch her, touch her.

"You can stay. . .if you want." She offered a shy smile before amending her words. "As long as we aren't fighting. Baths aren't for fighting."

I could agree with that. I would agree to anything that allowed me to stay with her. There were a lot more productive ways to spend bathing time than arguing. I also had no interest in upsetting her further. Kelan had set a high bar, but Melissa deserved nothing less.

Her hands circled her waist, her expression shifting in an instant. Panic flickered across her face. "Where's Ares?"

She took a few steps around the cavern, her gaze sweeping over the space before glancing back into the main room. Her eyes landed on where I'd hung her cloak and taken off her weapons belt. When she let out a deep breath, clutching her heart in relief, I realized—she hadn't been talking about the cloak. It was the sword. Even from here, the hilt alone spoke of time, craftsmanship, and considerable expense.

"Is that one of Kelan's swords?" I asked, unable to help my curiosity.

She met my gaze as if suddenly remembering what she had been doing, then stepped back into the smaller cavern.

"Oh, no. Ares is my short sword. Minithe took me to a weapon master after I slayed my first infernal beast. It was only a little one, but still."

Her voice picked up speed, words tumbling together in a rapid mash—nervous but excited as a different kind of blush spread across her cheeks. "He really helped me balance it for my use. You should have seen how Ares moved during the fight with the ravaian. I think if I'd had Ares with me on the solstice. . ."

Melissa fell silent again, lost in thoughts I was dying to hear. She seemed desperate to talk about it—yet uncomfortable at the same time. Perhaps Kelan being present would make it easier for her to share what happened. How could I help her work through the experience that plagued her if I didn't even know the extent of it?

"Kelan has two swords," she said at last, pulling herself from the haze. "But Ares is mine."

"It's a beautiful piece."

Damn. The confident way she'd claimed the sword was quite the turn-on. This was going to be harder than I thought.

"Fighting infernals and a wild elf? I had no idea you were such an accomplished fighter."

Melissa's laugh rang out like the most beautiful song. "No. It was a small infernal, and technically, I lost to Arbane. The curse lifted from him at the same time he bit me, so we called it a draw—but I know the truth."

Hearing that she'd been bitten sent a pulse of ire through me, but the joy in her voice over the memory kept it in check. I'd process that detail out later. "Are you training with the watchtowers or Kelan?"

She laughed again, shaking her head. Our bond hummed with her fondness as she thought it over. "Minithe trains me, and sometimes Ferox. I knew Kelan had to be somewhat powerful from his position in the guard, but he'd only ever used his magic around me during *other* activities."

A flush crept across her cheeks, but she continued.

"I'd never seen him fight though—not until he started sparring with Minithe a few weeks back. He's supported my monster-hunting dreams, but I'm pretty sure that's only because he didn't have to watch me get my ass beat."

That was a fair point. I wasn't sure I'd be able to stand by and watch her get hurt either. She turned her back to me and began undressing again.

"Kelan nearly short-circuited the electrical grid in Ylluna when he saw the bite wound from Arbane. I didn't think it

116

was that bad, but he was livid." Again, our bond flared with fondness. "I saw it all over his face, and you may not know this about Kelan, but he hides emotions very well."

A prickle of jealousy ran through me as I listened to her speak about our other bond mate. It was entirely my fault that she didn't know me now—but only time could fix that.

She hadn't even been in our world for a year, and already, she'd explored so many new things.

"Is monster hunting your goal?"

Melissa hesitated, fingers lingering on the hem of her tunic. A soft, but sad, smile settled on her lips. "I don't think so. Not anymore."

Her voice was quieter now.

"I wanted the watchtowers to have a reason to keep me before, but I don't think that's necessary anymore. I still train because I believe it's important to defend myself, but I'm better suited for teaching. That went well in Dytika with all their children, and now that I'm staying on Artemesia. . ." She trailed off for a moment, then met my gaze. "I'd like to live."

She finally pulled off her leather shirt and rose onto the balls of her feet, reaching to hang it on the offered rock hook.

Her hand slid over the wall, fingers brushing the carved stone as she turned the water on to fill the tub. As she moved, her hair shifted out of the way—and I froze.

Two perfect circles, marbled into her skin, stared back at me from her shoulders. Those marks hadn't been there when we met at the equinox, and they weren't bite wounds.

Then, as she fidgeted with her pants, she twisted back toward me—revealing a glimpse of her collarbones. A twin mark glared back at me on the other side. Something had pierced her—all the way through.

"Umm. . ." she mused shyly, glancing back up when she remembered I was still in the room.

"Feeling nervous now, little firefly?" I teased over the sound of falling water, watching as a soft blush returned to her cheeks. "I remember every inch of that beautiful body, but if you want me to look away, I will."

"It's probably silly," she said, a hint of embarrassment in her voice. "With how many women you've seen—grove life and all. It's only a body."

Something about the way she said it set off warning bells in my mind. Seeing her was nothing like seeing anyone before her—but I didn't think that was what she meant. "I haven't been with another since the day I saw you at the world meeting, if that's what you're implying."

At my words, she turned, surprise flickering in her eyes.

The new angle gave me a breathtaking view of the curve of her breasts, the taut lines of her stomach. And there, between her breasts, our fated mark called to me like a siren.

The surprise in her gaze stung. But she didn't know.

"Really?"

I closed the distance slowly, keeping her gaze locked on mine as my palm slid against her bare back.

"This wasn't what I expected," I admitted, voice low. "But I've been under your spell since the moment I saw you. I have a lot to atone for. If you give me another chance, I will love you right."

118

Her eyes fell to my lips, then back up, a renewed need burning behind them. "What about your dryad? I think I should meet with her before we decide anything."

I froze at her soft words. "I don't think that's a great idea."

"Because you love her, and you're being forced by the gods to choose another?" Melissa pushed back against my chest, even as I pulled her closer.

"No. Because she is lonely, and I don't want to cause her further pain. She knows everything I could tell her about you—she asks to meet you often. But the vasilissa is young for a dryad, and I worry that reality will be more than she can handle," I explained.

The vasilissa had already done strange, unpredictable things these past few weeks.

"Does she hate me?" Melissa asked quietly.

"I don't think that's a feeling she even knows how to express. Trees are much calmer than you or I. She just doesn't like the idea of me leaving."

Melissa considered my words for a long moment before finally coming to a decision. "Then we won't leave. I don't think Kelan would mind coming here."

If only it were that simple. A new ripple of sorrow stirred deep in my chest. Perhaps the gods would intervene now that Melissa had finally come to the grove—offering a new solution. But I couldn't help but feel like they had abandoned Voreios long ago.

Chapter 13 – Melissa

Even though Graak had made sure I bundled up in layers before we left his cave, I noticed he hadn't put his cloak back on. Voreios was colder than Dytika had been, even with spring only a week away. But I didn't think his lack of a cloak had anything to do with the weather.

Without it, the mark of our tied fate stood out against his muscled, darker skin—matching the one I'd seen on Kelan. A silent declaration to the groves. A sign that these men were mine—if I claimed them.

Graak walked ahead of me, shoulders squared, chest high as if proudly displaying what he had kept quiet for so many months.

When he promised that he wanted to choose me, I didn't believe him. I wanted to. But as they say back on Earth—the proof was in the pudding. I was still struggling to make sense of the timeline of events that had led us here. Kelan had been pushing for me to reunite with Graak for weeks, and now we were here.

We'd stayed up rather late, talking about little things— favorite foods, hobbies and simple stuff like colors, numbers, or subjects we'd studied. After my initial nervousness about being naked in front of him passed, it didn't feel awkward at all to take a bath with him there.

I wasn't ashamed to admit I found him handsome, but there was still so much left unsaid between us—especially the harder topics. We didn't really know each other. Everyone expected him to be with her, and I wasn't sure I believed he'd just change his mind and suddenly want this between us. It felt right and wrong all at once.

The humming beneath my feet lingered. I'd expected it to fade after sleeping in the grove, but the earth still called to me—as if there was more I hadn't yet uncovered. Maybe it was more than an agreement to a love match. Perhaps when the gods spoke next, I could ask them. Either way, Prafrum was right. If Graak was claiming me publicly, this would be an unexpected union indeed.

He took my hand in his, flashing me a charming, knowing smile as we navigated towards this meeting with the elders. I remembered Cassie mentioning that Graak and the elders currently oversaw some of the grove's functions, but I wasn't sure what to expect. I'd have to take my cues from Graak—follow his lead, if only for now.

An older satyr stepped into our path, bowing his head in greeting. He wasn't as tall as Graak, and his horns were less curved, poking out from between thick black hair streaked with white. Despite his age, the dense muscle packed onto his frame made me doubt he was an elder.

His gentle, dark eyes turned to me. "Melissa. It's a pleasure to finally meet you. You are even more beautiful than he could have prepared us for." His voice held warm amusement as he introduced himself. "My name is Zoq. I'm Graak's primary advisor."

"That's very sweet of you. Thank you for the warm welcome." I fought off the blush creeping up my cheeks, knowing he was just being friendly. "If you're his second, then you might be the man I need to speak to if I want the dirt on this guy." I gestured at Graak, and both satyrs chuckled.

"Zoq definitely knows my most embarrassing stories," Graak agreed, pressing his hand to my lower back as he guided us forward. "He's coming with us to meet with the elders. He was a ryne before the burning of Voreios, so he often keeps me from doing stupid things."

"I'm going to guess you didn't tell him about me?" I was mostly teasing.

Graak winced, but the flicker of guilt was brief before he smoothed his expression. "I didn't disclose the full details to anyone but the vasilissa for far too long."

"I can't save him from himself, though I try." Zoq took the lead, glancing over his shoulder with a knowing look. "But with the elders, I'm usually good to have around. It's early, so they should be in a good mood."

Something unspoken passed between him and Graak, a flicker of worry I didn't understand. Though they both tried to shake off the tension in front of me, it did nothing to soothe my nerves.

Wanting to shift the subject, I asked, "Are the watchtowers nearby?" I hadn't seen them since this revelation with Graak, and honestly, their absence made me wonder if our dynamic had changed.

"They're with the vasilissa in the new dryad grove," Graak replied. "But Cassie should be meeting us."

We climbed the steady slope of the mountains, the morning stretching on with each step.

Messengers kept finding Graak and Zoq, delivering updates in hushed tones. I wasn't sure how they always knew where to find them. It was an aspect of grove life I hadn't given much thought to before—how did everyone always seem to know where their leaders were in these vast forests?

Yet every single messenger also took the time to greet me personally. They couldn't see my tattoo, but the way their gazes flicked towards Graak's mark spoke volumes.

A female satyr approached, her steps brisk. "The south and the west are under heavy attack. They're requesting immediate assistance." She didn't bother to lower her voice.

Graak had walked through every other message without pause, but this time, he stopped. "Who is attacking us?"

"Infernals. Dozens of them," she answered, her gaze flicking to me.

Zoq rubbed his chin, eyes narrowing in thought before continuing the inquiry. "Where are the elves and the fae?"

"Not near our border today, sir. The infernals are focused on us alone." She passed Graak a leaf with another message scrawled across its surface, but I couldn't read it from where I stood.

Graak barely glanced at it before issuing orders.

"Ask Minithe and Ferox if they'll assist at the border. Zoq and I will split up and head over shortly. Send your partner to the other two borders—tell them to prepare for an attack." The woman gave a sharp nod, poised to run, but

Graak wasn't finished. "If any healers are in the main grounds, send them to the borders immediately."

"Yes, sir," she said, dashing off, swift as the wind.

"Wow." I marveled at her speed before noticing Graak's furrowed expression.

Zoq leaned in to speak first, and I appreciated that he wasn't excluding me from whatever thoughts he had. "Why would the infernals attack us? They know they can't break through the barrier, and we don't go beyond it. The only time we normally see them is when the elves or the fae are nearby."

"I'm honestly not sure. It could be coincidence," Graak replied, his tone dismissive—but the tension didn't ease from his handsome face. "Melissa, were there infernals at the borders of Dytika?"

"When I lived in the tower, we would see them from time to time. Once I moved to Dytika after. . ." I swallowed hard, fighting back the memories of the attack. ". . .the solstice," I forced myself to continue, "Kelan and Mebsec often fought on the borders, but he didn't tell me much about it. Kelan and the watchtowers would know more than I do. I hadn't left or been near the borders until I was told to come here."

Graak nodded. "It's unfortunate that the portals between the groves are down, but I'm willing to bet Minithe and Ferox will have those answers." His fingers slipped back into mine. "We'll talk with them."

The way he studied my face sent my heart racing. For a moment, I thought he might lean in to kiss me now that touch was coming easier between us. But instead, he lifted his hand and gestured towards a large cavern one ledge up.

"Almost there, I promise," he assured me.

"Okay."

I didn't really care about meeting with the elders. I had more pressing questions—like how this was actually going to work between us. The chemistry didn't feel as easy as it did with Kelan. Perhaps my expectations were unrealistic and needed more time to come to light. Patience had never been my strong suit, but it looked like I might need some in this case.

The elders' cave sat atop a landing in the mountains, on the opposite side of the main grounds. The entrance curved like a massive train tunnel, torches burning steadily along both sides of the path as we descended into the darkness. My nerves gnawed at me, but Graak's reassuring grip never wavered. He didn't tug me forward, but the firm hold of his hand told me he wouldn't let go. When the tunnel opened into a vast cavern system, the chatter inside fell silent.

"Graak and Zoq. We weren't expecting you for another few days," a short satyr called out to them, his tone initially warm—until his expression quickly soured. "Is that a fate mark?"

"It is," Graak replied, his voice dripping with returned hostility, his posture stiff. If I was taking my cues from my forced mate, then he really didn't like them.

A deeper voice cut through the tension. "The vasilissa has come out?" A satyr with white fur on his head and legs stepped into view, his brows furrowed. "Why were we not alerted that she was stirring?"

Of course, they would assume he was marked by her. Everything in me wanted to run from this meeting, but Graak squeezed my fingers.

"Is that her?" A second satyr gestured in my direction, and I realized I had unconsciously hidden behind my two massive escorts.

Graak didn't hesitate. "This is Melissa, my fated." His hands settled firmly on my waist as he guided me forward, pressing my back against the heat of his chest. "The vasilissa remains unchanged. I wanted to introduce you to my mate today so we could discuss next steps for Voreios."

Silence hung heavy in the cavern.

"The human woman is your mate?" The first satyr's lips curled like the words tasted foul. "How is this possible?"

"She is right here. Don't test my patience before you've even greeted her, Xhet." Graak nearly snarled. Apparently, there wasn't much friendliness between the two groups. "Her name is Melissa."

Somehow, the tension grew even thicker than it had been when we walked in.

"Did you know about this, Zoq?" another elder accused, his gaze narrowing.

I could feel their stares growing heavier—scowls sharpening, each one aimed at me.

"I did," Zoq answered swiftly. "It took some time to reunite them after the portals fell."

A murmur rippled through the gathered elders.

"How did this happen, Graak?" The older satyr's expression hardened, as if Graak's choice had personally offended him. "Melissa has only been here for an evening. Where is your other partner?" I stiffened, not understanding why he would be this invested.

"The how is easy. None of you can deny that she is beautiful. I was instantly ensnared by her at the world

126

meeting." Graak pulled me closer, and my cheeks burned as I wondered what he was going to say next. "We all heard Hairiko welcome her into Dytika. So, on the autumn equinox, after our rituals, I went to find her. The gods revealed our path that night."

"And you waited almost half a year to tell us?" Xhet pressed.

Graak exhaled, but his grip on me never wavered. "I had to make sure the vasilissa understood first." I felt his gaze on me before he sighed. "My intent was to bring Melissa back here during the solstice, but as we all know—that did not happen. But now that Melissa has been returned to my side, I intend to solidify our bond."

"He will have to be replaced," the white satyr whispered to another.

"How? The vasilissa is using him to ground our shield." The other satyr's voice dripped with disdain.

"Another trial will need to be held immediately." Xhet turned his glare back to us. "But you two will be banished this moment."

Banished?

They were going to cast him out of his own grove. I shook my head in disbelief, but before I could speak, Graak wrapped me in his arms, steadying my rising anxiety.

"I will host a trial as soon as Melissa and I return from the negotiations between the elves and the fae," Graak answered evenly.

Xhet's lip curled. "You should not be allowed to oversee anything concerning this grove. Not when your allegiance is owed to *her*." He spat the last word out—as if I were a disease.

127

"No one is being banned from Voreios." Cassie's voice rang out from behind Graak. She stepped up beside us, offering me a small smile, then shook her head at Graak.

"Cassie!" Xhet protested. "You don't understand. He is bonded to another. I know you haven't been here in some time, but there is a precedent for these things."

Cassie arched a brow. "It's true—I have been quite aloof these past few years. But given the circumstances, I will be returning here indefinitely. The watchtowers and I will oversee things until the vasilissa emerges to take her place."

I couldn't hide my shock at this sudden turn, but at least, it seemed, the elders and I might actually have something in common to bond over.

"Your mother tree is already aware of the situation as Graak has done his part in keeping her wholly informed of each change." Cassie gestured to me with another smile. "Melissa is a sister to me, despite her lack of roots, and she will be treated as any woman in our grove should be." Her tone was steady, leaving no room for dispute.

"A new ryne will need to be selected until the vasilissa emerges and selects her own druwid. But these are dangerous times—we will not act impulsively."

The elders considered her words carefully. Cassie held higher status than anyone in the grove while the vasilissa remained silent, and they knew it.

Xhet was the first to recover. "She will not accept another if he is still here."

I wondered how they knew what the dryad would feel towards Graak if she couldn't speak. When Graak spoke of her, they all seemed to understand this dryad held affection for him. If I'd loved someone for that long, I knew for a fact I wouldn't be able to let them go either.

Graak's voice startled me. "I will not do anything to jeopardize the future of Voreios. Nor will I apologize for the gods choosing a fate for me that differs from what we once believed was destined. However, that does not mean I take my responsibilities any less seriously than before. Once I have seen the transition of power to the next ryne, we will leave."

Leave?

Cassie said we could stay, but he was still insisting we had to leave. None of this made any sense. My face ached from how deeply I frowned at the mere thought of going.

Xhet finally nodded at my one-time lover. "We will have to treat this as a death once another ryne has been selected. Thankfully, the vasilissa has not bonded with you, so she will accept another if we can sever your energy from Voreios entirely."

Graak said nothing. The bond mark on my chest radiated an intense grief he may not have realized he was sharing with me. When I peeked a glance over my shoulder at him, his expression remained neutral, as if we were merely discussing the weather.

"Timing will be key so that Voreios is not left defenseless against her enemies. I can assist Cassie with the ritual for the border magic in transition to the new ryne."

Cassie's green eyes flicked between us. Graak's face remained stoic, but my stomach twisted in knots. Nothing about this felt right. I was going to be absolutely sick if I ended up costing another man his home over this stupid bond.

In the far corner, a grey and white centaur stroked his long beard. "We will be present to witness each phase of this transition. You should begin trials immediately."

"They have negotiations tomorrow. We will begin the trials in two nights. That will give me time to round up the appropriate warriors," Zoq interjected, emphasizing that a plan was already in place. "It will not be easy to replace Graak."

"Perhaps we should consider Zrif in this case," Xhet suggested. "He is currently unbonded. Unless the gods will allow an exception for you, Zoq."

"They will not. Nivy is the only bond mate I will ever have." Zoq shook his head and crossed his arms. "I shall add Zrif to the list, though he may be too similar to his father. We don't want her to be reminded of the ryne she lost— that could backfire on us all."

"Graak. . . I don't think this is such a great idea," I whispered, hoping only he could hear me.

"There is no other choice, little firefly." He gave me a gentle squeeze. "I know it seems hard now, but it will work out for the best. Cassie bought us some time, but even her hands are tied in this case."

Was he trying to convince me or himself? I sighed and tried again. "You really love her. I don't want to rip you away from your life. You were right—it's complicated. I'm sorry I gave you so much trouble. You should stay here. Let's put this aside. There must be a way to fix this."

Graak shook his head. "I won't do that. I simply cannot part from you again. I'm committed to this bond, Melissa. Let's get through the negotiations, and then we will discuss the future with Kelan. One of the other groves will take us in. I put everyone in more danger by running from you and avoiding my truth. Seeing you again after this time apart only solidified it for me—you are meant to be mine. The vasilissa is not safe with my recent behavior, and neither are you."

Dismay gripped my chest. "I don't know if I agree with the decisions of the gods. You were a ruler, and Kelan was a guard and because of this marking, neither of you are welcome in your homes." If this was ordained by the gods, I didn't understand all these consequences. I frowned.

Graak's expression softened. "I was only a de facto leader until she emerged from her tree. Given what happened between you and me, she likely would have found her true mate, and I would have stepped down anyway. When we return from the negotiations, I will search for her true partner."

"It is decided then," Xhet called out to the room, drawing our attention back to him. "Two days from now, we begin the process that will alter the future of Voreios forever. Perhaps the vasilissa may even emerge once these changes have taken place."

If I hadn't known before, there was no denying it now— my fated lover's heart was completely shattered. I wasn't even sure there was a way I could help him heal from a pain this deep.

Even as Graak held me tighter to his chest, the weight of his crushing despair through our bond felt like a blade driving through my shoulder all over again. If given the choice, I'd endure that pain every day just to spare him from walking away from everything he had ever loved.

When Lilly returned with Kelan, I'd ask her what I could do. There had to be a way to break the fated tie—so he wouldn't have to go through with this.

Chapter 14 – Graak

The mayhem at the two borders was far worse than I had expected. The sheer number of infernals slamming against the vasilissa's barrier was enough to darken the sun on this cloudless day.

The battle proved to be a much-needed distraction from what the rest of the week had in store for me. I hadn't been able to shield Melissa from the pain I was experiencing, and the pallor of her face made it clear how awful she felt about how the meeting had gone. None of this was her fault. Unfortunately, everything I said to ease her discomfort only seemed to make it worse. She could barely look at me as I departed for the borders with Zoq.

The attacks continued in relentless waves for hours, stretching well into the night. Having Minithe on the southern border and Ferox on the western border prevented far more casualties than we would have suffered otherwise. The only thing that had changed was Melissa's presence here. I recalled Cholios' threats from the world meeting, but I still didn't understand why. My intended mate had no magic. She couldn't possibly be a threat to him.

My hooves felt heavy as I walked the familiar path towards the vasilissa's tree. I hadn't been able to see her today, but I knew she'd still be awake. She always waited for me at the end of battles on the border—yet another habit that would have to come to an end in just a few sunsets.

Pink and green projections washed over me the moment I crossed into her private field. I could only smile as I settled at the base of her trunk. The comforts of our routine eased a bit of the pain—until she hummed the tune, asking for Melissa again. Oh, right. I still had to talk to her about that.

Selfishly, I wanted to pretend that nothing had changed—that we could exist in our little world one final time. But that wasn't reality, and waiting until tomorrow wouldn't make saying it any easier. She deserved to hear it from me.

"Vasilissa," I murmured, my voice barely above a whisper. Her leaves rustled, a silent acknowledgement that she'd heard me. "Two days from now, I'm going to hold trials to find a new ryne for you."

Her tree fell still. No wind, no projections, no chirps, no humming.

"I need you to understand that I will always care for you. But maybe we've been looking at this the wrong way. Perhaps you're like a sister to me—one I actually like, you know, not like Cassie. I know you like her, but she's stubborn and a pain in my neck."

A soft yellow projection and short hum signaled her amusement at my wording, but nothing more.

In my heart, I believed she already knew what I was about to say, so I pressed on with a bit more confidence. "Melissa needs me now. Something terrible happened to her, and I wasn't there to protect her. That can't happen again. I think you'll like her—I promise you will meet her someday. But the elders don't believe you'll find love if I don't leave for a little while."

A surge of pink energy flooded my mind, and the wind rose to embrace me. Her hum carried confusion and protest.

"I know we love each other, but. . .it's a little different from what I have with Melissa. My body and soul crave her. You'll understand when you meet your own mates—it'll make more sense then. I need to be the man she needs me to be now."

I had messed up my dynamic with Melissa so badly that I wasn't sure how to find my footing again. With a sigh, I pulled out my flute and prepared to play a few songs with the vasilissa.

I lowered my flute as another thought came to mind and said, "The elders are going to tell you that I died or something ridiculous. I'm not dead. I just have to leave for a while so you can have the chance to meet your fated and finally emerge from your tree. Once that happens, we can be family again. Do you understand?"

Her answering song, laced with the blue projections, told me she was saddened by this news, but she also seemed to accept our new plan. When I brought my flute back to my lips, the vasilissa joined in the song with her own happy chirps. Just like we'd been doing for decades.

Back on the main grounds, across the fire, I paused mid-step when I saw Melissa and Cassie still together. Their conversation looked serious, but Melissa also seemed exhausted. I knew Cassie was protective of my mate, but I hadn't realized just how deep that instinct ran. I had always thought of their bond as a matter of duty, but the way they looked at each other told me it was far more than that. To my wayward sister, Melissa was family.

I risked taking a few steps closer, knowing Cassie would sense my presence if she hadn't already. Her eyes snapped to mine. There was no longer anger in them over my claim on Melissa—everyone knew it was hard to fight the mark of the gods.

"I'm going to get a few hours of rest before the negotiations. Melissa, you should think about getting some sleep too. It's late."

"Don't turn into Lilise on me." Melissa teased, wiggling her nose at the earth watchtower.

"Or stay up," Cassie replied with a smirk. "I'm not the one who has to deal with elves and fae tomorrow. Perhaps a grumpy human will be enough to make both sides rethink doing this ever again."

Melissa's laugh was a beautiful sound. "Fair point. I can be a bit much in the morning."

Cassie headed down the path towards the trees where the watchtowers had taken up temporary residence.

Melissa and I watched her leave before she stretched and rose from the wooden bench, those beautiful brown eyes turning towards me. She couldn't fully mask the concern behind her laughter. The way we'd left things earlier was definitely unresolved.

I closed the distance between us and cupped her face, gently caressing her cheek with my thumb. Maybe it was a bit too forward, but I needed to express my care for her somehow.

"Are you ready for bed? Tomorrow is a big day—but at least you'll have Kelan back," I murmured softly.

"I am so ready to see him again. I think Lilise would have told me if something wasn't going right." Caution lingered in her expression as she stared up at me. I hated how insecure our dynamic made her feel.

"I'm willing to bet he's counting down the hours," I said easily. "That's exactly what I was doing when I got his message that you were on your way here."

Melissa blushed and tried to turn her face, but I was too close for her to look away entirely without stepping back.

"Where are the guest caves?"

"On the other side of this ascension. Why?" I raised a curious brow.

"Don't I need to find a room?"

At this, I couldn't help but laugh. "You'll stay in my cave while we're here. I'll not be parted from you for hours in the night."

Her eyes widened in surprise. "But. . ."

I scooped her up in one easy motion, and her blush deepened to the brightest red as the grove members still partying around the fire erupted into cheers. "You are mine, and you will sleep in my bed."

"I don't want you to get in more trouble," she protested, reaching for a shirt dangling from a branch near where she'd been sitting. It looked like the kind some of the female satyrs wore. "I don't want you to have to leave."

"Don't let the elders worry you. Cassie is taking charge of the situation until the vasilissa emerges and selects her druwid." Since my cave was just off the main grounds, we arrived within moments. I lit a few torches, letting the warm glow carry into the dark space as we settled in.

Melissa wiggled to get down as soon as we crossed the threshold, then darted straight into the washing cave the moment I set her back on her feet. When she reappeared a few moments later, she was wearing only the shirt that had been hanging from the branch earlier—it fell to her mid-thigh. My fated was so much shorter than even the female satyrs.

I was torn between concern over how little she wore, with snow still piled around the grove outside, and the hunger gnawing at me now that she was exposed.

"Are you going to be warm enough?" I finally asked, the fierce need to protect her winning out over my desire to have her.

"I sleep better with less on," she replied as she climbed onto the long bed—her ass flashing me in the process. The hem of the shirt lifted just enough to reveal her small panties beneath, teasing me with every movement. She had to know she was torturing me. A new, sharper hunger pain flared deep in my gut.

"Do you?" I crooned.

"If I get cold, I'll snuggle up to you. With that fur, I bet you stay plenty warm even on the coldest nights."

It sounded like an invitation to share the bed—but I doubted it immediately. It had to be the hunger talking.

With a sigh to myself, I pulled up a tree stool next to the bed. She frowned as I brushed the hair from her eyes.

"You aren't going to sleep?"

There would be no sleep for either of us if I joined her in bed at this moment—not in the state I was in. It was better to keep some distance. "I'm going to watch over you for a while."

"Like that's not creepy." She teased me, shifting to rest against the headboard. "Does the ground in Voreios vibrate all the time?"

I tilted my head in confusion, studying her for a moment. "What do you mean?"

"Ever since I got here, there's been—for lack of a better word—a vibration. It wasn't like this in Dytika. I keep hearing a humming and feeling a pull to go down certain paths."

I still wasn't sure I understood what she was asking, but my mind was instantly drawn to the vasilissa. Perhaps I should have introduced them today after all.

"Can you feel it now?"

She nodded, placing her hand flat against the rock wall beside my bed. "The vibration is everywhere. I'm guessing you all can't hear it because you're from Voreios—maybe

139

you've gotten used to it. I'll see if Kelan senses it when he gets here tomorrow."

Melissa shrugged it off, but then she studied me intently for a few moments. Maybe I should have brought her to the temple to speak with the gods instead of the elders. There was clearly something different about my mate—something no one seemed to fully understand.

"Did you see her today?" Melissa asked quietly.

"I did," I replied. I wouldn't lie to Melissa or hide anything from her any longer. "She knows about the trials and that we will be leaving—at least until she finds her druwids."

"Then we could come back here if you wanted to?"

I wet my lips and leaned forward, propping my elbows on the bed. "Maybe. It depends on the life we build. I'm not going to put any limitations on our options."

She huffed out a laugh. "You really are committed to keeping this up."

"Melissa, I meant what I said last night. I want a life with you. With Kelan. Yes, some of the loss will hurt, but I must trust in what the gods see. I have to trust what my heart tells me. I love her, but I don't think it will compare to the love I can have with you if I let it flourish."

The quiet contemplation between us was comfortable—almost as if she was finally letting my words match up with what I knew she was feeling through our bond. If she needed reassurance that I wanted to be in this relationship, I would give it to her every day until she believed me. Until she no longer doubted it.

"What can you tell me about the fae? I'm a little nervous about tomorrow, how tricky I've heard they can be.

I've met plenty of elves before, but I really don't know what to expect with the fae," she said.

I grimaced at the shift in conversation. Growing up in Voreios, there were few things I disliked more than the fae. If I could avoid dealing with them, I did. "I really wish you'd reconsider meeting with either of them tomorrow."

"Those were the terms. I won't go back on them now. I want to make sure Kelan is free from the punishment he only received because of me." She bit her lip and glanced down at her hands. "At least, if I do this, I won't have to go to the fae court for a year, and the fighting will stop."

"You will never be going to the fae court for any length of time." I reached over, placing my hand on hers, my thumb softly brushing over her knuckles.

"Graak, that's not the point," Melissa protested, her voice rising slightly.

I loved how she said my name. I wanted to make her moan it. . .and that was the wrong train of thought as I grew hard. Thankfully, she couldn't see it from how I was sitting. What were we talking about? Right, the fae.

I cleared my throat. "I'm sorry. I know no one can talk you out of this, so the least I can do is provide information that might help you be more successful." She settled back against the pillow, her posture attentive, telling me this was the right response.

"That would be amazing. How familiar are you with the fae? I know Voreios is isolated from most of the outside world."

I slid my hand over the bed to caress her arm, unable to resist the need to touch her in some way. She didn't shy away. Letting out a deep exhale, I knew I couldn't stall any longer.

"I'm fluent in their language and have traveled all over the world more than a few times. I was also well-trained in history at the academy, so I know more than it may appear. The forest folk who settled in these groves were the last major split from fae leadership many generations ago. However, in many ways, the fae and the forest folk are still alike because we were once considered a fey sub-class beneath them."

"The fae and the forest folk used to be the same?" Her eyes widened in surprise.

I shook my head. "No, the fae have always been as they are now—beings with wings, access to magic, and an obsession with contracts and tricky wordplay. The rest of the creatures under fae rule are referred to as fey. Fey even included elves and dwarves at one point. The power struggle is what caused our people to separate. The most important thing I can tell you is to be very specific and certain about everything you say to them."

"So, don't make any jokes about offering up my first born. Check." She gave me a wry smile as she pretended to scribble this information on her hand.

A growl ripped from my chest before I could contain it, and Melissa laughed as she stroked my cheek.

"I'm joking. I'll be very careful with what I say to them," she promised.

It was a fight to push down the surge of protectiveness still rising in my chest. She shouldn't be doing this at all. Even Kelan didn't want her to.

Then something shifted in her expression as she watched me—a tiny hint of fondness, the same look she'd shown when she talked about our elven bond mate before.

That calmed me immediately. I'd take the blessing. She didn't mind my protectiveness, as long as I didn't try to stop her from doing what she needed to do. I could agree to those terms. We were moving in the right direction.

Before I could continue talking about what I knew of the fae, she shifted subtly in the bed. Her eyelids were heavy as she fought the sleep. With a few strokes of my thumb across the top of her hand, she was out.

Chapter 15 – Graak

"No. . ." Melissa tossed in her sleep, her hand knocking against my shoulder.

I groaned, stretching out my stiff body from the uncomfortable position I'd been leaning against my bed. How early was it? No light seeped in from the front of my cave, which meant the fires had been put out, but the sun hadn't risen yet either. Outside, nothing seemed to be stirring, save for a light sprinkling of snowfall.

Melissa shifted again, a small cry escaping her as if she were trying to flee from the covers. The sound tugged at my instinct to protect her, but there was nothing here. I stood, leaning over to peer down at her.

"Little firefly. . .?" I murmured, rubbing gentle circles along her back when she tossed a third time.

At my touch, a sob tore from her lips, but her eyes remained closed. She was trapped in a nightmare.

I was left to wonder if she'd done this before the solstice, or if this was something new. Honestly, I had too many questions.

Ever so carefully, I slid beneath the covers beside her, wrapping my arms around her trembling form. Her heart pounded beneath my touch, frantic and uneven. It took a few moments of her struggling against me before I managed to catch her flailing arms.

"Melissa. . . I'm here. It's okay." I attempted to soothe her.

She let out a sigh, then buried her cold feet in my fur. I rocked her gently, matching the rhythm of her breath until it fell in sync with mine. When her fingers brushed over the top of my hands, I knew she was awake without needing to see her face.

"Do you want to talk about it?" I asked softly. This had to make her feel vulnerable, but I'd do anything to help her right now. Except let her go. Now that I had her in my arms again, I really didn't want to do that.

"Not really. Kelan usually helps me forget about them." Melissa shifted, pressing her body against mine, her bare bottom sliding right up against my groin. "I don't want to sleep anymore."

That couldn't be the full truth, but without talking to our other mate, I wouldn't know how he handled this if she didn't tell me.

She moved again, a slow, deliberate tease, and heat coiled deep in my gut, hunger igniting like a spark catching dry leaves. I wasn't strong enough to fight against what she was offering me. We both knew it.

"Then let me take your mind away from there," I replied, huskily.

In one smooth motion, I rolled her onto her back and climbed over her. She wet her lips, those heated brown eyes locking onto mine. I leaned down and kissed her roughly. Melissa moaned, her hips rising to meet mine before she sucked my bottom lip into her mouth. I growled

145

low in my throat, giving her a tormenting, slow thrust, showing her exactly how badly I wanted her. Her legs tightened around my sides, pulling me down into her.

This was absolutely an invitation. Bracing on one elbow, I slid a hand between us, tracing the curve of her beautiful, toned frame. My fingers glided over each defined muscle of her stomach before slipping beneath the line of her panties. Melissa's kisses grew more urgent, her breath hitching as she gasped the moment I found her clit, circling it with slow, deliberate strokes.

She was already so warm, so ready. The dampness at her core teased against my fingertips, but I wasn't in a hurry. I wanted to savor this.

Just touching her sent a rush of energy through me, dulling the hunger pains I'd lived with for months. Each second rejuvenated me, grounding me in the pleasure of her body. She wanted a distraction? I would give her one.

Each pass of my fingers wound her tighter, her body trembling with every swirl against her sensitive flesh. When I finally pushed two fingers inside her, Melissa cried out into my shoulder, gripping me as pleasure overtook her. The tight heat of her body made my cock ache, a raw need curling deep within me.

As grateful as I was that our triad would be complete soon, Melissa and I needed this time alone together. I watched, entranced, as she ground against my hand, chasing the pleasure I gave her. Her sexy panting grew heavier, each breath pulling her closer to the edge. I needed to see her fall apart, to feel her come undone beneath me.

Her breathing hitched, her body going taut as she tumbled into release. Pressing my palm against her clit, I curled my fingers inside her, wringing every last wave of pleasure from her trembling form. She was heavenly.

I didn't waste any time, kissing down her neck and sliding down her body as I withdrew my fingers from inside her. Melissa quickly realized my intent as I hooked my fingers into the waistband of her panties and tugged them down.

Once free, her legs parted for me—the most intoxicating gift. I had dreamt of her taste.

Melissa threaded her fingers through my hair, gripping my horns as I trailed slow, deliberate kisses down her stomach, teasing my way lower.

Her citrus and floral scent drove me wild, intensifying as I neared where I needed to be. My lips brushed over her clit, and she whimpered with renewed need. With a deep inhale, I traced my tongue through her folds, savoring her.

This scent. . .

I pressed my face into her, penetrating her with my tongue, drinking her in. But something was different. She tasted richer, fuller—there was something more.

I took another slow, exploratory lick, diving deeper, and realization hit me all at once. The scent was overpowering, demanding, speaking to something primal inside me. Melissa was entering a fertile cycle, and this would likely be the only clue we'd have since she wouldn't flower like a nymph.

A growl rumbled low in my throat as I pushed two fingers into her again. She gasped, jerking my horns downward as unintelligible sounds spilled from her lips.

Taking her clit into my mouth, I worked her with my tongue, curling my fingers into her wet heat, stretching her core to take me. Melissa fell apart, shouting my name, panting as I continued to consume her. But I wasn't done.

"You taste so good." I groaned as another orgasm rippled through her, sending tremors through her thighs.

I climbed back up her frame, keeping her body open to me as I carefully untied the first side of my chiton. My lips brushed over her neck as her hands slid from my horns to my shoulders. She turned to face me, lips parting in invitation to kiss her again.

I marveled at the beauty of her enraptured state. Still covered, I ground my aching length against her bare, dripping heat.

"Oh. . . Gods. Graak, please." She cried out, eyes squeezing shut as I slowly thrust against her. "I need you inside me."

"Don't worry. I'll take care of you right now," I promised, pressing a kiss to her neck, then to her earlobe with another teasing thrust. My restraint was hanging on by a thread, but nothing would be more satisfying than finally sinking into her.

"When we get back tonight, Kelan and I will mate you until you can't walk—until you are full with our child. All your needs will be more than met, little firefly."

She groaned and pressed her lips to mine. Her tongue ran along my bottom lip in a forceful display of need, and I growled as I kissed her back. I claimed her mouth with a passionate fury, and she tightened her legs around me.

The last of my bindings was all that remained between us. My fingers found the knot, my desire to finally consummate this overwhelming, unbearable—

All at once, everything stopped.

Melissa tensed in my arms, her body stiff against mine. She pulled back from our kisses, eyes wide with shock.

"What did you say?"

Chapter 16 – Melissa

Graak didn't bother masking the confusion on his face as I pushed against him.

"Did I hurt you?"

His eyes, glowing green just moments ago when his fingers had been inside me, were now returning to normal. I'd have to ask about that another time.

"No. You just reminded me of something very important." I shifted into a sitting position, putting some distance between myself and the heavy cock resting against my leg. My body protested, my core throbbing with unresolved desire, but my mind spun at how close of a call that had been.

I had been tracking my cycles well enough to know that, somehow, he had also figured out the timing. "I haven't taken my tea. My schedule has been off, and Lilise isn't here."

He didn't seem to know what to say. I couldn't imagine how my sudden rejection felt to him. I knew I wasn't in danger—Graak would never force me into anything—but I couldn't shake the guilt pressing down on me. Especially now, when we had been working to mend our bond.

"Lay back. I'd say it's my turn to take care of you," I purred. I could set this evening right again.

To my displeasure, he didn't move as I'd asked. Instead, he sat back on his heels, his cock tenting against his linens, and studied me with a curious expression.

"What happened?"

No. I did not want to have this conversation right now. My mind scrambled for the right words to shut it down quickly. We still had so much to learn about each other, and I wasn't sure how he'd react.

I forced a smile. "As much as I would love to ride your impressive cock until the meeting, I can't risk getting pregnant." Hopefully, I sounded reassuring. I wanted to give this triad thing a real chance, but there had to be boundaries. "I'd still very much like to help you out, though."

He was quiet for a moment, then nodded as understanding crossed his face. "You want to wait for Kelan. Of course, we can. He's been very excited about this prospect—we should do it together, just in case."

I blinked. "Wait. . .what?" I asked as he laid back on his side next to me.

"Come here. I'll hold you for a few more hours of sleep." He slid his hand along my lower back, encouraging me to lay down.

"You aren't seriously intending to impregnate me, are you?" I stared at him, and that confused look returned to his face.

A baby wasn't in the plan. I had barely wrapped my head around having two men who wanted to adore me as their mate. I had already caused both men to lose their

151

homes—how could a child even begin to fit into our lives? Especially right now!

"Of course I am. As soon and often as possible." Graak nodded, as if that was the only answer he had ever considered. "Kelan and I will take care of you and all our children."

Immediately, I saw red.

How dare he make assumptions about who and what I would be. There was no way this was going to work out. It couldn't. Mate bond or not, I refused to let anyone dictate my path.

"I am not going to be a breeding tool for you both. I will not be barefoot in the kitchen with a litter," I huffed out, trying my best not to yell. "Kelan may not even want them."

"I know for a fact that he does. I'm not sure what it is you're trying to imply." His head tilted slightly, his voice calm—too calm. "You can wear whatever footwear you'd like, though there are perks to being barefoot occasionally, or so I'm told. My hooves are always bare, but they're far sturdier than your soft little feet. Also, there are no kitchens in any of the groves."

I narrowed my eyes, my temper flaring hotter. "You didn't even ask if I wanted kids! Why would you just assume that?"

Graak frowned, stroking his fingers gently down my arm. "I'm sorry I've made you upset. Come here, sleep a little bit more, and we can talk about it in the morning."

"No." I climbed out of the bed like it was on fire. I needed space. I needed time to think. "I'm going to take a bath. . .alone. Do not follow me."

Chapter 17 – Kelan

The morning of the negotiations had finally arrived, and I had barely slept. I'd been scarcely able to breathe as I waited to reunite with Melissa again.

Never again. I would never be parted from her like this again.

I knew the exact moment Graak and Melissa found each other. Relief flooded through Graak's bond, soothing my soul. The watchtowers could protect Melissa, but knowing he was by her side—that he would take care of her the way I would—helped settle my anxiety at being apart from her.

What I hadn't expected was the hurricane of other emotions that followed over the next two days. I couldn't tell who was struggling more with the transition.

After the elven transports had dropped Lilise and me onto the mountain of Melladur with a handful of elven guards and ambassadors, I couldn't stop searching for her. I had never arrived at the world meeting this way, having only attended the last one through a portal in Dytika.

"It looks like they've arrived as well, just on the other side of this ledge," Lilise said, a knowing smile curving her lips.

I had been asking about her every chance I got, knowing that Lilise could communicate directly with the other watchtowers no matter how far away we were.

"I will never be able to repay you for all the kindness you have shown me," I replied politely. The conversation with Brokk might have gone very differently after I rejected Siraye if Lilise hadn't been in the room with me. For that, I was grateful.

The powerful dryad only shook her head, her eyes soft with understanding. "No payment will ever be necessary. Cherish your mate and build a life with her."

Lilise gestured towards Melissa and Cassie before joining Ferox, who was speaking with the fae ambassadors.

I could make that promise.

I didn't quite understand why the dryads had so easily accepted Melissa as one of their own, but they were her family. In the end, I supposed the reason didn't really matter—not if the outcome had led to this.

Melissa had her back to me, but I could pick her out from any crowd. The compass in my heart pulled me towards her, humming with each step I took in her direction. Her brunette hair was loosely braided down her back.

Graak stood a few feet away, his expression set in an unfortunate grimace, but he noticed my approach first. That was probably the best place to start.

"I'm glad to see you were able to escort her here," I said, greeting my bond mate with an easy tone.

Graak nodded. "Nice to see you again." Then, lowering his voice, he added, "We have a lot to talk about."

Melissa must have heard us because she flipped her dark hair over her shoulder and gave me the most breathtaking smile. But then her eyes fell on Graak, and she turned away quickly. That was not the welcome I was hoping for.

"What did you do this time?" I sighed, not bothering to hide my annoyance. "You were supposed to fix this. The bond seemed strong this morning, and now she's not speaking to you?"

Graak didn't look the least bit bothered by my frustration as he rubbed a hand over his face.

"I got caught up in the moment and mentioned putting our baby in her. She's entering her fertile cycle, so I didn't expect her to react this way." Graak kept his gaze carefully averted from her, but we both knew he was attuned to every shuffling step she took. "That was the most recent upset anyway. I think I've smoothed over the issue of my leaving during the last equinox."

At least that was something. Then my mind caught up to what he'd just said. I replayed every single word. "You're certain of this?"

"Very certain. I think she knows it as well, though she didn't verbally confirm it this morning. She smells so good." The satyr wet his lips, crossing his arms.

Everything in me had been waiting for this. I had no idea how often humans cycled. There wasn't any information on that in any of the forest folk or elven libraries. This might be a once-in-a-few-years opportunity.

"What exactly did she say to you about why she was angry?"

From what I had seen, Melissa handled emotions in one of two ways—she would either be completely honest about everything, or she would say absolutely nothing. I hoped she had at least said something to him.

"A whole litany of reasons, though I'm not sure I understand most of them," Graak admitted. "She doesn't think you want children. Something about not being stuck in a kitchen. And then she told me she didn't want them." He frowned, clearly still trying to make sense of it all. "At first, I thought she might be waiting for you, but she wouldn't stop asking about the tea this morning and would barely look at me."

I didn't fully understand the kitchen thing either, but there was another easy point to dispel. I'd start with that one and work our way through the rest.

"Come with me. I'll talk to her," I said, patting his arm.

The moment I closed the distance between us, my beautiful mate melted into my arms. I tilted her face up, brushing my lips over hers with a few soft kisses. She responded eagerly, her tongue tracing my lips with urgency.

"I'm so glad they brought you back to me," she whispered.

"I've missed you," I cooed, pressing another kiss to her lips.

"Never again, right?" She smiled brightly as the tip of my nose brushed against hers.

"Never again," I promised, my hands slipping down to feel her curves. "Graak told me something interesting."

Her cheeks turned an adorable shade of pink. "Yeah?"

"I would very much like to have children with you—just to clear that up." I pressed a kiss to her forehead, resisting the overwhelming urge to cover every inch of her skin with my lips.

"Ah, that." Melissa glanced down at her boots, the wind catching loose strands of her braid and tossing them into the air. She fell silent.

I cupped her cheek gently, tilting her gaze back to mine. "You know we will take care of you, right? You won't be alone on this journey."

Graak watched me intently, as if trying to figure out where he'd gone wrong. For my part, I could only be grateful that my satyr bond had opened a dialogue I hadn't yet broached with our mate. Even if he had gone about it differently than I might have.

"I. . ." Melissa flicked a nervous glance at Graak before continuing. "I want to take care of myself too."

I stroked her cheek, bringing those dark eyes back to mine. "You are more than capable of doing that. Having a baby doesn't mean giving up who you are. Whatever you want to do, you'll always have us to help." I could feel her panic rising through our bond. Something about this topic scared her.

"But it will change things," she murmured, biting her lip. A ripple of sadness pulsed through our connection. She paused, then whispered, "What if I'm awful at it?"

I smiled softly. "But my love, what if you're amazing? I don't have a shred of doubt in my soul that you will be an amazing mother. You know what I worry about?"

She tightened her grip on me, as if anchoring herself for support. "What?"

I gestured to Graak, whose expression had lifted considerably since the start of this conversation. "I worry that you will love being a mother so much that he and I won't be able to keep up with the demand."

Melissa let out a breathless laugh of disbelief and buried her face against my chest. "That's not a fear to have."

"And yet, it's mine anyway." I stroked her hair. "If you truly don't want to have children, you know we will support you." Melissa glanced over at Graak, who nodded his agreement. "But if it's fear holding you back, let's talk it through tonight. If you aren't ready, then we will wait."

As I placed a soft kiss on the tip of her nose, all the tension in her tiny frame melted away.

Then another shadow crossed her face.

"But I've gotten you both kicked out of your homes. . . We can't stay in Voreios."

I raised an eyebrow at my other bond mate. Something must have happened in Voreios. Had he known there would be trouble? It could explain why he had left to begin with— and that wasn't the kind of information we could risk putting in letters that might be intercepted after the portals went down. We had a lot to talk about indeed.

"Notos has graciously accepted our request. I received word this morning that they welcome us wholeheartedly. Kelan and I would be aiding their borders, and they would love to have you teach, if you're so inclined." The satyr studied us both, clearly gauging our reactions to his suggestion.

"Why Notos? Couldn't you come back with us to Dytika?" Melissa asked. But she chewed her lip, her worry shifting to something else. "We already have a home and a routine there."

Graak hesitated. "The southern grove is better prepared for. . ." He glanced at Melissa, seeming uncertain. "Infernals. Their structure is better suited to what we may bring to their borders, if my suspicions are correct."

A chill ran through me. "Has it been that bad?" I couldn't stop myself from asking.

Graak's jaw tensed. "It's been unexpected. Nothing we couldn't handle, but Ciol is confident they can deal with it like we do."

If Graak had already been discussing this with the druwid from Notos, it had to be serious.

There had been an uptick in infernal attacks along Dytika's borders after Melissa returned on the solstice, but they were manageable. This new information pointed to only one possibility—the attacks were growing more aggressive now that Melissa had gone to Voreios, just like the gods wanted.

This had to be leading up to something big.

"I'm glad she made it to you safely," I said.

"I suspect Cholios didn't realize she was traveling until they got to our border. Thankfully, he doesn't have eyes everywhere—but that's a small blessing," Graak mused.

Melissa's face paled, and she shook her head. "None of this is fair to either of you. Or the groves. There has to be a way to break the bond. To set you both free."

Graak caught her chin, tilting her face up to his. "I'm confident that I speak for us both when I say that we want this bond. I will go anywhere and do anything to ensure you have a long, wonderful life—with or without children. Notos is prepared for the challenge, and with us there to protect you, everything will work out as it should."

The longer he held her attention, the more heat I saw in her eyes for him. This was definitely an improvement from what I had walked in on moments ago. Their dynamic was fascinating—Melissa fought with Graak in a way I had never experienced between us.

"See? Graak is well connected, and everything is falling into place," I said, pulling her closer, reveling in the way she smiled up at me. I was entirely smitten with this woman, and I wouldn't have it any other way.

"You're really okay with all this? The move, him and me, all of it?" Melissa studied me intently, searching for any flicker of doubt. "I see how you two chat it up, but you don't have to pretend for me."

I met her gaze without hesitation. "Yes, I'm okay with this." I kissed her, and a small moan escaped her lips. Graak was right—she did smell delectable. "Graak and I are in alignment about the future. I don't care where we are, as long as we're together."

"Then I'm okay with talking about a future family," she said, giving Graak a small smile. "Just not until we get settled somewhere more permanent."

Graak gazed at her with fondness in his eyes as he nodded his understanding. "I think you're going to enjoy Notos. It'll only take half a lunar cycle to complete the transition in Voreios, then we can pick out our new home together once I'm done with the trials."

I tried to keep my emotions in check after Melissa agreed to consider having children, instead focusing on the logical first step. "I haven't been to Notos since I was a child with my mother, so it'll be interesting to see how much I remember. But more than anything, I've missed you."

"I missed you too. At least it was shorter than last time." She teased, running her fingers across my cheek. "How did it go in Aramore?"

I exhaled, shaking my head. "I will owe Lilise for the rest of my life. If she hadn't been there, I would likely have faced far worse consequences. I will never be welcome back on elven lands."

Her expression softened. "Oh, Kelan. . . I'm so sorry."

"No, love. Forget about all that." I cupped her face gently. "I'm more excited about our future than anything I've lost from the past."

Melissa was my future. I'd known it almost immediately from the moment I met her. Everything else—lands, titles, the past—none of it mattered. Not like she did. And if we could encourage her to carry our child, the tone of this dreadful day would change forever.

There were logistical questions that my elven brain wanted the answers to, such as how often she was fertile, how long the pregnancy would be, and how many years we'd have to try. Those could wait for later, though.

A blush spread across her cheeks as if she had somehow heard my thoughts. She turned her face away, trying to hide, but I wouldn't let her. I caught her mouth in a kiss, and she melted into me, wrapping her arms around my neck. I could get lost in her right now.

We had been having such a fulfilling conversation that, for a moment, I almost forgot why we were standing on this mountain ledge. Until Cassie approached and cleared her throat.

"Hate to interrupt, but Melissa, it's time." Cassie waited until Melissa looked her way before continuing. "You don't have to do this. We can still cancel."

Melissa sighed, taking her friend's hand. "Cassie, we talked about this. I gave them my word. They're all here already. Honestly, what could go wrong with you, all these guards, and the rest of our people here?"

I couldn't help but love her for her principles, even as everything in me screamed that this was a bad idea. I'd have to leave it in the hands of the gods.

Chapter 18 – Melissa

The elven ambassador was the first to approach as I followed Cassie up the winding trail to the meeting hall.

"Kelan." The man addressed him with authority. "You will have to wait out here."

My gentle elf shot him a glare as the ambassador's gaze dropped to our entwined fingers. The glasses perched on his nose were practically useless, hanging so far down the bridge that I wasn't sure how he could even see through them. Maybe he was going for an educated aesthetic, but even with his pristine white-and-gold robes, it wasn't really working.

"I'm aware," Kelan snapped. He turned to me. "Melissa, this is Larongar. He'll be representing the elves' interests today."

"I'll escort her from here, then." Larongar offered me his arm, but before I could respond, Graak stepped up beside me.

"Actually, I will," he said plainly.

"Oh, more surprises. How fun." The ambassador's face, however, said this was anything but fun. "Graak. What brings you to the world hall?"

The tension between them turned downright hostile, and a shiver ran down my spine.

"If peace negotiations are finally happening between the elves and the fae, then it's in the forest folk's best interest to be involved." Graak shrugged as if the matter were trivial, but there was a clear challenge in his tone. "I assume Neia thought about that, or she wouldn't have involved us to begin with."

Larongar unraveled the scroll in his hands, his expression unreadable. "We didn't involve any of the forest folk in these talks."

A dangerous glint flickered in Graak's eyes. "You can't be that dense," he snarled in a tone I'd never heard from him before, not even with the elders.

"You involved us the moment you put Melissa in the middle of this. She is an ambassador on behalf of Dytika. That means she has the direct protection of all the groves—including Voreios. If you think I'm letting one of our precious female ambassadors step into that room alone with the two of you, then allow me to reeducate you on how the groves function."

Larongar stiffened. "You had your chance to negotiate with us in the past. You outright refused."

Graak's expression didn't waver. "I'm not here to negotiate with you or the fae, Ambassador. You asked Melissa to sit in on your meeting to bring the fae to the table. I am here for her—to ensure that you both don't trample on your dealings with the forest folk realms." His voice was steady, but the steel behind his words was undeniable.

He turned to me, offering me his arm. I took it—perhaps more eagerly than I should have. "You have no right to deny me access to that."

"I see. So there's no way for her to attend this meeting alone, then?" Larongar looked at me like he expected me to say Graak couldn't go—which I absolutely would not do.

"Correct." Graak answered, pausing briefly as Zoq leaned in to whisper something to him before heading back towards the retinue of guards we'd arrived with.

"Neia should've cut out all the middlemen and dealt with Helio directly. We could've avoided all of this."

Larongar grabbed his robes and turned with a huff, storming up the path towards the meeting hall.

I gave Kelan's fingers a soft squeeze as Graak stepped away to accept something Zoq handed him.

It was a new fur lining, which he tucked beneath the mage's cloak he wore. The added layer covered more of his chest—more than I was used to seeing—and I couldn't help but miss the sight of his bare skin. It didn't take me long to realize why—he was covering up the mark of our bond.

I frowned. "Are you cold?"

A short laugh escaped him before he gave me a smoldering look. "My fur is plenty warm for both of us, little firefly. I'm covering up so that our markings don't distract from your hosting. I'm your shadow today. Larongar won't notice, but the fae ambassador will."

Seems I was going to have a very hot shadow today.

Now that Kelan had smoothed over some of our miscommunication, I let my guarded walls come down. He wanted this. He wanted me and a life together.

Standing between both of them, something inside me settled in a way I hadn't realized I needed. I'd have to unpack that later.

I glanced over his cloak, a teasing glint in my eye. "Is this your version of formal clothing, then?" I let my voice dip into a husky purr. Graak's eyes gleamed with a delighted spark at my playfulness.

"This is the sign of my mage rank. So long as you approve. . .?"

His smile sent heat through me, painfully reminding me that I had denied him last night. I was certain now that if I had given him rules, he would have abided by them. Instead, I had fled the fire between us, afraid of my own desire.

I still had so much to learn about this world. But one thing I already knew with absolute certainty: I didn't need to be afraid of them. I just needed to be vocal about my needs, because they would never push me to do anything I didn't want to do.

Taking an obvious, appreciative sweep of him, I gave a slow, approving nod. "I think it will do."

I barely had time to lean in and kiss Kelan again before Ferox's voice cut through the moment. "There you are."

Damn all these interruptions. The elves should have let Kelan come back to me earlier.

Lilise walked beside Ferox, her warm smile easing some of my frustration. I had missed her too.

Ferox waited until I gave him my full attention before continuing. "Just a few things before you go into the meeting."

Lilise inclined her head towards my satyr, amusement dancing in her eyes. "With Graak, apparently. You managed where even I could not."

I smirked, but the moment was short-lived as Ferox continued.

"The biggest thing to remember today is that you are only a medium. You are not negotiating for them—just hosting the space so they can speak freely."

I nodded. I could sit there and listen to stuffy men argue if it meant keeping Kelan with me. What I didn't know was if I could just sit there and listen—when all I really wanted was to try and help.

"Do not let them talk down to you. You are an equal among them," Lilise added with an encouraging smile.

All I could do was nod again. I supposed this was their version of a pep talk, but the nerves still fluttered in my stomach. I wasn't sure how equipped I was to stand on equal footing among well-educated ambassadors who were far older than I was.

At the end of the day, maybe none of that would matter. Just a few more hours, and we could begin our new life. I didn't even really have to speak if I didn't want to.

"While we may not be in the room, we won't be far from you. Okay?" Minithe promised, appearing behind the group. "If you need to take a break, tell them that."

"I don't like that we won't be able to be in there. What if one of them attacks her?" Cassie's voice cut in before anyone else could give me more advice. I hadn't even noticed the two dryads sneak up.

167

"I'm prepared for an attack." I pulled up the fabric of my skirt, revealing my legs nearly to my thighs. "Minithe helped me strap Ares up, so he'll be coming with me."

Ferox stepped forward, calm and certain. "We'll be just outside the mountain structure. We can be with you in minutes if needed." He had four contingency plans ready—one for each situation he thought might arise. I was as safe as I could be.

"A lot can happen in a few minutes. It means you cannot hesitate. Okay?" Minithe emphasized, pinning me with her gaze.

"I won't let anything happen to her." Graak's hand settled on the curve of my hip as I smoothed my skirt back into place. Every inch of me flared with heat from his touch. "The only reason I'm going in there is to protect her."

As I stood upright, Kelan leaned down and captured my lips. His mouth felt so delightful on mine that I practically purred into the kiss.

"Promise me. . ." he murmured against my lips, "if you feel unsafe at any time, please leave. Come out. Don't worry about the ambassadors—just protect yourself."

"I. . ." I couldn't even pretend I'd do that if someone else was in danger. I gave him an apologetic smile.

"I'm being serious, my love." Kelan stressed again, and I knew this brief separation was just as hard for him as it was for me.

"I will see you when it's over," I whispered, rising onto my toes to give him one last soft kiss.

He took my hands in his, brushing his thumbs gently over my wrists. "I can hardly wait."

Chapter 19 – Melissa

Following the trail leading to the world hall, I admired the beautiful views of the treetops and the large canal that ran along the northern side of the mountain. I hadn't gotten to see this view the last time I came here. Artemesia was home now. Views like this one were everywhere to be found.

Would I even remember the finer details of Earth in thirty or forty years? Part of me hoped I would, but I'd chosen a different life.

Graak stayed about half a step behind me, but I could feel his focus on each of my movements. He leaned in closer as we approached the landing that led to the entrance of the large hall.

"Located in the Dragon Lands and above the dwarven city of Melladur, this is the only neutral location in our entire world. As you saw the last time you were here, it's where all the leaders meet to discuss issues with one another. Fitting that the elves and the fae would meet here," he murmured.

"These are the Dragon Lands?" I asked, barely able to contain my excitement.

He nodded but didn't seem to want to elaborate on that point. "The southern hemisphere of our planet gets hotter much faster than the north, based on how our planet is tilted towards the sun. The border of Anatoli is across the water there, and Notos is not far in that direction." Graak gestured in each vicinity.

I drank in the details of this world, eager for more. Teleporting everywhere had its own drawbacks, since I rarely knew where I was. Not that I was advocating for days on unicorn back. That might work for others who lived centuries, but I had too much I wanted to see and not nearly enough time to get it all in.

Impressive stone archways rippled across the surface of the entrance as we crossed the threshold into the hall tunnels. The gold and red door in front of me was one of four entrances, and I could access the other three by turning left or right. I remembered this part from my first visit. Ferox had brought us straight inside. I chose the door in front of me.

Natural skylights and palm-sized magical lights sparkling in the walls lit the space. A hollowed-out cavern revealed a massive stone conference table and rows of stone benches. There was more seating around the edges of the cavern.

I really hadn't noticed much about the place after my first meeting here, too overstimulated at the time by all the people and tension. I'd been so nervous—yet to this day, I knew in my heart that staying with the watchtowers was the best decision. I took in each detail quietly until a pull through our bond reminded me that my newest mate was still watching me closely.

"Stop checking me out." I teased him, my voice soft.

"I don't know what that means in the context you're using it, but I won't stop admiring you."

"Be serious. You're going to blow our cover."

Graak raised an eyebrow and gave me a seductive smile before his attention shifted to the approaching fae ambassador. He could apparently shift between playful and stern at the drop of a hat. I could not.

Our talk about the evening's plans hadn't let my mind settle, but it had taken the edge off my anxiety. I was only a host. It didn't really matter if my thoughts drifted, as long as I didn't agree to anything stupid with the fae.

This ambassador—Gaelin—wore robes similar to Ferox's, indicating he had also been to the academy. Wings fluttered behind him for a moment after his arrival before vanishing. He didn't argue about Graak attending, though it was clear he wasn't thrilled about it either.

I'd only been here a few moments before I found myself surrounded by the gathered men, with Graak at my back. His palm pressed gently on my lower back, guiding me away from the others as he gestured towards the table. Both ambassadors took the hint.

"Are you sure you won't attend the Seelie Court with your teaching abilities? That alone could put an end to all this." Larongar addressed me before Gaelin could even speak as we all took our seats at the large, empty table.

"This was discussed with Fenian. Nothing has changed there. I am sure the Seelie Court is breathtakingly beautiful. However, I have my own plans," I answered firmly, smoothing my dress under my legs. I needed to be prepared to be here all day.

"But the gamayun said—"

I shook a finger at him. "Only that a human's arrival would be a catalyst for the next phase. I've gone over that prophecy innumerable times with the watchtowers and the forest folk priests. That part is complete. I have very little influence on your world's grand stage. Surely, two men with minds like yours can find a solution to this situation."

I glanced at Graak to find him smiling with amusement. His presence beside me was comforting—it gave me the courage to be a bit braver than I might have been otherwise. Drawing from his example in dealing with both of them already, I knew I had to be firm and concise.

My satyr didn't allow others to push him around, and I wouldn't either. Not with him watching.

"We will discuss a treaty once you make good on your original debt," Gaelin began, leaning in and placing his elbows on the table.

"When the princess was found murdered, we no longer had any chance of meeting that particular term. We need to speak reasonably about alternate solutions to the contract." Larongar did not appear as collected as I expected an elf to be, shuffling through the papers and scrolls he'd brought with him.

Gaelin frowned. "You can start by returning the land to us and retracting your guards. Once this has been completed, then we can discuss alternatives."

"The land was not in the original contract," the elf countered, pulling out what must have been the agreement.

I didn't recall land being mentioned in any of the previous conversations I'd overheard. None of this made any sense. Why was there such a fuss over a bit of land?

Kelan had told me about the princess, but even that felt like a lifetime ago. Graak didn't appear confused by any of this, so I told myself to let it go. I bit my lip.

Remember your role, Melissa. You're just playing hostess.

"There is another option," Gaelin offered. When he didn't elaborate further, Larongar pushed his spectacles up the bridge of his nose.

"Well, say it then." Larongar leveled the fae with an annoyed stare as the silence dragged on. "That's what we've been waiting for."

The fae ambassador shifted lazily in his seat as if entirely unbothered by the whole thing. "Helio would be agreeable to taking a different daughter as his consort. The contract did not specify which princess. That would—"

"Absolutely not!" Larongar cut him off, rising from his seat. "Your lands have already claimed one princess. We will not entertain any discussions over our last remaining princess—especially for her to be so poorly treated in rank amongst your people."

With a shrug, Gaelin casually dismissed the retort. "It is not our fault that you don't know how to work our land's magic. *Consort* is the best Helio is willing to offer after the humiliation of your runaway princess. Of course, if you do decide to make arrangements for a union, the land is not included this time. Your people would need to vacate."

I thought from most of the books and movies I'd read, that princesses were often in these situations—so I didn't fully understand why they wouldn't marry her to end the war. I also realized that if I didn't ask, I wouldn't know, and it was getting harder to keep my mouth shut.

"What's so special about these lands?" I blurted out in a brief moment of silence before they could continue.

Gaelin gave me a cocky smile, then cleared his throat. "What a great question that is, my lady. As everyone knows, fey magic is the most powerful in our world."

Graak scoffed quietly behind me at this remark, but the fae wasn't even fazed.

"In our lands, the ground radiates with its abilities. It's also our most valuable export. The elves were having trouble—like the rest of the world—with drastic population decline. When our late king offered them a solution to form a more permanent partnership, the land was included to aid them."

"This land was to give the elves access to. . .fey magic?" I still didn't understand. Some of it was the way he spoke. Magic seemed like an impractical solution to their declining population problem.

"It's more nuanced than that. This land connects to a special spring of water that can tell the future. It used to be home to the gamayun. The land was meant for Helio and Princess Aiyana to set up their own kingdom—between our two. There was a whole ritual to tie her to the well. So much wasted time." He tsked.

I mulled over what he said for a moment. "If you were going to share the land after the wedding, why not share it now? Helio is king of the fae, so he wouldn't need his own kingdom anymore, correct? Both of you could take a side up to the spring, so you'd have access to the prophetic waters?"

When he shook his head without a moment of consideration, it became evident there was no wiggle room with the fae.

"No, that will not work. The fae held up our end of the bargain, and now Helio is alone without a promised wife. Aiyana broke the contract, so the elves should be the ones to correct the situation."

My brow furrowed as I rubbed my chin. I wouldn't have considered Helio to be alone—as a king he would likely have plenty of options for a wife should he choose. But maybe there were other factors, like the land, that I wasn't aware of.

"So, we've heard what the fae are willing to accept. That's a start. Would the elves be willing to draw up a new marital agreement and return the lands?"

"No." Larongar dismissed the notion entirely, continuing to sort through his papers. "Our people resent the fae. This is not the time to talk about a union—even to end the war."

"What had you intended to offer, then?" I was genuinely curious. He'd said very little so far, and this didn't seem like a productive use of the opportunity I was supposedly giving them.

My question seemed to embarrass him; his cheeks paled, and he took a seat again before replying.

"Honestly. . .we hadn't expected the watchtowers and Voreios to show up. My job was to persuade you to go to the fae court for a year."

"Absolutely not." Graak spoke up for the first time, his voice a low growl. A chill ran down my body at the heat in his tone. Gods, what was wrong with me? Now was not the time to get distracted.

"Wait a minute." Gaelin held up a hand towards Graak. "Larongar is on the right track. You are the only reason we agreed to come to this meeting. It's worth a discussion, at least."

Waving Graak off his attack, I straightened in my seat.

"I was quite clear about this in my terms with Fenian for these negotiations. I also have nothing I could teach fae children—especially those I've been advised are much older than I am."

Gaelin laughed loudly, as if I'd just made the funniest joke of the day. Arrogant fae. "You were not going to be a teacher, my lady. Helio is prepared to have you as his primary consort. He's quite taken with you."

Graak's chill demeanor vanished as he rose to his hooves behind me. I needed to settle him before this took a bad turn. I grabbed my mate's arm and offered Gaelin a smile.

"He saw me once, months ago. He can't be taken with me—I barely said more than a few sentences. There would be no advantage to him with that union."

"Helio enjoys pretty, exotic things," Gaelin said, assessing Graak's display of possessive aggression with interest—and a hint of wariness. "And you are both. It's the whole reason he'd be willing to trade you for the elves' contract. Even without powers, you'd be something none of the others would have."

Each word out of his mouth stoked the flames of Graak's fury, and I needed to change the energy before this devolved into a fistfight—one my lover would clearly win.

It was time for a break.

I cleared my throat and met each of their gazes before responding, "I will say this simply: I will not be a tool for either side to end this war, and I will never be a consort to Helio. Go back and speak with your people. Find out what each side is willing to offer *that does not include me*. Let's try this again after a break."

Chapter 20 – Melissa

They both gaped at me in surprise, but with one glance at Graak, they decided not to push it. As soon as they exited through their chosen doors, I let out the breath I'd been holding.

Graak stepped up behind me and began rubbing and kneading my shoulders.

"You really know how to take charge of a room," he said, sliding his palm up my neck and caressing my skin. "Your expressions alone are captivating."

"They only left because of you." I laughed, leaning into his touch.

"That's not true. You're handling this much better than I am in a lot of ways."

"It's crazy for me to even be here," I said, my voice soft with wonder. "I never would have imagined sitting in a meeting like this back on Earth—let alone having a say in any of it. Even if I was in a meeting like this, no one would've even noticed me." I shrugged because that fact had never bothered me before.

"I can't imagine a world where you're not mesmerizing everyone you walk by." His husky tenor made my knees weak.

But now wasn't the time for those kinds of conversations.

I turned on the bench to face him before rising, my palms sliding up his chest beneath the mage robes.

"You know I would never go to Helio, right?" I said, a crease forming between my brows.

He only nodded as he studied my face. The new tension between us felt like it might burn me alive. I desperately wanted to put the past behind us. I was scared—but everything about the future we'd talked about felt right. Except for one thing.

"If we have to leave Voreios, there's one thing I want to do before we go."

Now I had his full attention, focused on what I was saying—not the chemistry about to explode around us.

"Anything," he promised.

"I want to meet her."

We both knew who I was talking about. A flurry of emotions rippled through the bond, most of them some variation of nervousness. It took a few beats of silence before he met my gaze again.

"We can do that. She's been asking to meet you too."

"And I can talk with her by myself?" I pressed.

Graak raised an eyebrow before replying, "You know she can't talk."

"But from the way you all speak of her, she has a way to communicate. I want to sit with her and try to speak anyway. I know how much she means to you, so this is important to me."

He cupped my face in his hands and rested his forehead against mine. "Yes, to all of it then. I have to run the new

179

ryne trials, so that should give you two days to spend with her however you'd like."

I smiled so wide my cheeks hurt, then wrapped my arms around his waist. Some of the weight on my shoulders lifted, knowing I'd at least have the chance to get to know the dryad my mate had cared for. I didn't know exactly what I'd say, but there was still time to figure that out.

"What do you think about all this? Is it even possible for us to come to a resolution today?"

Graak studied me again. He seemed to be carefully considering everything he said to me—and I wasn't sure why. Maybe he was trying to avoid miscommunication, but we'd have to sort that out. I wanted him to speak his mind freely.

"There likely won't be an agreement for another fifty years. The fae need to feel like the elves have paid the price for breaking a contract. How they negotiate with the elves will factor into every decision that comes with other contracts they have in play with other kingdoms."

My mouth dropped open in shock before I could school my expression. "I don't have fifty years for this! Why would they drag out peace talks for that long?" I exclaimed.

"Nothing moves quickly in this world when everyone has nothing but time," Graak said gently, reminding me that my life span—and everyone else's—was not the same. "Your presence here has made them do something they never have before: come to the table. You brought them here. But this doesn't have to be your life's work."

I sighed. "I guess some part of me thought I'd have a bigger role to play here. Especially with everyone talking about the prophecy all the time. If I'm not meant for this, then what other reason could I have to be here?"

The words came out with far more sadness than I intended. I didn't get centuries to leave a mark, like the rest of them might. It didn't always bother me—but right now, the reminder stung. A small part of me liked who I could be when sitting at the world table.

"He kisses you so easily." Graak's eyes fell to my mouth, and his words jolted me out of my forlorn thoughts. "So freely."

The sudden shift in topic made my heart race. I couldn't tell if his comment was a deflection or a response to my rhetorical question. "What stops you from doing the same?"

"Regret," he admitted. "I don't want to keep hurting you."

"Then let's try again—and see if we can get it right this time." I leaned up and brushed a soft kiss against his mouth.

The satyr took my invitation as I parted my lips to let him in. What started out as a gentle sampling turned heated, filled with a desire that raged through my entire being all the way down to my toes.

He left me breathless, torn between a need for air and the all-consuming ache in my body. It was just a tease of what would come when we were alone again.

"We have to. . ." I groaned as he kissed me again, "pause for now. They may come in here."

"I think they've had enough of your time." He growled, his hands cupping my neck.

That flicker of fury and protectiveness surged through our bond and with it, that sensation of hunger returned. I

181

needed to remember to ask him about that later. It didn't seem to have anything to do with food.

"I think we can make it one day, don't you?" My fingers dug into his back as he continued exploring me with kisses. "However, I don't need to be this aroused when we begin round two. Agreed?"

"If you won't leave, I'd prefer to take a longer break and call Kelan in here. I'll claim you on this table."

"Graak. . ." I protested weakly. My body was so wound up for him in every possible way. This mate bond was out of control. I could only imagine it was because we were all together again, with hints of the future before us.

"Fine." He relented before smirking. "Maybe you should sit on my lap, then. I'll work out some of that need."

His hand slid through the slit of my skirt, caressing my thigh. The touch instantly sent heat rushing through me.

"You are incorrigible," I purred against his lips. "Not in front of the ambassadors. I will maintain my own seat, as will you. Our cover, remember? No one's supposed to know."

Graak turned me around in his arms and gripped my waist, pulling me flush against him. There was a very subtle grind against my backside. "You have no idea how enticing your scent is when I know you're thinking about us," he murmured. "If they even dare mention trying to take you from me again, I won't be able to keep our secret. I think Gaelin already knows something is up."

I slid my hands over the tops of his. "Was it your growling that gave it away?"

"Probably. I also can't stop looking at you." He kissed the base of my neck where my shirt revealed my skin, then trailed his nose upward. "You know—beautiful, exotic things and all that."

My cheeks burned with the blush spreading across my face. Before I could reply, both doors opened, and the ambassadors walked in.

Taking a step away from Graak physically hurt my soul, but I adjusted my dress and took my seat like a proper lady. My thighs were soaked, and I wasn't sure if I wanted to curse him or kiss him for doing exactly what I told him we shouldn't do. Graak unapologetically took a seat much closer than before.

The two ambassadors didn't even glance at each other as they rejoined the table. Larongar sighed deeply, as if attempting to bury his disdain for this situation. Gaelin, on the other hand, appeared cockier than ever, reclining in his seat with casual ease.

Before I could say anything to them, two guards entered the meeting room—an elven and a fae male, dressed in black from neck to toe in uniforms that mimicked their respective guards' attire. It was almost accurate. . .but not quite.

A strange energy floated around them—almost like an aura—and it felt familiar.

Flashbacks of the mages in the Infernal Plane raced through my mind. Something wasn't right with these two, and I was putting the pieces together too slowly. No one else had been allowed into this meeting—except for the last-minute adjustment allowing Graak. Any outside communication should've taken place with their people.

Graak stood instantly, putting himself between the intruders and where I sat. I didn't mind his aggressive

183

posturing—not with how the darkness in their gazes stirred my memories. They didn't look anything like Xernath. . .but they felt like him.

"Excuse me. No one else is supposed to be in here," I said, gesturing towards the exit and adding authority to my voice.

The pair didn't alter their course. They strode forward into the center of the room, then one at a time opened their hands to reveal dark, glowing balls of energy. Four total. A strange smile spread across both of their faces. Even Gaelin shifted in his seat, stunned into silence by the display.

The balls of dark light floated forward, hovering in the air near where everyone sat. Two seconds later, they exploded—shaking the ground. Time slowed to nearly a standstill.

Graak spun me against his chest and rolled us out of the way as the table flipped in our direction. Stone spikes erupted from the floor, breaking some of the momentum from the blast. Wood and stone exploded from the other tables caught in the direct line of impact, showering us with shards and debris.

Smoke, dirt, and mist filled the air. The shadows from my nightmares crept in from every angle, elongating and twisting as figures emerged. We were surrounded. My ears rang from the blasts, muting the world around me. I couldn't hear whether these shadowy figures said anything—not that I was sure I'd want to.

The ground cracked and tore beneath us, green magic pulsing from where Graak stood. It radiated outward, striking into the shadows before they could fully manifest.

"You need to get out of here!" I shouted—maybe louder than necessary. "They're after me, not you. Go!"

"I will never leave you." He growled protectively, and a flash of green sliced through another cluster of shadows as stone speared down from the ceiling. "We need to move towards the exit quickly. I need a few moments to prepare the teleport magic."

"I'm sorry I dragged you into this. I don't see the ambassadors." I locked eyes with the shadow elf guard as he surveyed the damage.

"You can't think about them. They're either dead or gone." Graak raised his hand and the ground beneath us shifted, reshaping itself into a tunnel leading towards the exit.

The enemy's response was immediate. Another volley of shadow bombs detonated across the chamber. The cavern shook violently, and the ceiling cracked above us. They weren't going to let us go without a fight.

The infernals would not take me alive again. I'd relived that night too many times in my nightmares. I resolved to beat them here or die trying.

I pushed away from Graak before he could stop me and slid under the last remaining upright table. I reached through the slit of my dress and tore Ares free before emerging on the other side. I slashed my blade through the air with precision, pursuing the closest target. All my training had led to this—just as Minithe promised. I *was* the sword. And I would not fail this time.

The guard dodged my first strike, but I swung again. Our blades clashed, and I was forced to skid backward as he forcibly shoved against Ares. Then, the man landed a clean slice across my exposed chest. Blood splattered along the floor. I growled in fury, forcing myself to contain a scream of pain as I reset my stance.

The deep wound burned worse than any lash I'd experienced before. From the instantaneous bubbling I felt along my skin, I knew they had laced the weapon with poison.

More shadows began pushing up from the ground. Above us, the light from the sun tunnels dimmed, and thunder cracked through the sky. The storm felt like Kelan. He was coming for me—no doubt with the watchtowers. I just had to hold out. The earth ripped apart in bursts around me as Graak's magic tore through any shadows that got too close.

"Aurinia. . .it's time for you to take your place in our realm." The elven shadow guard raised his sword, taunting me with a twisted grin. "Cholios wants you—dead or alive."

What could he even do with me dead?

Did I want to know?

He'd been trying to kill me that solstice night—but the way they all threatened me, it didn't sound like death would be the end.

"I'm never going back unless I find a way to slay your master!" I shouted at the shadows surrounding me. A green glow radiated from my necklace. No. . .it wasn't my necklace. My *chest* was glowing green. I didn't have time to figure out if this came from gods on my side or theirs. I couldn't hesitate anymore.

With a quick feint, the guard fell for my bait. I drove Ares through his chest. Dark blood splattered me as I kicked him off the blade and let him fall. One down, one more to go.

I turned to find the fae guard already locked in a fistfight with Graak.

The guard slammed into the floor after Graak landed a perfect blow to his face.

We were gaining the upper hand. Maybe—just maybe—we could make it out of here. Together.

Green energy surged from Graak's right fist, blasting outward and eviscerating the shadows that had begun crawling towards me. Somehow, he was fighting a guard and protecting me simultaneously.

A mirror-like reflection ripped down the wall beside them, a near-paralyzing fear rising inside me.

That's how they took me the first time.

Not again. I won't go again.

I swung Ares through one of the shadows before quickly realizing it had no effect. I ducked beneath the smoky hand reaching for me and bolted towards the exit. It was the only way I could help Graak now—by getting out.

The fae guard's head snapped in my direction just as Graak gut-punched him into the stone wall. He knew he was outmatched. Then he spoke—words sharp and foreign. My translator didn't catch any of it. Dark energy orbs flared to life all around us. Before Graak could strike again, the fae snapped his fingers. A second series of explosions detonated in rapid succession.

I only had a second to react—but there was nowhere to go. I was completely exposed. A split second later, Graak was there, shielding me from the direct hit. Stone walls shot up all around us, but the power behind the blast was too much to fully deflect. The impact flung us backward. He pulled me close, trying to cocoon me from the worst of it.

The walls must have softened beneath Graak's magic—but it wasn't enough. As we slammed into the rocky surface, my head cracked hard against the stone. Graak's worry surged through our bond as a fire ignited from the wound on my chest. Dizzy with burning pain, darkness closed in. And then—everything fell silent.

Chapter 21 – Kelan

Being apart from her was going to kill me—even with this short distance.

Graak had opened a new conversation about our future, and this war could be damned for all I cared. The fae and the elves wouldn't come to an agreement today anyway. But she'd agreed to discuss the prospect of having children with us—something that gave me hope.

I would do anything to put her mind at ease. Something about the way they lived life on Earth made her nervous about this process. But here on Artemesia, she could have or do anything she wanted, whether or not she chose to have children. With Graak and I aligned in the belief that Melissa came first, the possibilities were endless.

If she wanted to fight monsters? Then she'd have everything she needed to do that. If she wanted to study a rare bug found only in one part of the world, we'd make sure she had the freedom to go wherever she pleased. It didn't matter how much or how little she wanted to do— we'd give her everything she asked for. I just had to find a way to articulate all this to her tonight. Her dreams didn't have to die because she had mates and a family.

My bond with them both helped keep my impulses in check. I could get a general idea of what was happening in the meeting hall. Graak was far more expressive with his emotional range than I was, and I appreciated the protective surges I felt through him. I was also relieved at the growing affection between the two of them. Though my partner was clearly committed to Melissa now, he still had a knack for getting under her skin. It'd be an interesting adjustment for all of us.

After the ambassadors returned to the hall, confusion and fear surged through Melissa—tightening in my chest like a vice. I turned towards the mountain entrance just in time to see Lilise gesture for the other watchtowers to move.

Something was happening.

It didn't take long for my eyes to catch on the shadows elongating from the cliffside edges. . .and a mage manifesting in the sky.

Everything felt *off* in the natural world around us and I took off in a full sprint, desperate to get to Melissa. The ground trembled beneath my feet, and thick clouds of smoke billowed from the meeting hall. The mountain shook like a volcano on the brink of eruption. Ferox was already airborne, challenging the mage—but then a second appeared, and then a third.

I expected a bit of panic since I couldn't see Melissa, but instead, a sense of clarity swept over me. Get to her. That was all that mattered. I needed to see her and protect her. After that, I could handle everything else as it came. For now, I just needed to clear the path between her and me.

Summoning a storm, lightning charged through me as I took aim between the mages. They deflected the strikes, too busy intercepting while I focused on running and the shadow infernals.

Cassie sprang up from the ground in front of me, her body half-contorted into a tree as the earth shook again with violent tremors.

"Solidae Terrae!" She growled through gritted teeth, her fingers elongating into roots that sank into the earth around her.

The trembling beneath my feet began to lessen. A green glow spread across every rock up and down the mountain. The once-imminent rockslide halted in place, and I used the opportunity to force myself to run faster.

Even with all my energy focused on reaching the tunnel, my eyes kept flicking to the entrance, watching for Melissa to emerge. I had no idea how long Cassie could support the entire mountain this way, so Melissa needed to exit or this whole thing could collapse with her inside.

Elf and fae guards shouted orders as explosions erupted behind me. They were fleeing the overwhelming ambush, but I would not leave here without her.

Lightning rippled out of the sky and crashed all around me. I could feel Lilise and Ferox drawing on the storm I'd manifested, reaching places I couldn't see. Tornados and fireballs struck down enemies alongside my lightning. Five of us against what felt like the entire world.

"Find her! Leave this to us!" Lilise shouted.

I didn't need any more prompting. I sprinted onward, and anything that got within feet of me was instantly eviscerated by wind, water, or flame.

As I approached the first level of stairs to the meeting hall, a fresh wave of explosions threw me back into the tree line. The ground continued to rumble, straining against Cassie's spell.

For the first time since that horrible winter day, my bond connection wavered. Both Graak and Melissa had been hit hard—and it felt like they were slipping away. Breaching the entrance, all I could see was smoke.

"Melissa!" I shouted, fighting back my rising panic.

I have to find her.

My chest seized in painful terror as her bond connection vanished entirely. I couldn't feel her anymore.

The ground shook again as the mountain groaned beneath the pressure of its unnatural shift. The hall wasn't going to hold for much longer.

"Melissa!" I pushed my way through the fog and stumbled over the dead fae ambassador. I leapt over his body without a second thought. "Melissa! Graak!"

What remained of my bond shattered, weakening again. Graak was fading too. Dodging around broken chunks of one of the massive tables, Ares skidded across the floor when my foot clipped its hilt. A trail of blood on the floor led to an open mirror portal, just like the one Melissa said had taken her to the infernal lands.

They would not take her again. Blind fury surged through me, clouding every other thought. She'd done all this to help my people. . .to help me, and it only put her in danger yet again. Not this time.

Unsheathing my swords, I lunged forward, straight into the portal. They would all die by my blades tonight. If she was dead, I would take as many as I could with me—before my heart followed her.

There would be blood in the infernal lands tonight.

Chapter 22 – Graak

The teleportation spell had barely gotten us out in time. My stone shields failed the moment we landed back in Voreios. The burns covering my body screamed, and dizziness threatened to overtake me—but I had to make sure Melissa was safe.

When the infernal guard mentioned wanting her dead or alive, I'd thought it was just a threat, not a promise. The power of those explosions made the truth painfully clear in a way I had never hoped to experience. Melissa was fading away in my arms.

I didn't have time to lament the fact that, for all my training and magical prowess, it hadn't been enough. Four watchtowers and Kelan outside, and none of it had been enough. Only the power of a mother tree seemed capable of holding Cholios at bay—and now, I was losing Melissa.

She never should have left the grove.

Blinding green light poured from her chest as I ran towards the main grounds, desperate to find a healer. I didn't know if it was coming from her necklace or from the injury on her chest. Part of me prayed that it was Montibus trying to aid her. But right now, I needed Thadal with his healing waters more.

The world shook like it had during the solstice as I broke the tree line. Birds burst out, startled in every direction, as renewed panic spread through the grove members around me. From the flickering I felt in my anchor to the vasilissa's barrier around Voreios, we were under a full-on assault. Zoq was already mobilizing the central guards to the borders. Then he noticed me.

"Graak! You—" Zoq fell silent as he took in Melissa's condition in my arms. "Get a healer!"

A messenger bolted towards the nereid's river cove to retrieve any who hadn't already been sent to the borders.

Zoq's voice was urgent as he said, "There will be time to catch up on what happened, but you need to get to the vasilissa. The inner grove portals are failing, and the borders are under siege. But the vasilissa needs you. She's in quite a state—like she was that night."

I gave him a stern nod. Why did this keep happening whenever something happened to Melissa? It was as if the two mirrored each other, but that couldn't be possible. Adjusting her in my arms, I got a better look at the slice across her chest. The way the infected skin bubbled could only mean only thing: poison.

"Send one healer to me at the vasilissa's tree. Everyone else goes to the border. No one comes through except the watchtowers and Kelan. Do not engage outside our boundary—only take the targets you can hit safely from within. Don't let any of that chaos breach the grove until I can assess the situation."

I could barely focus. So much needed to be done, and as Melissa's head rolled back in my arm, I didn't have time to do it. "If the watchtowers rejoin us, follow their commands. And send Kelan and Lilise to me immediately."

I didn't wait any longer, knowing Zoq would handle this. Each step down the path fell into a cadence that would test every ounce of my strength. I'd only scratched the surface of healing magic during my time at the academy, and with my aptitude for earth magic, I'd avoided it. Now, I desperately wished I'd studied harder.

Let me save her. Let me heal her. I inwardly begged to any entity that could hear me.

A stirring in my gut told me the magic was attempting to respond. Droplets hovered in the air, pulling up from the earth to my call—then froze. I was missing something, some step, and the magic wouldn't budge.

Fuck.

"Stay with me," I whispered to Melissa gently as I made the final turn on the trail out of the center forest. One more hill and I'd be at our dryad's tree. "I have you, little firefly. . .just fight a little longer. There's a healer coming."

Melissa didn't respond, but the green energy pulsing from her chest flared brighter. I'd never seen magic like this before. Was it helping or hurting her? I couldn't tell. She was so still. I needed Lilis. Or Ferox. Or any of the higher acolytes.

If only I could heal her. . .

When the vasilissa's tree came into view, her song rose to meet me—urgent and clear. Green light radiated from her bark, not just in the projections I usually only saw in my mind. Melissa's glow flared in response, as if the two were speaking in a way I couldn't hear. It had to mean something.

As I drew closer, I began to make out more of her song. It didn't sound distressed. . .it almost sounded joyful. The glowing intensified with every step I took. I hesitated, thrown off by the response she was projecting. Why would she be happy about this? Then again, maybe she didn't understand that Melissa was hurt.

"Melissa is in trouble. Can you help her?" I asked.

The vasilissa sang in reply, sending me vivid flashes of orange and yellow. She wasn't scared. She was excited.

"I have a healer coming—though you appear to be much improved," I said, eyeing the tree again, still unsure what to make of her mood. "Can you keep the colder winds away from her? She needs to hold on to every bit of warmth."

I gently laid Melissa at the base of the oak, then slipped off my cloak and began wrapping it around her.

The green glow from both of them pulsed in unison, synchronized like they shared a heartbeat. As I shifted her to slide the cloak underneath, Melissa's hand slipped from her lap and touched an exposed root. The light from her chest surged through her arm, down into the bark—and then vanished entirely into the oak. My lover's body went limp, and every trace of warmth drained from her in an instant.

"What happened?" My brain couldn't process any detail, any thought. What *was* the green light? Was that her soul? Did the vasilissa just absorb it? I had a thousand questions and no answers. And my mate was dying. . .or already dead.

The vasilissa tried to communicate, her song rising again, but I wasn't listening. I gripped Melissa's hand in mine, desperate for any sign of life. Another melody pulsed through the shock I was experiencing, accompanied by images in shifting colors—but I couldn't care. Melissa's lifeless body was more than I could bear. The deafening silence in our bond would break me.

"Vasilissa, you need to put that back right now. . .she needs it! She won't survive without it. If you care for me at all, you'll give her soul back this instant," I insisted.

The tree continued to sing, ignoring my plea. Soft projections entered my mind—of a beautiful day with green flowery fields swaying under golden light. This was how she used to tell me everything would be all right. But the projections had always been only the color green before. As much as I wanted her to feel joy, I didn't think she understood the full depth of what I was experiencing.

Where was Montibus? Any of the gods? Maybe they could make her give it back.

I barely noticed the nereid appear at my side. I stood there like a statue until the touch of her magic—cool, soothing water—brushed against my shoulder. I jerked away, the world snapping back into focus.

"Not me. Her." I spoke more harshly than I intended, gesturing to Melissa.

The nereid looked between us sadly. Her hands began to glow as she knelt beside Melissa, assessing her injuries.

"There is no soul left within her. I can heal her wounds, but there's no way to pull back the spirit once it's gone." The woman shook her head, refusing to meet my gaze. "She's gone, Graak."

Perhaps a nymph would understand what had happened with the glowing energy. As far as I knew, this sort of thing wasn't normal—but nymphs were nature. There had to be something else going on. I wasn't ready to accept that I couldn't save her.

I scooped Melissa into my arms, cradling her limp body against me. My fingers twitched at the proximity of the pure water the nereid had brought. My body ached, but I leaned hard into the core of my magical output, begging—pleading—for the strength to fix this.

At first, nothing happened. Then water exploded out of the pouch she'd brought, rolling towards where I sat with Melissa.

Grimacing, I knew it wouldn't matter. I didn't have the caliber of spell needed to pull her soul back from wherever it had gone.

"Her spirit went inside the vasilissa." I didn't want it to come out as an accusation. If the vasilissa had done this intentionally, there had to be a reason.

The nereid furrowed her brow, drawing the water back up from the ground. "That's. . .unusual. Given her close bond with you, she may be trying to protect Melissa—but that shouldn't be possible. Nature spirits don't take souls the way undead spirits might."

"Could this be a dryad thing?" I asked, grasping at hope. *Where were the watchtowers when I needed them?*

"If it is, then we might be looking at something only a mother tree can do. I've never heard of this before." The nereid hesitated, then added, "Unfortunately, the toxin in her body would prevent me from returning her soul even if we could. Her skin is already starting to break down. Let me heal you, please. Your energy isn't very stable either."

"Nothing else matters if she can't be healed," I rasped, voice thick with grief.

Reality hit like a boulder crashing down from a cliff—heavy, brutal, inescapable. Melissa had been dead the moment they landed a clean cut on her. Tears streamed down my cheeks like they were on a mission, blurring my vision as I looked at her. All the color had drained from her skin. Her lips weren't their usual soft rose color. I'd never see those warm brown eyes again.

I'd failed to protect her. Each step I'd taken regarding Melissa had been the wrong one, and for the first time in my life, I had no direction. Was this how Zoq felt every day after losing Nivy? How did he keep moving through each day beneath the crushing weight of a world without her? I should never have let Melissa go.

"Graak!"

Cassie's shout cut through my spiraling thoughts. The agony on my sister's face mirrored the manifestation of my worst fears.

"I have her, Cassie. She's here," I mumbled, hollow and defeated.

She closed the distance between us and sank to the ground beside me. Her face twisted in pain, and thick tears welled at the corners of her eyes.

"Why didn't you listen to me?!" she shouted, taking Melissa's hand. "I can't go through this again. You can't leave me. You promised."

Cassie collapsed onto Melissa's chest, and her wailing sobs tore at my heart.

"Let me see her," Lilise said, her voice calm, but carrying a quiet urgency that cut through the grief.

I hadn't even noticed others approaching. The vasilissa had gone silent, no longer singing or sending projections. My mind was shutting down as tears continued to fall, silent and unrelenting.

Lilise gently pulled Cassie away from Melissa, and strands of blue and white magic began to weave around the woman lying limp in my arms. My fingers twitched again at the familiar call of healing water, but I couldn't summon hope—not anymore. Not even the most skilled healer in the world could bring her back without a soul.

"Where is Kelan?" I asked solemnly. I didn't care who answered—I just needed to know where our other bond mate was. The connection between us was so faint I couldn't even sense his general direction.

This must be what it feels like to lose your heart.

"Kelan and Minithe are missing," Lilly replied curtly, her eyes flicking between Melissa and the vasilissa with a raised brow.

"Elaborate on *missing*," I pressed. There was no way the infernals had killed both the fire watchtower and Kelan. I refused to believe it.

"We don't think they're dead," she said. "There were no bodies. But there was a trail of blood that vanishes into the residue of shadow magic. Ferox found Melissa's sword, but there was no sign of the other two. Cassie guessed if you were still alive, you'd bring her back here."

A pulse of water magic tugged at the skin around the wound on Melissa's chest. As soon as it touched the area, the toxin surged, spreading rapidly through the water. Lilise recoiled immediately, hissing through her teeth. The sound that escaped her—low and guttural—reminded me of a growl. I'd never expected to hear that from her.

Lilise stood as Ferox emerged from the tree line. The thin frown on her face told me everything I needed to know—she couldn't heal Melissa either.

They seemed to be having an entire conversation of sadness and grief through expressions alone, without voicing a single thought to the rest of us.

The vasilissa began to hum again, sensing their attention shift to her. She wasn't happy anymore, tuning into the tumultuous energy around her. Lilise stepped closer to the dryad, her hand glowing with white light as the vasilissa allowed the watchtower into her aura. It was a form of communication unique to their kind—something I'd only ever seen when the watchtowers visited before.

"The vasilissa took Melissa's soul," I said again, though I wasn't sure if it meant anything.

Lilise's gaze flicked to me, sharp and unreadable, but I didn't offer anything more.

"This could explain Aurinia?" Ferox asked aloud, though it was clearly meant for Lilise.

"You don't think. . .?" Lilise's question trailed off, unfinished, as the vasilissa hummed a tone I'd heard for years—the one she used whenever I asked her for her name as a child.

The guard had called Melissa *Aurinia*, but I hadn't thought anything of it. Melissa had seemed to recognize that they were speaking about her. Could this be connected to the winter equinox as well?

"Who is Aurinia?" I asked, not knowing how this could possibly relate to Melissa. I was desperate for answers—yet somehow, everyone else seemed to have even more questions.

The vasilissa hummed again, that same haunting note— and this time, we all turned to face her.

"I have a feeling," Lilise said quietly, "we're about to find out."

Chapter 23 – Kelan

In the constant dusk of the Infernal Plane, I'd lost all sense of time. I couldn't tell how many days had passed since the negotiations went down in flames and shadows.

The adrenaline had kept me moving, pushing me into yet another sleepless day. Seeing her blood splattered across the floor and the weapon she'd forged discarded like nothing. . .it tore something deep within me.

I slaughtered countless infernal beasts rising from the shadows that crept through every corner of this hellish place. My muscles ached with pain and stress. Sweat, blood, and grime clung to me from head to toe, but I didn't stop. Even here, in their own dominion, they tried to flee—but once I caught sight of them, they never got far.

Memories looped endlessly in my mind, gnawing at my resolve. Melissa's smile. The way her heart would race when she embraced me. The open affection she offered. Those warm brown eyes, always full of love.

Now, all that remained was silence in our bond. A void where my heart used to be.

I'd felt the snap—the sudden, crushing silence of her emotions—the moment I crossed through the portal. This must have been his plan all along, but I didn't understand why. Why would a Shadow God want *her*? My sweet, bright-hearted mate didn't deserve any of this.

There were new questions I needed answers to. But the problem with answers was that they wouldn't bring her back. Nothing would change the fact that Melissa had gone somewhere I could not follow.

After some time, I finally registered that I wasn't alone. Someone else had followed me through the portal— Minithe, the fire watchtower. She fought silently by my side. In my bloodlust and fury, I barely noticed her presence. She didn't speak, didn't try to reach me, only matched my violence with her own as we hunted down enemy after enemy. She likely saved my life more times than I could count as I gave myself over to blind rage.

Eventually, hunger and the remnants of elven logic pulled me back from the edge of madness—but with that came overwhelming sadness. If Melissa was still alive, if there was some chance, she was being held captive. . . I couldn't waste time eating. But if she was dead. . .

The latest infernal beast had stood seven feet tall before I struck it down, spending the final shreds of my fury. I'd tried pulling information from them when moments of clarity allowed, but they all told me the one thing I couldn't bear to hear:

"Melissa is dead," the infernal spat, blood pouring from between its teeth.

A growl ripped from my throat as I paced around the fallen creature. My rage scorched my insides, threatening to consume everything until nothing remained but ash.

The clearing stood eerily quiet. Only Minithe and I remained. The rest had fled before I even saw them.

Not sure which way to go, I finally had to stop to process the rest of my emotions. The ones I'd been avoiding for days. The reality of a world I'd never wanted to live in.

Minithe tossed a small bundle of leather when I glanced her way. With my strong reflexes, I caught it easily.

"You should eat," she reminded me sternly. The first words she'd spoken to me since we'd jumped through the portal. "You won't stand for much longer if you don't."

"If she's dead, it doesn't matter," I replied. The words physically hurt to say.

In the Infernal Plane, the sky always looked as if the sun were perpetually setting. Endless dusk. It made it difficult to tell how much time had passed, though there were signs—if one paid close enough attention. The landscape was a graveyard of faded life: low hills of ashen sand, trees and shrubbery long dead, their twisting forms clawing at the sky.

Storm clouds rolled in the distance but never crossed my path, as if they sensed what I might do with their power. There wasn't much here beyond a few decaying rock structures scattered through the dirt.

For the first time since emerging from that damned portal, I stopped moving.

"You should eat anyway," Minithe insisted.

I tried not to glare at her, releasing a deep sigh instead. Anger wouldn't help me any longer. My rational mind was quickly reclaiming control—and with it came unbearable grief.

I unwrapped the leather bundle to find it full of dried meat. Minithe had taken the time to hunt and prepare food, even while we'd been chasing beasts for what felt like endless hours. I couldn't help but be impressed.

All our power hadn't been enough, though. Four of them. Four of the strongest people on our planet—and still, it hadn't been enough to protect Melissa. Even two bond mates hadn't been enough to save her.

She never talked about what had happened before the watchtowers found her the night of the solstice. But the way she came back to me. . .maybe there had been something in that moment. A key. A sign. Some hidden truth that could've warned us. Would she have been safer if she'd returned to Earth? No amount of wondering could change reality now, no matter how desperately I wished it could.

The redhead said nothing as she sat beside me, patiently cleaning her sword. The quiet comradery was my only comfort now, though I wasn't ready to admit it. She'd left her team to follow me. To help save Melissa. Dryads didn't need food, yet she hunted for me all the same.

"Why did you come?" I asked, taking another bite. The meat was as flavorless as the Infernal Plane was bland—but it did the job it needed to do.

""I saw you go through the portal," Minithe replied, as if that alone explained everything. "If Melissa had been taken again, you'd need backup. Fire will always follow fire."

"They all keep saying she's dead." I closed my eyes, trying to shut out the pain that thought brought.

"We haven't seen a body yet," she said simply, as if that was the only truth that mattered. "Have you satiated your need for blood?"

"I don't think I ever will," I said, my voice low. "Not now. Not after they took her from me." I stared into the endless dusk. "I honestly thought I'd be dead by now. I wish I were. There's no going back to who I was before Melissa."

"Your fire is tempered now, even if it's still hungry," Minithe said. "A tempered fire can be controlled. You need rest. Then we can work on a new plan of action. Without Ferox or moldavite, I'm not sure how we get back to Artemesia yet. We'll have to play by different rules if we're staying here for long."

"New plan of action for *what*?" I asked hollowly. I couldn't bring myself to care. How could I even begin to comprehend life after Melissa? My hopes for a family, a legacy. . .a future—gone with her. What future could I possibly claw together that would mean anything?

"For revenge. What else?" A faint smile tugged at Minithe's lips, but the pain behind it mirrored my own. "When we lose the ones we love, sometimes chaos is the only thing that gets us up in the morning. If there's no future, then there are no boundaries. Cholios clearly knew something that we didn't. Let's clog up their workings. Take out as many of the bastards as we can."

Before we die.

I heard the words she'd left unspoken and felt my resolve grow.

"Why *am* I still alive?" I murmured. "I was sure the bond mark would've taken me too." I ran a hand through my hair, fighting against the ache in my heart that still begged me to follow her.

"The timing varies between bonded groups," Minithe explained, "but considering you and Graak have barely seen each other in months, I think it's because you didn't complete the second part of the ritual." She gestured for me to eat more, and I ignored it.

"Second part?" I wasn't sure I even wanted to know.

"Well, yes. The gods approved your fated union—that's what the marks represent. But all members must consent to the bond in full. Melissa would've needed to complete a ritual during copulation with you both." She paused. "Considering she didn't want to discuss the markings with Lilise, I feel safe assuming she didn't know about it."

"I've never heard of this second part before," I admitted, finally taking another bite. The meat tasted like ash. "Graak may have told us about it after the negotiations."

"Unlikely," Minithe said. "It's a sacred honor, one that's only initiated by nymphs. Either Lilise or Cassie would've spoken with Melissa about it—*after* confirming she was satisfied with the union. For Graak to bring it up would've been presumptuous, and the satyrs do not speak of it." She leaned in and placed a hand gently on my knee, her voice softening. "What it *does* mean is that you and Graak are safe from the bonded death. . .if she has, in fact, passed away."

Perhaps some part of her thought this would make me feel better. It didn't. I didn't *want* to live without her. I had grown to rely on the feelings of Melissa and Graak surging through our bond. Now the deafening silence threatened to drive me mad.

"I can't feel them in my chest anymore," I murmured. "Does that mean they're both dead. . .or would Graak have survived somehow?"

The redhead finally frowned, and concern clouded her eyes. "Show me your mark."

I pulled my grimy shirt aside, exposing my shoulder. What had once been a vibrant green pattern now barely remained—a faint, dark outline clinging to my skin. Would it continue to fade until there was nothing, or would I always have at least this piece?

"Damn." Minithe let out a quiet sigh and looked down at the ground, the energy between us growing heavier, wrapped in sorrow. "There's no easy way to say this," she said softy. "Melissa is gone. Her death severed the link between the three of you."

The beasts had all been right. My mind could pinpoint the exact moment I lost her—even if my heart hadn't wanted to know. After days of rage, the only path forward was acceptance. And I still wasn't ready.

I'd lost my sun. The only thing left now was to embrace the flames and storms still burning in my soul.

Minithe slowly unbuttoned the top of her leather uniform, revealing the skin beneath her clavicle. A faint red pattern, similar to Melissa's, stretched across her chest. "I, unfortunately, know all about your pain," she said quietly. "All we can do is take it one day at a time. And if you're up to it—make sure no one else has to experience this."

"What about Graak?" I needed to find my bond mate. We'd loved Melissa differently, but I knew how deeply he cared for her.

"With Melissa gone, you won't be able to sense Graak. She was the anchor between the three of you." Minithe paused and I watched as her mind raced.

"He wasn't in the grand hall, so he was likely with Melissa—wherever she ended up. He could be captured or dead. But if she's gone, they'd have had to go through him. So odds aren't exactly in our favor."

"I have to know. I need confirmation. If he's alive and captured, I'll see him freed." That would give me something to focus on for now.

"I figured," she said with a faint nod. "Let's see what damage we can do to the infernals from this side—and maybe get your answers about him. I need time to find a way back to Artemesia, anyway. And I don't think Lilise and Ferox have any means of following us. We're on our own for now."

The fire dancing in her eyes said it all—she was ready for the fight, even if it was just the two of us against the infernals. For Melissa, I could fan the flames long enough to bring this world to its knees.

"I'm in."

Chapter 24 – Graak

The nereid healer had told her sisters about the human's soul entering the vasilissa. Nymphs never could keep secrets from one another. Now, the flower nymphs were sobbing along the tree line, lamenting that they couldn't be with the vasilissa while the pixies could. Not that I could stop the pixies from doing whatever the hell they wanted anyway.

Between the nymphs and the pixies, word spread quickly about the events of the last few days. Dread hung thick over our lands, and I could do nothing to ease it—only wait. My requests for privacy were ignored, despite Zoq's best efforts to keep the crowd away.

It had already been hours. No—*days*. The sun had come and gone more times than I could count, and still, I couldn't let go of her. I cried openly, off and on, no longer caring who saw. Zoq and the watchtowers were the only ones I acknowledged at all.

"I'm so sorry," I whispered to her limp form. Though the warmth had long since left her, the peace in her features only served to shred my heart.

I stroked her cold cheek, just as I had for hours without thinking. But this time, the skin all over her body began to glow, even from beneath the covering of my cloak.

I sat up startled, hating to admit how much hope I felt at the sight.

"Melissa?" I said carefully.

Like a wisp of smoke, her body dissipated into the air— as if she'd never been there at all. The slight weight I'd grown so used to no longer pressed down on me. In her place, the moldavite necklace hit the ground with a soft *thud*, followed by the elvish bracelet Kelan had given her.

The emptiness of my heart echoed the loss of her tiny body. Sorrow gave way to a fury that boiled my blood.

"What was the point?" I roared at the sky. "You asked me to bring her here—for *what*?"

Cassie came to my side and knelt to pick up Melissa's bracelet. I hated the broken look in her eyes before she followed my gaze upward.

It didn't take long for Montibus to manifest beside the vasilissa's tree. Sunlight gleamed off the antlers rising from his head. He was twice my size, every inch of him radiating quiet power—clearly prepared for my challenge, or hoping to dissuade one. But I wouldn't have it.

"Oh, so you *are* here to watch this," I spat, rising to my hooves with a glare.

"Watch your tone!" the god bellowed, his voice deep enough to make any man cower. But I didn't. He couldn't do anything worse to me than what had already happened.

"Where have you been?" I snapped, jabbing a finger at him. "You all *ordained* that she had to be here—and then you vanish as she *dies*? What the actual fuck?"

213

"Her death is a result of *your* failures. This is not something you can take out on us." The earth around me responded to his words. Magic deep within the soil surged upward, rising in thick mounds to trap my legs in place.

"You've taken everything from me! I love the vasilissa— yet you bond me to another. And I *choose* to love the one you sent crashing into my life—and now she's taken from me too?" My voice cracked, rage and grief merging into something primal. "Have I messed up so much that a *point* needed to be made?" The ground around me quaked, resonating with my fury. The vasilissa stirred faintly—but then fell silent once more. "Why hurt *her* to teach *me* a lesson? You could've come for *me* instead!"

Before I could continue, Cassie stepped in, her voice quiet but cutting. "Melissa trusted you. She *believed* in you. If you had told her not to go to the negotiations, she would have listened."

Montibus frowned at his watchtower. "We told her this would be a dangerous life if she remained. She chose to stay for all of you."

"That's not the same and you know it," Cassie snapped.

"Why did you even need her to come here?" I shouted again, fury rising like a tide. "Why did Cholios want her? None of this makes any fucking sense. If you'd been straightforward in our earlier talks, I would've taken her and Kelan away."

The god glowered down at me. "There are things that have not yet manifested into reality," Montibus said coldly. "But do not pretend you understand the world better than we do."

I waved him off and shattered the earth mound around my feet with a flick of my wrist. "I'm done talking to you. I'll find the next ryne for the grove. But after that, I never want to see you again. I'll never worship or honor any of you ever again."

Montibus appeared in front of me. "Do you need some time in confinement on our plane again?" he warned, his voice low and dangerous. "Mind who you are speaking to."

"Why does it matter?" I shot back. I'd been there more times than I could count for talking back to the gods. The one thing I knew with certainty was I would likely end up back there someday.

When I turned away again, I noticed only Cassie was still paying attention to the god who had arrived. Ferox and Lilise were fully absorbed with the vasilissa. Despite how angry I was, I couldn't find it in me to be upset with her. She didn't know any better, and placing Melissa near her had been my decision.

It all came back to this: I played a part in my mate's death. I hadn't stopped her from going to the negotiations. She was struck by a blade while in my care. And then— because I still hadn't put her first—she lost her soul. I'd tried to protect them both, and in doing so, I failed her.

Now she was gone. And I didn't even have anything to put to rest. She'd vanished like a nymph would.

I couldn't stay here. Everything had changed—by my hand. Now, I needed to turn my attention to the only other person who would understand what I was feeling. Even if he would never forgive me.

"Is Kelan alive?" I asked.

"Kelan is unattainable," Montibus replied.

"That is not an answer." I sighed, tired of playing games with the gods.

If I wanted answers, I'd have to find them for myself when I left the grove.

Turning towards the vasilissa, I placed a hand on her bark. She stirred at the touch, letting out a soft hum, and the green glow beneath her bark resumed, pulsing in steady waves.

This conversation confirmed that Kelan and Minithe were, at the very least, missing. Montibus vanished. The god knew me well enough by now, but he'd never seen me quite this angry before. Well, if he thought time would make this easier, he was gravely mistaken.

The deafening silence of our bond shook me to my core—a constant reminder of my failures. At least I knew where Melissa's soul was. Kelan didn't. I just hoped he wasn't dead.

But I wouldn't pray. Empty prayers were what had led us all here in the first place.

Prior to the merging of their souls, the oak tree would sing—radiating emotion through sound and brief projections. Now, all that remained were flickers of earth magic in response to the world around her. She still reacted to me more than anyone else—my touch on her bark, or any intense surge of emotion sparked by someone else's words, would pull a brief flash of color from her.

I slipped Melissa's moldavite necklace around my neck. It felt like the only piece I had left of her. If this was all that we were left with, then I wouldn't let it be lost in the chaos of what was to come.

"She's in there. I think they. . . She is confused," Ferox said, attempting again to reach her through the root network.

"What is she confused about? Did you get a response from her?" Cassie pressed, nearly as impatient as I was.

"No. She knows I'm trying to connect with her—but not when I call her by Melissa's name."

My heart slowed. I'd always longed to know the name of the one I believed to be my fated lover. I'd only ever called her by her title. From the first day we met, she'd hummed musical notes at me repeatedly, and I knew she'd tried to tell me her name. I just never managed to crack the mystery. Would Ferox hear it first?

With a sigh, I let the desire go. It didn't matter who heard it first. I just wanted to know she was safe. That *they* were safe.

"What should we do?" Lilise asked aloud, though her eyes were on Ferox.

He furrowed his brows. "I'm going to get Prafrum," he replied. "He's the only one who may have more answers for us."

"We can send a messenger for him," I offered. I wanted to keep all the watchtowers I could as close as possible—no more risks until we knew the vasilissa would be unharmed by this action. I couldn't save Melissa, but I wouldn't lose her too.

"No, keep your people here. It's still quite turbulent out there. I'll be able to travel more efficiently, and we need to reach him as fast as possible."

"If you think that's best. . ." Lilise said, giving Ferox a concerned look.

217

"I think we need to find Kelan before worrying about Prafrum. Melissa would come out for him." I tested a new train of thought. Melissa implicitly trusted Kelan. Between the two of us, we could draw her out together. With her body gone, I wasn't exactly sure how that would work, but we'd find a way.

"I know you want to find Kelan. I watched Minithe chase after him, so I suspect they're together. I hate to split our team any further right now, but we must resolve this quickly. They're both in danger if this continues much longer. Let me know if she emerges," Ferox said with a nod, then left quickly for the temple, which would enhance his magic for teleportation.

"Is there a chance Melissa was really a dryad? Or is the vasilissa still trying to protect her, and that's why they're struggling with communication?" Cassie asked with a thoughtful expression. "I can't believe there's a chance we found my only living sister wandering around the sacred grounds. Half of her anyway."

Honestly, I wasn't sure I believed it either.

Lilise pursed her lips, considering her words before she replied. "Melissa was human, but I'm suspicious that her soul might not have been. Heliria did something with a piece of moldavite right before she sealed the portals. I suspect it's the one you're wearing, Graak. Melissa spoke Druidic by default upon her arrival—not like the other humans who came before. Cholios had her secured to a tree when we found her. Then we must consider how strangely this young dryad grew up."

"A lot of Melissa's behaviors were like one of us," Cassie agreed slowly, casting a glance at me. "Even from the stories she would tell me about her time on Earth."

Lilise's attention also turned to me. "If you're still planning to leave, I think you need to reconsider. This isn't over. But now we need to lay out all the facts together."

"Yes," I agreed gruffly. There was one night in particular I needed answers about immediately. "The more I think everything over, the more connections between these two line up in a way that can't be coincidental. Every time Melissa was in mortal danger, the vasilissa screamed and reacted as if she were being attacked. She also began to act strange the week before the world meeting—when you introduced Melissa—as if she knew Melissa had arrived. How would she have known? What happened at the solstice?"

"Those are two very different questions—and yet, both add more to the puzzle." Lilise frowned. "I think Cholios knows something about Melissa's soul. You mentioned they said he wanted her dead or alive. He tried to kill her the night of the solstice. She won't speak much about what was said to her before we arrived—or what she overheard—but her human body may have only been a vessel."

If the two were tied, then that was why the gods wanted Melissa brought to Voreios. If I'd listened, none of this would have happened this way. She might have been safe. Right now, I didn't have either of them to confirm it, but so much could have been avoided by not running from destiny. At least Kelan would have been here to experience this instead of being out in the unknown.

"If Melissa had been killed that night, would that have killed the vasilissa too?"

Lilise offered me an apologetic shrug. "It's not like there's any precedent for this situation. We weren't aware of what was happening here in Voreios, so all we were focused on was protecting Melissa. It was only with Silva's guidance and Montibus' intervention that we made it in time."

"I don't understand why they didn't step in this time. What was the difference between the two occurrences?" I growled. They worked so hard to prevent the situation on the solstice, but not even lifted a hand to help this time.

"The only theory I have is that she was touching the wrong tree the first time." Lilise glared into the distance as she relayed her thoughts.

Flashes of Melissa came pouring back into my mind— the scars on her shoulders that had pierced all the way through her, the way her head would fall when she began to relive that night, the way she'd said no during her night terror. Her absolute determination not to show how terrified she'd been when the infernals attacked outside the borders of Voreios.

"I'm supposed to protect her." Defeat layered my words. I'd left her to the wind and now Ferox was out chasing a cure that might be the only thing to save them both. What was I doing? Clearly not enough.

"You are the only reason she's present in this tree right now—and not dead in the meeting halls or kidnapped back to the Infernal Plane," Lilise answered bleakly. Her face reflected my misery. "We wouldn't have made it to her a second time. Not with how quickly that poison spread."

220

This didn't make me feel any better. I gazed at the tree with a frown as I gently touched her. The vasilissa sent me an orange flash with pink sparks sprinkled in before falling silent again.

"But this tree has been planted for what. . .seventy-six years?" Cassie started again. "Why hadn't the gods brought her back to us sooner?"

"Melissa was only twenty-seven when she arrived here. What was going on during those remaining years—maybe we'll learn more when Ferox returns," Lilise replied with a wistful sigh. "I'm willing to bet they lost her soul for a time. If it was on Earth, perhaps that's how she ended up as a human."

"Oh good, you're all still here," Xhet interjected, and I groaned at his appearance. "I needed to find you as soon as possible. Solis filled in the last piece at our morning prayers."

Lilise gave him her full attention, but Cassie only looked as annoyed as I felt, not bothering to rise and greet him.

"Well, what did they say?" Lilise prompted.

"Everything makes so much sense now. The vasilissa will emerge soon, and Voreios will be made whole. The condition she was born with required a sacrifice—which Graak fulfilled by placing his dying mate at her roots." Xhet almost seemed proud to be relaying this to us. I shot a glare in his direction. Xhet noticed and had the good grace to appear shameful for his previous excitement.

Lilise had fallen still, which meant she was relaying this information to another dryad—likely Ferox—but I couldn't keep my mouth shut. That answer couldn't be right. "I think I'm going to need more. What condition? What sacrifice?"

221

"That is not the way of dryad magic—" Lilise started to argue, but Xhet cut her off.

"It was a curse the fae cast on us the day they burned our grove, before another dryad could take root. Ultimately, Melissa was the blessing the grove needed. The vasilissa put out a calling of the grove to her once she arrived. Melissa's life won't be in vain. The prophecy is coming into effect now." The elder beamed up at the tree. "She's going to rise and bring balance back to the world, ending the fae and elven war—and our morose state."

His attention fell to me again as the dryads talked, and an awkward silence settled over our small group.

"I'm sure this is troubling for you, Graak. Losing a mate is a hard situation. No one will fault you for your move to Notos. I'd advise you to leave before she awakens, so you don't hurt her with your split loyalty." He tried to pat my arm, but I shifted out of his reach. "Zoq can handle the ryne trials, so you can depart tonight."

"You don't need to have trials if she's about to emerge. That would be a wasted effort." Cassie finally spoke again, and it wasn't friendly. "Graak isn't leaving yet. That would destabilize the borders, and right now that's the only magic still holding. There isn't another member of Voreios who could survive the druwid rites. Graak nearly died to establish what we currently have—and she's full grown now. If she comes out, she'll be able to pick her own druwids."

I had to agree with that. If she was about to come out, I would not be leaving. I would embrace whatever was to come with an open mind.

"Something isn't adding up. Baccys never said anything about a curse on the vasilissa or the lands. Given all the troubles we had, it would have come up before. Perhaps we do need Prafrum after all. I need to hear this from Solis myself." I recalled every single conversation I'd had with my mentor and gestured for a messenger. "Call for Zoq immediately."

Xhet tutted as if I should have known this. "Baccys died before he passed that message on to you. You'd barely become a man—he wouldn't have shared that burden with you."

"Then why didn't any of you tell me? You know what, wait for Zoq. He would've known about this. He's the last ryne to the dryads from old Voreios."

"You'll be able to ask the vasilissa herself. However, I think she'll need to be protected from you when you find out the truth," Xhet said, eyeing me warily.

"I would never hurt her. It's my fault for placing Melissa here—not hers. If this is true, then she took what she needed. . ." Pain tore through my chest at the thought. How would my sweet dryad handle this information? She wouldn't want to hurt anyone. Maybe leaving was for the best. I would only hurt her—and myself—every time we interacted.

"I think it's too soon to assume anything," Lilise retorted, raising a hand in my direction to stop my movement. "Graak, please stay. Let's sort this out together."

"What if she doesn't fully wake up?" Cassie asked, and I hated the silence that followed.

Lilise recovered first. "I just don't know. She still seems to be responding to Graak, so we'll take that as we can. Only time will tell us what we need to know. For now, she's healthy—and we know that Melissa is in there. Let's hold on to whatever faith we can for a bit longer."

The wait was going to be the death of me in the end.

Chapter 25 – Aurinia

After the woman's hand touched my bark, everything changed. An influx of information and sensation poured through my entire being—from root tip to leaf. New sights and sounds. New meanings to actions. Impressions of the world beyond my isolated hill. Colors and music and sights unlike anything I could have comprehended before.

I could lose myself here for an eternity and never grow bored.

The woman had experienced the world around me in a way I had only ever observed in others. Her range of emotional responses was far greater than I'd thought possible.

From time to time, I felt something along my bark— something trying to pull my attention away from these overwhelming new experiences. I was too overstimulated to give it much thought. Sometimes the other dryads would reach through the roots, but I'd never spoken with them there before, so I didn't divert much attention to what they said.

They called for someone I didn't know. Oh. Yes, I did. That was the name of the woman Graak had bonded to.

Melissa. Were these all Melissa's thoughts and experiences?

In my consciousness, it looked like bright strands of pink, purple, and black twisted together from the sky, while various shades of green rose from the earth to meet them. One forest green strand wrapped around the nearest purple tendril—and the rest of the world faded away.

The bark I slept in didn't feel like mine. Strange vibrations in the ground, coming from miles away, drew closer with each passing moment. Trees were dying, and they sent warnings to the rest of us: danger was coming. It was a signal to move nutrients deeper into the ground—our only prayer for rebirth, whatever horror had come to claim us in this life.

The sense of impending doom overwhelmed my mind. Every fiber of my being had urged me to flee, to get far away before whatever it was got to me too. But how? The other trees had urged me to go—that I wasn't the same as them. Stores of nutrients had come to me, as if to help me carry out this new quest. I hadn't understood why they said these things. I'd always been here, the same as them.

Then one day, the vibrations became unbearably loud. The danger was near. Something rumbled above the ground around my roots, but it hadn't communicated with us or the other plants the way the trees and river did. A rough sensation scraped against my bark, sending a flash of pain, followed by another stab. I could scream at the pain. What was hurting me? Even the insects and earthworms had known to move away from this thing.

I needed to leave. I needed to go now, or I would die. Pressing my energy into the bark furthest away from the point of the pain, something new began to happen. Bark turned to energy, which turned into something else. Placing a branch on the ground, I looked down at myself. What I'd thought were branches had changed in a new way. Little stubby shoots spread apart in front of my vision, confusing me. Even the coloring of my bark had lightened. What had happened? What was going on?

"Help. . .help. . ." I began to cry as the sense of loneliness rose in my grief. I couldn't talk to the other trees anymore. I couldn't feel their connectivity—or their pain. I had been separated from the grove. The silence became deafening; I'd never experienced anything like it before.

I turned back to look at the tree that had been my home. I could now see what had happened to all the others. The field had been cleared. They had all been torn down, and the stumps were being ground away. My little mind didn't know how to process the horror of what I saw. They were just gone. . .and these beasts were doing the same thing to me.

A blade had been implanted in the lower portion of my tree stump. I stumbled towards the tree, my branches unsure how to move in this new form. I knew I had to stop the pain, even if I couldn't feel it anymore. I pulled at the blade lodged in my bark, but it wouldn't budge.

"Mom!" I called to the earth—I called for the spirit of nature, the one our energy had always become one with. I called for the grove I could no longer hear. Surely, they wouldn't leave me alone now to witness this.

"Hey! Is that a little girl? What is she doing all the way out here?" The words came in a strange language my mind didn't understand.

"Mom!" I shouted again, turning towards the field of trees behind me. Still, there was no answer.

"Are you missing, little girl? Come here—we can help you."

The man came closer to me. Man. I only knew what the other trees had called these creatures. We'd seen them walking in the forests, though I could never tell what they were doing.

The man stood with the big machine that was eating up the roots of one of my friends. My eyes widened as fear seized me. These were not good creatures. My branches moved so slowly, and I stumbled and tripped again and again. I could hear the creature shouting behind me before it began to chase me.

"Mom. . . Mom!" I cried in pure terror. Tripping in the forest, I felt a slice across my new lower branch, and a red liquid poured from the scratch. It hurt so much I wanted to scream—but moving forward only made it worse. Seeing a small opening, I crawled away to hide in the bushes.

As evening set in, I could hear more people shouting in the forest. Normally, they went away at night. Why were they still here? Trembling, I curled into a ball and tried to make no sound. My trunk hurt, and it kept making a strange gurgling noise. My head ached, and the red stuff had dried over my strange new bark. I was so lonely—but tucked against the bark of this tree, I found a small bit of solace.

A light flashed outside where I was hiding.

"Stand back, gentlemen," a softer voice commanded, using those words I didn't understand.

Quiet footsteps approached, and I tightened into the smallest ball I could become. Then the voice spoke again— but this time I understood her. The language of the trees.

"Come here, little one. We've found you. You're safe."

Her dark hair fell around her shoulders, and from the way the light illuminated her face in the darkness, I knew I was staring at a goddess. Was it Mother Earth come to save me? Why couldn't she save the forest?

Very slowly, I climbed out towards the woman's voice. The goddess wore a strange blue outfit with belts, but she lifted me into her arms and walked me past the men. She was taking me away from the trees, and my heart cried out—but she was the goddess, and I knew I should obey.

Melissa's thoughts pulled in the confusing details. The goddess had been Silva, and she'd worn a police uniform. The unusual language had been English.

Before I could go too far into that memory, another green strand tangled with a black thread from the sky—and the two began to combine.

This was my grove. I knew this place very well. A young satyr, likely around ten years of age, stood with Baccys. This was one of my favorite memories. My tree had been very young then; I could only partially understand what the two satyrs were saying at the time. The world was so new to me—I had only awoken a few days earlier. I hadn't learned how to sing yet.

229

"What's her name?" the boy asked, his voice barely above a whisper.

"We won't know until she tells us, but you can call her Vasilissa for now. Go introduce yourself." The older man gestured him forward.

The boy stepped up to my root sphere. He looked unsure but determined to follow through with the request. "Hello, Vasilissa. My name is Graak. I'm not ready yet, but I'm going to train hard, and I will protect you."

Though I didn't understand what any of those words meant, I liked the way his voice sounded. Having him talk to me made me feel so light. My leaves illuminated in response to my new feelings. Then he smiled at me.

Trees remember everything. So even though I didn't understand it then, I had replayed that entire conversation over and over again as he told me about training and his trial. We were going to be friends for the rest of our lives.

The thought shifted as another black thread collided with a green one.

I had been growing steadily for two full seasonal cycles. More and more people began to visit as Baccys grew more confident that I would survive.

A woman came by once every season. While she often cried during our time together, I could feel the love radiating from her. She felt like a tree, even though she didn't look like my other tree friends. This woman could understand my vibrations a little better than Baccys could. She said her name was Cassie. She would sing songs to me. Sometimes, *she brought others who would try to communicate with me as well. I couldn't talk with them either, though.*

Members of the community were starting to meet me. The trees around me would talk about these new visitors, and where they liked to travel in the grove. I was beginning to learn about the seasons from them—and how I should behave to survive.

Flower nymphs would visit my grove a few times each year, but those friends never stayed long and never returned. I sang often and projected colors to anyone who came close enough. They all seemed to like it when I did that.

Snap. Another tendril of memories fell into place.

A teenage satyr approached my tree roots with Baccys. I recognized him immediately, despite the changes in his physical appearance. It was my first friend, returning from training. I still didn't have many friends—everyone who came around never stayed long—and I had been lonely.

"Hello, Vasilissa. It's been a little while. Do you remember me?" His voice was deeper now. He was taller too. It felt like ages had passed since we'd last seen each other, but his energy felt the same.

I glowed a beautiful orange to show him how excited I was. His eyes sparkled as he smiled at my display. I wanted to leave my tree and embrace him, just as I'd seen others do when he greeted them on his way to me. Somehow, I knew I should have been able to do that too.

A slight frown tugged at the corners of his mouth as he observed me. "Nothing to say yet? That's okay, Vasilissa. I know you'll speak when you're ready. You might even come out soon. We'll all be very glad to meet you. You'll be able to wander wherever you'd like. I'll always be with you. I'll make sure you don't get into anything too crazy."

With a display of blue energy, I tried to express my sadness at not being able to speak with him. My friend was home, and he had been exploring. What had he seen and learned?

"Don't be sad. I will come visit you until you are ready." His hand gently touched my bark. "To be honest, I'm really looking forward to learning your name. We must keep you a secret from the rest of the world for now—but you are our guiding light."

My name was Aurinia. . .and I tried to tell him that. He still couldn't hear me, though I kept trying. He took a seat at the base of my trunk and began telling me all about his experiences over the past few years. I sang to him in colors that matched what I thought his stories were about, though I really didn't understand them yet. He would occasionally pause and smile, enjoying my version of talking—almost like he enjoyed hearing me as much as I did him.

Snap. More tendrils of my memories and Melissa's collided.

Now a young man, he had been true to his word. He came to visit me almost every day. He would talk, and I would express emotion. Only occasionally would he mention wishing to meet me or hear my voice. No one understood why I wouldn't come out—not even me. We had begun to communicate more effectively through this limited means,

232

thanks to the amount of time he spent trying to understand it.

"Baccys, I don't understand. Is it me? She should have come out years ago."

"This is a dryad given to us by the gods. She's in there—Cassie has confirmed that—but she's not even speaking to Cassie. You need to give her time."

"Maybe she needs someone else. Maybe she doesn't feel confident that I'll protect her if she does come out," he lamented.

"Don't say that. Look—you're upsetting her."

I could tell my actions were making him unhappy, but I didn't know how to change that. I gave off deep blues, and all my branches drooped. I didn't know how to be more than I already was. Didn't he know that I wanted so much more than this too?

"I'm sorry, Vasilissa. I don't know what to do. You should be exploring and roaming the grove. We need you."

"Why don't you bring the world to her until she decides to come out?" Baccys suggested.

"How?" Graak grew quiet for a moment, thinking. "Wait. . . I think I have an idea."

The next day, he began bringing new members of the grove for me to meet every few days. They would tell me who they were, what they did, and share their lives with me. I was happy to have more friends, but I noticed that sometimes his interest drifted towards some of the people he brought.

"Graak! Not in front of her. Trees remember everything!" Baccys shouted, swatting the back of his head.

Graak rubbed the spot he'd been hit, and the nereid he'd been talking to covered her laugh before running off with the others. "Oh, it's harmless flirting. She's probably not even going to notice."

"She will. She may not understand it now, but she'll remember. You'll absolutely want to follow your nature—but understand there's a chance you'll be her first bond, if you're fortunate enough."

"But. . .I'm trying to do what we're supposed to. We have to feed. I'll starve before she's full grown. Am I just supposed to wait for her?"

"Oh no, you'll want to be practiced. Flower nymphs don't remember—but give a dryad a bad experience, and she'll never forget it. Don't do it here, in front of her. Treat her tree like you would her spirit form."

I didn't really understand what they were talking about, but my friend's tone was upset. I sang to him and flashed angry reds at Baccys. Oh, how I wished I could speak. I just wanted to make Graak smile again.

The old satyr only laughed kindly at my response. "It seems she's already very protective of you," he said as I continued to yell at him with reds.

Graak turned to me with those sparkling dark eyes. "It's okay, Vasilissa. Baccys is right. It was something I needed to hear."

I calmed down as he placed his hand on my trunk and gave me that smile of his.

Snap.

Graak had become a full man. As he approached my tree, I could tell his energy was distraught and heavy. The root network whispered that a great battle had taken place, and much of my community had vanished. Friends who had shared their stories with me. . .gone in an instant. He came to me alone that day.

I sang to him, as I always did when he visited, and he let out a deep sigh.

"Vasilissa. . . I need you to come out. We need you more than ever. . ."

I didn't understand why I couldn't leave my tree. They all asked me to, but every time I tried, I simply couldn't. I was nearly twenty years old and felt like I could be so much more than what I was. Something was missing.

"Please. . . Where are you? Baccys is dead. I have to step into his role, but I can't do it without you. Please help me."

He sat among my roots, and I felt the weight of his sorrow. All I could do was wrap him in my energy waves and hold him while he cried. I mourned with the trees—for the fallen, for the lost community.

Cassie returned quickly after Baccys' energy disappeared. There was a ritual to be completed, and they had to ensure nothing went wrong. Her presence was comforting, and I could feel a pull from the tree—was this what I would look like if I ever left?

Though Graak was anguished, his energy began to connect with mine. Green light circled my tree as both Cassie and Graak chanted. Then a beam of green energy tapped into him, and he grimaced in pain. I wanted to make it stop—it was clearly hurting him—but he continued *chanting well into the next day. When the ritual was finished, he collapsed, exhausted, and took a seat at my base. I could sense him more clearly than ever before. If I focused, I could hear the beating of his heart.*

Zoq and Cassie checked on him frequently as he faded in and out of consciousness—but our hearts remained in sync.

After that, something else had changed. The two of us were linked in a new way. Graak became even more attentive to me than he had been before. Though he couldn't stay all the time, he started coming to me every morning and evening. He took care of my soil, trimmed my branches, and ensured I had enough water. Baccys and a few other satyrs had done that before—but now, Graak allowed no one else to care for me unless he was far away on the outskirts of the grove or traveling, which he rarely did.

"No one will hurt us like this again. Not if I have anything to say about it," he promised me.

Another batch of tendrils slammed together, spiraling me straight into another memory.

The other world came back into focus. The cold, sterile walls of the hallway blurred into each turn. When the officer gave me back my stuff, she gestured with indifference to the exit.

"Do you know who posted bail?" I asked as I signed for my few belongings.

I'd only wanted a soda, but I should have known better than to get in that asshole's car. Tomorrow, I'd enroll in the teaching program I'd been eyeing for months. With a few waitressing gigs, I could afford the classes.

"Don't know or care. Exit's that way."

I rolled my eyes and pulled my cell phone out of the bag. Catching up on the texts, I could only figure Stacye bailed us both out. I'd have to find some way to pay her back and stop depending on whatever jackass my girlfriend decided to hook up with. This one happened to be a mid-tier dealer that the cops tagged often.

Being felt up by a police officer, called a drug whore, and offered an exchange of sex for freedom had to cross a line somewhere, but apparently not in this stupid state.

A long bath and maybe a hit of something would help set my head straight.

"I knew there had to be a reason you weren't returning my calls."

The sound of his voice made my heart sink. "Jeff. What are you doing here? How'd you even find me?"

"You can run, kitten, but I always know where to look. It's time to stop partying in the woods." He buttoned up the jacket on his three-piece suit as he rose from the plastic seat in the waiting room. His short dark hair was cut in the corporate style reflective of his big investing gig. "You look good. Still not eating enough, though."

"When did you become my mother?" I turned to leave him behind in the station. "I'll pay you back for the bail. Somehow."

"Melissa, stop. I don't know what it is you're chasing, but it's not out here." His long strides brought him to the door before I could reach it. He opened it like the gentleman he always tried to be in public. I heard the click of his car

237

unlocking and saw the lights flash. "You'll want for nothing. Just come back with me to the city."

Oh, sure. Bring up that he'd flown all the way from New York to Arizona just to clean up my mess. "I don't need you to provide for me. I'll make my own way," I huffed.

He gave me a dubious look. "Sure. Looks like you're doing a great job of that. Prostitution? Seriously? I'm not a better alternative than prostitution?" Jeff stepped in front of me and grabbed my shoulders.

I flinched at his words but glared up at him anyway. "What I do or don't do with my body is none of your concern. I don't know when I became your pet project, but hooking up a few times doesn't make me yours."

"You're not a nymph, Melissa! Life has consequences, and the forest won't save you. I'm trying to."

"I don't need saving," I said with a growl. "I'm going to make something of my life—on my own terms. I'm meant for so much more than this. I know it."

Chapter 26 – Graak

The morning of spring arrived like an unwelcome reminder that time passed—even when I didn't want it to. The flower nymphs began their joyful song, greeting the season as they had every year of my life. But for the first time in hours, I questioned my sanity. Because today was not one I wanted to celebrate.

"You can't skip out on the ritual, Graak," Cassie pressed, using the earth to force me to my feet.

I'd fallen asleep beside the vasilissa again, exhaustion finally dragging me under. I couldn't even remember the last time I'd eaten.

"I think Zoq can handle it," I replied, not bothering to hide my disinterest.

"Oh no," Zoq called from somewhere behind me. "You remember what happened the last time I tried to do the ritual. What if we lose access to the inner grove portals as well? It must be you."

I'd forgotten about the world issues and the failing elemental magic. Easy to do when I'd lost both women I loved in the blink of an eye. I rubbed my face and studied the vasilissa for a moment.

"Sounds like the gods should figure that out on their own then."

"Graak!" Cassie shouted with exasperation lacing her voice.

"Fine. How about it, Vasilissa?" I asked. "Do you want to run through the spring ritual with me before I have to do it for the rest of the grove?"

This was our tradition. In the other groves, their mother trees would perform the ritual. Since our mother tree couldn't leave her bark, I performed it in her place—after running through a special routine I'd designed just for her. Sometimes I made new songs for the occasion, unless she found a favorite. Then I'd play that one every year. It was our way of coping with reality.

I waited for her to respond with anything. She would normally chirp and sing ecstatically. She loved the changing of the seasons, and all her new flower friends. But this year, I was met with. . .nothing.

Cassie drew my face towards hers before the flurry of depressing thoughts could fully seize hold. "Focus on the grove first today," she said softly. "Lilise will stay with her. We need the community to keep moving forward, and they'll look to you for guidance. If you can't pull it together, then everything you've worked so hard for is lost. Is that how you want to honor either of them?"

I closed my eyes and took a deep breath, letting it out slowly. "No. I'll do the ritual."

"Good. One step at a time. Zoq and I will be there to support you." Cassie gave Zoq a nod before returning to Lilise and the vasilissa.

Zoq wasted no time picking up where she left off, practically dragging me by the elbow towards the open field near the main grounds.

"They are all going to see right through me." I sighed, fighting back the urge to run to her tree the moment she slipped from my view.

"Show yourself some grace."

"I'm trying," I replied, frowning. "I don't care much about anything anymore."

"I know exactly what you're going through."

And I knew that he did—in a way that made my heart break with the new understanding of the pain he'd experienced.

"Does it ever get easier?"

"No. You just learn how to adapt because that's what they'd want for you," Zoq said thoughtfully, and I knew his mind was with Nivy and their children. "My brother getting sick was unfortunate but having you to care for gave me something else to focus on."

"Like this ritual will for me?"

Zoq chuckled, but it wasn't unkind. "No. Your real healing won't begin until we get some answers—about Melissa's soul, the vasilissa returning to normal, and unless we figure out what happened to Kelan. Until then, it's just going through the motions. And that's okay too."

As usual, he was right. I could handle going through the motions. At least until we had the next piece of the puzzle. The chain around my heart clicked into place. I would be controlled and level today. Zoq and Cassie would make sure I had the space I needed if I started to crack. But that wouldn't be today.

The vasilissa and our grove were counting on me, and I wouldn't let them down.

The spring ritual never took place at a set time—it was guided by the position of the celestial bodies. Being so closely tied to nature, as we were in the groves, I could feel the shift like an internal clock ticking over. It wasn't spoken, just known, like someone guiding me along a changing path. All the members of the grove were tuned into it too, so I wasn't surprised to find most of them already waiting or arriving as I began my ascent to the rising altar in the field where we gathered.

Whispers stirred around me, a flurry of questions I couldn't focus on—questions about my well-being, about the vasilissa. They were concerned, and I wouldn't begrudge them that. They loved the mother tree who kept us all safe within her barrier.

I'd like to say they loved and cared for me too, but it was different than the love they had for her.

The altar had already been covered by the grove members in a variety of offerings they wished to have blessed. Spring and summer rituals always carried more fire, with hopeful lovers looking to find their matches or bless the grove with new life. This was a day of renewal, after all the hard times.

I summoned every bit of strength I had to smile at those gathered.

"Hail and welcome spring!" I announced.

Immediately, the energy around us lifted. The crowd responded to my tone, drawing from the joy I offered. I lifted my hands to the sky and turned my face towards the sun.

"We thank Silva and Solis for the days that grow longer and warmer."

A chorus of voices rose in celebration, singing praise to the celestial goddesses. Drawing on my magic, I reached into the earth and pulled forth the ceremonial rod buried centuries ago for this exact purpose. A cluster of nymphs stepped forward, fastening long strands of fabric to the top. I raised the rod high, allowing the ribbons to unfurl and dance in the breeze as they drifted through the crowd.

"We thank Montibus for the blessing of the fertile soil at our feet, and the shelters for our homes," I continued, smiling at the renewed cheers. "We thank Ventus, Calor, and Thadal for the balance that provides stability—so that we may grow and be blessed."

That part was different in each grove, as we honored our own patron while keeping the elemental magic in harmony across our world. Now came the blessings.

"Bless the unions made here tonight with little cries. Bless the joining of hearts, so they may find their truest matches. Bless the community with growth and strength for the future."

I lifted a goblet from the altar table to the sky and took a deep breath.

"To the gods! Hail and welcome spring!"

Flower nymphs began to sing and laugh as they danced into the fields behind me, appearing with the shift of the planet into full seasonal transition.

"To the gods!" the crowd echoed, voices rising in celebration. "Hail and welcome spring!"

With a fake smile plastered to my face, I took the longest drink I'd had in weeks. After what the gods had taken from me, I could only hope this was enough to fool them all.

Chapter 27 – Aurinia

The memories slowly transitioned into more recent visions. I had no idea how long I'd been in this state. The underground root network spoke of the transition to spring as if it had already passed. The new flower nymphs sent back warm vibrations, and my pulses met theirs like a gentle greeting.

I'd missed the spring ritual with Graak. He was always so busy, but I cherished the moments we shared during those little traditions. And now, I'd missed it.

The deflation I felt after riding the high of reliving my life—and Melissa's memories—was sharp and sudden. The new world, the one that had opened through a window in space revealing a vast tree anchored among the stars, began to fade.

There would be time to revisit everything again. But now, I needed to connect with the grove. I turned my full attention to those gathered around me, scanning the space as I searched for him. I knew he was close by. My first friend.

He stood with his arms crossed, his shoulders sagging with exhaustion. A group of flower nymphs chattered at him, but I wasn't sure he was even listening.

"Please try to understand—I'm doing this for her safety and yours. It's not my intention to favor the pixies. I literally cannot stop them without using unnecessary force."

"Just a few steps closer, Graak. That's all we're asking."

"Fine." He sighed, rubbing a hand over his face.

They squealed, and two of them wrapped their arms around him before they all ran to sit in a cluster beside my tree. I loved listening to them talk and sing. They always brightened my days—but right now, more than anything, I wanted to cheer him up.

Melissa's memory of the first forest had revealed something I'd once tried—and failed—to do. But something felt different this time. Everyone always asked me to leave the tree, and she had done it, even though she hadn't been able to return afterward.

Would I give up my true body to do what she had? Flashes came to me—her hand, my hand—caressing Graak's skin, being held by him, kissing him. Yes. For that, I would give up this existence, if I had to.

I copied the sensations I remembered from that vision. Pressing my energy into the bark nearest him, I pushed once more. A bright pulse surrounded my consciousness. That had never happened before. I leaned into the light. I wanted this. I wanted hands and feet. I wanted to experience the world beyond bark and farther than my roots could reach.

As the light faded and my vision adjusted to the beautiful, familiar colors of my grove, I lifted a trembling hand in front of me. Delicate fingers stretched outward, longer than I'd expected from Melissa's memories. The nails were long and rounded, but along my soft, pale skin ran green lines—like those I'd seen on the other dryads—twisting up the length of my arm.

I followed them with my eyes. They crossed and curled in the most intricate, beautiful design, weaving all over my body. My brunette hair tumbled forward as I twisted to glimpse the back of my legs. That's when I realized it I wasn't just hair—tiny vines were elegantly wrapped between thick strands, like living filigree.

Unlike Melissa's memory, I could still feel my tree. I could still feel the grove. My roots and my feet connected to the soil, and all the messages flowed—passing through me as they always had.

I heard him before I saw his hooves come into view, and my heart raced with wild abandon. We'd waited so long for this.

Trusting myself not to stumble, I gave Graak a smile so big it made my cheeks ache—and I ran to him. He caught me at the waist before I could slam into him, my hands hovering gently over his chest.

"Melissa," Lilise said softly, but I was only half listening.

My eyes locked with his as my hands slid up to rest on his shoulders. I couldn't quite read the expression on his face as he watched me.

"My name is Aurinia," I said, loud enough for the others to hear—but I needed him to hear it first. Then I hummed the sound I'd been singing to him for decades.

"It's beautiful. . .you're beautiful," he whispered, tears pooling at the corners of his eyes. Years of complicated emotion—grief, longing, love—twisted in his expression like a vortex.

A soft laugh escaped me as my own tears spilled down my cheeks. I cupped his face in my hands, and he pulled me in closer until our foreheads touched.

The gods may have taken him from me—but they couldn't take this. This was our moment. And if it was all I could have, I would cherish it forever.

I don't know how long we stood there, but it wasn't long enough before I heard an elder cough behind me.

"Graak, we need to speak."

My first friend didn't seem to hear him. His attention remained solely on me, unwavering. But I didn't want him getting into any more trouble. I took a small step back, and Graak let me go. The elder offered me a smile.

"Vasilissa, we've all been so looking forward to meeting you. This will be a day of celebration indeed."

"Aurinia," I repeated, returning his smile. "Please call me Aurinia."

"Very well, Aurinia. Give me a moment to speak with Graak, and then we can begin going over what must happen now that you're to take full control of the grove." He didn't wait for my reply, just gestured for Graak to follow him.

Lilise stepped up and took my hands, inspecting me like she had often done with Melissa. Cassie hovered nearby, but she didn't approach me. I smiled at them both, uncertain of the nervous energy in the air.

"How are you feeling?" Lilise finally asked, and the tension immediately faded.

"I'm excited—and a bit confused," I admitted softly.

Lilise and Cassie shared a look, and I could tell they wanted to ask more questions. But before they could, I had a few of my own.

"How do I make clothes? I'd like to be a little less exposed for whatever comes next."

For the first time, Cassie smiled. "Nymph magic 101. You can make whatever you want. Tap into your core energy—right here." She gently touched the center of her chest. "You should feel your tie to your tree humming. Then just imagine what you want to wear. I'd recommend leaving your feet bare. It'll help keep your root connection strong, even when you're far from your tree."

"Give it a try," Lilise encouraged, squeezing my hands.

I thought through all the different types of clothes I'd seen before. This time, I could choose my own style—and add my own flare. It was still a bit chilly, even with spring's arrival.

Wait. . . I'd missed the spring ritual I remembered again, and the disappointment was renewed. I glanced towards Graak and Xhet, who were having what looked like a heated discussion—but that wasn't anything new. Graak never did get along with the elders.

"What's wrong?" Lilise asked gently, resting a hand on my shoulder.

"Nothing," I said quickly, brushing it off. I couldn't change the past. Only the future was in my control.

Leaves wrapped around my body as I changed into a pair of leggings cropped at the ankle with a green layered skirt. A long-sleeved white shirt hugged every curve of this new form, with cutouts at the shoulders. My skin felt as warm as my bark did, so that shouldn't be too much of an adjustment.

I wiggled my toes on the snow-dusted ground. The whole forest felt different now. I could sense the frequencies of every living thing around me. The sensations were overwhelming if I focused too much on any single one, instead of absorbing them as a whole—like I'd done all my life. Each blade of grass whispered a story; I could feel the insects, the wildlife.

Feeling it from two places at once was surreal. My mind now had two echo points—one in this body, and one in my tree. I could still sense everyone moving around the borders. I could feel everything under my protection barriers I'd anchored with Graak. And I relished that connection—his magic linked to mine, a hidden piece of him no one else could take from me.

"I wish you would leave it be." Graak's voice cut through the calm, short and furious. I tuned into the trees near the two satyrs, letting their voices carry to me. This trick only worked at short range—but they hadn't gone far enough to keep it private. "She just came out, and you're already trying to wrangle her into your control," Graak snapped. "Let her find her footing before you try to bombard her with everything."

"Think about what's best for her—not yourself. Losing a mate is hard. Ask Zoq," Xhet retorted. "You really shouldn't be anywhere near her as the truth comes out. How do you think it's going to make her feel when she realizes what she's done?"

"None of this is her fault."

"It's easy to say that now. But what happens when you realize she's not the mate you lost?"

Xhet's words were like a blade—sharp and cruel—slicing through the tree, just as Melissa had once felt. How could he be so certain?

"If you insist on staying, then it should be only to help her find her true mates. You need to sever whatever attachment you have for each other. That's the only way she's going to survive."

Graak let out a low, guttural sound. A stone slab rose from the earth—and with one brutal punch, he smashed it into a hundred jagged pieces. "I need to hear it from Silva myself," he said through clenched teeth. "Because everything in my soul knows—she is still my heart. And once I find Kelan, there will be no denying it."

"I understand that you feel this strongly," Xhet said, his voice calmer but still unyielding. "However, if there's even the smallest chance that things aren't what you think—then you'll only confuse her when the truth settles. I know you don't want to hurt her."

Cassie and Lilise were watching me now, their expressions filled with worry as I turned my attention back to them.

"How did this happen?" I asked, my anxiety growing with every heartbeat.

"We were hoping you might have more answers for us," Lilise replied gently. "What we do know is this: your seed was given to Baccys by Silva on the eve of Voreios' destruction. It was a way to ensure the grove's survival. A prophecy was given that night, and Baccys later told us Heliria threw a stone through the portal before she sacrificed her life to seal it. We believe that stone was meant to bring a human—Melissa—into our world, to fulfill that portion of the prophecy."

The weight of the revelation settled heavy on my shoulders. "But Melissa's memories. . .they're mine now. I still *feel* as though I lived that life and this one. Is it truly possible that we're not the same?"

"Anything could be possible," Lilise murmured, "but I think we'll need time to let the dust settle."

The mate mark I remembered from Melissa's chest wasn't on mine. I didn't bear her scars or the wounds from the Shadow God's attack. In their place were delicate green designs of leaves arranged in a circle. Graak's faded markings echoed Zoq's words—that his mate was dead. No matter what he said, it was my fault.

I grimaced. "How can I reverse it?"

"Reverse what?" Cassie asked, her brow rising in concern.

"I don't want her soul," I said, voice quiet but certain. "Even if it means I'll never live a normal life." I met Graak's gaze over Lilise's shoulder and frowned. "The price is too high."

Lilise pulled me into a tight embrace, and I let my head rest against her shoulder. "I don't think everything is as it seems. Let's discover those answers together."

I could only hope she was right. Because the best day of my life was swiftly becoming the worst one.

Chapter 28 – Aurinia

I walked arm in arm with Cassie as we headed towards the main grounds.

How many stories had I heard about the parties and late-night shenanigans the grove members got into here? Graak shared everything with me—except that he was an amazing dancer; the other nymphs had told me that bit of information.

Now I could finally see it all with my own eyes—and maybe get into a bit of trouble myself.

Every satyr or nymph who passed stopped to offer me a smile, a welcome, and some of them even tears. Okay, so I cried a few times myself. I knew all their names; as many had visited me at my tree over the years. They'd told me their stories, but most of them never thought they'd get to hear mine. Today, I was starting a whole new chapter.

"Voreios rises," Cassie said, with a smile that warmed my heart.

It was hard to imagine that something as simple as me coming out of my tree could inspire so much elation. I understood that my role as the anchor to the grove for our borders played a part in their safety, but I knew absolutely nothing about leading. Melissa's memories of Hairiko filled me with a different kind of nervous energy.

"This may be a silly question, but I'm still trying to understand—how do I get to be both a tree and a. . .what is this form? There are hundreds of trees in Voreios. Why can't they do this too?" I glanced between Cassie and Lilise to see who would answer first.

"It's a good question. I really didn't spend enough time with you to explain anything," Cassie admitted. "I wasn't sure if it would help or hurt you, knowing how different you were."

"I think you did the right thing. I was already sad that I couldn't come out like people asked me to. If I'd really understood what that meant, I think I would've gone crazy." I shrugged, trying to downplay how exciting this was for me.

"That's a very likely possibility. Dryads are trees—but not in the traditional sense," Lilise began, and my interest perked up. "We're a type of nature spirit who, upon creation, took the form of trees. Other nature spirits chose different forms, aligned with their essence. That's why we have nereids, aurai, oceanids, and so many more. What you're in right now is your spirit form—and all the nymph variations have one. This form has a few types of manipulations."

"Like what?" I asked curiously.

"Well, as you've seen, you can change your outward appearance with accents like clothing. You can also change things like your hair, skin tone—even body proportions. Those changes require more energy to maintain, though, so most of us only use them when we're undercover." Lilise gestured to a series of rocks by the fires where we could sit.

"Oh, undercover. Like a spy." I smiled broadly at the imagery that came to mind—mostly from movies Melissa had watched.

"Yes, exactly," Lilise affirmed, though I didn't think she realized where my mind had gone.

I cast another glance over my shoulder at Graak. Each time I looked, he was watching me—just like now.

But once the path widened into the cleared field with a large fire dancing in the center, he split off from our group to talk to Zoq, who stood at the entrance of a cavern. Judging by the cavern's distance from my tree, I could guess this was Graak's space. He was here often at night. Zoq bowed his head to me, and I blushed, caught watching the two of them.

Music swelled around us as the satyrs and nymphs jammed out—as Melissa might've said. I could feel the weight of their gazes on me, but none of them felt angry or heavy. Still, the sight of the fire and Graak triggered a memory that shouldn't have been mine. I didn't know if I had the right to ask, but my heart needed to know.

"Where is Kelan?"

The wait was torturous. I shouldn't love a man I'd technically never met, but I did. Maybe it was Melissa's affection, but I couldn't erase the feeling of him imprinted on that part of my new soul.

Cassie frowned and pulled me to sit beside her. "Kelan has been missing since the negotiations—along with Minithe. We don't think they're dead, but we haven't been able to find them. Graak has scouts searching every kingdom on the planet. He's determined to locate them."

"I thought you had a connection with Minithe—that you could all talk to each other?"

"We do. The link has been silenced, but not severed. That's why we believe Minithe is still alive."

I pressed my hand against my chest above my beating heart. "But you have no way of knowing if Kelan is."

"No, we don't," Lilise said empathetically.

"Is she still out of her tree?"

That was Ferox's voice—but it was in my head. He wasn't here right now, at least not from what I remembered. I glanced around the fire, trying to spot him.

"She's out for now. I'm not sure how much longer, though."

That was Lilise's voice—also in my head. I turned to look at the water dryad with a raised eyebrow, and she smiled at me.

"I think she can hear us."

Well, that confirmed I wasn't going crazy. "How. . .?"

"I'm approaching the fire now with Prafrum."

Ferox appeared on the far end of the main grounds and made his way towards us, flashing me a proud smile. I jumped into his open arms as he offered me a hug.

"Our little fighter turned out to be a dryad after all." He squeezed me tightly as I buried my face in his robes.

"How can I hear you all in my mind?" I wondered aloud.

"You've been added to our grove vibration. Normally, there is one for each grove, but as you are the only dryad here, you may have sought out the nearest one. That would be ours—located in the sacred grounds," Ferox answered as I released him and took a seat again.

The elders, Graak, Zoq, and Prafrum were now talking on the other side of the fire, and it wouldn't be long before they came over to me. So much was happening all at once, but I needed to be prepared for anything.

"The vibration allows you to sense the other dryads' emotions, as well as communicate with them no matter how far apart we are in the world," Lilise added.

Using this new information, I tried to reach for Minithe—but I finally understood what they meant about it being silent. I hit a wall in my mind. Not severed, just blocked.

"Now we can talk all the time. In grove vibrations, you can also speak directly to one member instead of all of them. It's pretty neat."

Cassie's enthusiasm was infectious.

"I think this is my favorite new skill." I beamed at her, then toned it down as I saw Xhet appear behind Ferox.

He plastered on a smile. "Vasilissa. Ferox has brought Prafrum, but I do not think we need to involve him or the other groves yet."

I tilted my head to the side and looked back at Graak, who still hadn't approached. "I thought Graak wanted to speak with Solis through Prafrum. I'm out now—I don't see the point in being secretive about my existence any longer. Plus, I hardly think the priest is going to share anything that we don't want him to."

"I see. Well, if that's what you think is best." But Xhet's tone didn't make me feel like he believed that at all. "Before Graak comes over, I do think we need to have a conversation about your new protector."

257

"You're trying to do that now?" Cassie rolled her eyes. "Let it go for a few evenings."

"I think that's a poor idea." Xhet winced when Cassie shot him a deadly glare. He turned back to me. "Do you remember the conversations we had before the negotiations?"

"Yes. Grove procedures dictate that because he's unwell, I would need to be prepared to have a new protector. Graak told me you were going to say that before he left," I replied, emphasizing the point. Graak never lied to me, even when I didn't want to hear the truth. I wasn't sure that was always true of the elders. "I don't want a new protector. If he wants the role, it's his."

Xhet stammered. "Vasilissa—"

"Aurinia," I corrected him.

"Aurinia, he is bonded to another. He cannot hold the position any longer. You need a partner you can run the grove with," Xhet implored. "He really needs to be sent away."

"No. Graak isn't going anywhere unless he and I discuss it—and that's what he wants." I was done having this conversation. If I was supposedly in charge, then to hell with the old grove procedures. I could speak now—and if I truly had a say in it, then they couldn't force him out of my grove.

"Xhet," Lilise interjected. "I think you're going about this the wrong way. Cassie has already informed you that the ritual to anchor the barrier cannot be undone at this moment. Aurinia may have another match in Voreios, but it's not something that can be forced. Give her some time to meet with grove members, and let's see what happens organically. Until then, Graak should remain."

I frowned at my hands. This plan would stop them from trying to force him out—but I didn't want another match.

"We really don't have that kind of time with the disturbances in the elemental magic realm. He will impede her ability to form connections with others."

"No, I won't." Graak's voice broke into the quiet conversation. He gave me that smile I'd always loved. "She should absolutely meet with all the other mages in Voreios. I will never get in the way of anything she desires."

Even if it's you?

I wasn't brave enough to vocalize that particular thought—not with all the other questions about the roles Melissa and I had played to get me here. But the gods had to know that I loved him. I'd always loved him. I wanted Graak—and from this new pit in my heart, I wanted Kelan too, whether he would be able to love me or not. He'd never met me before—not this part of me, anyway.

Ferox interrupted my forlorn thoughts by taking a seat beside me as Prafrum made his way over. The old satyr appeared just as I remembered him from Melissa's infused memories. He calmly took me, seemingly listening to something none of the rest of us could hear.

"Well, this is definitely not what I expected when we last spoke." Prafrum's words came out so softly, I almost couldn't make them out.

"It's a pleasure to meet you," I said politely. "Everyone says you might be the best one for answers. Is this what the gods wanted?"

"Perhaps." He considered me for a moment, then glanced at Graak. "Voreios has had a dryad tree all along?"

Graak nodded, and though his face was turned towards the old satyr, I saw his gaze flick back to me every few moments.

"It still doesn't explain how you've been doing the summer and winter rituals without her present."

My protector ran a hand through his hair and shrugged. "I don't think that matters now. What we need to know is how this happened. She looks like Melissa, but according to Xhet, Solis said that Aurinia needed a sacrifice. Everything in me rejects that as a possibility."

Yes. This was the answer I wanted more than anything.

"They haven't referenced anything about a sacrifice," Prafrum said, "but they have said that what occurred is as intended."

"So. . .the unlikely union you mentioned was about Melissa and I?" I frowned. "I thought you'd been talking about Graak and me—Melissa." I stammered over the words as her memories blurred into my own.

Prafrum turned to Graak and studied his faded marking. "Well, that is also a surprise. With everything Ferox told me about Melissa. . . I'll pray on it for a while. For now, it's best to assume nothing."

He looked back at me. "Aurinia, I would like to sit with you alone as we connect with the gods. Graak, I suggest you put aside some time to process what's coming—if you haven't already. Let Zoq run things while you grieve."

Graak's face fell, and for the first time since I'd come out of my bark, sadness consumed him. The worst part of this whole situation was that I couldn't comfort him the way I wanted to—because I was the cause of his pain.

My arms burned with the need to hold him, tell him I was sorry, beg him to forgive me. Instead, I stood there, deflated, as the person who mattered most in my life fell further and further from my reach.

Prafrum offered me his hand, and I took it—never taking my eyes off Graak as I was led away. This time, he didn't look back at me.

I couldn't blame him. But damn, it hurt. I didn't bother to wipe away my tears as the darkness of the forest enveloped Prafrum and I.

Chapter 29 – Graak

Aurinia.

I'd said her name over and over in my mind since she revealed it to us. I'd never heard a more beautiful name.

I could barely keep myself from looking at her. I wanted to see every expression, every movement. I needed to know everything she'd experienced from the moment we'd first met. She had all of Melissa's stunning looks, but none of the cautious manner in the way she touched me.

As soon as she'd emerged, she'd melted into my arms—and it was more perfect than anything I'd ever dreamt of. I hadn't been wrong to believe that Aurinia loved me. There was no doubt now. The outpouring of affection I felt from her was a glimpse of the life I'd been fighting for so desperately.

Except everything was different now, and it wouldn't easily fall back into place.

The elders and Prafrum all assumed that my true mate was dead, that I was simply thriving on denial. But I wasn't.

Aurinia was mine, in the same way Melissa was meant to be—because, to me, they were the same. That was the only way all the facts made sense.

Kelan and I had each found and fallen in love with one half of our woman—and now, those halves had united. I refused to believe this wasn't the truth.

Prafrum had kept her isolated in a cave in the mountain to speak with the gods. It had been two days. The watchtowers didn't seem disturbed by it, though I noticed that Lilise was quick to put Xhet in his place whenever he tried to mandate something on Aurinia's behalf.

To the elders, I'd been quietly demoted now that Aurinia had emerged, so I was grateful the watchtowers continued to step in. The rest of the grove behaved as if everything were the same as before, allowing me to maintain my position and keep the grove's usual functions intact.

As Zoq and I left the southern border after a routine check-in, I decided to ask again.

"Any word on Kelan?"

My faithful friend tossed me a pitying glance. "You know I'll tell you as soon as there is."

"He's out there, and I know he'd be able to sort this out in an instant. He'd know what I do!"

It wasn't that I wished for infernals to attack the grove, but honestly, where was an infernal portal when we actually needed one?

Ferox had talked me down from going to search for Kelan myself, reminding me I'd be leaving Aurinia without the protection she needed. He'd won the argument the moment he asked what Kelan would want me to do. That was an easy answer—she came first. It's the same thing I'd want him to do if he were in my position.

The only thing I could do now was resecure our bond to her and keep her safe—trusting that he would return, or that my spies would find him.

"You know I'm here for you when you're ready to talk about her," Zoq offered gently, as if he expected me to yell at him.

"I think I've been very forthcoming with talking about her. She's all anyone can talk about." Not that I didn't understand it. Aurinia was perfect.

"I meant Melissa." Zoq fixed me with a look that said he meant business. "I see the pain you're carrying—even if you won't admit it."

I hated that he saw through me so clearly. The fear that Melissa was truly gone—that my actions and comments to Aurinia had frayed whatever affection she might've once had for me—was eating me alive.

I wanted, with all my heart, to believe they were the same. But if they weren't. . .this wouldn't end well.

We hadn't had a moment alone since she stepped out of the tree. We used to talk every day—well, I'd talk, and she'd project. Now that I could actually hear her responses, I'd been deprived of her entirely.

"Prafrum said not to make any assumptions. Even though he implied Melissa had passed, I'm not ready to give up on the idea that they really were two pieces of the same soul."

Zoq took a deep breath, as if uncertain where to go with the conversation. "Have you tried speaking with Montibus about this situation?"

"Of course not," I grumbled, the reminder dragging up my recent fight with the god. Until I sorted things out with

Aurinia, I knew exactly how any of our conversations would go—I'd end up locked in the god's plane for my lack of faith and colorful vocabulary.

"He may talk to you if you apologize," he reminded me.

I shook my head. The trees ahead had the soft glow I'd only ever seen in other groves—the sign of a dryad nearby. Even Zoq seemed taken aback, hesitating as he studied the trees. As we made our way into the main grounds, the forest split to reveal her. My heart stopped in my chest as she took my breath away.

Aurinia stood beside Ferox and Prafrum, caught in conversation. Her head turned towards me, and she blushed before looking down with a small smile.

If Zoq said anything else, I didn't hear it. My feet carried me straight to her, and she easily stepped aside, making space for me in their cluster.

"They really didn't say anything?" Ferox pressed, though he gave me a quick nod in greeting. "It's been days."

"Nothing that provided any additional insight. I believe the fluctuations in our elemental magic may be limiting their abilities in this world."

"If our magic fails, and even the gods are unable to intervene on our behalf, this is going to be far worse than we originally thought," Ferox mused, the deep furrow in his brow emphasizing the weight of the news.

"It seems your timing couldn't have been more necessary, Aurinia," Prafrum added, his voice gentle but firm. "The summer ritual may be the only chance we have at restoring the balance."

I hated the displeased look she gave him in return.

"What if a season isn't enough time to master something I've barely had the chance to practice? We're not even sure I have elemental magic—and yet it all comes down to this?" She turned her hands in front of her face, then let out an adorably frustrated huff.

"You do have earth magic. We just have to find out how to unlock it," Ferox said, trying to lift her mood. "It will also be imperative to find your first druwid. If it's not Graak, as the elders claim, then we must discover who it is quickly."

Aurinia shot me a worried glance, and I offered her a reassuring smile. I knew in my soul she was mine, so this prospect didn't concern me. She could meet hundreds of other mages, and even if she found another partner besides Kelan and me, she would still be *ours*.

"It's a good idea. You should meet with all the mages in Voreios," I said encouragingly—and immediately regretted it when her shoulders fell.

"Okay," she replied softly. "What am I supposed to do, then? It seems like an awful lot of blind dates to cram in when I should be focused on practicing this ritual."

I didn't understand the term *blind* date, but Ferox laughed and shook his head at her.

"Don't think of it as dating, at least not at this stage. In most cases, you'll only need to meet them to know if there's a spark," he assured her.

From there, Ferox shifted to speaking to her through their root connection. I didn't enjoy not being able to hear this part of the conversation. I wasn't sure if they were trying to keep it from me, or from Prafrum. Aurinia's bright green eyes flicked to me briefly before she started to turn away.

266

I caught her wrist. "Aurinia, wait. Please. Can we talk? Just you and I?"

A mix of excitement and caution warred on her face as she took in my hold on her, then met my gaze again. "I'd like that."

Ferox gestured for Prafrum to come with him, but I didn't miss the slight smile on the dryad's face before they departed. The gods, the elders, and maybe even the rest of the world were against us—but I now suspected I had allies in my quest to win back Aurinia.

She chewed on her lip, lost in thought, and I hated that she was nervous to tell me how she was feeling.

"Come, walk with me," I said with a smile. I'd try anything to put her mind at ease.

Aurinia nodded and followed my lead, sliding her hand up my arm to take my proffered elbow. Missing the sound of her voice, I decided to start with small talk.

"How are you feeling today?" I asked softly.

The wind blew her hair around her shoulders as I waited for her reply.

"I'm okay, I think. It's been a lot to process, and I'm not sure if I'm doing anything right." She tilted her head towards the sky and basked in the sun with her eyes closed for a moment. "How are you?"

"Honestly, I'm good. Seeing you moving about the grove has been the highlight of my life. Everything feels different. It feels right."

Her face softened at my response, but then she seemed to think better of it. Before she could say anything else, I pulled the moldavite necklace out from the pouch at my side.

267

"I have something to return to you," I said with a smile. "Lift up your hair."

She turned around and did as I asked, allowing me to fasten it around her neck. When she twisted back to face me, I hesitated at the contemplation in her expression as she held the stone up in front of her.

"It isn't painful for you to be around me? I know you can never look at me without seeing what I took from you, and I'm so, so sorry. I wish I could give it all back."

I opened my mouth to respond, but she wasn't done. She dropped the necklace and met my gaze.

"I realize I've been saying you're going to stay, but we haven't had a chance to talk about what *you* really want."

"I want to be here," I insisted.

"I can't live with myself if I keep hurting you."

"Aurinia," I said her name gently, guiding her around to stand in front of me. "You've never hurt me. If anything, *I've* hurt you—made you believe I was going to abandon you."

"No, you didn't. You told me you would come back," she protested. "You told me exactly what they were going to say."

"You know I wouldn't lie to you. So believe me when I say that I want to be here."

She pursued her lips and considered me. "To be fair to all of them, they aren't wrong about their reasoning."

"What do you mean?" I asked, even though I suspected what she might say. But I had to wait for her to confirm the feelings. That's how it worked in the groves. If she would declare us, then I wouldn't let anyone get in the way.

Her face scrunched up with a sadness that tugged at my soul.

"I don't even know where to start. Graak, I miss you. I miss all the time we spent together. I would've stayed mute forever if it meant that you could be happy."

Tears streamed down her cheeks in thick bands, and I pulled her into my arms.

"Shh," I whispered, cradling her close. Her fingers dug into my skin as she held on to me. "I would never ask for that. Being able to experience you in Voreios is the beacon we've all prayed for. I don't want to go anywhere— especially not away from you."

She protested again, "But Melissa—"

"What happened to Melissa wasn't your fault—it was Cholios. Unfortunately, I wasn't strong enough to save her, and in the end, the poison won. I don't believe she was a sacrifice for you. Only time will reveal what happened. But please—don't think that I can't stand the sight of you."

"So. . .you're okay to stay? Even knowing that I may not be able to stop loving you?" She wiped her eyes as she took a step back. "I'll go on the dates like you all want, even if it's fruitless. I don't want to chase you away. So if I'm not overbearing with my affection. . .could you still be with me? Even just as friends?"

Oh, Aurinia. . . I'm never going to be just your friend.

But seeing the hope in her eyes—that spark that said she'd found a way to make things right between us—I knew this wasn't about how I felt. It was about her.

The words of the others finally sank in, even though I still didn't want to believe them. If there was even a small chance she wasn't my destiny, I owed it to Aurinia to let her uncover that truth for herself.

"I'll be anything you need, Aurinia. I couldn't protect Melissa, and that weighs on me. But I will work hard to protect you, as your friend and confidant. Let me hold your secrets like you've held mine. Let me be your strength as you navigate this new experience." I brushed a strand of hair from her face with a gentle caress.

"Meet the mages. Take the time to discover who you are—knowing that if you stumble, I'll always be there to catch you. Let's navigate this journey one day at a time."

The smile she gave me was the most beautiful thing I'd ever seen—just before she surged forward and wrapped herself in my arms again. I'd wait as long as she needed to know that this was where she would always belong.

Chapter 30 – Kelan

Grey. Bland. Void of life.

Everything, day after day in this world on the brink of dusk, dragged into a perpetual state devoid of joy.

My mood hardly helped that. When I pushed myself to the brink of exhaustion and finally gave into sleep, I only saw her. In my dreams, I couldn't guard my mind well enough to avoid focusing on Melissa. Between replaying our memories or living out imagined futures—what our life could have become—I couldn't find solace, not even in my own mind.

Going from her bright, beautiful smile to this depressing grey reminder ensured I wouldn't rise above the looming depression.

Shaking thoughts of my sweet lover from my mind, I rose with a groan. Who really needed sleep anyway?

Every day, Minithe and I slaughtered infernals until there were none left in the area. Then we'd continue, traveling deeper into the dark mists.

"You almost managed to get half the sleep you actually need to not go mad." Minithe teased, tossing me a sack of rations.

"Do the dreams ever stop?" I hated that I even had to ask, but the longing in my chest hurt more than giving in to apathy.

My companion gave me a pitying look before she replied, "Yes, but once they do, you'll only want them back. It took me a century to finally put them to rest."

A century? I didn't want to live like this for a century. Damn our long lives.

A thundering roar ripped through the air and immediately seized our attention. We both looked to the sky. When I squinted, I spotted a faint dark mass moving with incredible speed across the horizon. From this distance, the beast was massive.

I was on my feet without a second thought, the thrill of a fight like this bringing a new level of excitement to my being. "Infernal? That has to be the largest one I've ever seen."

Minithe shook her head and walked a few paces ahead of me. "That's a dragon. Come on."

She didn't wait for a response before dashing across the sandy, murky plain. I was on her heels instantly, my fingers itching for a combatant like this.

Dragons hadn't been in our realm for centuries, from what I understood. Their lands had fallen to chaos and violence long before I was born. The place we still held for them in world meetings was mostly out of respect for the lost. Even the fae wouldn't step on their lands—for fear that whatever plague had taken the dragons might spread across to the Feywilds.

The ground beneath us moaned as our rapid steps across the sand lit a beacon for every nearby infernal to rise from their morbid rest. Puddles of shadow and gore trembled, morphing into the grotesque forms of beasts all around us.

"Ignore them!" Minithe shouted, fire erupting in a violent halo around her. "Don't let that dragon get away from us."

With a new directive, I honed in on my own innate abilities. The best way to slow something down in the sky was a storm. There was little moisture in the air, but I gathered whatever I could find.

To my left, infernals lunged, and I drew my first blade, cutting through them without losing step beside the dryad. Ahead of us, the dragon looped upward, swerving to avoid flying directly into my brewing storm.

"It's working!" Minithe cheered as the flames around her intensified, heat melting the sand in our wake.

That's when the beast must have noticed us. The rising fire must've caught its attention. Another roar tore through the silent void as it twisted midair, turning to face us.

"I think we have his attention now." Minithe drew her sword from the sheath at her hip. There was something in her expression I couldn't place. Her eyes darkened as the red dragon grew larger in the sky.

The watchtower gestured for me to slow my pace, and I immediately complied, lightning sprawling around me to tear apart the infernals that still dared to approach. We didn't have time to waste on them, and I had a feeling we'd need all our strength.

As Minithe rolled her shoulders and came to a stop, I drew my second longsword.

Minithe must have battled dragons before. From the way she moved, this felt familiar to her. She was nearly five centuries old now, but I'd never thought to ask those kinds of questions.

A second roar echoed—this one from behind the red dragon. Breaking through the top of my storm cloud came a deep blue dragon. It had a longer tail and slimmer frame. Through the magic coursing through my storm, I could *feel* it: the new beast was siphoning off some of the water I'd gathered.

"I knew it," Minithe muttered, glaring at them both. Then she glanced at me, as if remembering I was there, as if she were about to fight the two dragons on her own. "Focus on the smaller one," she ordered. "If we hit her, it'll give us an advantage with the red."

"Do you know them?" I asked, shifting my stance to mirror hers, balanced on the balls of my feet. The sand around us had all turned to glass, but the grooves made it easy enough to find footing where we wouldn't slip. My magic, already aligned with fire, pulsed with the heat around us—but I'd never felt anything like *this* before. . .and now I wanted nothing more than to see if my power could reach this height too.

"Yes," Minithe replied, her flames flickering from red to orange, a bright yellow outlining her figure. For the first time in my life, I began to sweat from the temperature alone. "Red's fire is different than ours. Don't take a direct hit, but you can absorb the energy to retaliate. For the blue one, your fire attacks won't work, but lightning will. Your swords will be practically useless against their scales unless you can catch a wing or strike under a joint. Use them for defense and always keep moving."

The two dragons spiraled around one another in the sky, and I couldn't help but marvel at the beauty of something I never thought I'd see. The red was easily double the size of the blue, but the smaller one's tail trailed in a perfect circle around the other, hauntingly breathtaking in its precision.

I pulled my storm clouds in closer, holding back my lightning strikes until we could engage our new opponents. A part of me hated that this seemed to be an inevitable fight. But I wouldn't disobey Minithe.

"If fire won't work, we're at a serious disadvantage."

Minithe tossed me a cocky smile. "I said *your* fire attacks. Leave the red one to me."

I nodded and gripped the handle of my sword, channeling lightning along the length of the blade. The dragons accelerated, diving from the sky towards us. The smaller blue one charged a beam of light at the center of her mouth—then blasted it in our direction, freezing over some of Minithe's explosive flames and separating the two of us as we both launched into action. I tracked my target, careful to avoid sliding on glass or ice.

Fire combusted between all four of us as Minithe hurled herself straight into the red dragon's path. Her blade slashed through the ball of flame building between his teeth. I had to trust her to take on that monster.

Turning back to the little blue, I summoned three bolts in the sky beyond her as the lightning along my blades illuminated the path of my rapid steps. I lunged. My first strike deflected a claw swipe, and my second blade arced towards her scaled neck. Electricity sizzled down her flank, and we both felt the jolt. The blue dragon hissed, leaping away from me, and a low rumble built in her throat as she took flight again.

The dragon must've assumed she was safe in the sky, hovering just outside my jumping radius. I chased her along the ground. When she twirled back to face me, I pulled one of my lighting strikes—just as she unleashed a flurry of icy shards in my direction.

Fire ran in my veins, but I still felt the cold. My left side barely avoided being engulfed by a wave of frost that would've frozen a limb clean off.

I raised my hand and pointed at her, summoning the remaining two charged bolts into one powerful blast that shot vertically through the sky. She screeched and spun around the bolt with reflexes that shouldn't have been possible for something her size. I growled and twisted the bolt to follow her, tracking her through the air. I'd never controlled this much raw energy before—but I couldn't let it go to waste.

Heat rippled from behind me. I had only seconds to react. I leapt as a stream of flames shot past, barely clearing it in time. The red was responding to the other dragon's distress. My bolt shattered in the sky, fracturing into jagged streaks of light as my control slipped.

Fuck.

Minithe used the opportunity to slam herself straight into the red dragon's chest, toppling him over. Her flames had morphed from yellow to a blue so bright and pure, it felt nothing short of otherworldly.

The smaller blue dragon dove lower, aiming for Minithe as the larger one bellowed in pain, fire engulfing his body. Using the icy water she'd unleashed into the atmosphere, my storm clouds shifted into place above us. The dragon and I locked into a silent tug-of-war with the moisture in the air, but I was determined to win somewhere.

I timed my lightning blasts to her movements, letting them loose as she charged her own attack. Her wings scrambled to pull her back—until she pivoted towards me with a snarl. She slammed into the ground and charged, teeth bared, racing in my direction.

I raised my blades and crossed them in front of me just as we collided in a fury of force. Hundreds of pounds of beast and that icy breath on my skin sent the first real thought of my mortality surging to the front of my mind. Then—she reared back. Blood trickled down from four points around her mouth, where my blades had connected. She bared her teeth at me and let out a low, simmering hiss.

Goddess, these beasts were a dangerous beauty. But I didn't have long to marvel at her. She wound around me and snapped her jaws, missing me by inches. We kept dodging each other as we moved in this strange dance of lightning and ice. Whoever took the first hit would be in a world of pain.

A sudden suction of air in her direction warned me that she was about to charge another blast. I released a volley of lightning. She dodged the first two, but the third struck her square in the back. Sparks flew off her damp scales and fell around her like shooting stars in the night sky.

The sound she made was so heartbreaking that I missed the attack from behind, until it was too late. The red dragon crushed me beneath his paw, claws slicing into my skin. My chest was going to collapse in on itself.

Despite the pain, I knew this for what it was. And I could hardly fault him. The little blue must be his mate—and I wouldn't have done anything differently. The glassy sand shattered beneath me as his weight pressed me into the ground. I tried to call on my lightning. Bolts lashed out around me, but I couldn't focus. Couldn't breathe. I wasn't even sure I'd hit him. The dragon lowered his face to mine, flames blooming in the back of his throat.

Minithe's blue flames exploded into us both, dislodging him off me. Air rushed back into my lungs, and I stumbled to my feet, gasping. My vision faded in and out as I tried to reconnect with the reality of the fight around us.

But I wasn't fast enough. The red dragon scooped the blue one into his front claws and launched skyward— straight into my storm clouds.

"Come back here!" Minithe shouted, giving chase. "You will face me!"

The watchtower let out a string of colorful curses, and the air around her combusted into a chaotic spectrum of fire. I followed her as fast as I could, despite what I was certain were at least a few broken ribs. A black ring grew in my vision, and it took longer than it should have to realize it wasn't just pain—it was an infernal portal.

"Minithe!" I shouted. She snarled as the dragons veered towards it and vanished inside.

As the portal began to spin closed, she surged forward, preparing to lunge. We needed to prevent it from closing, but I wasn't sure how.

Pulling my storm into a tight, targeted line of clouds, I hurled it into the edge of the swirling darkness. The barrier cracked and quivered—but held just long enough.

Without another word, we both leapt inside. Magic tore at my skin and clothing as we left the dusty lands behind and entered the unknown.

Chapter 31 – Kelan

A bright flame burst to life beside me, hovering above Minithe's palm. She glanced at me briefly, noting I stood beside her before turning her attention to our surroundings.

The tunnel we stood in was devoid of any markings in the dark stone. No light appeared on either side of us.

Sweat rolled down my body—partly from the thick humidity of this new place, and partly from the continued heat radiating off the dryad's magic. A sharp pain pulled at my core. Something internally was broken.

"The dragons aren't all dead—and they sided with Cholios?" I don't know why that was my first question, but it seemed the most obvious. "That's why we don't see them anymore."

"There weren't many dragons to begin with," Minithe said quietly. "Not even before the infernals arrived."

"Why would they choose to side with him, though? How does no one else know about this?" Or. . .did the world's leaders *know*—and simply chose not to share it with the rest of us? Given everything that had happened since Melissa arrived, I was starting to doubt every truth I'd ever been told.

Something shifted in Minithe's expression—a reminiscent sadness that I felt all too deeply in my own soul. "I don't know if *all* of them did, but I know these two all too well. I was there. . .when they killed their king."

I rubbed along my ribs, testing each one for pain as I thought over what she'd said. Three were definitely broken, and two more felt sprained. "You were there?"

The dryad turned away, staring into the flame cupped in her hand. "That was the day I lost my mates." Minithe's voice was low, flat—but not emotionless. "It was the battle that cost me everything. Valk was blinded with rage when they snuffed out Cenara. I'd been trying to move her into Notos, but she wouldn't go. As an esper, she was particular to the mountain she'd been birthed in. Valk was powerful, but even he couldn't go up against all of them. I got there too late." She paused before continuing. "I saw his dragon fall out of the sky. The fading of these marks is still the worse pain I've ever felt in my life."

I didn't know how to comfort Minithe as she swam in the memories of a past she probably hadn't spoken about in centuries. The raw pain in her features told me that this was something I'd carry with me for the rest of my life. I opened my mouth, unsure what to say. But then she turned back to me, her expression wiped clean, as if she'd never said anything about this memory.

"I swore the next time I saw them, I'd take my revenge. When I became a watchtower, I gave myself over to the flames. Focused only on the missions and protecting the guardian. On honing my abilities." Minithe let out a furious huff and began to pace, her boots stirring the soot-marked sand. "They still managed to slip away!"

281

I winced. "That's on me." While she had been ready to battle dragons—clearly, I wasn't on her level.

Yet.

She sighed, and the tension evaporated. "You did very well. I wasn't sure if you'd be able to hit her—yet you landed a few solid strikes. And from the looks of it, she'll have a longer recovery than you."

I took the praise with an easy nod. I didn't feel it was entirely deserved, but I'd battled two dragons and hadn't died. That had to count for something.

"Which way do we go?" I asked, changing the subject.

Being dropped in a tunnel was hardly ideal. Someone could approach from either direction, and we wouldn't know what to expect—or where to go.

We paused, both studying the ground for any hint of a trail, any mark that might indicate where the dragons had gone. When I pointed to a muddy scuff and a few drops of blood, Minithe's eyes lit up.

"That way." She offered me an encouraging smile. "I'm not sure we're up for another fight right now, but we need to know where we are."

She likely was, but I was not. Each step sent a sharp pain through my chest as my cracked ribs rubbed against tender skin. Once we found shelter, I'd need to bind them so they could heal properly.

"Can you take over the light for a moment?" Minithe asked as I sheathed both of my swords. Instantly, her flame vanished.

Lightning danced around both of my palms. The white light wasn't nearly as effective as her fire had been, but it was better than standing in darkness.

"Do you ever use flame instead of lightning?" Minithe turned back to me, one eyebrow raised.

"It's never manifested as fire—only lightning," I offered with a shrug.

"That shouldn't be possible. The magic always appears as fire before lightning can be channeled."

I wasn't sure I liked the way she looked at me, like I was a puzzle she intended to solve.

"I might have, as a child," I admitted. "But my trainers in the guard focused only on my lightning once I showed it to them."

After the fire had claimed my mother in Elranmel, and I couldn't save her. . . I hadn't seen a lick of flames in my magic. Not that I'd truly put in an effort to revive it either.

"They should have trained you in the base element," she insisted. "You fall within the realm of fire."

"The elves don't understand forest folk magic. We had other fire users, but no one else had lightning."

She rubbed her chin, thinking for a moment. "It's rare. Even in Notos, there are only four of us in this world who can wield it."

Now she had my full attention. "You can use lightning too?"

"Of course," Minithe replied in her usual cocky tone. "I don't use it often. Summon a flame for me. Just a flame."

I frowned. Opening my palms in front of me, I pictured a flame, like the one she'd held just moments ago. A spark lit for a second, then faded.

Screams filled my mind. The trees that made up our town were all burning. I tried to calm the flames, but instead, they grew stronger. Every time I pushed forward, trying to reach our house, the fire leapt higher.

"I don't think I trust myself with fire," I replied honestly.

"There are worse things to have to admit," Minithe said, softer now. "But if you're going to grow, you *will* have to master the base element. If we're going to stand a chance against what's coming. . .we both must leave some things behind in the infernal sands."

I couldn't argue with that. As I followed Minithe down the path, I knew I had to rise above the traumas if I wanted to get my own payback on the Shadow God who had taken my world from me. For Melissa's memory, I would walk straight into whatever fiery hell awaited.

The dragons had gone farther than we could've predicted. After walking for hours, we'd taken shelter in a cove to rest and recover. Minithe helped me bind my ribs with shreds torn from my shirt. Hardly ideal, but until we found better resources, it would have to do.

The pain and aches in my body kept me from slipping too deeply into sleep. The faint red pulse around Minithe's form dimmed slowly as I rubbed my face. This was her version of rest—still connected to her tree somehow, even without the root connection to the other watchtowers.

"We need information," she said, rising to her feet and stretching. "I think today we just keep moving until we find someone. Anyone."

"I agree." We'd wasted enough time in the infernal sands, and my sensibilities were returning. If Minithe could survive the loss of both her mates and keep walking, then I could find my way through this too. If there was any chance

Graak was still alive, I needed to find the thread that led to him. Somehow, I knew he'd do the same for me.

"We're also going to start working on your fire basics."

I nodded my consent. Of course she was right—time was a luxury we might not have.

She poked her head out of our alcove, looked both ways, then stepped onto the trail. "There are four phases of fire that are the most prominent and will influence your control: Ignite, Growth, Control, and ultimately, Decay. They move in a cyclical nature. We're going to focus on the first: Ignition."

I fell into step beside her, turning the concept over in my mind. "But what if I can't control what I ignite?"

"Then I'll put it out," she said dismissively. "You cannot hurt either of us—so now is the time to practice."

That was a reasonable assessment. This tunnel of rock and dirt wouldn't catch fire, and there was no one else around to get hurt. "What do I need to do?"

"Create a flame in your palm."

She meant to pull it from inside, like how I summoned my lightning. But what were the core differences between fire and lightning? Both were dangerous. Both could destroy. Lightning was unpredictable—until I learned how to guide it. Fire could be chaos too. . .but it was also heat. Light. A conduit for life. It wasn't my lightning that had kept Melissa comfortable that day in the snow, when she trusted me enough to go out. It was the *warmth* of my magic. My *fire*. It was the way her kisses animated my soul with something I'd never known before.

My hands heated as the magic raced up to the edges of my fingertips. Tiny embers sparked along my skin. I exhaled the breath I'd hadn't realized I'd been holding. Turning my hands in front of me, I didn't bother to smother the smile that slowly spread across my face.

"Good," Minithe said simply. "Now pull it into a ball—and hold it."

"For how long?" I asked, concentrating as I gathered the flame into a circle in my right hand.

"Until we find another person."

The more I shifted and manipulated the fire, the more it flickered. It was fragile, always threatening to go out. The dry, stagnant air in the tunnel didn't help. But if it was truly mine, it had to thrive by my will alone.

Minithe didn't seem concerned that I couldn't help her scout while focusing on this task. After watching her face down two dragons without a hint of fear, I found myself wondering if there was anything she was truly afraid of.

We didn't speak as we walked. Instead, I kept my eyes trained on the ball of flame, watching the flickers of color that flashed within. My main goal right now was to maintain its shape, but a secret part of me also wanted to see if I could turn the flame yellow or blue.

Exhaustion from the constant drain of magic—and the sharp pain of each step against my ribs—nearly caused me to lose the flame once. But then my mind began playing tricks on me. Once I saw *her* face in the fire, I knew I would protect it at all costs.

Suddenly, Minithe raised her hand, and with a twist of her fingers, my flame vanished. A surge of protest rose in me, protective and furious that she'd doused it so easily. But the alertness of her expression sobered me instantly.

Faint voices teased down to us from an opening in the distance. We were approaching someone. Light spilled from the entrance, and I blinked as my eyes adjusted. Minithe paused and placed both hands on the tunnel wall. I'd seen other dryads do this in Dytika—a way to sync their roots to the world when they weren't barefoot.

When her eyes snapped open, she gave me a quick hand signal indicating to go left. Slinking as close to the wall as we could, I moved ahead of her, taking point.

The tunnel we'd been walking through opened into a massive cavern. Stalagmites rose from the ground like jagged teeth—perfect cover to hide behind as we crept closer to the voices echoing ahead.

"I didn't say you were dismissed, Lawry." A man roared, and the entire cavern shook. Dust rained down over Minithe and me. The words weren't in any language I recognized. Yet somehow, they came through in Druidic, clear in my mind.

"We're done here," another man snarled. "Those were the terms, and I'm not discussing this further with you. I've told you all I know and given you everything you've asked for over the years. Izo and I are out."

"Are you really that much of a coward?"

I risked a peek around the rock I was crouched behind. A dozen or so figures stood with their backs to us—mage cloaks unmistakable. We'd found their hiding spot.

The irate man standing on a ledge had short, choppy red hair and wore black leathers instead of mage robes. But shadow magic clung to him, dripping off his body like toxic oil, ready to strike out at any who dared oppose him—like this Lawry did now.

287

And yet, the man challenging him didn't flinch. His dark skin was marked with thick bands of red tattoos that wrapped around his mostly bare body—nothing like the thin, intricate dryad lines I'd seen in the groves.

"This isn't about me. We got you to the battlefront. We've done our part. As soon as she wakes, I'm leaving."

"We all knew this wouldn't be easy. This is only the first stage. Nothing has gone off-plan yet. Aurinia has been made whole and is within our reach. Once we have her on the solstice, if you still want to leave—then you may depart."

"Your guys are fucking this whole thing up! This shouldn't have even happened," Lawry shouted, smoke pouring from his throat.

Was he one of the dragons? Were they both dragons? Something about the other man didn't feel right. I wondered what Minithe thought, but we'd have to discuss it later.

Then, from the far-right tunnel, a woman emerged. Pale, with jet-black hair, she wore a cropped icy-blue dress and moved fast, leaving an icy trail of frost behind her.

"Izo."

The relief in Lawry's voice hit something all too familiar. It was the same way I'd felt when Melissa had woken up after the solstice.

"I'm fine, Lawry," she said, waving him off and turning her attention to the man on the ledge. "Aedan, you have bigger problems. They're still out there. This is your mages' mess—have them clean it up."

"Look she's already back up and moving," Aedan said, gesturing towards Izo as if she hadn't just spoken. "It's the fire watchtower and the elf in the Infernal Plane?"

"Yes," they replied in unison.

Aedan turned to the cluster of mages and commanded, "Send a message to Declan with this information. He will find them."

Two of the mages vanished in a dark puff of smoke.

"I don't think Declan alone will be enough," Lawry warned. "Minithe is problematic on her own, and the elf is considerable. I recommend sending Keane."

Aedan only laughed and hopped down from the ledge to stand in front of Lawry. I couldn't hear what they said next—even with my heightened hearing—so I leaned back against the rock and scanned the wall across from me. My eyes trailed upward, through the floating fire lanterns suspended in the air as if tethered by a magic. And then I saw her.

Melissa.

But it wasn't.

This woman had bright green eyes and green markings that traced across her face and down her neck. Her dark brunette hair tumbled in waves over her shoulders, elegant vines woven throughout. A dryad—from Voreios, judging by the color of the markings.

A second image shimmered beside Minithe: a full projection of the dryad standing next to Graak. She wasn't looking at him, but I recognized the affectionate expression on his face.

Graak's markings were faded like mine, and this woman's chest was bare where Melissa's design had once

289

been. She wasn't *my* Melissa. . .but I couldn't shake the feeling that this had to mean something.

Minithe tapped my shoulder, snapping me out of the trance I'd fallen into. I hadn't even noticed the others leave.

She moved a boulder aside, revealing a hidden tunnel, and slid into it without a word. I followed silently, wishing I could go back and stare at those images once more.

The tunnel opened into a small cavern. Minithe picked up what looked like torches and placed them into holders she clearly knew were there. There was a familiarity in the way she moved—like she'd been here before.

"That was a lot of information," she said, lighting the room. "I'd say this was a pretty lucky break for us."

Today had twisted in more unexpected ways than I could've imagined. "Did you see the images of the woman?" I asked.

"Yeah," Minithe replied, still walking around the space lighting torches. "I'm wondering if she's the mute dryad. Aurinia, perhaps?"

Aurinia.

Melissa had mentioned that name once before—she'd said Aurinia was in danger, that we needed to find her first. If they already knew where she was, then they were a few steps ahead of us. I couldn't shake the sense that they looked so similar for a reason.

"Melissa looks like Aurinia," Minithe said, voicing what we were both thinking. "But we both know from your marking that Melissa is dead."

"What if she's not?" I asked carefully, trying to keep the flicker of hope in my chest from creeping into the words.

Judging by the look Minithe gave me, I failed. "Could Melissa have been a dryad on Earth and not known it?"

"Ferox and Lilise had her blood tested," Minithe replied quietly. "She was completely human."

"This can't be a coincidence." I rubbed my face, exhaustion sinking into my bones. "Aurinia just *happens* to be the same dryad Graak was chosen to protect decades ago—and now we're all bond matched? I don't know why our markings are faded. . .but I know that look on his face. He loves her."

"We can't make any assumptions yet. There's too much magical influence to trust anything we're seeing—or hearing." She shook her head and paced a few steps.

"Let's talk about that we do know: Declan is hunting us both now. Don't know who he is, but I'm sure we will find out."

"Aurinia has entered the picture, but she also happens to look exactly like Melissa," I added, and Minithe gave me a look that said I needed to stay on topic. "If she's from Voreios, then she's the only dryad there."

Minithe nodded. "Aedan is pulling the strings with the dragons, probably because he has dominion over fire. There was a third name—Keane but seems we may not have to worry about him yet."

I hadn't pieced together the bit about Aedan, but Minithe could sense fire on every level, so I'd take her word for it.

"We have also found the mages' lair," I offered.

"That's true," she easily agreed, taking a seat on a smooth stone that looked almost like a bench. "Now that we're here, we need to infiltrate the mage ranks. It's the only way to gather more information."

I hesitated, then asked, "How did you know about this place?" I hoped my question didn't sound suspicious—I trusted Minithe. But still, the circumstances were. . .odd. "You moved one boulder and knew exactly how to get in."

"Because I've been here before. A long time ago."

I waited for her to elaborate, but the silence stretched on until she sighed.

"Kelan, welcome to the land of the dragons."

Chapter 32 – Aurinia

"Have a good rest of your morning, Aurinia." Graak kissed my hand before he departed.

We'd fallen back into a modified version of our old routine now that we'd made our pact to be friends. He came to watch the sunrise with me and caught me up on everything going on in the grove, just like he used to. I loved being able to sit next to him on the ground by my tree.

I fought off every single urge to scoot closer or touch him, even if I wanted nothing more than to crawl into his lap and listen to him talk. That's not how friends behaved, though.

"One day, you should let me come with you on your border walks," I called after him, completely failing at not admiring how gracefully he moved.

"I would prefer it if you stayed off the borders, my sweet dryad," Graak replied, as he did every time I brought it up.

"What trouble could I possibly get into if you are there?" I said wryly.

Graak gave me a single heated look and wet his lips before shaking his head, obviously deciding not to take the bait.

Just friends. We are just friends.

I'd already been true to my word and had started becoming reacquainted with a few of the "eligible bachelors" that the elders directed my way. That hadn't gone as planned, since I already knew everyone in my grove. They'd all been by to see me at one point or another. There were no sparks, even though they were clearly handsome men. They just weren't *my* men.

Instead, I spent the time asking them for details about the stories I remembered them sharing with me in the past.

The elders were visibly disappointed, but Lilise shook it off immediately. Since then, they had pivoted to the two available border leaders, Haz and Zrif, but both dodged every request to come visit with me. The flower nymphs informed me of a coup brewing among the guards in protest on Graak's behalf. That suited my agenda just fine, so I didn't push any further.

"You ready to meet Lilise for training?" Cassie asked through my mind.

I smiled broadly as I turned to face her. *"Yes, but I believe you said you also have something to show me?"*

"I do." She laughed, showing me her palm.

As she neared the tree with her hand, it began to glow. Cassie's spirit form then started to disappear into the tree.

"But that's not your tree!" I exclaimed.

"That's true. Dryads can tree walk through the root network. You merge your essence into any tree, and then you can move through as long and as far as you'd like." Cassie vanished into the tree. Through the roots, I could feel her energy moving, hopping between them as if she were skipping ahead of me.

She emerged and waved at me. *"Your turn. Come on, let's go meet Lilise."*

"Okay." I stepped up to the tree Cassie had entered and placed my palm against its bark. The sensation was different from merging with my own tree, but the energy was welcoming. I could feel its life force making room for me.

A flash of Melissa's first shared memory came back to me. That hadn't been her tree—it had simply shared its space with her. Trees were like that on any planet it seemed. They looked out for one another, sharing warnings and messages, passing along nutrients and water when it could be spared.

"Can I be trapped in a tree that isn't my own?" I asked all three of the watchtowers in our group network.

"Not here on Artemesia, but in the days of portal hopping, yes. It was a common problem, actually," Ferox answered. *"When that happens, you need a member of your grove to set your essence free again. Same thing can happen if your spirit form turns into a tree on another planet."*

"I can turn into a tree as well?" There were so many things that I could do now!

"Yes, any type of tree you want—though that one's only helpful if you're trying to hide from something. Tree walking is the more commonly used skill."

"Makes sense." Maybe it was practical, but I was excited to show Graak tomorrow morning. Which tree would I pick to turn into first? There were so many options.

As I fully entered the tree, I felt a gentle tug from the roots, indicating the direction Cassie had gone. Each movement between trees felt like gliding on the wind or drifting down a river. If I was being honest, it took even less energy than walking. Best way to travel ever.

"Come out here," Cassie called to me.

Pressing against the bark of this new tree, I grounded my feet and reestablished my connection to the grove. I was a long way from my tree—almost to the mountains along our southwestern border.

"That was amazing!" I exclaimed with a grin.

Lilise and Cassie both smiled at me, enjoying my obvious excitement.

"We don't even have to use the inner grove portals to travel when we do that," I said, sitting down beside Lilise.

The water watchtower had a sack on her lap, but she waited until I'd settled before she began to tell me what we would learn today.

"As a nature spirit, there are gifts that are innate to what you are. I know Ferox has already mentioned elemental magic—and we will get to that—but not today." Lilise held out her hand to me.

"But isn't that the most important thing for me to practice, considering the ritual?" Just mentioning the ritual made my stomach twist into knots. Everyone was counting on it to go perfectly, and I still hadn't even caught a glimpse of the earth magic.

"These will come more intuitively, so I don't think it will take us much time at all for you to grasp," Lilise said, rubbing the tops of my hands with some water to calm my nerves. "There are abilities all dryads can do— communicating with trees, fostering plant growth, and providing seasonal updates to the ecosystem."

"Oh, so I've been doing two of those even while I was trapped in my tree." The more I thought about it, the more I realized that, even subconsciously, I had still been doing it. Messages had passed through the roots of my tree, and I'd been offering insights on how the ecosystem should behave in order to thrive. It was as natural to me as breathing.

"Yes, you have been," Lilise agreed. "The one we're going to focus on now is plant growth. One of your main roles will be controlling the entire root network of your grove. You can grow and hinder roots to shape the forest. Voreios has been unhindered with her wild lands, but some forms of control are essential to maintain balance between the plants and the creatures that live here."

That made sense. Most of the trails we walked didn't follow any clear logic—there were tangles and disconnects, even in the root network, where too many plants competed for the same resources.

"I can control all that?"

"Yes. You and your daughters will. For now, that task will have to be taken in small steps to reorganize a century of chaos."

I scrunched my nose in displeasure at the sound of that. I didn't have any daughters, so the task would fall entirely to me.

"I'll try to help where I can," Cassie offered. "But since my tree is severed from this land, it won't listen to me the way it does to a dryad rooted here."

"I appreciate any aid you can lend." With a deep breath, I steadied myself. "Where do I begin, then?"

Lilise gestured to the field where we now sat. "Lesson one: growing a seedling."

She opened the pouch in her lap and pulled out a few seeds. They looked like the flora the satyrs often planted this time of year. Then she placed one in my hand.

"Connect with the seed's essence first," she instructed.

The energy was tiny, almost like trying to pinch a grain of sand from the desert. For something so small, it was actually a quite daunting task.

No matter what I tried, I couldn't connect to the seed. I would either overwhelm it—pulling life into myself—or I'd give it too much, and it would nearly explode. I tried again and again.

This should have been a skill that came easily to me. I was born to do this. If I couldn't grow a single flower seed, then I wouldn't be able to fix the forest. I tried again, and just before the essence burst, Lilise clasped her hands around mine.

"I need you to take a deep breath. You're putting way too much thought into it." Lilise waited until I met her eyes, her concern clear as I frowned.

"I don't understand why I can't connect with it," I huffed.

"Let's work on something else," Lilise said, rising to her feet and moving to sit on a rock that jutted up from the ground.

I followed with a pout and tried to hand the seed back, but she shook her head. Cassie and I sat on either side of Lilise now, and I waited for further direction.

"Channel into the ground here. Listen to the messages being passed along to you," she said, her voice barely louder than a whisper. "Hear the few and hear the many.

Don't try to pick out individual ones—just breathe and let them flow."

"Okay." I closed my eyes. When I'd been trapped in my tree, I could still *see* the world around me, but it had felt more like sensing energy—movement and connection—than seeing in a physical sense. My eyesight in this spirit form was tunneled in a way that made it easier to focus in, but harder to feel everything around me. I was still learning to merge those two experiences.

With each deep breath, I sank further into my mind. I felt the tingle of a passing message, the tremor of a cluster arriving with new data points as they passed from me to the rest of the earth. This was often how I slept. I could feel myself slipping into the dream world.

"What does spring look like here?" Lilise asked—or at least, I thought it was Lilise. I didn't really want to look.

Spring was soft pastels and a warm breeze. It was basking in the sun for a little longer. Spring was fresh air and growth, as new grass poked through the snow and my leaves began to sprout from the rest. It was movement after a long rest—or running into Graak's arms after a lifetime of being frozen.

"There you go," Lilise said proudly.

Still anchored into the messages, I snuck a peek at my hand. A small shoot was now emerging from the seed. I leapt up excitedly, watching as it continued to grow in my palm. Cassie opened a hole in the dirt, and as I tucked the seedling into the soil, it began to hum a song. The flora of each season had their own melody, and as I hummed along, others in the ground began to glow.

Stepping back from the seedling, I clutched at my hair, overwhelmed by the warmth of affection heating my soul—and then came the fire. But this wasn't dangerous fire. This was the fire that shielded me in the winter. This was lightning, the kind that messed up grids in Ylluna. This was a picnic and a blanket anywhere at all—because he had never given up on me.

"Kelan." I breathed out the name like a prayer. I could feel him in the soil. I could feel him in the air around me. And then I heard it—the crashing lightning to the south as a storm crept by in the distance.

I wasn't sure when I began to move, but as soon as I entered the tree, I took off. Each rumble of lightning in my path charged my soul, flooding me with new life. I didn't care what was between us—I wouldn't let anything stand in my way. I had to see him. I had to hold him.

When I emerged from the tree on the southern edge of Voreios, there was chaos. A violent storm tore across the lands beyond our rock barrier. My guards fanned out, shouting messages and warnings to one another as they battled infernals as far as I could see—but none of that held my attention for long. Bands of long white lightning slashed through the sky, some of them shredding apart infernals and aiding our satyrs.

"Kelan!" I shouted, my skin breaking out in goosebumps. I ran towards him.

"Vasilissa on the border!" a guard called from my left, jolting me from my pursuit. His words echoed across the field until a satyr emerged from the waves of smoky ash, a green band tied around his arm—like Graak's.

My steps towards the border grew more cautious as he approached, but I continued to follow the lightning strikes.

"Vasilissa, please stop." I recognized the border leader as Haz. He was still catching his breath from the fight, but he gave me as gentle a look as he could manage.

"No. He's out there." I wasn't turning around without him.

"None of ours are too far out. We have eyes on everyone, but it isn't safe for you to be here."

Lightning crashed again, and I tore my gaze away from Haz back to the sky as rain poured down on us. Visibility was poor, but I could find him.

"I'm sorry. I have to go for Kelan." My body vibrated with the call of the earth as a green glow began to radiate from my fingertips.

My eyes locked on the horrifying tangle of limbs and monstrous mouths tearing at the barrier, trying to break through and attack the guards.

The last time I'd been surrounded by infernals like this, Graak has shredded them all with the earth. I wanted to do that now, and immediately the earth began to tremble. Haz gripped my upper arm as if to steady me—but I was the one causing the quake.

The soil split, tearing away beneath the feet of the beasts and leaving a narrow path just wide enough for me to walk into the heart of the storm. Kelan had to be close if he could strike from this far out. Perhaps he would see me, and I wouldn't have to go too far.

I knew the exact moment the infernals saw me past the illusionary border—even before I crossed it—as hundreds of red eyes locked onto me.

301

"Vasilissa!" Haz's voice rang out behind me, trying to draw my attention. But I couldn't look away from the beasts. I refused to believe that this was what they saw every day on our southern border.

The darkest clump of clouds split open, and what looked like an elven man flying through the air stepped into view. He hovered closer and closer, and all the blood drained from my body. I recognized him. Our brief encounter was forever etched on my soul.

"Aurinia. . ." Xernath called to me, his arm outstretched and a sinister smile twisting his lips. "Finally. We've been waiting to meet you again. Come out and meet your destiny."

Any confidence I'd had before wavered as flashes of boney fingers digging into my skin, poles shredding through my shoulders, and blood running down my body seized control. I was dying. All over again. I was anchored to the tree where my life had once been ripped from me.

What once was water now ran like blood over my skin, coating me in a red that would never fade. Each pair of glowing infernal eyes were his—watching me, seeing into the very depths of my reborn soul. I sank to my knees and screamed. The earth answered my pain, spiking outward in jagged fury, severing some of the infernal beasts that dared to come too close.

"Get her back in the grove—now!" Graak bellowed from somewhere behind me. His voice cut through the spiral of chaos like a tether catching me mid-freefall.

Ferox appeared at my side just as the wind turned icy. His presence merged with Lilise's magic, the two of them clearing away the storm.

"Aurinia! Don't run away now—we've only just begun to play." Xernath taunted, causing me to lift my head from the ground.

Graak walked past me, excess magic pouring off him in waves. He was furious—but in that calm, collected way that was somehow more terrifying than his normal anger.

"Don't speak to her," Graak commanded, his tone chilling. I'd never seen this side of him, but it echoed Melissa's memories of the negotiations.

There were too many infernals. Ferox lifted me back to my feet and pulled me away as my protector stepped beyond the barrier. He was completely unshielded. He was walking straight into danger—alone.

But when I glanced up at Ferox and saw the yellow glow in his eyes and the fury of the winds howling from the north, I knew Graak wasn't alone. Green and blue magic tore through the eastern and western fronts—Lilise and Cassie lending their elemental power to the defense.

Then I heard it: Graak's voice, but it came from the earth itself. "Terra Spica Silva."

Large spikes of rock erupted along the battlefield, ripping up the terrain in every direction and shredding anything in their path—as if drawing a new, brutal border in blood and stone. The earth launched Graak into the sky as he collided with the mage midair in a clash of fury and power.

As the infernals began to dissipate, they left behind a trail of ominous black scars streaking the sky as the storm began to break.

Tossing Xernath to the ground, the mage exploded through three massive pikes, and shadows ripped up from the earth, trying to deflect Graak's stone attacks as he closed in. I couldn't take my eyes off him—even as I wondered why Kelan wasn't moving towards the border now that the way was clearing.

The mage couldn't put any distance between himself and my protector. Graak moved with the earth, his grace impossible for a man his size. He landed on top of Xernath, and from where I stood, all I could see were brilliant flashes of green as his fists struck again and again.

As the smoke and rain faded, revealing a brilliant, cloudless sky, I felt like I could finally breathe again.

"Aurinia," Ferox said as he led me slowly back into the grove, "you cannot do that again."

Sure, it had been impulsive, but I didn't understand the edge in his voice. Then I noticed the visible relief on every guard around me as I moved deeper inside. Haz bowed his head and let out a deep breath he must've been holding in for some time.

They had been terrified. And not because of the monsters beyond the border. It was something *I* had done.

"But Kelan. . ."

The moment the words left my mouth, I realized I couldn't sense him anymore. He had vanished with the storm and the infernals. That shouldn't have been possible. Unless this had all been a trick. One I had almost fallen straight into.

"That was not Kelan," Ferox said, confirming what I had already begun to suspect. "I'm not exactly sure how they did it. But it doesn't change the fact that this situation could have been infinitely worse—if you hadn't had a panic attack."

"I don't understand. Why were they so afraid?" I asked, rubbing my arms to shake off the chill of the rain.

"You're not just a tree anymore. Just because that part of you is safe doesn't mean you're free to act without consequences. If anything, it's worse now. You are their shield. You are the last dryad of Voreios. If something happens to your spirit—or your tree form—and you die, this barrier and Voreios will fall."

My eyes widened in horror as the truth settled over me. I had come so close to charging headfirst into a battle I wasn't prepared for.

Shame hit me hard. I turned and bolted from the border, back to my tree. Next time, I had to do better. The grove had protected me up until now—and for them, I expected more of myself.

Cholios would not use my desire for Kelan to destroy my home. I would find another way.

Chapter 33 – Kelan

It hadn't been restful sleep, but as Minithe's red glow began to fade and darkness claimed the space between us, all the details of yesterday came flooding back.

"Light the torches, Kelan," Minithe demanded—though I doubted she even needed the light to see.

My fire training was to begin again immediately. Taking a deep breath to center myself, I imagined a flame growing in my palm. But my thoughts were conflicted, flashing between Melissa and Aurinia. A new seed of hope had taken root overnight, and I wasn't sure I could descend into despair again. Not if there was a chance my mate had survived.

"What's taking so long?" Minithe pressed, though I could hear the amusement in her jab.

"There's something missing," I admitted. "I'm distracted. With Melissa, there was this undeniable pull—I couldn't focus on anything that wasn't leading me to her. I don't feel that now."

"I shouldn't tell you this," she said, pausing as if weighing her words, "but that doesn't necessarily mean Aurinia isn't your mate."

The dryad snapped her fingers, and small flames danced at the tips of each before she locked eyes with me.

"You need to be in her presence. You can't experience her energy through the images here. There's no telling how this will play out until you stand in front of her again."

That seed in my soul grew incrementally bigger, and the element poured out in relief. A steady, compressed ball of flame formed in the center of my hands. I'd never felt fire come so easily—and this was only the beginning.

Minithe waited patiently as I lit each of the torches. Her back was turned when I headed in her direction, but at the entrance of our little cavern was something I hadn't expected.

"Is that. . .?"

"Supplies. Mage outfits, food, water, and even a healing tonic." Her voice held a hint of surprise, but it didn't match the alarm bells ringing in my head.

"Someone knows we're here."

"Yes," she agreed. "But they didn't attack when they could have. Something to ponder. Take this."

The dryad tossed me a small blue vial, and I caught it.

"You don't think it's poisoned?" I asked, raising a brow.

"That would only kill one of us, so I'm willing to gamble the odds on you." Minithe's lips curved into a mischievous grin, and I rolled my eyes.

Without any further thought, I popped the lid off with my thumb and chugged it back. My throat burned as the liquid went down. The taste was awful—like drinking decaying flesh—but the relief in my ribs came quickly.

"It *was* a healing tonic," I muttered, gagging at the aftertaste and clearing my throat, hoping for a splash of water.

"Awesome," Minithe said, tossing me a mage cloak. "We'll need to do something about your hair. How do you feel about a new facial scar?"

"Whoa, whoa." I tried to laugh it off, but she'd caught me completely off guard. "Why all the changes?"

"There are two things that could be happening here, and we need to act the part for both of them," she explained, turning to face me as she fastened her own robe. "Either this mountain is enchanted and new people are automatically inducted into the lower mage ranks—given everything they need to begin—or the serpent creatures that live here assumed we were new mages and left us these supplies. The Infernal Plane has never been breached like this before, and I'm willing to bet they don't have protocols for what we did."

That would be immensely helpful—if it were true. I wrapped the cloak around my shoulders and tied it into place. "If that's the case, then we can't look like ourselves. We'd blow our cover."

"Exactly." She gestured for me to lean down, and in one swift motion, she singed my hair to a short cut—without burning a single inch of skin. "When we leave, I'll try to find some ink so we can dye it. But for now, this should help."

"What about you?" I asked, running a hand through my hair. It had never been this short in my life.

Without responding, Minithe's red dryad markings faded from her fair skin. Her eyes shifted to a soft brown, and her bright red hair dulled into a plain brunette, stripped of its vines. Her ears elongated to match mine. In a blink, the nymph had transformed herself into an elf.

It was a skill they all possessed, but I'd never seen it in action. On Artemesia, the nymphs had no reason to use it—not like they had on Earth, where they'd once been hunted and stalked.

"How long can you hold that form?"

"Weeks, if I need to. But I'll let it drop when we return here in the evening. It drains more energy than I like—and we need to be prepared to fight another dragon."

As I pulled the mage cloak shut across my chest, my body vanished. We both stared at the spot where I'd been standing before. I could still feel my legs—my whole body—but I couldn't see any of it. Minithe stepped forward and shoved her hand into my chest, pushing me back a step.

"Interesting," she murmured. "Pull the hood up."

My body briefly came back into view as I opened the cloak to pull the hood over my head, then I closed the cape back up. "Did I vanish?"

"Yes. There's a very faint outline when you move, but if you stay still, I can't tell you're there."

"Now the real question—can you still sense my fire?" I asked.

Minithe smiled at that. "Yes, I can."

For the first time in weeks, it felt like we'd been given a boon. "Then, let's give them hell."

We wandered through the tunnels for hours, piecing together a makeshift map in our minds. Even though Minithe had been here before, centuries had passed—and with mages infiltrating every nook and cranny, a lot had changed.

Most of the places we explored were filled with nothing but empty beds. Not a single personal belonging in sight. The only indication that anyone had been there recently was the way the linens were arranged, and the lingering sensation of magic in the air.

I began to look forward to the moments when we'd weave our way back to the main cavern, where we'd seen the dragons meet with Aedan—because then I could see her.

There were different images of her scattered throughout the space. She was beautiful. I hoped she was still mine. Living in a world where Melissa's likeness roamed but was destined for someone else would be a different kind of torture entirely. Perhaps that was what Graak struggled with as well?

"Finally," Minithe whispered, her voice low with excitement. "When I say so, I need you to create three spheres like the one you did this morning and hover them around the room so we can see."

I followed the soft sound of her voice down to a cave tucked into the back of the meeting space. "What did you find?"

"Now," Minithe said as she rifled through stacks of books and maps on the surprisingly elegant desk at the center of the room. "These are plans, from the looks of it."

I struggled to form the third sphere of flame but eventually got it to stabilize. Only then did I move to her side to see what she was looking at.

"Tons of references to the solstice," she said, flipping pages, "though it might take some time to decipher—this is written in a bunch of different languages. Which ones can you read?"

"Only Druidic and Elvish," I admitted with a frown. "You?"

"All of the ones spoken on this planet—and quite a few from others," Minithe replied as she turned one of the pages around for me to see. "Though this one is new to me. The letters are Draconic in origin, but they're smudged, morphed into something else. There's a lot of pages written in it, so I wonder if it's the mages' unique language?"

"There has to be some way to translate it," I said, sifting through papers piled on the far corner of the desk.

"We won't have time for that," Minithe replied, sliding a sheet towards me—an image of the sun and Artemesia aligned, arrows and lines radiating in every direction. "This is referring to the summer solstice specifically."

The negotiations had taken place a few days before spring. If this event was planned for the solstice, that meant there were only a little more than two lunar cycles left before the attack. I didn't even know what day it was.

"We need some way to tell time while we are down in these tunnels." I glanced around the room, looking for anything that might help. In the elven city, we had devices that kept time both indoors and out, in addition to our innate sense of rhythm from nature. The dwarves likely had a great technique for this—too bad I hadn't studied them more.

Then my eyes landed on the pillars of wax scattered around the room. "Could we use these?"

Minithe followed my gaze. "Candles? That could work! We'd need a few different sizes."

"Or," I said, circling around to the largest candle, "we could check back in here every day." It sat inside a brass holder etched with markings.

"At the rate this one is burning, it would take a full planetary cycle. Good thinking."

I was about to reply when I heard the scuff of footsteps approaching. Minithe and I locked eyes, then moved swiftly to the back of the room. My fire spheres blinked out instantly, leaving us only with the dim candlelight. I pulled up the hood of my cloak and willed my body to ease into a meditative state. The less movement, the less likely we were to get caught.

"All I'm hearing is that it almost worked." Aedan's voice sounded calm compared to the panicked muttering of the person with him.

"But we almost lost Xernath in the process," the mage protested. "He's not so easily replaced on the elven council."

Xernath.

I'd heard that name before. Melissa had mentioned him—he'd been present at the winter solstice ritual.

"It would've been his own damn fault," Aedan snarled, and the mage recoiled as every candle in the room suddenly burst to life. "He's obsessed with what's not his. Cholios grants him a favor—and this is how he repays it? With such a poor display? This won't happen again."

"Yes, sir. We all understand. But the council. . ."

"I don't give a damn about the elves." Aedan shoved the mage aside as he strode towards me. "Just the one. Do you think it could work again?"

"Our sources haven't seen her today. She's isolating in her tree, from what we can tell. Lilise won't let anyone talk to her," the mage added, falling silent for a beat. "Between Graak and the watchtowers, I don't think we'd be able to pull it off. They're suspicious."

Aedan stared directly in my direction, rubbing his face thoughtfully. "Declan says the two intruders are no longer in the infernal sands. But there've been no reports of the elf or Minithe in Voreios?"

"Not yet."

"They couldn't have just vanished. One watchtower alone can't create a portal."

"Maybe they got eaten by infernals?"

Aedan chuckled and shook his head. "Sometimes I forget that you all aren't as bright as we give you credit for."

I held my breath as Aedan took a step closer and grabbed a book from the shelf embedded in the cavern wall—just inches from my shoulder. The warmth of his breath brushed my face and sent a chill down my spine.

"A watchtower is the living embodiment of their element," he said, flipping open the book. "They can only be killed by the acts of a god, or the highest laws of nature. To suggest that Minithe is dead from infernal wounds is to say that fire itself has ceased to exist." He turned and showed the mage a page I couldn't see. "Let me assure you," Aedan said, his voice edged with quiet reverence, "fire is not dead in this world. Not yet."

"Why haven't we tried to infiltrate their ranks, if they're so powerful?" The mage asked—and I was dying to know the answer too.

"Oh, we did attempt it once." Aedan snapped the book shut. "Lost a lot of mages with those plans. Lilise and Ferox are impenetrable in their commitment to the roles they play. Ultimately, the only way to break a watchtower is to make them care about something more than their oaths to the other gods."

"Impossible, then." The mage sighed and bowed his head.

"Not anymore," Aedan murmured. "There's a crack in the ranks. And it's a gift that the other gods haven't noticed yet. It wasn't one we anticipated, but a present nonetheless."

This was a shocking revelation, one that seemed almost too outlandish to be real. There had never been an oath breaker among the watchtowers.

Who were they referring to?

If it were true, it would only upset the balance on our planet further.

314

"Is this something we need to act on?" the mage asked, more alert now. "I can make some arrangements."

Aedan gave him a smooth, knowing smile. "We'll let you know when that becomes necessary. For now, we focus on the lost duo—and keeping our fae-elven war from stagnating too long. Come, let's check in with Keane."

The two men strode from the room as quickly as they'd entered, Aedan slamming the book down in the middle of the map as he exited. I hardly breathed until their footsteps faded completely into the distance.

"It's helpful that Aedan seems to be quite chatty," Minithe said as she lowered her hood. Her faux elven appearance threw me off for a few seconds.

"Way too close for my liking," I muttered. "An inch or two more, and he would've touched me and revealed our location."

"Much too close," she agreed, though she didn't appear as worried as I was.

"Lilise and Ferox have encountered them before?" I pressed. If there were more details we didn't know, we needed them fast.

"Not that I remember them mentioning. But those two have a long history with mages. I doubt they would've forgotten meeting someone like Aedan, though. He's not a god, but there's something. . .ethereal about him." She grabbed a book off the shelf with a frown. "I wish I could talk to them now, but at least this should help with the translating."

"How'd you find that so quickly?"

"I was scanning the shelves while they were in here."

She'd had her back to them the entire time. Maybe smarter, but I'd always been trained never to turn my back on an enemy.

"Do you think there's any truth to what Aedan said? About the crack in the watchtowers?"

That finally earned her full attention.

"Maybe. Maybe not. Could be all smoke and mirrors, But. . .we did miss the glaring reality that Melissa and Aurinia are tied somehow." Her voice softened. "I do know that for me, nothing can bring back Valk or Cenara. So I'm out of that equation, my tie to the gods is all I have left now that the guardian is also dead."

Almost unconsciously, she rubbed the place where her faded mate mark lay.

I cleared my throat and glanced around the cavern, pretending to refocus. "We should probably retreat for today, so we can study that book you found."

"Already working on it. But yes—this isn't the best place to hole up for any length of time. Do you have the candles?"

I swiped a handful from the lower shelf and stuffed them into the pouches of my mage cloak. They vanished from sight, but when I reached back in, I could still feel them. Another effective feature of these cloaks.

"What do you mean you're already working on it? You haven't opened up the book yet."

"Tree gift," she said with a shrug. "You know what paper's made of, right? Well, the tree still leaves imprints of the details on the pages. I can absorb that into my root memory."

"Explains how you know so many languages. That's a useful trick," I mused.

I flipped the hood of my cloak over my head and turned to exit the library—only to stop cold. Aedan leaned casually against the tunnel wall to my left, staring straight at me. From the smirk curling his lips, I knew the bastard could see me.

"You two appear to be quite resourceful," Aedan said as Minithe came up beside me. "What a pleasant surprise it was to find you in the library."

Her hood was down now, and I watched as her elven glamour faded. Her magic stirred and flared to life—and Aedan's responded in kind. Within seconds, the air between us grew heavy, the pressure dropping as their powers clashed in silence.

He tsked and shook his head. "My brother has been looking for you all night. Would've been far more courteous of you to stay put in the infernal sands. Care to share any details on how you escaped?"

He was taunting us.

"Fuck you," Minithe spat.

I wasn't sure how we were going to get out of this. Aedan might not have been a god, but he sure as hell wasn't a normal mage either. I reached for one of my blades, fingers brushing the holster on my shoulder—when the entire tunnel trembled, a deep rumble shaking dust loose from the ceiling, like a stampede of unicorns was charging up behind us.

I didn't dare take my eyes off Aedan

"I'm going to go out on a *branch* here," Aedan said, pausing as if to give us time to groan at the joke, "and guess you can't communicate with the others here. Can you?"

"I don't need the others," Minithe gritted out.

"Oh, I very much doubt that," Aedan said with a laugh, turning his gaze over Minithe's shoulder. "Hello, brother."

I shifted, adjusting my stance so I could keep them both in my line of sight. The resemblance was striking—same bright red hair, similar facial features—but the newcomer was nearly bare, wearing only shreds of linen across his open chest. His long hair flowed like a waterfall over every curve of his form.

He spared me a quick glance before focusing entirely on Minithe, offering her a smile that might've been charming under different circumstances.

"Declan, I assume," Minithe drawled, though her face remained deceptively calm, as if she was speaking to someone she merely detested.

"What a pleasure it is to finally make your acquaintance," Declan purred. "Although, I never enjoy having to snuff out the fire of a beautiful woman."

"Yes, yes. How droll of you." Minithe cast a glance between the brothers. "You know we aren't going to surrender, so how are we playing this?"

"Surrender, don't surrender—it doesn't make a difference," Declan said nonchalantly. "I'm your executioner, and today, you will die."

Water began to lift from the ground—slow bubbles at first, but then it started to spread outward from Declan's feet. Minithe shoved me in the opposite direction, away from the wall where Aedan stood. She slammed her arm into Aedan's chest, and fire exploded out of both of them.

"Run!" she shouted, twisting him out of her way—and we took off.

I tossed a quick glance over my shoulder and immediately wished I hadn't. The men were shifting shapes into something I'd never seen before.

Where Declan had once stood, dark grey stretched across his skin, and his bright red locks darkened to a black as pure as night. Rows of teeth protruded over the edges of his elongating mouth. A second set of horse-like legs burst from the lower part of his torso, and his lower half shifted to flippers—soon swallowed by the rising surge of water. The fae had something like this. . .kelpie, if I recalled correctly. But this one was far larger than anything I'd ever seen.

Aedan's transformation was just as extreme. Four wings erupted from his back, and smoky red scales trailed up and over his black leather. His mouth elongated into a fierce, lizard-like snout as he grew.

Another dragon?

"Run and don't look back again!" Minithe shouted. "Find *anywhere* to get out of this tunnel. This isn't like the dragons from before. Do *not* come back for me." Her magic heated up around us.

"We do this together or not at all, Minithe," I replied, voice steady with resolve. If they made her this nervous, there was no way I'd survive them on my own at this point.

The stampeding sound echoed again, followed by a rushing roar of water coming straight for us.

319

She groaned in frustration. "We're going to work on the rest of the fire cycle *now*. Aedan is fire energy, and Declan is water. Don't blast Aedan with fire—he'll absorb it and strike back. Transform the magic into something else. Depending on the intensity, push it into decay and dissolve it. And do *not* get swept up in the water."

"The bigger chamber's here—to the left!" I shouted and she followed my lead.

Water chased close behind us with every step. A roar shook the cavern as a dragon loomed on a rocky ledge overhead. Flame burst out in all directions—he didn't even have to charge the attack. Minithe diminished the fire with practiced ease as we pushed deeper towards the center. Even now, she left a few smaller areas for me to practice in.

Ignite. Growth. Control. Decay.

As we twisted around the stalactites, I focused on each flame core I could reach, taking them under my control. I shrank and expanded them, testing the limits of my abilities while adrenaline surged through my blood. Then, one by one, I snuffed them out.

Suddenly, water exploded from the tunnel behind us, sending a cascade of droplets raining down. Steam hissed off Minithe's skin as they burned away in her proximity. Dragon Aedan launched into the air, unleashing a supercharged wave of fire in our direction to keep us in the path of the oncoming flood. Minithe stepped forward, arms raised. The flames bent around her, shifting away from us in a powerful arc.

I was used to calling storms to fuel the element I'd trained in most.

I mirrored her stance, siphoning some of Aedan's flame into myself. It was dark and twisted—hot and deeply cold all at once. My instincts screamed to repel it, to push it back. But instead, I turned towards the rushing water and slammed my hand into the layer building at our feet.

Declan, now fully transformed, swam inside a cresting wave—his kelpie form the stuff of nightmares. His eyes locked onto mine, and for a moment, it felt like he was staring straight into my soul.

I summoned every spark of power I had, calling lightning from my core. It surged out of me and cracked through the cavern, illuminating every crevasse. The blast was so fierce, even Aedan veered higher into the air to avoid the arc. Minithe didn't waste a second—climbing up the nearest rock wall in pursuit.

The kelpie burst from the waves, looking thoroughly singed—but he charged at me without missing a step. Teeth were all I could see as his long jaw snapped forward, faster than anything I'd ever faced.

Even with my swift elven feet, I barely stayed out of range of those snapping jaws.

"Fire has gotten you far, but I'm here too," a woman's voice urged in my mind.

That didn't sound like Minithe.

I didn't need another voice in my head right now. I was barely holding onto my sanity as it was.

Above us, the ceiling of the cavern burst into flames, and I watched as Minithe launched off the wall—crashing into Aedan mid-dive. The kelpie retreated, vanishing into the swirling waters that somehow remained locked in a circular wall around me.

"Follow the wind. It's your only way out. Embrace me," the woman urged again.

I furrowed my brows.

Wind?

A blinding explosion of flame and lightning collided with the water, and Declan reappeared—slamming into my left side, ramming me into the opposite wall of my watery cage. He swam past me again and again, each pass allowing him to carve into my arms, my back, my legs. I fought to breathe, but the murky water blurred my vision, turning him into nothing more than a slicing blur before the next hit came.

Wind.

It sounded like she was saying I could work with air as well.

"Tell me how," I pleaded with the woman in my mind.

"You know how. How do you summon the clouds?"

There were no clouds in here. Just suffocating water

Declan slammed into me again, and the force sent me spinning. My chest burned, the lack of air making me dizzy.

A glow sparked in my chest, faint at first. I reached inward, searching for the same tether I used to summon storm clouds.

Something graceful and fluid wound its way through my inner magic—something I'd never noticed before, hidden beneath the intensity of my flame.

I need air.

I pulled on that hidden strand of magic with everything that I had—and the wind answered. A violent gust collapsed the pool around us, slamming Declan and me into the stone ground. The wind surged, lifting Aedan into the air and forcing him back. It ripped the oxygen from the room, snuffing out every active flame.

Was this all me?

Stunned, I glanced around the cavern. In the far upper corner, I spotted a small hole—wind streaming towards it like a beacon.

Declan and Aedan roared in unison, a sharp reminder that we were still very much in danger. Aedan twisted midair, trying to dislodge Minithe as he flew—straight towards the very exit we needed.

I bounced off a stalagmite and called the wind again, knocking Minithe off Aedan's back and into my path.

She braced for impact, but I caught her with one hand while the other grabbed the ledge of the small opening. Her eyes widened as realization hit.

Aedan swooped around, launching another ball of flame just as we scrambled up and into the new tunnel.

Minithe slammed her fist into the tunnel wall, her hand shifting into roots that burrowed into the stone. They spread quickly, sealing the entrance behind us.

This fight wasn't over, but we'd survived the first round.

Chapter 34 – Aurinia

I'd replayed the incident over and over in my mind, trying to understand every mistake I'd made. Three full days had passed, and a few things stood out. First: the watchtowers inquired after me, but when I told them I needed time, they respected that and let me be. Second: Graak hadn't come by since then.

The time to myself didn't only allow me to dwell on what I did wrong. It also gave me a chance to evaluate what I wanted to do next. Time wasn't on my side. Only focused action would do if we had any chance of surviving as a grove.

Cholios and Xernath hadn't come for Melissa. They'd come for *me*. And I didn't understand why.

As far as I knew, I'd been born in this grove. No one outside should even know I exist. Even if they did, there was nothing about me that they couldn't find in the other vasilissas.

The only thing I couldn't rule out was that Voreios was the weakest link. *I* was the thread holding the balance together. If that was true, I wouldn't let us fall without a fight. And that started with how I chose to run this grove.

"I need to speak with you all," I sent to the three watchtowers through our root link.

"We will be right there," Lilise replied immediately.

I pushed out from my tree, the breeze brushing against my face as the wind gently rolled by. Taking a moment to collect myself, I felt optimistic despite all the things I would set into motion today.

Then *he* appeared just beyond the trees, and my breath caught in my chest. My protector stood at the edge of the grove, calmer than the last time I'd seen him, but the hard set of his jaw told me his anger hadn't passed.

His expression didn't soften when our eyes met, and I braced myself. He instantly looked away, as if just seeing me stirred fury in his chest.

"We need to talk," he said gruffly.

"Yes," I agreed, through my throat felt dry. This was good. I needed to talk to him about my plans too.

"What were you thinking?" Graak growled. He paused, but I knew he wasn't done. "You could've been hurt. Captured. Or worse! We talked about this *that morning*. How could you be so reckless?"

I frowned and parted my lips, trying to figure out what to say.

"Do you understand what is at stake?" He rubbed his forehead, clearly trying to rein himself in. "I don't want to yell at you, but I don't know how else to make sure you hear me."

"Graak," I said softly, pouring all my affection for him into his name. I wanted him to calm down, to look at me.

"Answer me, Aurinia. No deflections. Not on this."

"Graak," I pressed. This time he sighed, but didn't speak. "I'm sorry. I thought Kelan was out there, and I acted impulsively."

"You attempted to leave for Kelan?" Graak raised an eyebrow, though his tone had softened. The tension between us still lingered, so I continued to push my affectionate thoughts towards him.

"Yes."

"You know Kelan would never want you to leave a protective barrier—especially if he was surrounded by infernals," Graak replied.

I chewed on my lip for a moment. He was right. Kelan would've been just as upset if I were Melissa.

"Of course, you're right. I just. . . I need to know that he's safe. That he isn't dead too. I wasn't thinking straight, but I promise I won't act that way again." I twisted my hands together nervously. "I really am sorry for how it all played out. There are realities I *think* I understand, but I don't. And that collided horrifically."

Graak studied me for a long moment before he gave me a small nod. "As long as we are in agreement that you are *not* to leave the borders like that again."

I hesitated, knowing he was likely going to yell at me again, but I was going to say it anyway. With the pressure still on this vibe in my heart, I took a small step closer.

"Well, about that. Tomorrow morning, I want you to escort me to a border of your choosing."

He growled at the request, but now he seemed distracted. "Aurinia, no."

"I'm including you in my plans, please just hear me out."

Graak balled his hands into fists a few times, then squeezed his eyes shut. As if he was trying to not look at me, out of anger or something else, I wasn't quite sure.

"I will not be doing that."

"Yes, you will," I replied with a calmness I didn't entirely feel. "I need to be aware of what's happening around *my* grove. If I go with you, then you know I'm acting appropriately. It will also make the guards feel more secure if you're there."

He groaned and sighed in frustration. "Aurinia, I am your ryne. It's my job to keep you safe. The borders are far from that."

"I must know what is going on, Graak. You cannot shield me from the pain of my people." My fists curled tight as I met his gaze, unflinching. "Is that what the southern border looks like every day? This isn't the same as what happened at Dytika. I will not remain ignorant. That's not protecting me—and it's not helping them."

"You help us all by staying safe in the center of the grove." He leaned in, and the air shifted—charged, electric. Static danced along the scarce space between us. "Which is exactly where I expect to find you moving forward."

"I will not abide by that," I said, voice shaking slightly as the space between us disappeared. "To make informed decisions, I need to. . .see what. . .is going on." I stammered when he pressed me against my tree, his nose and lips trailing slowly up the side of my neck. "You either go with me," I whispered, "or I take myself."

"I will take you," Graak replied huskily, placing a kiss on my neck that sent a full-body shiver rippling through me. "Using glamour to win your position is hardly fair. I'm only

327

so strong, little firefly. You're playing with forces that have their own consequences."

I wasn't entirely sure we were still talking about going to the borders.

I panted as his hands slid up the sides of my body, lifting my skirt with every inch. One of his knees parted my legs, and he cupped my ass, pulling me flush against him so I could feel the full length of his erection. I whimpered, overcome with this new, crushing need. I didn't know what had shifted so suddenly between us, but I pleaded to all the gods that it would stay. I wanted him to be mine so badly.

"You smell so damn good," he murmured, nipping at my ear.

"Graak," I begged, my hands sliding around his shoulders, my fingers gripping him for balance.

In a flash, I was standing upright, feet on solid ground, with him a full arm's length away, his back to me. I stared at him, breathless and confused, not even trying to hide it. His shoulders rose and fell like he was struggling to steady himself as well.

"Aurinia," Lilise called, and I silently cursed myself for summoning them and not seeking him out first. "You wanted to speak with us? Oh, good. I see Graak is here too."

"Just a moment," he muttered, turning his face towards the sky. It sounded like he was counting.

"Yes. . ." I exhaled, shaking off the harsh transition.

This would be yet another thing we'd have to talk about later.

Cassie, Lilise, and Ferox stood nearby, their eyes focused solely on me. If they knew what had just happened, none of them showed it. I appreciated that they were ready for whatever I had to tell them. This is where Melissa and I differed. I knew exactly what these three were capable of. Their presence here was a blessing to Voreios, and I wouldn't squander it any longer.

"The other day was an absolute mess. I'm sorry for how I behaved." I paused, meeting each of their eyes so they knew I meant it. "I've had some time to reflect, and I'm going to need your help. All of you—if you're willing."

I directed the last part towards Graak, who had finally made his way back over to the group. His expression was forcibly neutral. I knew him too well for that, but at least I had his attention again.

"I'm done sitting on the sidelines. Voreios is a home for warriors. I've seen it in our people, and I won't stay disconnected from them like this. I know Minithe isn't with us right now, but I want to start training with Ares again."

Ferox was the first to respond, offering me a smile. "Done. I think this is a fantastic idea. You and I will begin tomorrow—after your lessons with Lilise."

He didn't even blink at the mention of Melissa's sword. When no one protested this first part of my plan, my confidence grew. I could do this.

"Graak has agreed to take me to the borders so I can get a real picture of what's happening in my grove. Cassie, I'd like you and Graak to fill me in on everything you can— our history, our dealings and alliances, our place in Artemesia's structure. Any details that can help me better understand Voreios."

Graak gave me an incredulous smirk, but he didn't dispute my claim. He ran his tongue over his lips like they were dry, and my insides twisted. Damn him for being so handsome, and damn Melissa's memories for the new hunger rising inside me.

"That's good with me," Cassie agreed. "After you're done with Ferox, we need to work on your control of earth magic. Now that we've seen a tremor of your ability, we must grow that rapidly. Summer will be here before we know it."

As soon as she mentioned it, I remembered the green glow radiating from me and the way the ground tore apart beneath my feet.

That was me.

That was *my* earth magic finally revealing itself. All the pieces were starting to fall into place, and I hadn't even realized it.

"We should also stop by the temple to talk with Montibus," Cassie continued, unaware that I'd been lost in my own thoughts. "I know they didn't speak much during your time with Prafrum, but we should try again."

"We have a temple?"

Now my earth sister chuckled. "Of course we do. Every grove has one dedicated to its patron god."

I still had so much to learn. I sighed, accepting the fact that curveballs were going to keep coming.

"That's a lot of training for such a short period of time," Lilise said gently, concern flickering across her features. "Perhaps we should keep the focus on the summer ritual. There'll be time for weapons training afterward."

"I'm ready," I insisted. "For all of it. I've thought through everything, and I want to do this."

"Counter proposal," Lilise said, gesturing at Graak. "And I think he may agree with me: three days of training, one day off—so you can experience Voreios. Not the borders. Not magic. Just living in your grove. That way, you come back refreshed and connected to your community."

"That follows academy structure." Graak nodded his approval. "I'm in support of this plan. Also, due to the intensity of your training, we won't be going to the borders every day." He held up a hand as I opened my mouth to protest. "I won't shield you from what's happening. I promise not to be a barrier on your path to becoming a great leader."

Finally.

From here on out, I would steer my own destiny.

Chapter 35 – Aurinia

The morning workout had been just as intense as I remembered. Minithe and Ferox had completely different training styles. Where Minithe focused on slow, precise movements, Ferox came at me with blitz of speed that knocked me entirely off balance.

As I rubbed my aching calves before our ascent to the elders' cave, I thought of Minithe and Kelan's sparring match. A few months ago, the idea of that had felt impossible. But Ferox seemed to think otherwise—or he was showing me just how far out of practice I really was.

Lilise waited for me patiently as I rose to my feet. I nearly blushed when I caught the fond look in her eyes as our gazes met. Nothing had changed in how they treated me—not since Melissa, not since the negotiations. And I couldn't put into words how much that meant to me.

"*Lilly?*" I asked as we entered the trees.

"*Yes, Aurinia,*" she replied patiently.

"*You once said that fighting felt counterintuitive to who you were born to be, so now you focus on healing unless called to fight.*"

I paused, listening to the hum of the grove—the gentle thrum of life radiating from every root and leaf.

"I think I finally understand what you meant. But I don't know how to balance that with what I feel is coming."

"Being a vasilissa means the community thrives—or declines—on your efforts and choices. It wasn't a role meant to be mine for long, but the instincts remain," Lilise explained. *"Voreios has been in fight mode for decades. And after your experiences these past few months, you're forced to face the challenge. But you are not alone. Life continues, even in adversity."*

"But is that still living, if it's only to fight?" I asked.

My mind raced with the faces of our guards, the stories Graak had shared, the loss our community had suffered since the fae attacked.

We exited the trees, arriving at the caverns nestled high in the mountains. A memory surfaced—Graak and Zoq standing behind me as I was introduced to the elders. Well. . .not *me*. Melissa. But it felt like my memory now, and I was tired of pretending these feelings and emotions didn't belong to me too. Hopefully Montibus would have more answers when I visited the temple with Cassie after this.

"Aurinia," Lilise's voice came softly in my mind. *"There are times in life when only the fight seems to matter."* She tilted my chin up to meet her eyes. *"That's when it's your job to show them exactly what they're fighting for. Give them something to live for—a dream, a future. Give them hope. And don't let them lose sight of that."*

Hope. Such a simple word, but there was so much weight to it.

I smiled at Lilise. *"I think I can do that."*

"You're already doing it every day—just by existing. Now imagine what you could do with intention."

A shiver ran through me at how much power she'd given me with that one statement. Everything was strengthened by intention—and weakened by doubt.

Together, we walked into the cavern. Skylight holes had been carved along the tunnel, letting sunlight spill through in quiet beams. There was no harsh adjustment to the darkness this time. It had felt so dim when I first came here—but not now.

A cluster of older satyrs sat in a tight circle ahead, and I felt him in the earth's vibrations before I saw him. Graak. I had no idea how he moved so quickly around the grove, but I also hadn't paid attention to his movements this morning while training with Ferox.

"Vasilissa," Xhet said, surprised, as the group turned their attention to me.

I was coming to understand that I had this effect on meetings. My presence seemed to command immediate attention from those in the vicinity. Perhaps it had always been that way with Hairiko, and I'd simply never noticed. Or maybe she was more predictable. Most of my grove seemed to forget I could move about freely now, so they were often surprised to see me.

I flashed Graak a smile, meeting his gaze from under my lashes, letting the space between us charge with tension. I was tired of pretending I didn't want him. His gaze darkened with heat, but he didn't move.

"I apologize for interrupting this meeting," I said, letting my voice carry. "But I've made some decisions—and I'd prefer you be the first to hear them." They had been running the grove before I emerged. According to Cassie, the transition to irrelevancy had been difficult for them. My grove sister could be brutal sometimes.

"Of course, we'd love to hear your thoughts. Graak, you're dismissed," Xhet said, turning away from my ryne. Graak responded with an astonished chuckle at the blatant disrespect.

"Graak, please stay for this," I said, leveling my voice. "We all need to be on the same page." I glanced at Lilise, who gave me the slightest nod of encouragement. "I'm done dating the mages. I do not have any matches among the warriors at the borders."

"You haven't met with Zrif or Haz," Xhet protested.

I shook my head.

"I met with Haz earlier this week. Aside from me apologizing to him, there is nothing we need to discuss on the this topic. As for Zrif—he is Graak's eldest son. I've met with him many times over the years, especially as he grew up." I let my tone harden just slightly. "I see no purpose in continuing this charade of courtship. It ends today. My time is limited, and it must be spent preparing for the ritual."

"Strong delivery," Lilise praised through our private root link. I beamed.

"You should still meet with him. Things could've changed, now that you're out and you've both matured," Xhet insisted

Lilise clicked her tongue. "I believe Aurinia has said her piece on this matter."

"He's the strongest mage we have in the grove," Xhet countered again. My patience thinned.

"Zrif *is* powerful, but he is a water master—and I must bond with an *earth druwid* first." I kept my voice steady. "And he is *not* stronger than Graak."

It took everything in me not to look at my protector, though I imagined he enjoyed the ego stroke.

"I'm concerned that you're pressing this because you think I'll be distracted by how much he looks like his father. I hope that's not your belief—because I'm acutely aware of the movement and presence of every person in this grove. I will not be duped into affection based on appearance alone."

I let that sink in before finishing.

"He's also avoided every opportunity to meet with me. So again, I say—no more dates. If we're all on the same understanding, I'll be on my way to the temple."

"Vasilissa, please."

"Xhet, we've had this conversation. You *will* call me Aurinia. There is no need for the formality in small meetings like this." I looked around at the elders, and most appeared shocked into silence. "I've even considered taking it a step further. Lilly has a nickname, so maybe I should have one. *Aura.* How's that sound?"

"That feels improper," he muttered.

Lilise smiled at me again, that fond gleam back in her eyes.

"Well, *I* like the way it sounds," I said simply. "I'm literally the only dryad rooted here in Voreios. There's no confusion for anyone that I'm the vasilissa. The others announce it everywhere I go. But in a simple conversation, I don't want to be addressed that way. Can we agree on that?"

He swallowed. "Yes, Aurinia."

"Great. I'm so glad that we found an understanding today." I turned on my heels and made my way towards the entrance to meet Cassie at the temple.

"You will need a druwid soon," Xhet reminded us all before I crossed the threshold.

I paused mid-step, took a breath, and convinced myself not to turn around.

"As always, I appreciate your attentiveness to my needs," I said over my shoulder. "But I'm going to handle that particular item my way. Thank you."

"Do you think Montibus will actually speak with me?" I asked Cassie as we walked along a softly worn path through the northern portion of the grove.

"Yes, I'm actually surprised he hasn't attempted already." The branches moved out of our way with a simple thought.

Being a tree and hiking this way definitely beat some of the shady forests I'd wandered through on Earth. While the plants had never hurt me, quite a few of my friends back then had come out of a pathless trek sliced to pieces.

"I haven't seen them since that day," I said with a frown.

They'd seemed so willing to speak with me when I was Melissa. But after I was trapped in the tree. . .they never came to visit me. And now? Still nothing.

Had Graak offended him so badly that Montibus had abandoned Voreios? Despite their absence, I could feel a familiar hum the farther north we walked—as if the Earth God's light pulled me forward.

"The gods are strange sometimes," Cassie said, brushing off my concern. "You wouldn't have earth magic if he hadn't blessed you at some point." She came to a stop and gestured ahead.

I took in the sight of ancient, crumbling stones. A haunting, harmonious chant floated on the breeze, weaving itself around me. Roots and vines crawled up the edges of the structure, threading through every crack. Nature was reclaiming it, slowly and without apology. It must have been falling apart for at least a century.

Priests and priestesses—primarily satyrs—moved quietly in and around the temple despite its decaying condition.

The chant called to me, beckoning me forward. I stepped past Cassie, unable to take my eyes off the way the earth attempted to claim this space for its own. It was poetic in a way. Life in Voreios echoed nature left to its own devices. It would find a way to thrive, given even the smallest opportunity.

Lilise had spoken of hope. And maybe. . .this temple was hope. Another thing broken by the past—but not beyond restoration. All of us could be *more*.

As the grove members began to notice me, they paused their activity, and the chanting fell gradually silent.

"Vasilissa," the nearest female satyr said, greeting me formally with a deep bow. One by one, the others followed, lowering their heads and bending at the waist. I wasn't sure I was a fan of the bowing.

"I didn't mean to intrude. Please, continue as you were." I tried to wave off the attention, but I already knew this would be a losing battle. "Cassie and I are here to speak with Montibus. Your songs were lovely."

"The gods wait for you, Vasilissa," the woman replied, stepping away without turning her back to me. I'd have to deal with that another time.

Within moments, the rest of the worshippers had vacated the temple, leaving Cassie and me standing alone.

"I'm never going to get used to this." I sighed.

"This may not be about you," Cassie countered. "Montibus might've requested this before we even arrived."

That was a point I hadn't considered. "But why would he need so much privacy?"

Cassie shrugged, unconcerned. "He and Graak talk in private all the time. Your ryne can be. . .quite blunt with our patron. Perhaps Montibus doesn't want you to feel the need to censor your thoughts for fear of being overheard."

As I stepped onto the stone-tiled patio of the entryway, the room ahead fell into a hushed silence.

"I'm going to be right here when you come out."

For the first time, nervousness stirred in my stomach. "You're not coming with me?"

"Some things you'll have to experience alone, Aura," Cassie said with a soft smile, using the nickname I'd chosen earlier. "I think they owe you some explanations—and other things that aren't meant for me to hear. That said, no matter what's revealed about what's to come, you're my sister. You will always have my unwavering support."

Tears stung the corners of my eyes, but I blinked them away. She was right. And it wasn't like I wouldn't tell her everything afterward. This was *my* journey, and I needed to walk this step alone. "Okay. I'll see you on the other side."

Crossing the intricately carved doorway, I paused as the niches along both side walls lit up, like torches guiding me towards an open bench in front of the altar. I stepped carefully over the cracks and settled breaks in the tiles.

My fingers itched to clean out the space and set it all right. I didn't want to be disrespectful of what had been, but I also wanted to leave behind something of my own intention.

Perhaps for now, my intention was just to embrace what was—so I could help enhance what was meant to be. But it was not the time. I was here to speak with Montibus.

"Hello?" I said softly, feeling strange for speaking to an empty room, but they'd always been listening before.

Graak had rarely mentioned this space in all our conversations—especially after I'd had time to sift through the memories rooted in decades of stillness.

Prafrum hadn't returned to Voreios after the fae attacked. Part of that was because they were hiding me, and the other part was because the grove's devotion to Montibus had shifted to becoming more individualized.

Honestly, I was surprised we had as many priests and priestesses as we did. So much of our culture had changed. What was once a society of art, culture, and religion had transformed into one focused solely on defense and war preparation.

Knowing that Notos had adopted a similar mindset, maybe it would be wise to see how Aconi handled the balance.

"Montibus?" I asked again, standing before the empty stone slab that served as an altar. I realized then—I had nothing to offer. Even Melissa's memories gave no real insight on what to do now.

There were so many questions tangled inside me, I wasn't even sure where to begin. As a tree, I had existed with nature, threaded through the energy of the gods. Melissa had grown up agnostic—until the gods appeared in her classroom. How much of this was by design? And how much was chance?

"I can feel you," I said softly. "But I don't know how to comprehend the last few months." I paused. Hopefully honesty would be the right offering for this conversation. "This would be easier for me if I could see you."

Lights flickered on the far side of the altar, and then—she appeared. A woman with long black hair, bright green eyes, and a flowing white dress that sparkled like stardust. Thin, delicate antlers rose from her head like branches touched by moonlight as she placed her hands on the altar.

"Aurinia," Silva said, smiling with a cheeky grin. The goddess I'd seen in my dreams. The woman who had found Melissa as a child in that memory.

"I'm surprised to see you and not Montibus," I said, a little breathless. "But I'm grateful to be able to finally express how thankful I am for all of your protection so far."

Start with gratitude. That was my plan. I didn't want to begin my new relationship with the gods in timeout, the way I'd heard they'd done with Graak.

The goddess tilted her head, studying me for a long moment. "You're welcome," Silva said at last. "But I know that's not what you really want to talk about."

It was worth a try. "I need to understand what happened—so I can move forward. Melissa. . .me. . .all of it."

"You're not ready for all those answers yet." Silva walked around the altar slowly, then hopped up to sit on the edge in front of me. Her dress spilled like a swath of the night sky over the floor in a long train. "It would only confuse your mind from the task at hand. Our powers have been strained by what has occurred over the past century. *That* must be your focus."

"You're referring to the summer solstice ritual?" I asked. She gave me a small nod. "I'm already working on it," I said quickly. "But please—just answer this. Are Melissa and I. . .the same?"

"How could you be the same? You lived two very different lives—until the moment her soul collided with yours."

I hated how immediate her response was. Like she'd been waiting for this question.

"But our memories merged," I pressed. "She was living in a tree on Earth at first—I wasn't able to speak until she joined with me. How can we *not* be the same? I think she

342

was a piece of my soul." I'd gone over this time and time again, trying to make sense of all the details.

Silva pursed her lips thoughtfully. "Does it really matter? Or is this answer for your conscious?"

Did it matter?

I gaped at her in shock, struggling to recover from what felt like a slap. "If you want me to focus on this ritual," I said, voice tight, "then I need to know. I can't think straight—and even I know if this doesn't go perfectly, it could be the beginning of the end. Maybe for all of us."

Silva's brow twitched almost imperceptibly. "Are you threatening me?"

Smooth going, Aurinia. Maybe think about what you say before it falls out of your mouth in front of the gods.

"No, of course not. I'm second guessing everything," I pleaded with her. "I think if I knew at least this, then it would clear away the unnecessary waste preventing our success and your rise back to full affluency."

"That is not an answer I can give you," Silva stated firmly, her tone final. "The only person who can decide who you are—is you."

Well, that's cryptic.

I pulled my bottom lip between my teeth as I mulled over her words. Perhaps it was permission—permission to claim that Melissa and I were the same. I had her memories and feelings, in the same way that she now had mine. We were one mind now. I could hum her favorite tunes, feel her deepest insecurities, follow all her dreams, incorporating all her pieces into who I define myself as.

The only question left was whether the gods would bless my intended mating union—the same way they had when it was Melissa. Would I give up Graak and Kelan if they didn't?

No. I wouldn't.

I was fairly confident that if I claimed Graak, he wouldn't abandon me—even if the gods' blessing never came. Kelan was the unknown. I hoped that he would be able to love me as I am now—with or without the gods' mark of destiny.

"Thank you, Silva," I said, bowing my head respectfully. "I'll think on what you've said. But I came today to discuss a key component of the ritual: earth magic."

The temple rumbled as the words left my mouth. Dust and dirt fell from the ceiling, and I winced at the fresh cracks splitting across the tiles. I wouldn't be able to leave this place in disrepair for much longer. I'd have to discuss this with Cassie afterward.

When I turned my attention back to Silva, another woman sat in her place. Her skin was darker than Graak's, though lighter than Lilise's ebony tone. A spiked crown the hue of a golden orange arced around her head in a perfect semi-circle. Her yellow eyes glowed with a force so intense, I had to look away. Instead of a dress matching the night sky, she was wrapped in a sheer heavenly glow.

"Who are you?" I asked, my voice strained with discomfort.

"I'm Solis," she replied, her tone almost a haughty dismissal. "I'm the twin form to Silva. We are the same and separate of the celestial beyond."

That made no sense, but I really wasn't in the mood to press any further on that. "Does this change have something to do with the summer solstice ritual?"

"Yes. We are approaching my season of higher power. After the failure of the winter equinox, lunar elemental magic is weakening across the realms. That failure cannot be repeated."

"I understand," I said quickly. "I'm doing everything I can, but my earth magic has only just surfaced."

"We do not have time for delays," she insisted.

Before I could reply, the ground trembled again. The floor sank into a perfect circle, taking the entire altar room down with it—until we were surrounded by the very soil that had once rested beneath us. Solis slowly rose toward the ceiling above me, leaving me in the new pit alone as she watched expectantly.

Out of the earth, a form emerged. He walked forward from the dirt, manifesting into a figure I knew all too well. The god who had saved me from Cholios that night. His moose-like antlers were so large they tore into the earthen walls around us. The weight of his power was overwhelming, trying to force me to my knees in his presence—but I would not yield.

Instead of appearing annoyed by my insolence, the god smirked.

"So much has changed, and yet everything is the same," he said thoughtfully, his deep voice calling to me. The voice that had called my name in this world for the first time. The one that had revealed Melissa's tie to me all those months ago. "Three have been running the world, yet the fourth is the foundation."

"Earth," I whispered to myself, thinking of the other vasilissas. "It's been a century since the last earth vasilissa participated in a ritual. How has the balance lasted this long? Why now?"

The two gods exchanged a look—and I hated the long pause. Why wouldn't they answer me?

"Because of the tie to you," Montibus said at last. "But that no longer matters." Another deflection. He didn't give me enough time to protest before speaking again. "Things set in motion the night of the winter solstice are still in effect, and the final countdown has begun. Are you ready to receive full access to your gift?"

I took a slow, deep breath, fighting the fear curling in my stomach. After this, there would be no more excuses— only action. Once I received my full power, there was no returning to what was before.

"I am humbled that you find me worthy," I said, bowing my head.

Montibus stepped through the altar like it was only a projection and pressed two fingers to my forehead. My body immediately seized, as if the dry earth cracked through my veins. Heaviness filled every cell, every bone. I was falling apart—and being rebuilt faster than I could comprehend.

"You are earth," Montibus chanted, but it didn't sound like spoken words. It felt like truth pouring into my soul. "I see your strength. You are earth."

The words bubbled up inside me, begging to be released, so I followed my intuition. "I am earth."

Though I couldn't see his face—his hand still rested on my brow, and Solis nearby, her radiance too blinding—I *felt* the joy in the energy around me. The planet itself seemed to echo its approval.

"You are earth," Montibus continued. "I see your fortitude. You are earth."

"I am earth," I repeated, stronger this time. The cracks inside me reformed as a solid wall—an impenetrable fortress surrounding the well of magic within.

Where I go, I move with intention. I don't merely channel the earth magic. Words had power—and mine were sharpened by purpose. I was the magic itself.

The lines across my body began to glow—the same radiant green as the moldavite necklace had when Melissa and I first merged. I turned my hands before me, watching the energy roll off my skin—lost to the sensation of possibility as the gods began to fade away. For the first time since this task had been set before me, I was beginning to believe I could succeed.

I was born for this.

Chapter 36 – Aurinia

Days passed in a blur as my training grew more rigorous. My mentors reminded me repeatedly that we were cramming years of lessons into weeks, but I refused to let that excuse soften me.

"You must keep your elbow up to hold the block. How would Minithe feel about this posture?" Ferox stepped back from me, crossing his arms. "Reset and go again."

"Minithe wasn't training me against tornadic winds at the same time," I snapped back—then instantly regretted it.

"Aura, the stakes are higher now. You know that."

"I thought we were focusing on weapons training," I grumbled, tightening my grip on Ares' pommel. "You've been using magic the entire time."

"Very few people in this world *don't* have some type of magic," he replied. "You need to be prepared to manage any advantage an attacker might have."

"And I didn't before?" I asked, resetting my fighting stance, waiting for his next strike.

Ferox paused. When he met my eyes again, there was something soft there. "This may hurt to hear," he said gently, "but we never intended for Melissa to fight monsters on missions."

My mouth fell slack in disbelief. I hadn't expected that to be his answer.

"A border challenge now and then, maybe. But after the fight with the ravaian, we knew it was too much. You were capable, but against any true powers. . . It was a risk we weren't willing to take."

"But. . ." My voice cracked. I looked down at the sword in my hands, fingers flexing over the hilt as I lowered it to my side. "Minithe took me to make a weapon. I took on five shadow guards—and beat four of them."

"I know you don't want to talk about that night," Ferox said, his voice lower now, "but that only emphasizes my point. You were unsupervised for one moment—and we almost lost you." He paused.

"Minithe was more willing to bet on your fighting spirit. But the other three of us? We just wanted to keep you safe. You needed to be able to hold on long enough for us to get there. Nothing more." Ferox sighed as he finished the confession.

"And that's different now because I have magic of my own? Or because I'm a vasilissa?" I asked, hating how disappointed I was at hearing this. I really couldn't argue with him. On the solstice, I'd had no real way to fight Xernath or Cholios. If Montibus hadn't intervened, if the watchtowers hadn't come when they did. . .I would have died. Or worse.

"If you were only a vasilissa, then you'd be in the same boat as Melissa. Hairiko and Sabina would never be training to fight like this."

"But Aconi would be," I stated flatly. It wasn't a question.

Ferox gave a small nod. "This goes beyond being a vasilissa. Can we leave it as I know you're capable of more? You want to train, so we're all in."

Could I leave it at that? They were giving me exactly what I'd asked for, but I wasn't so sure they'd offer what I hadn't known to ask about.

"No," I said, shaking my head. "I need to understand *why* I'm different. If you have any clues, then I want to discuss it together."

"Very well." Ferox's agreement came much quicker than I'd expected. He gestured for us to take a seat on the ground before continuing. "Lilise and I don't have all the facts yet," he warned. "We're still speculating. So don't hold this as definitive."

"Okay," I replied softly. Speculation was more than nothing.

"The Shadow God is targeting you personally. That much is certain," Ferox said. "It's the *why* we aren't sure about. By all appearances, you're nothing more than a very young vasilissa. And yet. . ." He hesitated. "He intended to kill Melissa from the start—the ritual, the poison, even the attacks. That was always the plan. But now. . .we have a worse problem."

"Worse than death?" I gave him an incredulous look.

"Yes." Ferox's expression darkened. "We don't think Cholios is trying to kill you anymore."

"He wanted access to Melissa's soul. We believe he decided the best outcome was either to extract her essence through death—or to unify your two pieces." Ferox paused, considering his next words carefully.

"What could he have done with her soul?" I asked. "That still doesn't explain how I'm different."

"I'm getting to that." He sighed. "The timeline doesn't align with you being the last daughter of Amalithea. There's a twenty-year gap. If she'd been carrying you then as a seedling, you would have burned up in the fires along with them."

I frowned. "But the only earth dryad left after the attack was Cassie—and we all know I'm not hers."

Ferox nodded grimly.

"Yes. Which means you are—quite literally—a dryad from the gods. And we believe that's why Cholios knew about you when no one else did."

My breath caught, the mere thought stirring dread deep in my soul.

"Now," he continued, "we need to figure out what else he knows about you. . .before it's too late."

I didn't feel like I had any more answers—just more complicated questions.

"You need to separate the dryad magic from the earth element," Cassie corrected me for the eighth time.

"I thought I was doing that!" I protested, flinging a boulder out of my way.

"Not quite. You are using the roots to move things, not the earth itself."

"Ugh." I threw my hands in the air and plopped down on the ground ungracefully. "How am I supposed to get this straight before the ritual? I don't have time to keep messing up."

Cassie took a seat next to me, placing a reassuring hand on my knee. "You were born to do this. We just need to find the method that clicks. Using the different types of magic is like using different muscles. We have to train them."

"You make it sound easy—and I'm running out of time." *Days.* That's all I had left. This was way too close for comfort. My confidence was slipping fast, and I didn't know how much more I had to give. It didn't help that even with the added nutrients Graak had been giving my tree, I felt like I was starving.

"It's not easy," Cassie admitted. "Take a deep breath. Then I want you to concentrate on the rock over there." She pointed to a basketball-sized rock about three feet away.

As I assessed the rock, I sighed, finally deciding it wasn't going to move itself. I shifted to stand, but Cassie grabbed my arm and gently pulled me back down.

"Stay seated. I want to try something."

"But I feel more grounded if I stand," I protested. The surges of magic often threw me back if I wasn't well centered before trying to access it.

"Exactly. Try to move that rock while sitting here," Cassie repeated, calm but certain.

Closing my eyes, I focused on the green energy welling inside me and mentally reached out to the rock. At first nothing happened, but then inch by inch it levitated off the ground as if lifted by invisible hands.

"There you go! That's it. A little higher," Cassie said encouragingly, and I loved the excitement in her voice.

Turning my palms upward, I called the magic to myself. The rock crept closer to me until I was able to pluck it out of the air.

"How did that work?" I asked, but I couldn't hide my gleeful smile that I had somehow done it this time.

"When you're standing, it's easier for you to channel through your root network," Cassie explained. "That taps into your dryad magic. But rooting from a different part of your body takes more time—so sitting allows the earth magic to flow freely. Good."

"That's great, I guess. . .but I can't sit during the ritual."

The reality hit like a gut punch. There were stairs to climb and movements to perform. If I remembered correctly, there wasn't a way to sit comfortably on top of the pyramid.

"You won't need to. You just need more time to strengthen that magical muscle." Cassie rolled more rocks down from the mountain edge we stood beside. "Let's go again."

Taking a moment of silence, I relished the warm feelings of family bonding. This was low-level basic training for her, but Cassie never showed a hint of impatience.

All of them had been with me in one form or another for months. They'd been determined to stay with me when I was Melissa because I had nowhere to call home. But they'd rarely spent time in Voreios before then.

Now I was nervous they might leave me after the ritual—finally free to return to their own calling, because I had a home of my own.

"What happens after the solstice?" I asked, and Cassie's bright green eyes flicked to me in surprise.

"In what way?"

Looking away towards the boulders, I chose my words carefully. "Well. . .let's say everything goes smoothly. We restore the magical balance of the world. Crisis averted." I hesitated. "Will you all be leaving again?"

I'd never resented Cassie for staying away before. I had Graak. I had the community. And she needed the rest of the world to be happy. But now, I couldn't imagine life without her. If they left, I knew I would feel the void of their energy.

"I hope you didn't feel abandoned by me." Cassie glanced down at her hands. "I couldn't stop crying when I first came home," she admitted. "And for weeks after. It destroyed my mental state." She shook her head gently. "You and Graak don't understand the world that was lost because it was before your births. I couldn't be here and watch it all fall away."

I studied her—the way her head fell, the shallow breaths she took, caught somewhere between grief and memory.

"Does it still hurt like that now?" I asked gently.

"Sometimes." She paused, her voice thickening. "But things changed the day I met Melissa. I couldn't see how it

354

was connected to Voreios then. . .but for the first time in all these years, I didn't feel so alone."

Cassie turned her face towards me, eyes shimmering. "Then you sang the songs with me—like I used to with my sisters. And suddenly, I'd found a kindred spirit to build a family with again. So, to answer your question. . .no. I won't be leaving Voreios again. Not for any long length of time. This is my home."

I smiled and leaned my head against her shoulder. To know she felt the same way soothed my soul. "I'm so glad to have you here," I whispered. "Share with me what hurts—and let's heal together. For everyone. You've always been there for me, so let me do the same. One day at a time."

Cassie exhaled softly. "First, we've got to get past this ritual."

I groaned at the reminder, and we both laughed as she handed me another rock.

"What are you ladies doing?" a playful voice called. "That doesn't look like training." Lilise stepped out from a tree to my right, her voice laced with teasing sing-song.

"Look!" I grinned, floating the rock from my lap to hover in front of her. "Cassie found a work around—so I wouldn't accidentally use the roots."

"I knew you'd figure it out," Lilise said with a proud smile, catching the stone and setting it down. "But now we need to practice the ritual. How are you feeling about the lines?"

I put my hand to my chest and recited with dramatic flair, "Something, something, at this time of year we honor the longest day with offerings and dance."

355

Cassie snorted, and I smirked—knowing it would get a rise out of the older dryad. The words were as important as the magical steps, but they were the easiest piece of the ritual for me to memorize with enough repetition.

"Please tell me you're joking." Lilise frowned.

I laughed. "Yes. I promise I know my lines. I'm more concerned about how to move the earth magic when I am standing than forgetting the words."

"I can help with that while we run through it," Lilise said, already gesturing for me to stand. "On your feet, little one."

I rose, bracing myself.

Immediately, hundreds of root pulses rushed through me—weather fluctuations, ground vibrations, movements of grove members. It all came at once, slamming into my senses like a tidal wave of information. I swam in the noise, trying to get my bearings once more. But this was what I needed to fight through. These were dryad functions—not earth magic.

My feet slicked with a cool drizzle, Lilise's magic coating the ground beneath me. My connection to the roots grew slick and murky. Looking down at my toes, I saw they were now encased in a water bubble. I wiggled them against the sensation of swimming. What a unique feeling this was.

"This was a trick they used on the dryads in training at the academy," Lilise explained. "Move your rock now." She gestured to a nearby boulder nestled by a cluster of trees.

A surge of focused magic burst out of me and practically threw the boulder at Cassie—who crushed it into dust, letting it drift out all around her.

"A little too much magic for the task," Lilise observed with a knowing smile. I winced. Of course she noticed the imbalance. "For the ritual," she continued, "you'll need to add the precise amount of your element into the center of the pyramid. Harmony between the elements is essential. If it's off, everything falls out of alignment—like it did during winter."

She formed another structure on the ground with water. A shallow basin that looked to be about two feet by four feet with round corners.

"I want you to fill it up in ten percent increments. Since it will only allow that much magic at a time, you'll have to deliver it with precision," Lilise explained. "Too much, and it will spill it over. Too little, and you won't complete the task."

I stared at the water cauldron in horror like it was an infernal bear about to eat me alive. I was not a fan of this task at all.

"When you are ready. . .begin."

She raised an eyebrow when I turned my expression to her, waiting for the question bubbling up inside me.

"What happens if I can't bring it back in alignment?" I wondered, holding my breath for her answer.

I'd been afraid to ask before, but as the final pieces of the ritual fell into place, I couldn't avoid the answer any longer. Cassie glanced at Lilise, silently passing the answer to her.

"After two failed rituals, both lunar and solar magic will have failed. Then the elemental magic will begin to fade— starting with the element most out of balance."

She didn't have to say it. I already knew it would be mine that went first.

"Those with elemental magic will start losing access to their magic until it fades completely. The protective barriers surrounding Voreios and the other groves will fall."

This was worse than I thought. "How do the barriers keep out the infernals?" I asked.

"We don't fully understand," Lilise admitted, moving closer to the water cauldron. "But from our estimation, it's due to our ties to celestial magic, channeled through the elements."

"What Lilise is trying to say is. . ." Cassie bumped my shoulder, her voice light, "don't screw this up."

I laughed despite the seriousness of the new weight on my chest.

"We're all counting on you," she said with a wink. "But really, do your best. You're not alone. That's why we practice, right?"

I could only nod and try to calm my racing mind. Practice would help me understand this balance. I brought my hands forward and formed a circle, projecting energy from my core. This would give me a way to visualize the amount I wanted to pull from within.

At first, I barely tugged at the energy and nothing happened. Then I pulled harder with my mind. Green light shimmered in the air, dancing around me as bits of excess magic missed my visualized tube completely. Tamping down the pull of energy, the flow leveled out, magic funneling into the cauldron.

"That's it. Good adjustments, but you're going to need to be a little faster than that," Lilise urged.

I didn't want to go faster. I could barely keep it from ripping out of me as it was.

Still, I breathed deep and tried again, focusing on the amount of energy I could manage and pushing it to move faster.

Within thirty seconds, the flow burst free, spiraling into chaotic flares of green light around me. Cassie tapped into my mind through the roots with a soft, reassuring buzz. The energy responded—siphoning towards her—and she channeled it straight into the earth.

We repeated the flow, again and again, until I finally cut it off, sinking to my knees in exhaustion. The cauldron was only half full, and the amount of overflow had been staggering.

"How am I supposed to focus on this *and* speak my lines?" I gasped for breath. "There's too much happening at once!"

"Practice," Lilise replied, her tone never wavering. She dispersed the water and earth magic from the basin and reshaped it into a new container. Then she caught my gaze. "Recenter yourself, and then we're going to do it again."

Chapter 37 – Graak

The sunlight filtered through the treetops and down onto our small gathering. I turned my face towards it, basking in the warmth against my skin. I'd been doing that a lot more lately. Her presence in Voreios continued to shift the way nature responded.

The more she explored—anchoring her magic and her very essence—the more that changed. Some of it had to do with the way Aurinia was claiming the land.

The ritual that tied me to Aurinia when I began leading the grove had pulsed through me the moment she was granted full access to her element. Earth magic in its purest form. I'd never felt anything like it. Being her anchor to the barrier meant I had access to her power. I'd always known she held an overwhelming reserve of raw magic. It was why I'd been able to do things I never should have—like participate in the solstice rituals. But this? This was something else entirely.

"How's she handling the training?" I asked, turning slightly towards Cassie where she sat a few feet away.

The watchtower glanced at me with a raised brow. "You already know. Don't think I haven't noticed you watching us the last few days," she remarked wryly.

It was true. After Aura had declared her "dates" had come to an end, I'd had a difficult time staying away. Aside from a few heated looks—and a few stray glamour pulls— she'd stayed focused on her training.

But we were running into a new issue. One I didn't think she was prepared for. Hunger.

I'd starved for months waiting on Melissa. I knew what it meant to ache from the inside out. I'd learned how to live with it. But Aurinia wasn't used to this kind of deprivation. Her eyes gave her away. Each day, they darkened to a deeper shade of green.

"I'm asking since you can speak honestly," I said, my voice low. Only Cassie, Zoq, and I sat in the ring. The dryad was a good pulse check on how Aurinia was actually feeling. It was insight I cherished immensely.

"She has an unexpected amount of magic," Cassie admitted, running a hand down her face. "For a normal nymph, this would take a decade to master. And that's with academy study. But she's a vasilissa. She has weeks and can never train at the academy."

Cassie gave me a hard look. "The ritual is going to depend on you just as much as it does her. There will be a lot for you to regulate and ground out."

"I'm happy to practice with her if you think it would help." I offered, already knowing what her answer would be.

Cassie's lips twitched. "Lilise was clear. She needs to learn how to manage it on her own. If she knows what you can do to help, you'll become a crutch."

I couldn't argue with their logic, but I had another motive for my suggestion. As soon as our energy connected,

361

it would bring her straight to me for what we both needed—to feed. The intimacy of our magical bond would tear down whatever remained of the wall she'd tried to keep between us.

Zoq gave me a knowing look and shook his head. Old man always called me out on my nonsense. But at this point, I barely had thoughts beyond pleasuring her if I wasn't fully distracted.

"How about any leads on the portal to find Kelan?" I asked, shifting the subject.

Normally, the longer one goes without their other bond mate, the more certain they become that the other has passed away. But for me, it was the opposite. The more Aurinia's magic grew, the stronger mine became. And since then, I'd felt a pull in the ground as if the elf's energy had brushed against a barrier. But I couldn't get a lock on the direction.

"Ferox has gone through every book and spell he knows," Cassie replied thoughtfully. "Since we can't create portals without a guardian, we may have to hijack one of the infernals and go over there ourselves."

"If you find a portal, I insist you take me."

Zoq leaned forward, but Cassie shook her head, holding up a hand. "No. I can't believe you're even trying to pull that," she scolded.

"He's my bond mate. Even with the mark in disrepair, I bet I could find him faster." I shrugged off her concern.

"That's not the point," Cassie snapped. "If we get trapped over there, you could end up separated right before the ritual. Aura and Voreios need you here."

"I honestly don't think you or Ferox should go either," Zoq added with a grimace. "From what I've heard about Kelan, he's strong. If he's with Minithe, they should be able to hold their own for a few more weeks. It's not ideal, but this ritual must go perfectly, or we're all done for. I think he'll understand the delay."

I frowned. We'd lived our entire lives separately, but now that Aurinia was relatively safe, I couldn't deny the urge to find him. I'd seen the way her expression changed at the scent of a storm or the flash of a unicorn through the trees. How she bit back the ache. How she tried not to let herself miss him—because she wasn't sure he'd still love her. But I didn't have those doubts.

There were only a few moments in my life where everything felt simple and uncomplicated by the rest of the world's circumstances. Two of those times were when the three of us had been together.

"I have this feeling in my core," I admitted quietly, turning the cup of mead in my hand, "that either he will find his way here. . .or it will have to be me who finds him."

"That may be so," Zoq said gently, "but I implore you to wait." Always speaking with his sage advice. "The day after the ritual and once you're officially named our druwid— then you can leave. But not before."

As much as I was frustrated, he was right. The moment I left, Xhet would press Aurinia again to make a different match. I was surprised that after her declaration, we hadn't gotten any closer to claiming each other. Nothing more than fleeting glances, quick touches, and blushing smiles.

"Did she say anything to you, Cassie?" I asked, but nymphs were tricky about things like this. I wasn't sure I'd get a straight answer.

"She's said a lot of things." My sister pressed her lips firmly together. Not even a subtle hint. "But you know right now, she's focused on the ritual."

"Sure," I muttered, trying not to show how badly that response gutted me.

To my surprise, it was Zoq who spoke next.

"Dryads will always do what they want," he said with a small smile. "You didn't get to witness the full cycle because of their nature—because of how she grew up. Of all the nymphs, dryads are the most thoughtful before they act. Allow her this time to process."

My mentor's eyes glazed over in that far-off way they always did when he shared a story about her. The love of his life.

Zoq set his drink down, his voice softening. "From the day that I became her protector, Nivalis and I had always been close. She was my entire world, even as a seedling. Each transition of my role with her presented its own challenges. Nothing was like the change when she matured—she pulled away from our friendship so hard that I felt like I was spinning. When I finally found her, she wouldn't look at me. Then Nivy escaped to her tree and refused to leave without so much as a word. I tried to soothe the new tension between us, but she still refused. Eventually, Amalithea asked me to leave."

Amalithea. The last mother tree of Voreios and likely Aurinia's mother. Cassie's smile had grown faint and distant. Zoq was the only one left who remembered Voreios *before*. Maybe that's why she let herself grieve with him in a way she couldn't with the rest of us.

"She asked you to leave?" I asked, knowing there was a happier resolution ahead.

He nodded. "Yeah. She said I was upsetting the seedlings, and that if Nivy wanted to talk, she'd find me." Zoq chuckled before continuing. "Six days went by. Six! I finally caved and went to Baccys. After being with her for almost every day of my life, I couldn't handle it anymore. He only smiled and said I needed to wait for her. So, I did. There was nothing else I could do. She went out of her way to avoid me and wouldn't speak to me if we did run into one another. My little sapling to protect. . .she'd grown into something extraordinary, and I was losing her."

His voice cracked slightly, but he kept going. "It went on like that for three more weeks. Not hearing her voice. . . I would be fine if she didn't care for me, but I needed to hear her voice. I thought that I was going out of my mind."

I understood that all too well. Not being able to speak with Aurinia all our lives had gutted me. If I truly lost that now, I would go mad. "How did you get her to speak with you again?"

Zoq looked at me briefly, tilting his head. "I have no idea why she chose that particular moment to break our silence. It was a summer evening two weeks after the solstice, and I felt her heading my way through the trees. At first, she stared down at her hands. I was so elated and relieved to have her so close, I pushed aside all the pain I'd been carrying and greeted her warmly. When she finally met my eyes, she blushed."

He closed his eyes for a beat. "I caught that first hint of her glamour—a glorious combination of spice and plums. She took my hand, and nothing was ever the same after that. Life may have moved on after the fires, but my heart never could."

Cassie reached over and took Zoq's hand in both of hers, silent tears shimmering at the edges of her eyes.

None of us spoke. We just watched the flicker of the nightly fires through the trees, each lost in our own thoughts.

Zoq had lost everything—Nivy, his other bond mate, his daughters, his grove. Sometimes when I'd see him having a particularly difficult day, I wondered if the gods had spared him just for me. So I had someone to guide me along this path. How could I ever repay him for that?

Zoq cleared his throat, his voice steady again. "My advice is the same as what I was given. You've waited this long. Give her all the time she needs. I promise you that nothing can compare to being loved by a dryad."

That was exactly what I would do. My heart already belonged to Aurinia. In my dreams, it had always been us. She was worth the wait.

"Am I interrupting?" Zrif's voice broke the silence behind us.

"Just a much-needed trip through a memory," Cassie said softy, patting Zoq's hand as she offered Zrif a smile.

I gestured for him to sit beside me and handed him a mead as he joined the circle.

"I know I'm later than expected, but we ran into some trouble today. I didn't want to leave the border until it was resolved." He spoke rapidly, still hyped up on adrenaline.

"Elves?" I asked curiously. Zrif led the western border—where our land ran along the mountains and brushed the edge of elven territory.

"Infernals. The elves have been sticking to the southern front primarily." He took a long drink, then met my gaze. "Is there something specific we need to discuss?"

"Always business," Zoq said with a chuckle. "Graak, tell him what you told me."

"Is there a reason you are avoiding Aurinia?" I asked. Zrif choked on his drink before giving me a confused look.

"I thought she wasn't meeting with mages anymore?" He *almost* sounded innocent.

"You're the only one who avoided meeting with her," I said, arching a brow.

"Haz didn't do any initial courting either." Zrif hesitated, then added, "I thought. . .we all thought she was going to. . ."

I hated the bit of amusement I felt watching him dance around the fact that they'd all assumed she would take me as her druwid. "Zrif, how do I feel about loose ends? The elders insisted on this, and yet you declined to meet with her. This is our vasilissa—our one dryad—and you made her feel unwanted."

Cassie tossed a handful of pebbles at me with a snort. "You're being mean to him, Graak. Look how brightly he's blushing!" she exclaimed.

Zrif waved off her comment. "I'll talk to her, if that's what *you* are asking. It was never my intention to hurt Aurinia. I understand the elders had a larger role to play in the absence of Aurinia's direction, but we in the guard don't report to them. We answer to *you*. They've disrespected you for some time, and we won't allow it any longer."

"Meet with her for me, then," I said, rising to my hooves and leaning against a tree to watch Aurinia in the main grounds below us. My chest warmed at the sight of her laughing at something Ferox had said.

"I appreciate the guard's loyalty," I murmured. "But you're all right—Aurinia is mine, and I am hers. Everything else. . .is just biding time until she declares her intentions."

Chapter 38 – Kelan

For weeks, we moved from place to place in this cavernous hell. I never thought I would miss the cloudy haze of the infernal sands, but tunnel life wasn't much better.

I was grateful I didn't experience claustrophobia in here because these pathways weren't meant for a man my size. That, however, was what made it easier for us to escape the battles with Aedan and Declan as we ran into them.

The woman's voice came through a few more times. Minithe didn't have much to say about the new revelation of air magic, except that I was likely hearing Ventus—the forest folk goddess of wind. She wasn't aware of anyone else on Artemesia with two elemental gifts, so we put a pin in that conversation until we could get out of here.

With her guidance, my fire magic had grown to new heights. The adrenaline from almost dying every day didn't hurt, either. Declan never made the same mistake twice, and even lightning wasn't working as effectively as one might hope on a water creature.

"How long has it been since we've seen either Aedan or Declan?" Minithe wondered as she lit another one of our candles.

"We've slept at least twice since the fight in the food pits." I rubbed at the deep gash in my left arm Declan had managed to leave that day. It didn't hurt much anymore, but the phantom pain still pulsed through occasionally.

"I don't think they're chasing us anymore."

"Why would they stop?" I asked, though I suspected I already knew the answer.

"Because we are out of time." She flipped open the book she had stolen from the library. "I've never imagined something on this scale before. With all these fronts being amassed, they'll likely need time to coordinate."

"Time to risk returning to the main chamber, then." We needed to see what we were dealing with beyond the plans. For all we knew, the men had already changed things up based on where they'd found us.

"My thoughts exactly," Minithe agreed, wiggling her way into a tunnel heading north. "I think we need to try to blend in again if possible. Of course, that depends on how many there are."

Risky—but this was what we had been waiting and training for.

It took a few hours to weave our way down to the main caverns low in the volcano. We didn't talk much since our voices could carry in unpredictable ways through the small holes in the path. We'd learned that hard way. Still, I'd picked up a few tricks with the wind to mask our voices if we really needed to converse.

Minithe came to a halt as we approached the viewing holes in the tunnel—typically used by the serpent slave race the mages had imprisoned here. Since she could speak their language, they didn't mind us being in their space. They also didn't seem willing to reveal our location to their masters, which had been helpful on more than one occasion.

The entire cavern was flooded with a variety of infernals—from beasts to elves, fae, and wraiths. On the higher pavilion, Aedan and Declan stood with their backs to us. On pedestals among the infernals were twelve mages, and behind the pair of brothers, Lawry and Izo clustered with three others. More dragons?

A man with two pairs of horns growing from his head and rock-grey skin stepped between Aedan and Declan. He approached the edge of the overlook and glanced around at all those gathered below.

"Blessed solstice eve to the entire legion. Tomorrow, there is only one mission," he proclaimed.

Shouts in the crowd echoed Aurinia's name. The man smiled—but it was cold and cruel.

"That's right. Aurinia." A series of explosions erupted, leaving images of her imprinted in the air above the masses. One of them moved, as if it were a live display of her among the floral nymphs, the land swelling with new life, turning plush green. "She needs to be brought to Him *alive*."

The crowd went silent, clearly watching as I was. But I didn't have time to be enraptured by her. I needed to focus—scanning for strategic ways to defeat this large group.

"To make this simple, there are two vasilissas with dark hair. Grab them both. We'll dispose of the one we don't need. Every other attendee is fair game. Slaughter them all. If you tie up a watchtower or kill a druwid, you'll be given a reward from us. If you bring Aurinia to Cholios, eternal life—no conditions—shall be yours."

Eternal life in exchange for delivering one woman. It was a steep gift to grant, and I didn't have any guesses as to why she was so important to him.

I glanced up at the moving image of her. Minithe and I had agreed to call what I was experiencing a longing for my potentially lost mate. These teases tore at my heart—but even if Aurinia wasn't Melissa, I wouldn't let these bastards have her.

"Due to recent events, all mages will be given the sand to close the portals. If you catch her, then you will create a flare like this." The man paused, and an explosion of black and purple went off over his head. "The mage will follow behind you and seal up the portal. No watchtowers can come through."

"We already know that Ferox can track her. What happens in that case?" The question came from a mage.

It was a good question. The watchtowers had found Melissa once before—surely, they could do so again.

"With this sand, he will not be able to. However, I will deal with him if we have her."

"Do you think this sand closes all infernal portals?" I whispered to Minithe.

She pointed to where a few bags were floating towards the mages. "That's a gamble I'm willing to take—especially if they don't want people like us coming through again."

"Infernals! You will receive your assigned mage momentarily. This is only for your departure through to the sacred grounds from the transports. Once you are in the forest, you are all on your own assignment. Destroy everything. Catch Aurinia."

The man raised his hands above his head and tilted his head back, letting out a roar that shook the cavern.

"Tomorrow, the final assault begins!" he boomed.

The crowd erupted in pure jubilation at the declaration. I glared at all of them.

Hundreds of infernals, twelve mages, five dragons, and these three monstrous men were coming after this woman and all the attendees of the solstice ritual. I hoped that the others had the good sense to be prepared for something like this. Otherwise, it would be a bloodbath if we couldn't put a dent in these numbers.

"We need to see these transports," Minithe said, leaning closer. "I'm going to follow those mages heading south. You follow the one who broke off to go east."

I nodded in agreement, and we parted ways in an instant. Last bit of reconnaissance. He didn't go very far—this room appeared to be a supply corner. Knives for rituals, stones, candles, robes, and an armory. The center was the most interesting space, though. On a platform raised about knee-high off the ground sat a large pile of glowing sand. The mage took a bag from the back corner and scooped up a good chunk of it.

If this could do what we thought, then I needed to bring as much with me as possible. I was going to test the limits of these pockets.

"Who's there?" the mage suddenly called out. "I can sense you. Reveal yourself."

I didn't move at first. With my hood up and tucked into this tunnel, I hoped he couldn't see me too.

"You know I outrank you! Reveal yourself to me, and I won't have to tell Keane of your dishonor."

He turned and twisted, magic wrapping around him like a viper ready to strike.

"Xernath!" a woman called from down the hall. "Two minutes. I don't have time for your delays today."

"Coming," the man muttered.

Something inside the fire in my core snapped when I heard his name. This was the man who had touched my Melissa. Who'd been part of her worst nightmare.

While his back was turned, I climbed out of the tunnel and grabbed a few of the longer knives off the table as I passed.

Starting a wind loop at the entrance to muffle as much sound as I could from the outside world, I lowered my hood with my free hand.

"You!" Xernath growled. "You have the audacity to follow me here?"

I waited until he turned to face me fully, then threw two blades into both sides of his shoulders—amplified by the force of the wind. The impact bolted him to the wall.

The sound of his startled scream felt a little too good. All the mages needed to die, but this one might be the most satisfying. Xernath would never hurt her again. He'd never even look at her again—not after I was done with him.

"You are surrounded! You two will die here before you ever get out!" the mage shrieked as I turned the last knife in my hands.

Blood ran down from the wounds in his shoulders, staining his robes.

"As long as I get you, then I guess it won't matter."

He began to chant, and a newly formed shadow lashed out at me. I dashed forward and caught his chin, silencing him mid-incantation, and slammed him back into the wall. He grunted as his head struck the rock.

I pressed the final knife into the sensitive flesh of Xernath's gut, even as his muscles tried to resist. Still, the metal sank further in. Xernath could only whimper as blood poured from his mouth.

"Somehow you survived my bond mate, but I can promise you won't endure this."

Lightning pulsed from me into the metal tips of each blade, and his body jolted ferociously. His flesh cooked and boiled under the extreme heat.

"Honestly, I didn't think you had that in you."

I spun around to glare at Izo, ignoring the ashy remains of Xernath. She had managed to sneak past my wind barrier. The female dragon didn't seem overly upset about the state of her mage.

"You look like you've healed up since your last beat down." I taunted her, forcing out more cockiness than I ever had before. From my many years on the battlefield, I knew I couldn't show any hint of nervousness at the power of my opponent.

The woman hissed at me. "Don't get arrogant. You got in a lucky strike that won't be repeated. You're nothing but a speck of dust compared to me—acting brave when you don't have a shield."

"Looks like yours isn't here either," I pointed out.

At the mention of Lawry, the temperature dropped to below freezing as she stalked towards me. Ice daggers formed in her palms. I saw the attack coming as she swiped at me. With just enough time to duck, I pulled out my longer blade and deflected her next two strikes. Ice spread rapidly across the floor, locking the tables and debris in place.

Keeping my feet up, I sprang off the side wall and slammed my blade into her scaled hands. The room was much too small for her to shift to her full size, but as armor, her scales almost worked too well.

Cold air preceded her snarl as she lunged for my throat with elongating fingers. She wanted to play a game of temperatures—fine. I had my own moves.

The wind cloud blocking the room from the outside twisted into a funnel as I commanded it to siphon her magic. The flames in the torches around us surged higher.

Shadows and ice burst from her as she launched another flurry of jabs. Her scowl deepened as she still couldn't quite land a hit on me.

Fire exploded down the blade of my sword, and I smirked as the surrounding ice began to melt. This dragon wasn't stupid—she knew about my lightning. If enough of the ice melted, she'd be outmatched.

She vanished briefly into the shadows, then reappeared behind me on the right. A claw sliced across my cheek as I ducked under the rest of the attack. With an elbow to her chin, I forced her back, then swung with all I had into her side as she tried to recover.

My blade lodged into her stomach, between rapidly growing scales. Izo screamed in pained fury as flames licked up her half-shifted form and she crumpled. Using the pommel of my blade, I struck her hard in the head, sending her into unconsciousness.

I should let her burn up. She was the enemy, and she was fighting for Cholios—just like Xernath had been. But I didn't have the heart to. Especially when I knew she was someone's Melissa. I'd have to deal with the consequences if it came back around to haunt me.

I dispelled the flames quickly and yanked my blade out of her. I only had a few minutes, so I grabbed a few bags, filled them with the special sand, and hid them away in my mage's cloak.

With one last look at the female dragon bleeding out on the floor, I hoped that my time in the infernal domain hadn't cost me too much of my soul. Then I climbed back into the small servant's tunnel and made my way towards Minithe.

Chapter 39 – Aurinia

Everything came down to tomorrow. All the training had to pay off. My only job was to keep my community safe, and all I could do was pray that it would be enough. Lilise had mandated that I take the day off to save my strength. She insisted I needed to have confidence in what I'd done so far—and that no amount of "crunch studying" would help us any further.

Sure. Now I had no way to distract myself from the stress eating at the rest of my nerves.

Every grove member I encountered seemed occupied with their own preparations. I didn't remember this much activity in the past, but I could feel the undercurrent of anxiety in all their actions. Even the watchtowers had their own assignments in the sacred grounds, clearing out the overwhelming amount of infernals.

It was just me, left with nothing to do today.

"Graak has called a meeting of the border leaders. Come meet me there?" Cassie asked through our bond as the roots relayed the meeting location.

"On my way," I replied, trying to mask my excitement at finally having something to do—even if it meant being in close proximity to him.

The past few days had been harder than ever to keep my mind out of the downright gutter whenever I saw Graak. To stay focused on the ritual, I'd been avoiding him entirely—only speaking to him through my tree. It was the only way I could be sure I'd keep my hands to myself.

I was just about to enter a tree when I heard someone approach from behind.

"Aurinia, may I have a word?"

Turning on my heels, I found Zrif standing a few feet away. He was usually stationed on the western border. Though it had been a few years since I'd seen him in person, the similarities were uncanny. His face was softer than my ryne's, not as battle worn.

"Zrif, what a pleasant surprise," I said with a casual smile. "Are you going to the meeting as well?"

He hesitated, then nodded. "I had a feeling you would be attending. Perhaps we can walk together?"

"I'd like that," I agreed. But then the conversation lapsed into a slightly awkward silence as we moved through the forest.

I thought I'd made my point to the elders before, so we could've avoided this—but poor Zrif seemed to be struggling with how to start talking about whatever was on his mind. I could take the initiative here.

"How has everything been on the western border?" I asked.

His eyes gave away his gratitude in an instant. "It's going well. We aren't the hardest hit front by any means, but the encounters with elves have been minimal. Only infernals."

"Oh, you haven't seen the elves lately? That must be a nice break."

"They're keeping to their appropriate boundaries. Well, all of them except the ravaians." Zrif frowned again and met my eyes. "I feel that I must apologize for my actions as of late. I wasn't purposely trying to avoid you, and I hope I didn't cause any offense."

I smirked at his word choice, not bothering to hide my amusement. "I'm not any more offended than I have been for the past few years. You haven't seen me in some time. Graak used to bring you over all the time, and then all of a sudden, you're grown, getting promotions, and too busy to come say hi?"

Zrif ran a hand through his hair, his cheeks tinting in embarrassment. "You both are teasing me, I think."

"I take it Graak gave you a hard time as well," I said, bumping him gently with my shoulder.

Zrif may have been taller than me now, but I could still see him as the kid who used to play by my tree.

Then I added, "Zrif, we both know that you are not my druwid, but I do want to be someone you know you can come to. I think sometimes you're nervous in a way that other grove members aren't. I'm here for you too. Even if it's just so you can say, 'Hey Aura, I'm not in love with you like that.' Okay?"

"I may not be *in* love with you," Zrif said with a bright smile as he accepted the branch I offered him, "but I will protect you with my life. I am grateful every day that you have been made whole."

"I pray it will never come to that, but the sentiment is appreciated," I replied, a part of me wanting to push the thought away. "After tomorrow, we focus on growth. No one will hurt us like this again. Not if I have anything to say about it."

Repeating the words that Graak had declared to me all those decades ago gave me a sensation of power—because I meant them. No god, no fae, no kingdom would hurt my people again. They would have to go through me. And I would not fail them.

Zrif's eyes glossed slightly as he studied me. "Voreios rises. I'm grateful to be part of it."

He offered me a polite bow and took his leave to join the other border leaders, whose voices had begun to break through the silence of the forest.

The leaders and their seconds stood in a cluster in front of Graak. With a quick glance around, I noticed Cassie seated on the edge of the trees on a rock that had just enough room for me. I made my way to her—but I felt his eyes on me the entire time.

I stifled a groan when I finally met his gaze. Graak sat opposite me, and the lean of his body had all those flexed, bronzed muscles on display. A hunger cramp tore through me, and a tease of a smile played on his lips, as if he knew exactly what I was feeling. I wet my lips and pretended to look away, ignoring the furious blush burning my cheeks.

"Thank you all for coming so quickly," Graak said to the group. "There are a couple of major last-minute changes. I know the community is going to be disappointed, but I need all your help. Cassie, I need you to relay this information to Lilise and Ferox as well."

The energy among those of us gathered shifted into something more somber as his words sank in. No one spoke as we waited for him to continue.

With a deep breath, he finally went on. "With the influx of infernals and the situation in general, it's not safe. No grove members will be attending the ritual at the sacred grounds. Only those essential to the ritual will be leaving the grove. All the groves have agreed to this."

A few of the guards flicked their eyes to me, then back to Graak. No one responded immediately, though I could see their unease written across their faces.

Haz broke the tense silence after another glance in my direction. "I'm sure this decision was made after taking everything into consideration. However—if you'll humor me, please—I think I can speak for most of us when I say we do not feel comfortable having Aurinia go without more protection. If the groves attended as normal, that would place almost a hundred more guards nearby to protect her. To aid you. We've had a taste of what a full grove can do. If the situation is that dangerous, you should bring some of us too."

Graak nodded as he listened, as if he had expected this response. "I hear you. But we need you here to protect Voreios. I'm counting on you to do your part to keep our borders safe. If things go down, I need to be able to focus all my attention on her—knowing you're here to protect each other."

"Our borders only exist because of her," Haz countered. "Some days, she is all we have in the south. If you're overwhelmed, and the watchtowers are spread out dealing with other threats, you'll need backup. She'll be entirely exposed, and I don't think that's a risk we can take."

"I will be Graak's backup," Cassie interjected. "Ferox and Lilise can handle the rest of the grounds without me. Trust me—we understand your concerns, and they're valid. Unfortunately, now is the time to prepare for all possible outcomes. If the borders fall, we're counting on you to gather your areas to safety until a new order can be established."

"There is no order without her," Toq mumbled, though he looked away when Graak turned his head in his direction.

"That's why you're all being tasked to stay here," Graak replied, without addressing the last comment. "Zoq will be your primary point of contact after we leave tomorrow. He'll remain near Aurinia's tree until we return, so she can communicate with him."

I hummed my approval at that information. I could speak to people at my tree even if this spirit form was far away, so that would give us a way to keep tabs on what was happening here—and vice versa.

"We will be leaving and returning only for the ritual window. There won't be any extended gathering for us. There will be no unnecessary risks," Graak continued. "If I could put her at the top of the altar, I would."

"Can you take half the centaur clan at least?" Zrif pressed. "We can handle the borders, but that way you'd have some extra support."

Graak looked at me, but I didn't know what he wanted me to say. If it was going to be that dangerous, then I'd prefer they all stayed home.

"Would that offer some peace to your minds that she will be safer?"

A low wave of murmured affirmations rippled through the group, and Graak sighed. He knew when he'd been beaten.

"I'll speak with them today and make arrangements. Please believe me—if it's the last thing I do, Aurinia will come back to Voreios, regardless of the status of the ritual."

I didn't like the sound of that. I had to finish the ritual, or elemental magic was going to fail. Graak and Ferox could teleport, so I needed to make sure he didn't pull me out too soon.

"Advise those in your areas that all celebrations will be held here. The other groves have agreed to allow a flexible border policy once we get the inter-grove portals back up. Hopefully that will help offset some of the disgruntled responses you're bound to receive."

Graak paused, looking over each of them. "Any other questions?"

The group had fallen silent again, most appearing lost in their own thoughts.

I hated leaving this meeting with all those miserable looks on their faces.

"Planning for the worst is what keeps us safe," I said. "Tomorrow is the start of something new for all of us. Knowing you're so concerned about my safety warms my heart—but I worry about you too. I'd rather celebrate when we return with all of you than take the chance of losing someone before we've reestablished our magical balance."

I took a breath before continuing. "Between Graak, the watchtowers, the centaurs, and all of you all keeping my tree safe, I promise—I will be the most protected dryad in all our long history. Let me do my part, so we all walk out of this stronger."

Cassie smiled first from the corner of my eye, and a new sparkle lit up the eyes of a few guards. Hope.

Graak's job was to protect me. My job was to inspire them to hope. I had one chance to get this right tomorrow—so it sort of felt like hope was all I had left. I would be enough. My magic would be enough. It had to be.

"And on that note, this meeting is complete," Graak said as he rose to his hooves. "Zoq and I are on standby for any questions or concerns you have, as always. I'll be stopping by each border today to do a final check-in and shift some personnel."

I frowned as I realized that meant everyone was, once again, going to go back to their busy days. This meeting hadn't lasted nearly long enough—but Graak was always efficient like that. With everyone but me, anyway. I hovered around aimlessly as the others dispersed to their locations.

With a sigh, I decided to head towards the southeast forest. That's where the flora had gathered for the day. They might offer some easy company, especially since the nereids were busy too.

Before I could step into the nearest tree, Graak's arm blocked me. I stopped just short of touching him, grazing against him instead. My cheeks flamed as I turned to look at him. We were alone, and the heat in his gaze sent chills down my body.

"That was a mighty big sigh." His gravelly tone set my body on fire. "You've been avoiding me, and I can't take it anymore, Aurinia."

I tried to sound innocent. "Just focusing on the task ahead."

"You can do that and still talk with me." He leaned in closer, and I pressed back against the tree until our lips were almost touching. "You're denying what you need. Let me take care of you."

"Aren't you already?" I whispered, brushing the tip of my nose along his. The proximity was torture, stroking that deep ache between my thighs that screamed for his touch.

My question caught him off guard—as if he hadn't been referring to the fact that he tended to my tree's needs every day.

I pressed my palm to his chest and slowly traced the grooves of his muscles upward. I wanted him to desire me the same way I obsessed over him. As that feeling grew, I heard him groan.

"You don't have to glamour me, little firefly. I'm already all yours," he promised—and I wished that were true. His other hand slid to my waist, then down to my ass, pulling me fully against him. "But I love the scent of it. Dance with me this evening?"

"I'm worried I won't be able to let you go after one song," I admitted with a soft laugh. "I remember what happens when we dance together."

"Then we will dance for two. Or three," he pressed, not making it easy for me to deflect. But this was my losing battle.

I closed the distance and kissed him, sliding my body suggestively up his, feeling that massive erection dig into my stomach. Everything inside me screamed for release as

386

we exchanged soft kisses, and he tortured me with slow, grinding thrusts.

Finally, I broke away and eased some distance between us. He had borders to check, and if I caught him now, he wouldn't be doing any of that. I could behave a little longer. "Yes. One dance. I'll pick the song."

Graak let out an amused chuckle. "Anything you want, Aura."

I smiled and vanished into the tree, heading towards the flora. Within moments, I was in a completely different part of the forest.

All the flower nymphs were swaying in a circle, some sitting and some standing, singing up to the sun. They used to do this around my tree at the apex of the day, starting near the end of spring. They didn't miss a beat as a few of them held their hands out to invite me in.

A couple dozen pixies floated above us in beautiful chaos, flashing on the winds in their pastel variety. As I walked over to sit among the flora, a purple pixie flew down to me, dangling something sparkly with a giggle.

"Is that—?" I started, my heart racing. It looked like Kelan's bracelet. "Can I have that, please?"

The pixie chortled, darting just out of reach. "My treasure."

"Hmm," I mused, trying to think of what I could offer the pixie. Even being the vasilissa earned no favors with them—they simply did as they pleased. "How about a trade?"

A pink pixie flitted closer, looking pleased, but that wasn't the one I was negotiating with.

"What trade?" the purple one cooed, hovering further away.

"Hey, come back here, please," I said as sweetly as I could. "What do you want?"

"Treasure," it said, hugging the bracelet.

"What about anything else?" I asked. I wanted this particular treasure too, but I couldn't take it by force.

"Magic," the pixie responded decisively, spinning in a circle and sprinkling dust all around.

They already possessed their own magic, so I didn't understand why they would want mine. I held out my palms, and earth magic bloomed between them. "This is all I have—but whatever you need, you can have. Can I have the bracelet, please?"

All the pixies descended, mesmerized by the magic in my hands. Around me, the ground grew soft and plush with new grass and fresh life. The purple one stayed back, but the others came closer, each plucking little pieces out of the glowing mass in my hands.

When the rest had flown away, the purple pixie finally dropped the bracelet so it looped around my right pointer finger.

"Life. . ." the little thing purred, then zipped away.

Exhaustion settled into the well of my magic from all the extractions, but as I flipped my palm to examine the bracelet, peace settled in my heart. I had a small piece of Kelan. Whatever they needed my magic for—it would be worth it.

He hadn't given it to me. He'd given it to Melissa. But until we found him, I didn't think there would be any harm in me keeping it.

Pressing the bracelet to my bare chest, where I longed for the mark of mates, I closed my eyes.

"Please be mine. But even if you aren't, I pray that you're safe—and that we meet soon."

Chapter 40 – Aurinia

I could pretend that I hadn't counted down every moment until they lit the fires this evening—but I had. The pixies had taken more of my magic than I'd initially realized. I was exhausted, but the hunger tearing at my insides was so much worse.

I should have known it would come down to this. I'd been purposefully ignoring a key part of being a nymph—and that was the simple way in which we fed. If I didn't do something to take away this pain before I slept for the night, I'd be too distracted during the ritual.

Then he appeared at the edge of the fires, coming from the south. He looked about as worn out as I felt, but then he met my eyes. Heat and desire surged through me, strengthening my resolve. I left the group of women talking to me mid-conversation, beelining straight for him. I'd apologize later. Right now, I needed him.

"Aura," he greeted, taking in my appearance with a growing, confident smile. Damn him for still acting cool.

"I was beginning to wonder if you were going to show up for our dance." I teased, brushing past him to take the mead he'd grabbed for himself. Though I would likely fail, I could try to be as smooth as he always was.

"There's nothing that would keep me from being here knowing you were waiting."

I took a long sip of his mead, but it wasn't what I wanted. He watched me closely, calculating, as I handed the mug back. He chuckled softly at the way I scrunched my face at the aftertaste.

"I thought you weren't training today." Graak downed the rest of the mead and used his finger to tilt my face up towards his.

"I didn't," I replied quickly.

My pulse raced as he leaned in closer.

"You're not lying to me, are you?" he asked, gently stroking my cheek. "You've used up a lot more energy since the meeting."

I didn't want to talk about this. I wanted him to fix it— like I knew, instinctively, he could.

Wrapping my arms around his neck, I rose up on my toes. "Will you be upset if I want a rain check on the dance?"

He brushed his lips against mine. "Depends on what you say next. Is there something else you need to do?"

Oh, how I need you. Do I really need to say it?

A woman's laughter rang out behind me, shattering the perfect, dreamy world where we were alone. Suddenly, nervousness coiled tight in my chest—like everyone was watching me. They probably weren't. Not really. But it felt like they were.

"Aura?" Graak prompted, making me blush.

"I need to tell you something. Privately, if possible."

His eyes lit up when he smiled. "Done. All you have to do is ask. Follow me."

He stepped towards me and reached for my hand, ready to lead me somewhere—but I had a different idea.

Brushing my fingers up his arm to his bicep, I unhooked one of his bands. Lifting it high with a teasing smirk, I bolted away from the group and into the darkness of the forest to the west of the grounds.

"Don't you dare," Graak said with a playful growl.

He was hot on my heels, trying to catch me before I could slip into a tree—but he was a second too late.

"You'd better run fast!" he shouted after me, the sound of his voice igniting a new excitement deep in my core.

Being bound to me by the ritual, he could sense every turn I made. He kept pace better than I'd expected. I controlled my movement in the grove, and once we found our rhythm, I headed for the river.

We passed the temple, and the rushing water came into view. North or south? I veered left, heading towards the forest in front of the ocean.

Even if he hadn't been able to track me through the druwid rites, my laughter would've given me away. Every glimpse I stole of him behind me warmed my heart. Seeing that smile. . . The only problem now was that I wanted him to catch me.

Manifesting just outside a tree, I stifled a giggle as he lunged to scoop me up—barely missing. I was still just outside his reach.

Dodging around another trunk, I wasn't fast enough this time. His arm snagged around my waist.

"Oh, I'm not sure you were trying very hard to evade me," he said huskily, wrapping me in his arms. "Where did you hide my band? Or are you telling me I've been demoted?"

I laughed and shook my head. "Never."

With a flick of my fingers, I summoned vines from the ground and tugged him towards me. We tumbled over a small slope, and Graak instinctively shielded me as we rolled. We slid to a stop on a patch of softened grass I'd prepared, and then he smoothly flipped us, so I was beneath him.

His eyes roamed over my face as I tried to calm my racing heart. I refused to shy away from the intensity of his gaze. Propping himself up with one arm, he ran the other hand across my exposed midsection where my shirt had lifted. "You have my undivided attention in this isolated place, my sweet dryad. Tell me—what do we need to talk about."

"I've come to a decision about my first druwid," I said softly, "and I thought I should tell you first."

Graak swallowed hard and leaned down, brushing his nose along my neck before kissing my shoulder. "I'm dying for the reveal. Is it someone I know?"

Another laugh escaped me as I placed my hand over his and guided it lower, to the edge of my shorts. "Yes," I purred. "I think you know him quite well."

"I'll have to apologize to him later—for what I'm about to do to you now," Graak murmured, before kissing me hard. His hand slid under my shorts between my thighs, cupping me gently. One finger stroked through my slit and pushed inside, making me gasp.

In and out, he worked with a steady rhythm before adding a second finger. Kissing him was a dizzying sensation—but I had to say it before this went any further.

"It's you," I whispered as we paused to catch our breath. "It's always been you."

"My heart," he replied reverently. "I'm honored."

His pupils began to glow with a green hue as he continued working me up. This was a sign of him feeding, and I briefly wondered if mine were also glowing. My whole body trembled as he lowered himself down onto me, never slowing his strokes.

I was done with foreplay. In an instant, I dispersed the glamour of my clothing between us. Graak groaned, pressing kisses to every inch of skin from my chest up to my neck. He pressed closer, pushing my legs farther apart as I gave into the pleasure coursing through my body, knowing this was only the beginning. My head rolled back, and what started as a soft moan soon became a whimpered plea of his name. I needed him inside me.

With nothing more than a whispered word from him, a polished stone pressed against my chest and teased down my stomach into his working hand. It began to vibrate as he rubbed it over my clit. I jerked in surprise, but he easily pinned me in place and pumped his fingers faster. With nowhere to escape, I came—hard.

"That's my good girl." I basked in his praise as the vibrations continued. "You will learn not to run from what you need—not when I want to give it to you. Do you understand?"

"Graak," I pleaded as his fingers slowed.

"More is coming," he promised. "There's something else you need to know. Open your energy to me."

Graak didn't wait for a response as he feathered kisses down my body. He hooked his arms through my legs and pulled my core straight to his mouth.

A cry escaped me as his tongue swirled around my clit. *What had he said? Open my energy to him?*

I couldn't think about anything beyond this moment. But if he kept licking me like that, I'd give him damn near anything he asked for.

I wasn't sure I had anything left after the pixies, but my magic flared to life the moment I called for it. His earth magic twined with mine, just like it had on the day of that painful ritual beneath my tree. Our energy swirled together—and then, a surge of emotions that weren't mine slammed into me. As if I could hear his thoughts, his affection for me.

His tongue pierced my core, and I cried out. I came again, caught up in the sensations I was experiencing, and he greedily drank down my pleasure. The essence of his affection stirred an overwhelming need in me—to never be parted from him again. He clutched me tighter, his tongue penetrating deeper as I screamed his name. I didn't care who heard me.

"Graak, please," I begged as I climbed a third wave of ecstasy, but he wouldn't stop.

He sucked harder and pushed his fingers back in to stretch me. Finally, I heard him undo his chiton as I panted—breathless and desperate for air.

He slowly released me from that cycle of pleasure as he kissed his way back up my body, claiming my mouth. I could taste myself in his kiss, my desire caught in his beard. His thighs pushed mine wider.

"Aurinia," he murmured, groaning as his thick cock glided through my drenched slit. "Last chance—if we do this, you're mine. You're ours. Do you understand?"

I nodded, locking my legs around his thighs, pulling him down to me. "You're mine. You know it, and so do I. Graak, I need you now."

He slowly pushed inside me. My vision exploded with a mixture of pain and pleasure. He took his time, gently rocking until he was fully seated. Tears pooled in the corners of my eyes as I adjusted to his girth. We'd done this before—wait, no we hadn't.

He didn't rush, savoring every sensation, every taste, as he kissed along my lips, my jaw, my ear. I was going to explode from the fullness—both physically and emotionally.

Graak kissed my forehead sweetly before speaking in a strained, husky voice. "You feel so good. Are you okay? Ready for me to move?"

"Please. . ." I moaned, digging my fingers into his ass. Graak obliged me without hesitation. He thrust deep, setting a steady pace as his kisses continued, my desire slickening his movements.

For a moment, green light danced between us—almost like the last time. But nothing settled on my chest. No painful etching on my skin. If they wouldn't bless this union, then the gods could fuck right off. His thrusts increased, his breaths rapid. Within moments, I was ready to explode again.

"Come for me, Aura," he commanded, and I gave myself over to the pleasure, helpless against his pull. Graak came with me this time.

My heart soared as he leaned in to kiss me again. It was going to be a long night—and suddenly, I wasn't tired any more. As if all my energy reserves had been restored.

Using vines to flip him onto his back, I straddled him before he could recover. His hands were already roaming, hungry and urgent, as we built each other up all over again.

Tomorrow, I would rise to meet my destiny—but tonight, I would claim that which should have always been mine.

Chapter 41 – Graak

Ritual Day was upon us. I knew I should be nervous and pensive over the situation we were in, but I couldn't shake the euphoria of waking up with Aurinia in my arms.

Even now, as I watched her talk with Lilise a few feet away, I couldn't stop smiling.

"You are beaming like a second sun. It's almost unbearable." Zoq taunted as he came up behind me.

"Can you blame me? It's everything I've ever dreamed about—and so much more." I forced myself to look away from her and give Zoq my attention. "Is everything set for today?"

"It's quiet over there," Zoq said with a frown. "Too quiet. I don't trust it."

"We don't have any other choice, or I'd take it."

He leaned in closer and lowered his voice. "I notice that there's not a fate mark. Did you at least confirm your status?"

"We both know I've always been her druwid. Aura and I decided that, with or without the gods' blessing, we do this together." Screw the gods and their ideals if they still tried to get in our way.

"It could be that her soul already knows Kelan," Zoq mused, and I had to admit that made more sense.

"All the more reason that, starting tomorrow, I have to be out there looking for him."

"I already expanded the team searching for portals with Ferox. We'll go double time on that as soon as we know how the ritual went," Zoq agreed, nodding his head as Aurinia came my way. "All ready to go?"

Aura's bright smile took my breath away. "You all have done your part. It's about time that I did mine, don't you think? Plus, all the flora keep teasing me about this one." She gestured at me, and we all laughed. "Best to give them something else to talk about."

"I'm happy to keep discussing that point," I replied as I pulled her into my arms, cradling her back to my chest. She settled into my embrace as if it were the most natural thing in the world. When she looked over her shoulder at me, I kissed her.

Before I could get lost in the space between us, Lilise came up on my other side.

"Time to go. Remember, you both must keep your guard up—but the ritual comes first. Trust in us to take care of any assault."

Aura and I both nodded. We'd heard that now quite a few times. Aurinia's focus would be key, as she was still new to all of this. I'd been doing it so long that a little multitasking wouldn't bother me.

"It's the first time I'm meeting the other vasilissas like this. . .as me. Do you think they'll be surprised? Upset?" Aura asked, and I immediately picked up on the nerves in her voice.

"They're going to be happy to meet you whole." I reassured her. "If they're upset, it'll be at me, not you. You haven't done anything wrong."

She scrunched her nose, as she always did when I told her that none of this was her fault. "From the meeting we had yesterday, I know things are going to be different today. What is this supposed to look like on solstice morning?"

The main grounds around us were empty—void of the hundreds of members who would usually be going with me to the festivities planned at the sacred grounds. I wanted to curse the gods again that Aurinia wasn't getting to experience the ecstatic crowds and vibrant energy I had for decades.

"Normally, Zoq and I would hold a teleportation ring open as about a quarter of the grove goes with us to the sacred grounds."

"That many?" Aura gaped.

I nodded. "That number includes guards, but it's never been an issue before. The infernals are usually easily managed by the watchtowers and the second and third druwids. We take that many with us so we can intermix the populations of the groves with new genes. A lot of children are conceived at these events—and some members find their mates."

"Aww," she cooed, turning to look at me with soft eyes full of affection. "I love that so much."

I couldn't help a small chuckle at seeing how happy the thought made her. "I love it too—when a nymph brings home a guard or two. Not so much when the reverse happens."

She hit me in the stomach playfully. "If we don't bring them, they're missing out on that opportunity."

"That's why, after we succeed, all the groves are allowing a one-day window for our people to move between them with less scrutiny—certain areas, at least."

"Extra motivation for me to succeed," Aura said as a new fire lit in her bright green eyes. "If it's going to be this dangerous, I feel like I should have Ares on me."

"Cassie has Ares now," Lilise said, meeting my glare head-on. I'd told them repeatedly I would be removing Aura from the situation if it became overwhelming. "She'll be the closest to the ritual and able to provide it to you should it become necessary."

"Oh, okay. That makes me feel better." Aura took a deep breath and then smiled at me. "Shall we go then?"

Lilise nodded, signaling that she'd gotten the "all clear" from Ferox, who was in the sacred grounds now. Both dryads stepped closer to me as the dirt lit up with glowing white letters in Latin. Aura grabbed my arm—she must have remembered this magic from when Ferox had used it.

The academy had taught us all transportation magic; it was the most common skill. I pulled her into a tight embrace and felt her smile against my chest as we vanished from Voreios.

The shift was instantaneous, and with the blink of an eye, we were surrounded by the sparse woods of the sacred grounds. The altar where we performed the solstice rituals sat equidistant from each of the temples in our groves.

"Lilly! I can feel all your trees here, but I can't locate them. I even sense Minithe's!" Aura exclaimed as she ran her hands along a nearby tree.

"That's how we know she's still alive—somewhere. Even off-world, we're usually able to talk to one another, at least somewhat. The silence has been. . .unnerving. Our trees are masked so that enemies can't find them since we do not have a mother tree's protection on these lands." Lilise followed behind Aurinia before gently turning my lover around. "The other vasilissas are that way."

As Aura moved closer to me again, I took her hand in mine and led her towards the usual meeting spot.

"This is where you found me, isn't it?" Aura asked quietly. "It's all so familiar."

"Yet another sign," Lilise agreed. "Before the infernal startled you, you were walking up the stairs you're about to climb now, I believe."

My eyes widened at the new piece of information I hadn't heard before. When Aura nodded, I mulled it over but let it go. I didn't need more proof that Melissa was a part of Aurinia. Still, I tucked the detail away in case she ever doubted herself again.

A few more steps in, and I began to hear the others talking—though at first it was mostly indistinct voices.

"I don't understand why Graak isn't here. He *cannot* miss this ritual too." Sabina's shrill whine caused me to wince.

"He said he'd be here," Aconi snapped. "I can't believe you had the audacity to—"

Her voice fell away as I moved the brush aside and stepped through. Turning to help Aura up and through the foliage, Sabina didn't wait to pounce.

"You cannot put this off any longer. I've trained Celeste in both parts of the ritual so she can step in for Voreios. She'll use your magic for the ritual."

I knew the exact moment Sabina saw Aurinia—because the silence was so thorough I almost sent up a prayer of gratitude to Montibus.

"I appreciate your concern, but I'm ready—and more than capable—of doing my part," Aura said politely. If I hadn't been watching her, I would've missed the quick assessment she gave Celeste, who stood beside Sabina. "Besides, Graak is mine."

The subtle warning and decisive claim sparked a fresh wave of desire. She gave me a sexy smirk as she brushed by me to stand in front of the others.

"Hello, everyone. I believe it's time we do a re-introduction." Aura's tone was calm and collected. Confidence radiated from her and into the land. "My name is Aurinia, and I am the vasilissa of Voreios."

Hairiko was the first to break the silence. "You look exactly like Melissa. . .but she was not a dryad."

"Here, I'll share the information—since we're limited on time," Aura said, and then fell still along with the other dryads.

The other druwids all turned their eyes to me, but they'd have to get the details from their partners after the ritual.

Aconi closed the distance and embraced Aura. "We didn't know how he was doing it, but now we can set everything right again. Voreios has never let us down before, and here again, in the final hour, you arrive to change the course once more."

"I'm not sure about all that," Aura replied, returning Aconi's hug, "but I know we're ready for today."

"It's because Sabina brought a secondary failsafe—one that Aconi and I have not agreed to," Hairiko said with a disapproving tsk.

The moment Helio stepped up from behind Sabina, where he'd been talking with Ferox and Jax, I immediately pulled Aura back into my embrace. It didn't matter—the king of the fae had seen her, and from the gleam in his eyes, I knew there would be trouble.

"What an interesting twist this is," the fae king purred, and Aura stiffened. "The news of your death had ranked as one of the worst tragedies this year. And yet, here you are again."

"What is he doing here?" I growled, not bothering to mask my open hostility.

"Would you like to explain this to Graak and Aurinia, or shall I?" Aconi asked sharply, glaring at Sabina as she made her way back to her druwid, Ciol.

"Helio and I have been discussing the situation with the elemental magic," Sabina said, smoothing down her dress. "After you didn't show at the winter solstice, we couldn't let this fall apart because you were unreliable. If we return to fae rule, they can protect us."

From the furious expressions on Aconi and Hairiko's faces, this was clearly not a mutually agreed-upon plan.

"The fae would gladly take you back into our fold," Helio said, unconcerned by our reactions. "Going back to how it was would simplify many of your current problems. Now that. . .Aurinia, was it? Now that Aurinia has revealed herself, I think we may be able to come to some even more beneficial terms."

"How considerate," I replied snidely. "But as you can see, your valiant services and contracts are no longer needed here. You may take your leave."

"What does your vasilissa say?" Helio pressed, taking a step forward and earning another snarl from me. "I know she has a very pretty voice that can speak on her own."

"I believe Graak has made *our* stance very clear. We are not in need of contracts with you for protection, as I intend to take care of my people—with *our* power," Aura snapped.

That's my girl.

I squeezed her gently. For her first time out on the world stage, she was handling it remarkably well.

"Hell yeah!" Aconi cheered. "Now we have a ritual to get to, if you don't mind."

She flipped her bright red hair over her shoulder and sauntered down the hill before Helio could reply. The fae king, though, only had eyes for my dryad—and I'd beat him to a pulp if he didn't stop looking at her like he would devour her.

"We aren't done talking about this!" Sabina shouted as Aura and I fell into step behind Hairiko and her druwids.

"Yes, we are," I called back over my shoulder.

I kept Aurinia in front of me, but movement to the side drew my attention—Lilise and Ferox in rapid conversation a few feet away in the forest. Something else was amiss, and I hated that Helio was here as a further distraction.

Cassie appeared at our side, and my heart sank when I saw Ares in her grip.

"Cassie?" Aura asked, her voice wary, before Cassie slipped Ares into the holster on the side of my dryad's leg. They'd planned this all along.

Damn dryads.

"What's going on?"

"The energy isn't right. You both need to be prepared. No matter what happens—you *must* survive." Cassie tilted Aura's chin up, ensuring she had her full attention. "Do you understand me?"

"I. . .yes. I understand," Aura agreed, but she didn't sound certain. "I *am* finishing this ritual, though, Cassie. I won't leave prematurely. No matter what comes."

Watching the two of them in a battle of wills was interesting. Even more so when I saw Cassie concede. Nothing more was said between them, but a decision had clearly been made.

Now I realized the difference: everything had shifted. The way the watchtowers handled Melissa wasn't how they responded to Aurinia. They weren't directing her actions. They were guiding—helping her make the moves *she* chose.

Aura crossed the cleared land to stand beside the pyramid that was ours. She flared her hands out, feeling the energy of this ancient space.

"It's calling to me. Just like it did that day." She took a deep breath and turned around to face me, her palms extended. "This is our destiny. We didn't go through all this to fail now."

"When did you get so wise?" I teased, taking her hands and leaning in to kiss her.

When our lips brushed, the earth magic within me tied into hers—and I loved the way she gasped. *This* was why I'd

406

had her experience it last night. All the innermost thoughts, all the affection, rushed out into the other when our energy synced. A green line danced like a visual tether between us. Aura pulled back slowly, but our power remained in perfect harmony.

Then she turned her face up towards the altar and took that first step onto the pyramid. Magic from all four of the vasilissas powered on—the display of water, fire, and air dancing around the foundation. It had never been this vibrant when I performed the ritual alone. But Aura was a deep well of earth—and the magic responded.

Without warning, a black portal tore open in the sky to our left. Screams and roars poured out. Lilise and Ferox reacted instantly—the portal burst into flames and snapped shut. Another one ripped the sky apart to the right—before it too went up in flames.

"Aura, keep moving," I urged, even as three more portals tore open—infernals pouring through and blowing apart sections of the forest around us.

When Mebsec appeared at the base behind me, I knew the others were truly concerned. The second and third druwids typically stepped in to defend when the first druwids were engaged in ritual. Yet another reason we needed to find Kelan. Aconi and Aurinia both only had one druwid right now, while Sabina and Hairiko had three.

Cassie's arrows shot past us, shredding a new group of infernals that were quickly consumed in flames. Water and wind surged through another cluster of portals, but they were popping up faster than we'd anticipated.

Aura stopped again, just a few steps from the top, her gaze lifting towards a portal forming directly above the altar. Black masses oozed and sizzled as heavy smoke poured down towards her and the other vasilissas.

A haunting laugh echoed through the forest before the Shadow God spoke.

"There's no running from me today."

Aura trembled—just slightly—but with me at her back, she took another step forward, staring defiantly up at the ominous shape beginning to manifest.

"You will not stop me," Aura promised, her voice steady as she claimed the final step and raised her hands to the sky.

That was the only confirmation I needed. Even if we were to die fighting a god, we were going to complete this ritual.

Chapter 42 – Kelan

We hadn't found a moment of peace since I'd dropped into the assistant tunnels after my fight with Izo. High alert had been raised, and Minithe and I were now essential pieces that needed to be dealt with.

The servants had all vanished, replaced by infernals crawling everywhere, trying to kill us or push us away from the transports. They hadn't succeeded—though we'd led them around in circles more than once. Minithe had started carving out new tunnels by adjusting the soil with plant roots from the volcano's surface.

"It's beginning!" Minithe shouted back to me from farther ahead.

"I still don't think we should let the first one get through," I repeated, standing firm. I didn't want *any* infernals to get through—even if it meant being outnumbered.

"I hear you. But if we don't, we won't be able to make sure we reach the last one before they catch on."

"We'll get to them all."

Minithe chuckled and rolled her eyes at my bold declaration.

"If there's a chance for me to send you back through, I'm going to take it, okay?" she said, glancing away. "Just don't hold it against me."

It was another conversation we'd had a few times now—and I still wasn't budging.

"We go together or not at all, Minithe," I said firmly. "It'd be an honor to fight and die beside you. But let's go for the win. Demi-gods, dragons, infernals—none of it matters."

She didn't look convinced, but she smiled anyway. "Together, then. You go left. I'll hit the ones on the right, and I'll see you in the middle."

The transports were lined up on a floating platform suspended over the lava bed at the center of the volcano. Once we left these walls, we'd be completely exposed. Most portals we'd seen before were made entirely of magic, but these were anchored with a mix of magic and technology—similar to what I'd seen back in the elven lands. Each had a power source we'd need to strike to disable it. If we hit them right, the mages wouldn't be able to use them—trapping them and their infernals here. With us.

We both tossed on our cloaks and vanished. Using my wind magic, I picked us up and hovered us towards our first targets. The platform was teaming with mages and infernals—screaming orders, charging spells, general mayhem.

I didn't see Aedan, Declan, or Keane—but that didn't mean they weren't watching. It all came down to this. They were here somewhere.

Halfway through our flight, I caught a high-pitched chirp that quickly turned into a roar. Glancing up at the volcano's mouth, I locked eyes with a monstrous beast that was coming in fast. I hurled Minithe the rest of the way—straight into immediate chaos—then blasted myself out of the dive's path. The creature pivoted midair and lunged at me again.

Another monster? This one looked like a bat on steroids—almost as big as Aedan in dragon form. I didn't have time for this—not with the portals beginning to surge to life.

Minithe's first target exploded in a cloud of flame. I caught a quick glimpse of her, already fighting her way towards the second.

Landing hard, I sent out a pulse of lightning, clearing infernals from my path. The bat-like creature screamed again—another high-frequency burst aimed right at me. I had seconds.

Drawing my blade, I slammed it into the portal's magical core. The image of the world through it flickered, then blinked out—just before an explosion threw me back and nearly off the platform. The bat landed on me, shrieking as it lunged, trying to tear my face off.

Instead, I slid out from underneath it and rolled away as it swiped at me. Summoning winds, I pushed the beast in the opposite direction just as it tried to take flight and come after me again.

Transports two and three were much of the same chaos—battle the infernals, dodge around the bat, and blow up the port. But when water and wind magic began to blast through the portals, my heart lifted. Lilise and Ferox were assisting us, helping to take them down as they opened.

As I approached the fourth one, I was forcibly slowed by a larger cluster of infernals. So many limbs twisted together that I couldn't tell where one ended and the next began. Twisting my blade, I carved through the entire writhing mass.

Then my eyes snagged on the image through the portal. The vasilissas stood atop the altar, magic rolling around them, weaving across the pyramid. Then *her* face turned—looking directly up towards the portal in front of me. Could she see me?

I sliced through the final bodies and slammed flames into the magical port, exploding it—just as the bat-like creature landed in front of me again. I ducked beneath its attack as it lunged. . .only for it to pull back with a mouthful of infernals instead. My fifth transport exploded before I could reach it.

Last one.

I spotted Minithe heading my way. Above us, lightning I wasn't controlling crashed down from the sky as a roar split the air. A massive black dragon—almost as big as Aedan—flew overhead. Everything seemed to come to a halt as lightning bolts shredded through everything they touched, reducing chaos to stunned silence.

Only the giant bat remained unfazed, hovering out of the way.

Minithe slid to a stop in front of the final transport, her eyes fixed on the dragon. The beast slammed into the pavilion—and the entire platform cracked apart in a spiderweb of fractures. It was barely holding together.

The dragon roared again, and lightning shot down at us. I deflected all of it, but Minithe had gone completely still.

I glanced over my shoulder at the open transport. It was our only way out—and we had to go *now*. Lilise and Ferox were already working their magic to destroy it.

"Minithe! Come on!" I shouted, bolting towards it.

But she didn't move. She only stared at the dragon.

"Valk?"

The word tumbled from her mouth so quietly I shouldn't have heard it.

Valk? As in her dead dragon mate?

Fuck.

This had to be a trick, but we didn't have time.

I wrapped an arm around her waist and dragged her with me. The dragon roared the moment we moved. The shattered pavilion shifted—the beast was charging at us.

The edges of the transport began to pop and sizzle as the entire thing crumbled. The explosion was imminent. So I did the only thing I could—I threw us both through, praying the whole time that we would make it.

Chapter 43 – Aurinia

I have one job to protect my people: finish this ritual. The flood of infernals, the portals, and even the god taunting me in my mind—can all wait.

Trust the others to do their job, so I can do mine.

Easier said than done, with all the roaring and screaming in the background. The best thing I could do was weaken Cholios' hold on this planet by restoring elemental balance to its rightful place. This was what I'd been working towards these past few weeks.

I lowered my hands from the grounding process and took a long, deep breath.

Let it begin.

"At this time of the summer solstice, we honor the longest day of the year with our offerings and dance," I announced to the sky above. My voice was calm and confident, rooted in the knowledge that as the foundation—I wouldn't let this crumble. "Each year, we are stronger. Each year, we are brighter. From the height of this day, we revere the light that has been provided."

A white energy sphere appeared at the center of the altar between the four of us, pulling power equally from each vasilissa. Wanting to give it everything I had, I pushed out my magic—until I noticed Graak tugging some of it back. He was siphoning excess energy away from the sphere so it didn't take more than it needed!

That. . .would've been helpful to know earlier.

"By the powers of the east and the element of air, we receive your blessings of intelligence. Please accept our offering of music," Sabina called after a moment of silence.

The sphere began to radiate yellow. A soft chant rose from the trees around the pyramid, sounding like songs lost to an ancient time past as Sabina hummed along with it.

A portal exploded overhead, sending wind whipping dirt and leaves in a blinding spiral. Pressure slowly built behind my eyes as that dark, familiar laughter rang in my ears.

"By the powers of the south and the element of fire, we receive your blessings of passion. Please accept our offering of sacrifice," Aconi said, jumping in as soon as the chanting subsided. The ball shifted once more to a deep, blood red.

She unsheathed the blade at her hip, slicing open both palms. Blood pooled in her hands before she pressed them on the altar, and it spread outward in intricate designs— symbols of all our elements etched beneath the floating sphere.

"You think this will really be enough to stop me?" Cholios purred inside my mind.

I had to ignore him. This was all a distraction. The battlefield below lit up with sparks and magic as the mages clashed with the watchtowers, but my focus couldn't waver.

"By the powers of the west and the element of water, we receive your blessings of wisdom. Please accept our offering of libations," Hairiko offered in a sing-song voice.

She poured mead across the bloodied design Aconi had made. It shimmered as the liquid hit the altar, and I knew the gods had heard her.

The sphere transformed to blue. We were almost there. Now it was my turn to seal the deal.

"You can't protect them." Cholios taunted as soon as I opened my mouth. *"Give into me now and let's avoid all the death that's coming."*

"Get the fuck out of my head!" I snarled silently.

"By the powers of the north and the element of earth, we receive your blessings of strength. Please accept our offering of gathering," I intoned.

As the final offering was spoken, the sphere pulled on me harder, drawing so much magic that I could barely breathe. Graak was still pacing it—gently feeding back some of what he'd pulled off earlier. The sphere glowed a vibrant green as the gods and the earth accepted it.

Almost there.

Cholios pressed against my psyche like a clamp, trying to shut me out from my memories—and the final words. But I wouldn't let him.

"The gathering assembled here today honors you and calls witness to the balance of the energies in this world and the universe."

"I'm coming for you!" Shadows bellowed up around my feet, and flashes of the winter solstice screamed through my mind.

My body trembled involuntarily, and my vision grew darker—whether from the pressure in my skull or the depletion of energy, I didn't know.

"Guide us, hear us. Grow the energy so we may better connect with you," I said—then shouted, "All hail to the elements! May they forever reign."

The sphere in front of us exploded, releasing a shower of glittering light across the world as far as I could see.

The pressure in my head became too much. It felt like he was trying to seize control of my body. He shouldn't have been able to do that, but anything with a god could be possible.

I screamed, clutching the side of my head near my ears. Graak rushed up and caught me in his arms.

"You're done," he said urgently. "You did it. We're going home now."

Cholios only laughed louder, echoing through my mind, over and over—repeating, *"You're mine."*

My root connection with the land flooded with information, the entire world shifting beneath me. In the torrent of insight, I almost missed the moment Minithe joined our root channel.

Graak's magic swirled under our feet, dispelling the lingering shadows as he summoned a teleport back to Voreios.

I don't know what made me look up. Maybe instinct. Maybe fate. But as flames erupted from the final portal—I saw him.

My knees nearly buckled. I gripped Graak's arm for support as I slowly rose, needing to see clearly—needing to be sure.

The man in the mage's cloak had short white hair and golden eyes rimmed in red. Though his appearance had changed, I knew exactly who was standing before me.

"Kelan."

To be continued. . .

Thank you for reading! If you enjoyed this, please leave a review.

About the Author:

Callie Pey is the steamy fantasy romance author responsible for The Dryad Chronicles. She loves fantastical worlds and epic stakes that embrace love in all its forms with a heavy dose of adventure. A current Austinite, she enjoys reading almost as much as writing, painting, and finding even the smallest moments to capture joy.

With the Dryad Chronicles set to be re-released in 1st POV, Callie isn't done working on new material! Revolt of the Marked is a dark fantasy series not for the faint of heart along with a paranormal romance series that will feature parts of Texas! There is so much adventure coming, so stay tuned!

Keep up with her at:
www.calliepey.com

List of books based on timeline order:

The Revolt of the Marked

The Lament of the Dendron (TBD) Book 1
To Make a Monster* (out of print)

To Ignite a Pyrite Spirit*

The Dryad Chronicles
Daughter of Earth ~ Book 1
To Poison a Pearl Tome (TBD)*
Calling of the Grove ~ Book 2
Whispers of the Wind (12/21/25) Book 3
Summoning of the Flames (4/30/26) Book 4
Cursed*
Tides of Healing (12/21/26) Book 5

The Root of Fey Magic*

When the Veil Meets the Moon* (out of print)

* can be read as a standalone *

If there isn't a date. It means the book is out!!